also by
SCARLETT ST. CLAIR

When Stars Come Out

HADES X PERSEPHONE
A Touch of Darkness
A Game of Fate
A Touch of Ruin
A Game of Retribution
A Touch of Malice
A Game of Gods
A Touch of Chaos

ADRIAN X ISOLDE
King of Battle and Blood
Queen of Myth and Monsters

FAIRY TALE RETELLINGS
Mountains Made of Glass

a GAME of GODS

SCARLETT ST. CLAIR

Bloom *books*

Copyright © 2023 by Scarlett St. Clair
Cover and internal design © 2023 by Sourcebooks
Cover design by Regina Wamba

Sourcebooks and the colophon are registered trademarks of
Sourcebooks. Bloom Books is a trademark of Sourcebooks.

All rights reserved. No part of this book may be reproduced in any form or by
any electronic or mechanical means including information storage and retrieval
systems—except in the case of brief quotations embodied in critical articles or
reviews—without permission in writing from its publisher, Sourcebooks.

The characters and events portrayed in this book are fictitious or
are used fictitiously. Any similarity to real persons, living or dead,
is purely coincidental and not intended by the author.

All brand names and product names used in this book are trademarks,
registered trademarks, or trade names of their respective holders.
Sourcebooks is not associated with any product or vendor in this book.

Published by Bloom Books, an imprint of Sourcebooks
P.O. Box 4410, Naperville, Illinois 60567-4410
(630) 961-3900
sourcebooks.com

Cataloging-in-Publication data is on file with the Library of Congress.

Printed and bound in the United States of America.
WOZ 10 9 8 7 6 5 4

*This book is dedicated to my readers.
This series is a soap opera.
I'm glad you're here for it.*

"Everything is more beautiful because we're doomed."
—HOMER, *THE ODYSSEY*

"We lovers fear everything."
—OVID, *METAMORPHOSES*

"My vengeance is my guilt."
—OVID, *METAMORPHOSES*

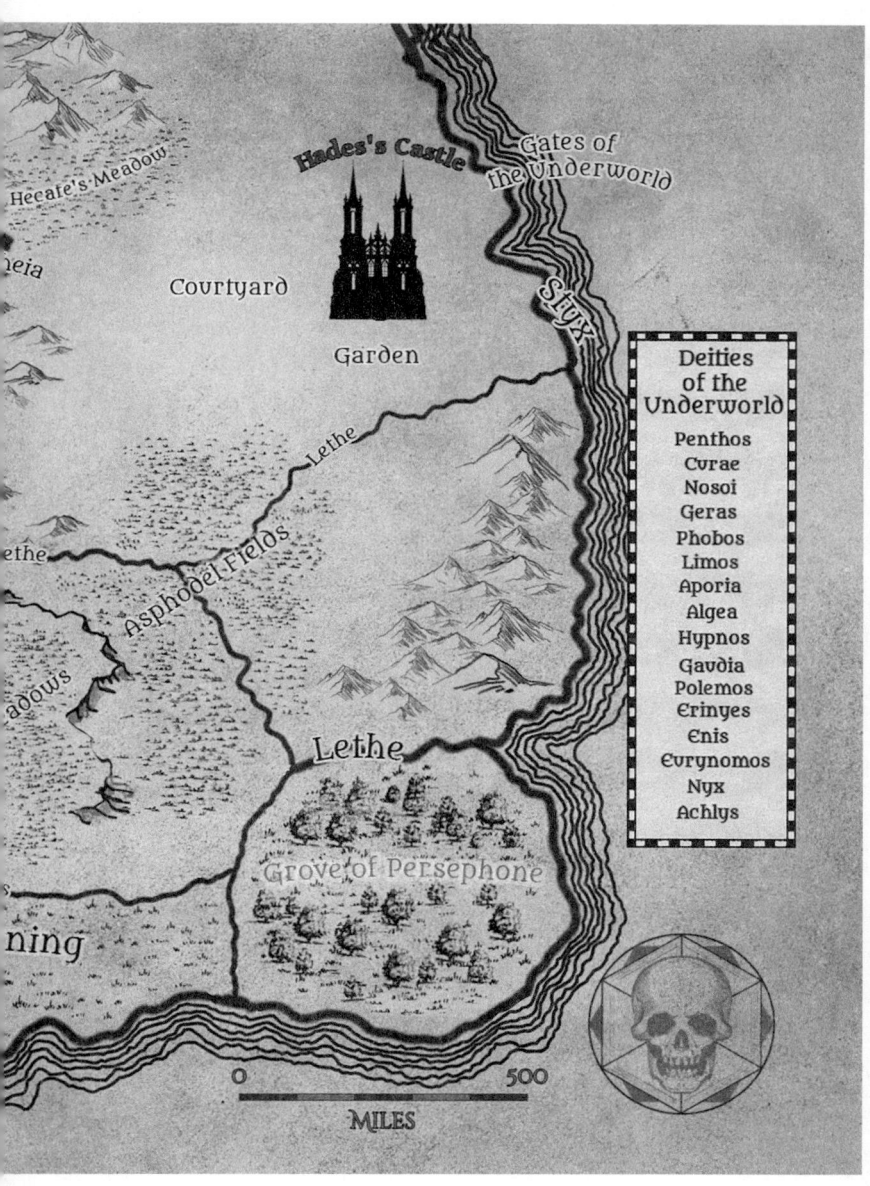

CHAPTER I
HADES

Hades stood a few feet from a burning farmhouse.

All that remained was the frame, a faint outline of what the house once was, and yet the flames still raged, filling the night with smoke and ash. At his feet was the corpse of an old man, the farmer who had lived within, his back full of bullet holes. Nearby, his soul drifted, unaware that it had departed his physical body, executing what Hades could only assume was his nighttime routine. That was usual for any mortal who experienced sudden death.

The old man had not seen this coming.

Not that he should have. The only thing this farmer was guilty of was seeing the ophiotaurus, a half-bull, half-serpent monster that was also a prophesied god killer. Someone had caught wind and visited the farmer to learn more under the guise of authority, and once they had what they wanted, they killed him.

Hades felt Thanatos's magic flare as he manifested

beside him, a slice of shadow that blended in with the night. Even his pale hair and face caught the reflection of the flame.

Neither of them spoke—there was no need. Nothing could be done beyond guiding the farmer's soul to the Underworld. Once he was settled in Asphodel, it was possible he might be able to give them information on who had murdered him, but Hades worried it would be too late. By then, there would be more sightings of the ophiotaurus, and whoever was after it would continue to leave a trail of bodies behind until they caught up with the monster.

"I mourn deaths like these the most," said the God of Death.

"Murders?" Hades asked.

"He did not have long left on this earth, and yet his life was taken anyway."

Hades said nothing, but he agreed.

This farmer's death was not necessary. The only useful information he might offer was confirmation that the ophiotaurus lived, but there were other ways to validate that rumor, and they did not involve killing.

Hades would find whoever had done this, and their punishment would be swift and fitting.

His eyes shifted from the fire to the farmer's soul, which was now frantically trying to enter the burning barn, likely attempting to reach the animals within, but they were already gone.

"Give him peace," Hades said.

At this point in his long life, he did not often feel sympathy for the dead, but in these moments, when the cruelty of humanity was most evident, the burden of granting relief weighed heavily.

Thanatos nodded, stretching his wings as he made his way toward the soul.

Hades left the scene, wandering into the vast field beyond the farmer's home, far from the glow of the fire.

Overhead, the stars glimmered so bright, they cast shadows, his the greatest among snow-dusted blades of grass. It was freezing, though it was summer—an untimely gift from Demeter, the Goddess of Harvest.

There were no coincidences.

On the night he had officially proposed to Persephone and she accepted, the storm had begun. It was Demeter's declaration of war and the weapon she would use to tear them apart. It seemed insignificant, just a few frozen drops, but it was just the start of something worse to come.

People would die. It was a matter of time.

And when that happened, would Persephone fight for their love, or would she give in to her mother to save the world?

He hated that he believed the latter.

He realized it was a horrible position, an impossible one. If Demeter truly loved her daughter, she would never have given her the ultimatum.

Hades considered these things as he searched the sky, eyes connecting stars. Among the sketches they made, he noted Cetus, the sea monster slain by Heracles; Auriga, the Greek hero raised by Athena; Aries, the golden ram whose fleece could cure any living thing; and Orion, the hunter who dared to cross Gaia, but Taurus, the constellation set at their center on the ophiotaurus's death during the Titanomachy, was gone.

It was the evidence Hades had been looking for.

What Ilias had said was true—the monster had been resurrected. Not that he hadn't believed him, but rumors did not make something true.

"*Fucking Fates*," he growled, and he was right to curse them. Lachesis, Clotho, and Atropos had orchestrated this resurrection, though he knew it had only come about because he had killed Briareus, one of the Hecatoncheires, the hundred-handed giants who had aided the Olympians during the Titanomachy. Hera, the Goddess of Marriage, had seen an opportunity for revenge against the giant who had helped Zeus escape his bindings when she, Apollo, and Athena attempted to overthrow him.

"*A soul for a soul,*" the Fates had said.

He felt a pang in his chest, remembering how Briareus had died. There had been no grief, no begging or anger, only peaceful acceptance. Perhaps that was the worst part, the trust the giant had placed in him, that it had been his time to go and not that his death had been ordered by another god.

And even as Hades had taken Briareus's hand and drew his soul from his body, like a slice of shadow shaken from the darkness, he had known the consequences would be far reaching, beyond even what the Fates could weave, because once Zeus and Briareus's brothers, Gyges and Cottus, discovered what he had done, he would no longer have their support or allegiance. Not that he believed either brother would choose him over Zeus. He was not the one who had rescued them from the darkness of Tartarus. Still, they had been allies to the Olympians in the war against the Titans, helping drive the elder gods into the depths of Tartarus. It meant that if Hades found himself in opposition to Zeus, as he was certain to, especially given his engagement to Persephone, he would not have the help of the two remaining giants when things came to a head, and he could not blame them.

Hades had repaid their loyalty with an execution.

The God of the Dead left the field, manifesting in his office at Nevernight. As soon as he appeared, silence descended, thick and heavy. He looked at those gathered—Ilias, Zofie, Dionysus, and…Hermes.

Hades's eyes dropped to the God of Mischief who was reclined in his chair, feet propped on his desk. Their eyes met, and a sheepish smile broke out across his golden face. Hades scowled, showing his teeth, and sent the god scrambling to his feet.

"I was just keeping it warm," Hermes defended.

Hades glared and took his seat. It was indeed warm, which only made him stare harder at the god.

"Nothing but the best for the King of the Dead," Hermes added with a cheerful grin as he moved to sit on the edge of Hades's obsidian desk.

"If so much as *one* of your ass cheeks touches this desk, Hermes, I will turn it to lava."

"It's not as if they're *bare*," Hermes argued.

Hades gave the god a withering look.

"You know what? The couch is far more comfortable anyway," Hermes said, perching on the armrest.

Hades turned his attention to those gathered, in particular Dionysus. He hung back, not quite part of the group—likely because he did not wish to be. He was dressed far more casually than usual, in dark trousers and a beige sweater. His thick braids were tied back, and his arms were crossed over his chest. He looked frustrated, and if Hades had to guess, it had little to do with his summons to Nevernight and everything to do with the mortal detective Dionysus was harboring at his club, Ariadne Alexiou.

Hades was surprised he had come, though it likely only had to do with his curiosity. Dionysus had a strained relationship with the Olympians, mostly due to Hera's hatred of him, which was why he had finally decided to take a side. But Hades was not stupid. He knew that did not mean Dionysus was loyal to him. It only meant that the God of Madness was loyal to himself.

"The ophiotaurus has been resurrected," Hades said. "Its constellation is no longer in the sky."

There was a certain amount of dread that came with saying the words aloud that Hades had not expected to feel, but he was responsible for this, which meant he was also responsible for the fallout if the creature fell into the wrong hands.

"Ilias," Hades said, meeting the satyr's gaze. He stood beside Zofie, hair as curly as the horns jutting from his head. "Tell us what you have learned about the monster."

"So far, there has only been one sighting. A farmer outside Thebes claimed he heard a strange bellow in the middle of the night. He thought one of his cows had been injured, but when he went to investigate, he found a half-bull, half-serpent creature coiled around it. Once it had spotted him, it slithered away into the grass." Ilias paused and glanced at everyone gathered. "The cow did not make it."

There was a beat of silence as Hades added, "Neither did the farmer."

Ilias's jaw tightened.

"He was perfectly well yesterday."

"And today he is dead," Hades said. "Full of bullets."

"So someone other than us wants the creature," said Dionysus. "Not surprising, but who?"

"Isn't that the question of the hour."

Hades stared hard at the God of the Vine, not that he suspected Dionysus had anything to do with the farmer's death. He was, however, aware that he enjoyed collecting monsters as much as Poseidon. It was one reason he preferred keeping the god close, even with their new and fragile alliance.

Dionysus narrowed his eyes. "How did the creature come to be resurrected, Hades?"

The God of the Dead did not like the accusation in his voice, but Hades was not Dionysus, and he would not hide from his responsibility.

"Because I killed an immortal."

Dionysus's harsh features softened, but not out of sympathy.

It was shock.

"This is the work of the Fates," Hades said.

"So you summoned us to handle the aftermath of your actions," Dionysus said, his voice dripping with disdain. "Typical."

"Do not act so superior, Dionysus," Hades said. "I know how you like monsters."

He could have attempted to explain himself. He knew the god hated Hera, and one mention of how she'd had a hand in all this would quell Dionysus's judgment, but in truth, he did not feel like it mattered. Either way, Dionysus wanted to be here, and he would want the ophiotaurus in his possession, which meant he would search for it, even if he chose not to help Hades directly.

"If this is the work of the Fates," said Zofie, "can you not just ask them what they have woven?"

"The Fates are gods just as I am," said Hades. "They are no more likely to tell me their plans than I am to admit mine."

"But they are the Fates. Are they not already aware?"

Hades did not respond. There were times when he appreciated Zofie's naivete. Tonight, it was frustrating.

It was difficult to pin down how the Fates operated. Much of their decision-making was based on their mood, as with most gods. It was possible they had only orchestrated the resurrection of the ophiotaurus to fuck with him, but it was also possible they wanted to see an end to the Olympians; Hades could not say which or even if they had chosen. He only knew one thing to be true—fate could not be avoided, just prolonged.

"Whatever their plan, we must have one too," he said.

"I do not understand," said Zofie. "The Fates have already chosen an end. For what do we plan?"

"We plan to win," said Hades.

It was all they could do—and hope that if the Fates had not given him or the Olympians their favor, they could be swayed, but that would never happen without action. He knew better than anyone that the three sisters took joy in watching the gods play into their hands, especially under the weight of suffering.

There was a beat of silence, and then Dionysus

spoke. "What is the prophecy that makes this creature so dangerous?"

He would not know, given he had been born after the Titanomachy.

"Whoever burns its entrails will obtain the power to defeat the gods," said Hermes.

"Are you certain that's the prophecy?" asked Dionysus, raising a dark brow.

"Maybe it's just one god?" Hermes wondered aloud and then shrugged. "I might have gotten a word or two wrong."

"A word or two?"

"It isn't as if it hasn't been four thousand years," Hermes said defensively. "You try remembering something after that long."

"You seem to have no issue recalling grudges from that long ago."

"I suddenly regret helping Zeus save your life," said Hermes.

Sometimes Hades forgot the two had a history, though it was minor. Hermes had helped save Dionysus after he was born by taking him to be raised by the Nysiads, ocean nymphs who lived on Mount Nysa.

"Perhaps it would have been better for everyone if you had not," said Dionysus.

The God of Mischief blanched at his words, and before a strained silence could descend, Hades spoke. "It's a prophecy, Hermes. A word or two can change the entire meaning."

Hermes threw his arms in the air. "Well, I never claimed to be an oracle."

"Then we will have to ask one," Hades said.

Perhaps the prophecy had changed. Maybe there was no prophecy at all. Just as that thought rolled through his mind, he knew it was too much to hope for. The Fates would not bring the creature back if they didn't want it to challenge the gods.

"And we must find the ophiotaurus before anyone else."

"Who are we racing?" asked Dionysus.

"My money's on Poseidon and his offspring," said Hermes. "That fucker is always looking for power."

Hermes hit on something Hades had also been thinking. The ophiotaurus could live on land, but it also thrived in water. Poseidon would jump at any chance to overthrow Zeus, but so would Theseus and Hera. Hades already knew the demigod and the Goddess of Marriage were working together, though he also suspected the God of the Sea fed Theseus's desire to overthrow the Olympians. Whether he actually believed his son was capable was another matter.

Sometimes, Hades wondered who was orchestrating the game and who was just playing it, but he knew one thing: if he could become the mastermind, he would.

"We cannot let it take refuge in the sea," Hades said.

It would be in his brother's territory and virtually unreachable. Even if Hades were to offer a bargain, Poseidon would not give up such a weapon.

"Then we are wasting precious time talking when we should be hunting," said Dionysus.

"The issue, Dionysus, is where to begin," said Hades, looking at the god. "Unless you have information the rest of us do not."

Dionysus did not speak.

"We must be careful in our inquiries," said Ilias. "Word has already spread among the market. Everyone within those channels will expect your involvement."

And they were right to, though Hades knew that would not be a deterrent. In the seedy world of the black market, few feared his wrath, though he hardly saw that as an insult. It was hard to fear death when faced with it every day. Still, it meant that he would be locked in a competition to locate perhaps one of the greatest weapons ever created against the gods.

"Then perhaps my maenads should make the inquiries," Dionysus suggested, but Hades ignored him and looked at Ilias.

"Put Ptolemeos on the case, but watch him. I trust no one in this matter."

"Even me, apparently," Dionysus said.

Hades returned his gaze to the God of Wine. "Let's not pretend you haven't already sent your assassins to scout. You don't wait for permission; you take it."

Dionysus pursed his lips and looked away. Hades could not tell if he was amused or annoyed.

"And what is to be done with it when it is found?" asked Zofie. "Will you kill it?"

Hades did not respond because he did not know the answer to her question. He supposed it depended on what the oracle had to say about the creature's powers, though he doubted anyone else searching for the ophiotaurus would think twice about whether the prophecy still rang true.

That creature had a bounty on its head and a ticking clock on its heart.

"You're all dismissed," Hades said.

He was ready to be back in the Underworld with Persephone. It was where he should have been this entire night, curled around her warm body in the aftermath of their lovemaking. It made him irate that he had not been able to remain at her side. Even on the night of their engagement, he had been away while she slept, gathering intel on the ophiotaurus and attempting to discover where Demeter had taken refuge.

He tried not to think of this as an omen for what was to come, but he knew a battle lay ahead. He had always known it would not be easy to make Persephone his wife, given that her mother was one of his most vocal critics. And while the snow swirling outside in the middle of summer concerned him, he was more worried about Zeus.

His brother liked control, especially where other gods were concerned, and that included a say in who they married.

Hades clenched his fist at the thought.

He would marry Persephone no matter the consequences, because in the end, a life without her was not a life at all.

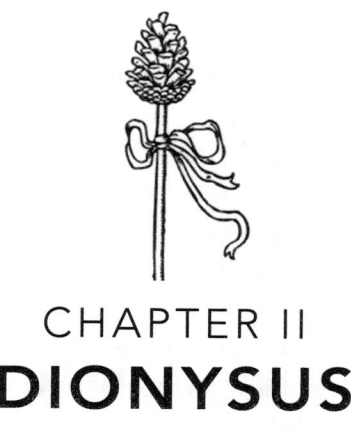

CHAPTER II
DIONYSUS

Dionysus left Nevernight and returned to Bakkheia, to the suite where he usually stayed despite having an estate of his own on the outskirts of Thebes. It was not that he found one place more comfortable than the other—he found no place particularly comfortable—it was that he could not handle the quiet of his home. Peace did not calm him; it only gave rise to louder, more incessant thoughts.

Even now, he was not completely free of them—of the endless voice in his mind that told him he had not done enough, that he was not enough. But at least here he could drown it out with the noise, the revelry, the *madness*.

He looked on it all now from the quiet of his suite, which had been abandoned by the usual carousers while he had answered the summons to Nevernight. Despite the early morning hour, his club teemed. Music vibrated his very soul and made his heart stutter in his chest. Laser lights cut through the darkness, highlighting sweaty and flushed faces, illuminating acquaintances and lovers locked in carnal embraces.

The musty scent of sweat mixed with the noxious odor of drugs seeped through the vents and burned his nose.

He was used to it—the sounds, the smells, the sex. It was part of the culture that had formed around his cult, one he had led with his maenads from town to town, leaving a trail of blood in his wake, and while he had long abandoned that life, he would never quite be free of the madness Hera had stricken him with.

Now and then, he could still feel it. It was a subtle tremor that consumed his body, and as it spread, it was warm and made him feel pierced through with pins and needles. It made it impossible to sit still, impossible to rest.

Just the thought made his fingers shake. He curled them into fists and held his breath, hoping to quell the feeling before it moved up his spine and into his veins, before it consumed him again, but as he focused, he became aware of a sound coming from somewhere inside his suite.

It was a panting moan.

He turned from the window overlooking the floor of this club and peered into the darkness but saw no one.

The sound grew in rhythm and was accompanied now by a knock.

Dionysus crossed the room toward a storage closet behind the bar. He pressed his ear to the door, which was soft, covered in the same black velvet that lined the walls. When he was certain the sounds came from there, he opened it.

Inside were Silenus and a woman he did not recognize. The satyr leaned against one side of the closet while the woman rode him, her legs wrapped around his waist.

"Fuck!" Silenus said, and they froze.

"Gods-dammit, Dad," Dionysus snapped.

Silenus laughed, breathless. "Oh, Dionysus. It's just you."

It was not as if this was the first time he had caught Silenus engaging in sexual acts. The satyr had become part of his cult after he was cursed to wander the earth. They'd spent days at the center of orgies, giving and receiving pleasure, as was his way of worship. Still, over the years, it had become something Dionysus wished to see less and less from a man he'd come to view as his father figure.

He closed the door with a sharp snap and then plucked a bottle of wine from the selection at the bar and poured a glass. As he took his first sip, the door opened again, and the woman stumbled out.

She cleared her throat and pushed her hair behind her ear.

"I am so sorry, Lord Dionysus. I did not mean—"

"Nothing to be sorry for," he said quickly, not looking at her. He took another sip of wine. "Go."

She bowed her head and stumbled away. A slice of bright light from the hallway cut through the dark as she left.

Behind him, Silenus emerged. "I was not aware you had returned," he said. Though Dionysus was not turned toward him, he could hear the clink of his belt as he secured it.

"How long have you been in that closet?" he asked.

The satyr paused. "I don't actually know."

Dionysus lifted a brow and glanced at his foster father. "Then how did you know I left at all?"

"I always know when you leave," Silenus said. "Because I feel like I can breathe again."

"Fucking rude," Dionysus said as Silenus elbowed his way beside him at the bar. The satyr was a head shorter than him but taller than any satyr he had ever met. It was likely because Silenus was not just a nature spirit. He was a nature god. He even looked different from others of his kind. Dionysus had seen satyrs with horse or goat feet and tails, but Silenus had the long ears of a donkey and a tail to match. Though it was a form he kept hidden mostly by his glamour.

"You have never faulted me for honesty before," said Silenus as he poured a glass of wine, only to down it like water. It was typical of him—he was the God of Drunkenness, which was why they had paired so well for so long, their lives revolving only around revelry.

"Should I start today?"

Silenus finished the last few gulps of wine before setting the glass aside with a clank. "Dionysus, even you know of what I speak," he said.

"If you are going to spout wisdom, you need to be far more drunk."

"This isn't wisdom. It is true. You have become unbearable."

"Why? Because I don't party with you anymore?"

"Well that is *a* reason," the satyr said. "But it's more than that. You know it is."

Dionysus pushed back from the bar, angling toward his foster father. "Enlighten me."

"You are not having fun," Silenus said. "At all. How long has it been since you let loose?"

Dionysus ground his teeth. "I am not the same person I once was, Silenus."

"None of us are," the satyr said. "But that does not mean we cannot enjoy life if we are to live it."

"Was it not you who said it is better not to have lived at all, and if we must, then it is best to die soon?"

"Well, you have yet to die, so why not spend a little more time having fun?"

Dionysus rolled his eyes and stepped out from behind the bar.

"You cannot go on like this," Silenus said. "You have let her have too much power over you."

Dionysus turned to him. "If we are going to speak about this, say her name."

Silenus stared, frustration in his gaze. "This quest for vengeance has made you...someone else."

"Has it occurred to you that perhaps *this* is who I am?" Dionysus asked. "And the person you met all those years ago, the one you miss so badly, was created by Hera?"

Silenus started to shake his head. "No. I don't believe that."

"You don't believe it because you don't want to see it."

"I don't believe it!"

They spoke in unison, voices raised and vehement, and once the words were out, the silence that stretched between them stung.

It was Silenus who spoke first. "I want to see you find happiness," he said and sighed, running a hand through his thin, graying hair. "Even if it is just an *ounce*."

"Perhaps I am not meant for happiness," Dionysus said.

"It's a *choice*, Dionysus," Silenus said, clearly frustrated. "You have to choose."

"Then I choose vengeance," Dionysus said. "And I will choose it until I have secured it."

"What about the girl?" the satyr asked.

Dionysus felt his body tense at the mention of Ariadne. "She's a woman, not a girl. What about her?"

"She's pretty," Silenus said.

His observation already irritated Dionysus. She wasn't just pretty. She was beautiful, and he was reminded of it every time he looked upon her face, *felt* it every time he entered the same room as her.

"She hates me," Dionysus said.

"Because she doesn't have anything to like at the moment," Silenus said.

"Perhaps I do not want her to like me at all."

"Your cock tells a different story."

"Don't look at my cock," Dionysus said. "It's weird."

"A cock never lies," his foster father said. "You like her."

"I want to fuck her. I don't like her," Dionysus said.

"Sounds like the perfect start to a relationship."

"Yes, an unhealthy one."

"Have you thought about…I don't know…turning her into more than just another one of your maenads?"

"I can't *turn* her into anything."

"Of course you can. You have already made her an unwilling prisoner."

"To protect her."

Whether she realized it or not, though that had

initially not been the case. Originally, he'd kidnapped her and brought her to Bakkheia because he'd suspected her of posing as a distraction so Hera and Theseus could abduct the Graeae. While she had done exactly that, she'd also told him she'd only made the decision to do it once she'd met him and found him completely unbearable.

He clenched his teeth.

"So you care about her," said the satyr.

"She is a means to an end, Silenus."

And she would be nothing more.

"Well, if she is a means to an end, let us hope she ends up on your cock."

Dionysus left his suite and took the elevator down to the basement, which was too simple of a word to describe what the underground of his club truly was. Most of the credit belonged to the maenads, who had made it into its own small city. It was a vast network of tunnels that connected to various parts of New Athens, and through it, they spied and killed and built a new life on the ashes of their past.

It was the complete opposite of what Ariadne had suspected, which was that he ran a sex trafficking ring. It was not the first time someone had accused Dionysus of such abominable behavior, but the fact that *she* had irked him, and it insulted the work of the maenads who spent the majority of their time *rescuing* other young people from fates similar to the ones they had escaped.

He wasn't sure why he was so bothered either.

They would not be so effective if their secret was known, and the fact that the world outside his realm believed he participated in trafficking usually benefited his agenda. It meant that people seeking those services often came to him to make connections, eventually becoming the target of his assassins.

It was hard work, precarious work...and for some reason, Ariadne's readiness to assume the worst stung.

It was not as if he should care either. He had only known her for a few weeks, and yet there she was, under his skin and burrowing deeper.

Sometimes when he was near her, he felt as though Hera had struck him with madness again.

When the elevator door opened, he stepped out onto the metal platform that overlooked the maenads' main living area. It was large, to accommodate the number of women who had joined over the last several years, though not all his assassins lived here. He expected to find the room abandoned this early in the morning, but a few maenads were still awake and alert, standing with their arms crossed, looking up at the industrial ceiling where large, metal ducts and bright lights hung. Some women looked frustrated, others annoyed, and a few were amused. Despite their mixed feelings, he knew they were listening.

He sighed because he knew exactly what they were listening for: Ariadne was trying to escape again.

He shook his head and stepped closer to the platform's edge. He wondered how long she'd been in the duct and when she'd stopped moving—likely as soon as he had arrived. She was probably up there now, cursing him, though he had no doubt she would wait him out as long as possible.

Then he heard a soft sneeze and concentrated his

power there. Screws popped out of holes, and the structure bent and folded. Ariadne gave a sharp cry as she fell from inside and crashed to the floor. For a split second, Dionysus worried that she had hurt herself during the fall, but she rolled onto her ass and glared at him.

She wore ripped jeans, a fitted shirt, and a leather jacket; her dark hair hung heavy over her shoulders. She was beautiful, even when she was pissed, which was all the time, at least with him.

"Leave," he commanded, and the maenads dispersed, disappearing down one of several darkened archways, leaving him alone with Ariadne. He stared at her a moment longer before taking the stairs to the lower level. As he crossed to her, she rose to her feet, dusting herself off, wincing as she did. "What hurts?" he asked.

She froze and glared at him. "If you were worried about hurting me, you should have thought twice before using your powers against a mortal."

"I did not use them against you."

"Then we have very different ideas of that meaning."

He took a deep breath to quell his frustration, but it didn't work. "If you are going to try to escape, you could at least accept my offer of training. Perhaps then you'd be successful."

"I am trained," she snapped.

"To interrogate and to use a gun," he said. "What useful skills against gods."

She reared back and tried to punch him in the face. He wasn't sure if this was her attempt at demonstrating skill or an instinctual reaction to her anger, but he caught her fist before she could even drive it toward him.

Her cry of pain surprised him, and he immediately

released her. She wrapped her fingers around her right wrist and held it to her chest.

"Let me see your hand," he demanded.

"I'm fine."

"For the love of the gods, Ariadne. Let me see it!"

She kept her teeth clenched and he held her gaze as she extended her hand. It did not appear to be obviously broken, and when he placed his palm over it, the energy confirmed his suspicions.

"You sprained it," he said.

"You mean *you* sprained it," she said.

Guilt struck him hard like a dizzying wave. He met her gaze. "I'm sorry."

His apology seemed to catch her off guard because she blinked. After a moment, she realized he was still holding her hand and tugged it away to hold it to her chest.

He cleared his throat. "You need ice," he said and started to walk around her. "Come."

He crossed the main living area and headed down a long, dark hall to the kitchen. He flipped on a switch, and fluorescent lights illuminated a sterile, stainless steel space, made so that it could feed hundreds at a time. Given that this underground network could house thousands if needed, it was a necessity.

He crossed to a row of tall shelves, located a box of sandwich bags after some digging, and filled one with ice. When he turned, he found Ariadne standing inside the door, staring.

"What?"

"Can't you just…magic a bag of ice out of thin air?"

He tilted his head and his lips quirked. "I don't think that is the correct use of magic."

"You know what I mean," she huffed and tried to cross her arms over her chest, but the pain seemed to remind her she shouldn't.

He approached and handed her the bag. "I suppose I could have," he said. "But I can also get it myself."

Besides, he'd needed to create distance between them, even if it had only lasted a few seconds.

She took the ice and placed it on her wrist. "Thank you," she said, so quiet he could barely hear, though in truth, he did not deserve the thanks. He owed her this.

"I am not joking about training you," he said.

"I don't want to be one of your maenads," she said.

"Then don't be," he said. "But if you are going to stay in this world, you are going to need to know how to do more than just carry a gun."

"Stop assuming all I am capable of is using a gun."

"Can you use any other weapon?" he asked.

She was silent.

"A gun cannot help us if we are to go against Theseus," he said.

She bristled at the mention of her brother-in-law, though he knew if she ever heard him call Theseus that out loud, she would rage. Ariadne hated the demigod, and from what he knew, she had every reason. Theseus kept her imprisoned beneath his will by holding her sister, Phaedra, hostage.

"Where were you going?" he asked after a moment. When she didn't respond, he continued, "Were you going to him?"

He knew the answer, and yet the thought of her sneaking away to Theseus in any capacity made him burn with jealousy.

"No," she snapped. "I was going to see my sister."

"Going to see your sister is the same as seeing Theseus," he said. "Do you really believe he will let you have access to her?"

"No!" she snapped. "But at least she will know I have *tried*."

Her eyes glistened with unshed tears, and the sight did something to his chest. He didn't like it because it made him want to do stupid things for her.

"Did I not agree to help you save your sister?" he asked.

"Hades agreed, *not* you," she said.

He ground his teeth together so hard, his jaw hurt. "He might have agreed to the deal, but we both know I am the one who will have to see it through," he said.

"If I am such a burden, then let me go," she said.

"I never said you were a burden."

"You don't have to," she replied, casting her gaze to the floor.

Dionysus just stared. "I'm not interested in rehashing how we came to be at this point or even how we feel about it," he said. "What's done is done, and we have work to do. You want to free your sister and take down Theseus, but what you fail to understand is that Theseus is not just one person, and even if he were, he's a demigod, the son of Poseidon. He's thousands strong, and to take him down, we will need more."

"More what?" she asked.

"More of everything," he said. "More time, more planning, more people, more weapons."

"I am not preparing for battle, Dionysus," she said. "I just want my sister."

"Too bad," he said. "Because you won't have her without a war."

She took a breath, her chest rising sharply, and he tried not to stare too long so she wouldn't notice how his attention had wandered.

"You have no idea what you stumbled into," he said.

"So what do you want from me?"

Her question surprised him, but not because of what she asked but because of how it made him feel—aware of both how empty he felt and his desire to fill that void.

But he quickly quashed those thoughts. "We have to find Medusa," he said.

Medusa was a gorgon who was rumored to be able to turn men to stone with a glance. If true, she would make a valuable weapon. The moment he had heard whispers of her power in the market, he had hired the Graeae to help him find her, but his plan backfired when Detective Alexiou decided to help Theseus and Hera capture the three sisters.

She likely had no idea what she'd been assigned to do when she'd arrived at Bakkheia. Theseus had made a wolf into a sheep, and Dionysus hated to see how well she followed him.

His eyes narrowed.

"What if she does not wish to help you?"

"It's your job to convince her," he said.

"I thought you said you did not need her power."

"In this game, it is not about needing her power, it's about who gets to it first," he said. "And you want me to get to her first, I promise you."

"Why don't you send your assassins?"

"This is not a job for them," he said. "She must be convinced that it is best to side with us."

"And what if I am not convinced?"

"Then let us hope by the time we find her, you are."

CHAPTER III
HADES

Hades appeared in his chambers, darkened except for the fire, which was too bright, like the blinding fire of the Phlegethon. He almost wished it wasn't lit, that he did not have to face more flames tonight, because the glow reminded him that the world outside this space did not wish for his happiness.

It made him want to become a recluse again, to shut out the world as he had at the start of his reign as King of the Underworld, but as he cast his gaze on Persephone, who lay sleeping in a sea of black silk, he knew that was impossible. She was too social, too loving, too invested to leave the Upperworld behind. She wanted to save the world, even the parts of it that did not deserve her kindness, and because she wanted that, he would want that too.

He sighed and ran his fingers through his hair, pulling out the tie that held it away from his face. He crossed to the bar and poured himself a shot of whiskey, downing it quickly before undressing and joining Persephone in bed.

He lay on his side and watched her, not wishing to disturb her sleep despite how he ached for her. Even in the shadowed room, he would know her face because he had memorized it—the arch of her brow, the curve of her cheek, the shape of her lips. She was beautiful, and her heart was so *good*. He was sure a part of him would always be in disbelief that she was his, that she had agreed to marry *him* despite everything that he had been and everything he continued to be, though there was a darker part of him that recognized engagements could end and so could marriages.

It wasn't so much that he expected Persephone to leave as much as he expected the world to tear them apart.

Persephone sighed, and it drew Hades from his thoughts. He focused on her face and noticed her eyes moving behind her lids. She frowned then, and her breaths became harsher, her chest rising and falling faster and faster.

"Persephone?" he whispered, and she whimpered, her head pressing into her pillow, her back arching. Her arms remained over her head, fists clenched as if someone were holding her down.

Then she went rigid and whispered a name that made his blood run cold.

"Pirithous."

Hades rose onto his elbow, fear flooding his veins. That man. That name.

Pirithous had kidnapped Persephone, encouraged to do so by Theseus after weeks of stalking her. Hades could still recall the entries the demigod made in a journal he'd kept at his desk, describing what Persephone wore, their interactions, and everything he wanted to do to her. It was chilling to read and added another layer of horror to the nightmare that was her abduction.

Those same feelings rose within him now, tearing open his chest.

It was a familiar feeling. He had been here with her before. Since the day Pirithous had taken her, he had haunted her sleep.

"Persephone," Hades said and pressed his hand flat against her stomach, but at his touch, she whimpered. "Shh," he attempted to soothe, but a sob erupted from her throat. She wrenched away and sat up, breathing heavily. He let her collect herself, fearful that touching her immediately after her nightmare would only upset her further, though he was desperate to take her into his arms, to help her feel safe, to never let her leave.

She turned her head and seemed to relax as her gaze fell on him, and he suddenly did not feel so useless. Sometimes he worried that he had done nothing right in the aftermath of her abduction and that one day he might unknowingly trigger some memory from that night, and then what would he do? How could he atone?

It felt impossible to keep her safe.

"Are you well?" he asked.

Her chest rose as she took a breath, studying him just as intently as he watched her. She was beyond anything he had ever imagined for himself—beautiful and gracious, far too good for the things he had done in his many lifetimes—and yet she remained, a steady light at his side, a beacon he could follow through the dark.

It was in these quiet moments when he felt most overwhelmed by his love for her.

"You haven't slept."

Her voice was a whisper that slid over his skin. It made him *want*, which felt wrong.

"No," he said and rose to sit, angling so that he could look at her face.

She was flushed, and her eyes were too bright, an indication that she had drawn on her magic as she dreamed.

Hades brushed his thumb along her cheek, and her eyes fluttered closed, as if his touch brought her a sense of comfort. The thought made his heart beat erratically. There was power in how she made him feel, and she was the only one who had ever possessed it.

"Tell me," he said, though he knew what she would say.

"I dreamed of Pirithous again."

He let his hand fall from her face, fingers curled into fists. It was one thing to know and another thing to hear.

"He harms you, even in your sleep," Hades said. Pirithous haunted her even though his soul was trapped in Tartarus—haunted *him* no matter how many times he had tortured the demigod to death. "I failed you that day."

"How could you have known he would take me?"

"I should have known."

Hades took pride in knowing everything, anticipating everything. He had taken every precaution, ensured Antoni took Persephone to and from work, assigned Zofie as her aegis to guard her at all times, even from afar. He had allowed her as much freedom as he possibly could, which was likely more than he should have, given she was a target for so many—enemies she could not even fathom. But he could not keep her locked in a cage, even if that cage was the Underworld.

"You are not all-seeing, Hades," Persephone said, her voice a whisper.

She was trying to ease his pain, and she could not know that her comment only made it worse. It did not matter that he was not omniscient. He still blamed himself for what happened. He had blamed Zofie too, and when he had tried to relieve her of her assignment as Persephone's aegis, his goddess had defended her.

He was not proud of his actions. He should have been comforting Persephone. She struggled. He knew it. Even when he made love to her, he could feel the tension in her body, highly aware of the time it took to make her comfortable.

This man, this demigod had invaded their most private and intimate space, and it enraged him.

And this, he recognized, was the power of the semidivine.

Their power was unknown, their numbers were unknown, and one insignificant son of an Olympian had managed to kidnap not only another goddess but *his* goddess.

He refocused on Persephone and what should have been comforting words.

"You are right," Hades replied. "Perhaps I should punish Helios, then."

She gave him a look, unimpressed with his comment.

"Would that make you feel better?"

"No, but it would be fun," Hades said. He did not

admit that he had fucked with the God of the Sun so much over the last few months Helios was likely to never assist him again—which was not so much a loss as it was a relief despite the fact that he suspected the god either had or would side with Hera in her quest to overthrow Zeus.

Hades had only managed to threaten the Queen of the Gods to submit to his will, ensuring that when Zeus protested his marriage to Persephone, Hera had to come to his defense. She had agreed, though reluctantly. It was not that Hades did not wish to see an end to Zeus's reign as King of the Gods; it was that he wanted Persephone at his side when he did. They were far more powerful together than apart, but then, Zeus would know that, which made him the greatest threat to their happiness.

"I wish to see him," Persephone said.

It took him a moment to process what she had said because his thoughts had been in a completely different space. He felt guilty that he had been thinking of Zeus and Hera while she had been agonizing over Pirithous.

But there was a determination in her voice he knew he couldn't fight—not that he would deny her request. He had made this promise to her the night he had rescued her, though not exactly as she had asked.

When you torture him, I get to join, she'd said, and while he had agreed, it had not kept him from going to Tartarus that night to torment the demigod alone—or returning nearly every night since to do the same. It was not that he did not wish to honor Persephone's request. It was that he had been waiting for her to make it, because then, he knew she would be ready.

His only hesitation was that once she visited this part

of Tartarus, she would know the darkest part of him. He realized she knew the purpose of his Underworld prison, but it was an entirely different thing to see it, and that triggered him, the fear that she might finally understand who she had fallen in love with and realize she was not in love at all.

He held her unwavering gaze and replied, "As you wish, darling."

Hades took Persephone to the white room—one of his more modern torture chambers. It was used to deprive its occupants of their senses. Sometimes, Hades would leave a soul in here alive for weeks, and by the time he returned, they had lost all sense of themselves. He particularly enjoyed granting this punishment to those who used their status and power to wound and kill in the Upperworld. It made it all the more satisfying when they finally lost their sense of self.

It was here where Hades had last left Pirithous, having spent the better part of his time in the Underworld cycling through other methods of torture, both old and new. He had broken bones and cracked knees, cut off his balls and his dick, covered him in honey and let insects and rats mince at his body until his bones were exposed.

He had done all that and more, and his rage had not lessened. Even now he could feel it welling inside him as he looked at Pirithous, who was slouched in a chair at the center of the room, only held in place by rope that wound around his arms, waist, and legs. His skin was pale white, almost gray, and spattered with layers of dried blood from his previous torture. He was not a pleasant sight, and Hades wondered what Persephone thought now that she was face-to-face with the demigod.

Beside him, Persephone was still and quiet, her eyes fixed on her attacker. After a moment, she took a breath, which sounded sharp in the silence of the room.

"Is he dead?"

He assumed she whispered for fear that she would rouse Pirithous.

"He breathes if I say so."

It occurred to him then that her only fear was that this man might be able to hurt her again. His hands fisted as she made her way toward the soul. He was overwhelmed with the urge to pull her back, to keep her near, to only let her observe him from afar, but he knew if she felt she could not do this, she wouldn't.

"Does it help?" she asked, turning to look at him. For a brief moment, all he could think about was how strange it was to have something so beautiful in a space like this. "The torture?"

Hades studied her face.

There was something innocent about her question. Perhaps it was the assumption that he used torture to heal his wounds instead of feeding them, as was the case with Pirithous. No matter how Hades made the demigod suffer, it would never be enough.

"I cannot say."

Her gaze lingered on him a moment longer before she turned and began walking around her prisoner. She could not know what this did to him, how this made him feel. She commanded this place like a queen, and she wasn't even aware of it.

She paused behind the demigod, watching him, and

all he could think was that she had never looked more beautiful, despite their surroundings.

"Then why do you do it?"

For a moment, he scrambled to figure out if she asked because she disapproved, but she did not appear to be horrified by him or the demigod restrained before her, so he answered truthfully.

"Control."

It was something he sought daily because it had been the first thing taken from him when his father had swallowed him whole upon his birth, and then, just when he thought he was free of that horrible prison, he faced another ten years in battle. In the aftermath, control had meant a dark existence. It meant that everyone in his realm had to feel like he felt—wretched and tortured. He had believed no one was deserving of a peaceful afterlife after what he had seen.

Over time, his idea of what it meant to be in control evolved, and his empire bled out into the world above. He sought to make the darkest parts his own, feeding the underbelly of New Greece until power and status could only be obtained through him and anyone who operated outside that did not last long. There were few exceptions, but among them were Dionysus and, most recently, Theseus, who was helped mostly by his father.

But not even they challenged him like Persephone.

She had crashed into his life and defied him at every turn, and he had not been able to exercise any sort of control over her. She would not be contained, and in many ways, he could not blame her. She had only just escaped the confines of her mother's authority, and then to come face-to-face with him—a virtual stranger who had attempted to give her rules—it was no wonder she had resisted.

In the end, she'd only wanted what he had wanted.

"I want control," she said, and Hades felt like she was squeezing his heart.

He wanted to give her that.

He extended his hand. "I will help you claim it."

She did not hesitate and came to him, placing her hand in his and drawing in close. He turned her so that her back rested against his chest, his fingers splayed at her hip, possessive and aware that Pirithous would soon awaken. Hades wanted the demigod to be reminded of what he had done, that he had taken the wrong goddess and challenged the wrong god.

With her safely in his arms, he summoned his magic like a spear and aimed for Pirithous. The demigod sucked in a sharp breath, as if he'd felt the pain of Hades's power, and at the sound, Persephone went rigid. Hades shifted closer, as if he could shield her from her fear with his body. He let his lips brush the tip of her ear as he spoke.

"Do you remember when I taught you to harness your magic?"

He had taught her one evening beneath the silver eaves of her own woods. As he recalled that evening—how his body had cradled hers, how he had touched her, how she had slowly grown warm and aroused beneath his hands—desire kindled low in his stomach, and as much as he would have liked to suppress it, to focus only on the point of their visit to Tartarus, Persephone made it just as hard.

She shuddered, and her ass and shoulders pressed into his body.

It seemed he did not even need to know her answer, her reaction telling him she remembered that and what came after.

Still, she spoke.

"Yes."

The corners of Hades's lips lifted, and as he spoke, his mouth skimmed the edge of her ear down the column of her neck.

"Close your eyes," he whispered as the demigod began to stir because he did not wish for her to have to look at him.

Pirithous's eyes blinked open, brows furrowed in confusion as his sleepy gaze fell on Persephone, at which point he seemed to fully awaken. Then he spoke Persephone's name, and it took everything in Hades's power not to cross the distance between them and rip out his tongue.

Instinctively, he pressed closer to her, his fingers digging into her hip. Touching her made him feel grounded and reminded him why they were here—so Persephone could take back her power, and maybe then, she could finally sleep in peace.

"What do you feel?" he asked, concentrating on her. Everything was about her.

He spoke against her skin and felt her take a breath as Pirithous began to beg.

"Persephone, please." His voice shook. The longer the demigod was awake, the more he recalled the torment at Hades's hands, and it made him desperate. "I–I am sorry."

Sorry.

That word burrowed beneath Hades's skin, calling to

the darkness that lived just beneath the surface. It made him feel…

"Violent," Persephone said, and he knew it because there was an edge to her power that he had never felt before. Beneath the warmth and the flora was something sharp and desperate. He wanted to taste it, run his tongue along it.

"Focus on it," Hades commanded, his hand twining with hers. "Feed it."

In the quiet moment that followed, Hades remained still, relishing the feel of her magic as she concentrated on gathering it into her palm. It was a rush, a great wave of power that hit him deep in his stomach.

"Where do you wish to cause him pain?" he asked.

"This isn't you." Pirithous's voice turned to a keen whine, and Hades wished more than anything that he would shut the fuck up. "I know you. I watched you!"

Yes, he had watched her.

He had targeted and stalked her. He had taken pictures of her in her home, where she was meant to be safest. He had felt entitled to her body for no other reason than the fact that she existed.

And he would be punished eternally.

"He wanted to use his cock as a weapon," she said. "And I want it to burn."

Hades grinned wickedly.

"No! Please, Persephone," Pirithous screamed, struggling violently against his restraints. "Persephone!"

"Then make him burn."

He let her go, and she lifted her hand, which burned with magic, sending a current of energy straight to Pirithous's cock. He began to writhe, his body jerking against the ropes that restrained him, cutting into his skin. His head snapped back and he bared his teeth. Hades imagined her magic felt much like being electrocuted. Even he could feel the current, like the residual heat from a fire, and it raised the hair on his arms and the nape of his neck.

"This...isn't...you," Pirithous ground out.

Hades felt Persephone stiffen at his words, and she straightened, lifting her chin as she stared at the demigod, and while he could not see her full expression from where he stood behind her, he knew she must look like a queen, because something changed even in Pirithous's contorted expression—something that made him realize just how futile his appeals were.

"I am not sure who you think I am, but let me be clear," Persephone said, her voice clear and resolute. "I am Persephone, future Queen of the Underworld, Lady of Your Fate. May you come to dread my presence."

Her words tangled in Hades's chest, stealing the air from his lungs. He had never felt so in love and so desperate to protect someone in his life, and while he had desired for so long to hear her embrace this part of herself—the title and power he had to offer—he wished it had come under different circumstances, that it had been born out of a love for the happier parts of the Underworld and not the darkest.

But there were few in this world who learned the truth of their power without strife. He and Persephone were no different.

"How long will he stay like this?" she asked.

Hades looked at Pirithous, who was still convulsing. "Until he dies," he said, and for a moment, he wondered if she was disturbed by the sight of his torture, if she would ask him to end it, but instead, she turned to him, tilting her head back to look at his face. He knew in that moment she was changed. He couldn't exactly say how, but it lingered between them, as tangible as the violence that had punctured her magic.

His goddess was no longer made up of innocent things, and there was a part of him that did not know how to feel about it, that wondered if she had never met him if that would still be the case.

"Take me to bed," she said.

Hades touched her cheek and then threaded his fingers through her golden hair. There were things he wanted to know, things he wanted to say. Did she still love him the same way she did before they came here? Would the trauma of this night fester in her mind until she realized she had become someone she did not wish to be? And would she blame him?

But he said none of those things and instead bent to kiss her. She welcomed him, her lips parting as his tongue sought hers, and his desire, which had not ceased, grew stronger than ever. He groaned and his arm tightened around her back, sealing every part of his hard body against every soft part of hers, and he considered that perhaps Pirithous's greatest punishment of all might be that he had to watch them make desperate love to one another as he died for the thousandth time.

But that was a desire he would not speak, and instead he drew away and met her gaze.

"As you wish, my darling," he said as he transported them away from the depths of Tartarus to their room, where he let her lead them to release.

Persephone slept.

She lay on her side, her hands folded under her head, her breathing easy and even. Hades sat on the edge of their bed, watching for signs that another nightmare had taken root within her dreams, but she remained quiet and still. There was a part of him that feared leaving her unattended. What if Pirithous returned? What if he was not here to comfort her when she woke?

He felt a keen sort of turmoil roiling within him as he wondered if her sleep would take on a new horror. Perhaps it would no longer be Pirithous that haunted her but the torture she had inflicted on him.

Hades raked his fingers through his unbound hair.

He was restless and anxious, and he had only found reprieve while he was with Persephone. His comfort came with her, whether she was astride him or beneath him. He wanted to be near her, inside her, filling her. The need was acute and primal, and in the hours after, it gave him the greatest pleasure to know some part of him remained within her.

If he could take refuge in her body every minute of every day, he would, but that was a sign of his addiction. It wasn't healthy, but if he were to have a vice, it was the best of the lot.

He sighed and rose. It was too warm, his body still slick with sweat. Unlike Persephone, who drifted off after sex, he'd remained awake, his body a live wire.

He poured himself a drink and then stepped outside onto the balcony where the night was mild and breezy. The reprieve from the heat was pleasant, and he felt at ease, knowing he was near in case Persephone spiraled into another nightmare.

He looked out on a fraction of his realm where silvery moonlight pooled in the shadowed garden outside his palace. It was the garden where everything had begun, where he'd brought Persephone to plant the seed of her bargain. *Create life in the Underworld*, he had instructed, *or be mine forever.*

Gods how he'd hoped she would fail, because at the time, he'd believed that was the only way he'd get to keep her. She'd been so angry, and it had only gotten worse when he'd brought her here, to the Underworld.

She, like so many, had expected a barren landscape of ash and fire. What she had gotten instead was a lush world full of color and flora. It had also been the first sign that what her mother had told her about him over the last twenty-four years was not the truth, and that had devastated her.

She'd fought him. *Hard.*

But the more he'd learned about her, the less it surprised him. She had been so traumatized by her mother's control, she'd resisted the idea of belonging to anyone. The stronger her feelings for him grew, the more she refused to love him, except there was no way to stop it once it had started, and when she finally succumbed, she'd opened the most powerful part of herself.

This...it went beyond love. It was devotion. It was worship. It was the power that began and ended worlds, and if he had to, he would do so in her name. He knew those words were true because he felt them so deeply, it hurt.

"Why are you naked?"

Hades was drawn from his thoughts and looked down into the garden where Hecate lingered, nearly invisible in the darkness.

"Would you really like an answer to that question?" he asked. "I can give details."

She scrunched her nose in mock disgust. "I think I can guess. It is not as if you are *quiet*."

Hades chuckled and Hecate arched a brow, though he could not help being amused at the thought of Persephone's cries of pleasure echoing throughout the Underworld.

"Come off your high horse," she said. "It is not as if you excel at giving pleasure. Some of us are just sensitive to sound."

He rolled his eyes. "Fearful I will become too arrogant, Hecate?"

"I do not have to fear it," she said. "You *are*."

"Arrogance does not make something untrue," he said.

"No, but it does make it annoying."

He could not help laughing. "No one said you had to endure it," he said. "Why are you here anyway? Aren't there some pathetic souls in the Upperworld deserving of your haunting presence?"

"No one is *deserving* of my presence," she said. "I am a plague upon men."

"You are definitely a plague," he muttered.

"I heard that," she snapped.

"I'm aware," Hades said.

"And you? Why are you sulking on your balcony instead of lying with your love?"

"I am not sulking," he said.

"You always sulk," she said.

Hades glared, unwilling to argue with the goddess. "I cannot sleep, if you must know."

"Worrying too much?" she asked.

He did not respond.

"Perhaps you should not worry when you are with her," said Hecate.

"That is when I worry most," he said, because he thought of what he stood to lose if anyone got in his way.

"Trust that your love is stronger than any god," said Hecate.

"It is not our love I worry about," he said. "It is what I will destroy to keep it."

"Since when have you ever worried over carnage?" she asked.

"Since I decided to marry the Goddess of Spring," he said.

"Foolish man," Hecate said. "You never had a choice."

Her words made him uneasy. There was something he disliked about the truth of the Fates and their threads. He'd have liked to think he would have chosen Persephone no matter the weaving of their lives and that perhaps she would have chosen him, though he knew she feared that all they had was what Fate had given them.

He wondered if she still thought that or if she had begun to believe their love might be greater than ethereal thread.

There was a part of him that did not wish to know.

"Do not pretend Persephone does not know who she has chosen to love," Hecate said. "She sees all of you. She is the Goddess of Spring after all. She is used to life and death."

CHAPTER IV
HADES

Hades returned to Persephone but did not sleep, a fact that did not escape her notice. She had risen around noon and frowned at him when she woke. She traced the high point of his cheek. He took her hand and kissed her fingertips.

"I am well," he said.

"Why do you lie?" she asked.

To protect you, he wanted to say.

"What will you do today?" Hades asked instead.

She gave him a strange look. "I am assuming you are asking because you do not intend to stay?"

"I have business in the Upperworld," he said.

"On a Sunday?"

He knew she did not ask because she was suspicious but because it was unusual. He normally spent the weekends sequestered in the Underworld with her. Sometimes they did not leave this room; other times he took her to explore parts of the Underworld she had never seen.

Whatever their day, it was time he cherished with her, and while he hated to give it up, he knew this could not wait.

He had to know if the ophiotaurus had reincarnated with a prophecy.

"I will make it up to you," he said.

She did not respond, and there was something about her silence that made him feel like he had hurt her. She sat up and swung her legs off the bed. He kept his eyes on her bare back, mesmerized by the way her hair caught the light, glinting like spun gold.

"I will visit Lexa," she said, answering his earlier question.

At the mention of her best friend, guilt and pain lanced through Hades's chest. He had always liked Lexa, but he had to admit, he'd had no understanding of the depth of their relationship until Persephone was faced with her death.

It went beyond being friends. They were soul mates, and he had failed to understand that Persephone would need more from him in the face of her death than he had managed to give her.

That was something he would never forgive himself for, because it had led Persephone to seek help elsewhere, the worst of it coming from Apollo, whose arrow had healed Lexa's wounds but not her psyche, which had effectively sentenced her to a different existence in the Underworld, one that ensured Persephone suffered just as much as Lexa.

Her best friend would never be the same, and Hades did not know how many visits it would take to Elysium before Persephone realized she wasn't coming back.

The version of Lexa she had loved was dead.

"How long?" he asked, because he did not know what else to say.

"Until she gets tired," she said, and he knew she was trying to keep the sadness from her voice. "Which will not be long…she tires easily. Is that usual for souls in Elysium?"

"Yes," he replied. "It is usual."

He did not wish to tell her that Lexa probably tired faster because Persephone challenged her. Though she'd been given instruction not to talk about their past together or speak long on the mortal world, it was something she likely could not help, which meant Lexa's mind was working hard to process or relearn what it had forgotten. Even emotions were a new experience in Elysium.

Persephone was quiet, and after a moment, she rose, naked and beautiful, and entered the bathroom. The sound of the shower followed. Hades considered joining her, but he had the distinct feeling that she wanted to be alone, so he got up and dressed.

This day felt strange, contrary to his usual routine.

He hated it.

He considered just staying with Persephone, but there were greater things at work, and it made him anxious to delay. The ophiotaurus was not something that could exist for long in the world without consequence. It was not only a threat to his happiness but a threat to all gods, and while some deserved to die, he'd rather that power not fall into the wrong hands.

A cloud of steam wafted into the room as Persephone left the bathroom, wrapped only in a towel.

"You're still here," she said.

He frowned. "Since when do I leave without saying goodbye?"

She did not answer, and he approached, touching her chin.

"I know you are upset with me."

"I am not upset. I just thought this day would be different," she said and paused to take a breath. "Yuri and Hecate want to meet about the wedding."

"Is that a bad thing?"

"No," she said and hesitated. "I...just don't know what you want."

He studied her, and when she tried to look away, he brought his other hand up to cup her face.

"I want you," he said. "You are all that matters."

He did not like the way she looked at him, as if she were searching for the truth of his words in his eyes, but he likely only felt that way because of his own fears.

Fuck, he had issues.

"I love you," he said and kissed her, drawing away quickly before he changed his mind and stayed.

The sounds of playful screaming reminded Hades of the Children's Garden in the Underworld, though the comparison made his heart ache. He rarely grieved anyone who entered the Underworld, but children were the exception. He had never gotten used to it, and he never would.

He hesitated to even approach this park where clusters of children played on large, colorful toys despite the cold and the dusting of snow on the ground, their parents either participating or watching idly. He was not invisible to their eyes, and his presence would likely strike fear.

The mortals above did not always realize there was a difference between him and Thanatos, one the God of the Dead, the other the God of Death, and they assumed he arrived to reap souls, but he was here for one person, and he did not require her soul.

He was usually good at ignoring the unease that settled on the world when he arrived, but something about being here made it far less easy. Still, he kept his eyes on Katerina, who was dressed in a brown jacket lined with fur. She was one of his employees, the trusted director of the Cypress Foundation.

She was also an oracle.

"She's gotten big," Hades said as he sidled up beside Katerina, who stood a few feet from one of the playsets, watching her young daughter, Imari, play.

Katerina jumped at the sound of his voice and then laughed when she saw him.

"Oh, Hades, you scared me!" she said, pushing his shoulder. Her breath frosted the air as she spoke.

He chuckled while Katerina's gaze returned to her daughter.

"She is big, isn't she?" she asked and then sighed. "I can't believe so much time has passed."

"Six years?" he inquired, though he did not need to ask. He knew.

"Yeah," she said. "You're good at that."

"Good at what?"

"Remembering," she said. "Or is that a god thing?"

"Is what a god thing?"

"Can you just look at someone and know their age?"

"I suppose," he said. "Though I have never really needed to."

Death was death, no matter the age.

"What are you doing here?" Katerina asked after a moment. "It's Sunday."

He took too long to answer, and Katerina's smile faded.

"I need your assistance," he said. "I would not ask if…"

"Hades!"

He turned his head to the sound of his name as Imari jumped from the play set to the ground. He laughed and knelt as she raced into his arms.

People had stared before, but not like they did now.

"There's my girl," he said, and she laughed as she pulled away from him, taking his hand in hers, which looked like a giant's in her small one.

"Come play with me," she said, tugging on his arm.

"Imari," Katerina began. "Lord Hades is busy."

"It's all right, Katerina," he said.

A wide smile broke out across the young girl's face, and she pulled Hades along toward the play area. He felt far too large and awkward, but Imari was too young to see him like that—too young to know what others feared.

He watched as Imari climbed a set of steps to a platform and reached over her head.

"Help me on the monkey bars, Hades!"

"Up you go," he said, and as he took hold of her legs, Katerina approached.

"What is it you would not ask?" she said.

As Imari swung from bar to bar, they followed.

"I need your gift of prophecy," he said.

Katerina wasn't in the habit of using her abilities as an oracle to help him outside the work she did for his foundation. She might comment on the potential success or failure of one of his endeavors or organize timelines for the greatest outcome, but he had never asked her for anything like this.

He continued. "There is…a creature called the ophiotaurus," Hades said, his voice quiet, his words slow. "In ancient times, a prophecy foretold the death of the gods with the burning of its entrails. I need to know if that prophecy still exists."

Katerina stared at Hades for a long moment and then looked away.

"The ophiotaurus," she murmured and then was quiet.

Imari came to the end of the bars.

"Catch me, Hades!" she said and let go.

He snatched her about the waist and spun with her in his arms. Her screeching laugh filled the park and made Hades smile.

As he set her down, she ran for a swing.

"Push me, Hades!"

As they followed, Katerina spoke. "If a person slays the creature and burns its entrails, then victory is assured against the gods," she said.

Silence followed her answer.

It was as Hades had feared—the prophecy remained true.

Imari began to swing, and Hades pushed. She giggled as she rose higher and higher, a happy backdrop to their somber conversation.

"What will you do?" Katerina asked.

"Try to find it before anyone else," he said.

The creak of the swing filled the quiet between them.

"What if you don't?" she asked after a moment.

"Then I suppose we will all die," he replied.

―――

Hades realized as he vanished from the park that he had left Katerina with an ominous prediction.

In truth, he did not know what would happen if someone found the ophiotaurus before him. It was possible that anyone might kill it out of fear, not realizing the true importance of the creature or the danger they would suddenly find themselves faced with.

If the ophiotaurus died, it would not be as important as the person who killed it according to Katerina's prophecy. Whoever slayed the creature must burn the entrails. Then victory would be assured against the gods.

The gods.

He knew there was no sense in trying to figure out who would be a victim of the prophecy. The Fates would not divulge the future they had woven, and it was possible they had only done this for their entertainment. During the Titanomachy, the ophiotaurus had caused such a melee as both sides scrambled to find the creature that would end the war, but in the end, it had all been for nothing. The Titans had managed to slay it, and Zeus's eagles had stolen the entrails, foiling the prophecy.

The Fates' message had been clear: there was no easy end to this war.

But things were different now, and it was possible

they wished to usher in a new era faster. He could only guess as to their motives. His fingers curled into fists as he felt his control slipping away. That was the worst part of dealing with the Fates.

Their future was final.

But that did not mean Hades would not attempt control. He would protect the few who were closest to him—Persephone most of all.

If she would let him.

Hades manifested in a wooded meadow, and he was immediately overcome by the oppressive smell of Demeter's magic. It bore down on him like a weight on his back. He could feel his body curling in on itself. The only reprieve was Persephone's magic—a sweet undercurrent that called to his soul.

Something crunched beneath his feet, and when he looked down, he saw shards of shimmering glass amid blooming carex and foxglove, all sprouting from a bed of green grass, untouched, as Hades suspected, by the winter storm ravishing New Athens.

His gaze shifted to the ruins of a greenhouse. It was the source of Persephone's magic. Her early magic too, for the thing that blossomed from the earth was a strange, black trunk with long limbs that curled around the metal frame of the greenhouse, and crushed beneath those branches were many of Demeter's flowers—prisoners who found themselves at her mercy and found none.

Now he understood where the glass had come from.

He wondered at what point she'd come to wreak havoc on her crystalline prison, and for a brief moment, he let himself marvel at how far Persephone had come—from creating life that mimicked the dead to coaxing blossoms from the earth as she stepped.

Hades took a step, and as he did, the glass beneath his feet was like thunder in the quiet meadow. He was well aware he was not alone. He could feel eyes tracking him but was not surprised that fear had driven any living thing from the meadow.

He turned, eyes roaming the scattered tree line.

"I know you're there," he said. "Come out."

There was no action that followed his words.

"Come out or I shall come to you," he said.

It was not an idle threat. He knew exactly where the nymphs had taken refuge. Beyond the tree line was a river, and from its banks, they watched.

They were naiads like Leuce.

He waited with far more patience than they deserved as they negotiated.

"Lady Demeter will murder you," said one.

"She will turn you into a bird as she has always threatened," said another. "And force us away from our home to the sea."

"He would not harm us," another countered. "He loves Lady Persephone."

"It is not his wrath we fear," said another.

Hades sighed, vanishing from the meadow and appearing on the bank of the river where five nymphs were gathered. They were half in water, their fingers digging into the muddy bank, faces obscured by tall grass.

When they saw him, they gasped and likely would have fled if he had not held them in place with his power.

"One of you will tell me what you know of your mistress," said Hades.

They shook.

"We know nothing about our mistress, my lord," said one who had hair like the sun shining on water.

It was not a lie.

"When was she last here?" he asked.

"It has been quite some time," said another. This one had hair the color of the darkest parts of the river. "Since Lady Persephone left."

"Left for the mortal world?"

"No, since the greenhouse was destroyed."

"And you have no idea where your mistress might be?"

The five of them shook their heads.

Hades studied them. "I need you to find her."

Their eyes widened and they paled.

"My lord, she will know!" This one who spoke had red hair like two others. All three were crowned with white lilies.

"We will already be punished for this," said the one with dark hair. "You ask us to die for you!"

Hades tilted his head, narrowing his eyes. "You will already die for me, Hercyna," he said. "The only uncertainty is how."

"Do not scare her!" the blond one snapped, wrapping her arms around Hercyna's head, crushing her to her breast.

"I cannot help it if you fear death," said Hades. "It is the truth of any existence."

"Lady Demeter was right about you," she seethed. "You have no care for anyone save yourself!"

"If you knew what drove me to this meadow, you would choke on your words," Hades said. "Imagine if

I had brought Persephone here to witness your loyalty wither in the face of her abusive mother."

"You don't know what it's like!" one of the three redheads—Peisinoe, Hades remembered—said. "Persephone knew! She would understand!"

"Perhaps she would," Hades replied. "But I am not Persephone, and I need to know where Demeter is hiding."

Their anger reminded him of Persephone's when they'd first met, their opinion of him colored by the way Demeter had painted him.

"Let me give you an idea of what you are about to face if you do not help me," said Hades. "Your fountains and wells, lakes and springs, rivers and wetlands will all freeze. You will be driven from your homes—you and all your sisters and friends. You will attempt to find reprieve from the cold but will discover that the whole world is frozen, and in that state of despair, you will know what it is to beg for death." He paused and let his words linger in the air between them. "That is your fate, brought about by none other than the goddess you protect now."

The five exchanged looks, a different kind of fear present on their faces. It was the acknowledgment he needed, that what he said was already coming to pass.

"I will do it," said Hercyna.

"No!" the other four said in unison.

"We will all do it," said Cyane. She looked from her companions to Hades, her eyes alight with anger. "Even if it is only to inform her that you are looking for her."

"I imagine she already knows," said Hades. "I'll be waiting."

Hades returned to the Underworld.

He found Persephone asleep, so he undressed and poured himself a glass of whiskey, hoping it would ease his anxious thoughts.

Katerina's prophecy was still at the forefront of his mind but so was Demeter. He thought of the task he had assigned to the five nymphs, biting back the guilt. He knew it was dangerous to send them searching for Demeter. The nymphs were likely to be punished just for speaking to him, which made it even less likely they would return with any news on Persephone's mother.

It was not as if he thought he could appeal to the goddess either. He only wished to know where to find her when Zeus became involved and either demanded an end to the snowstorm or his engagement to Persephone.

He felt the air stir. Glancing over his shoulder, he found Persephone had risen, and she gazed at him from their bed, sleepy and flushed, her beautiful body half concealed by the robe she wore. He'd have liked to rouse her from sleep with a kiss between her thighs, but he no longer felt that was possible given the last few weeks, so he had waited, wondering if she might rise before sunup.

"You're awake," he murmured.

He faced her fully, and her eyes fell to his cock, which was hard and tight. He needed some sort of release, because the longer he went on like this, the more uncomfortable he would be, but with the way Persephone was looking at him, he did not think he'd have to agonize much longer.

He downed what remained in his glass before approaching her, and as he sat, he cradled her face in his hand and brought her mouth to his. She let him lead, and he plied her mouth with his tongue until he could no longer taste the whiskey on his breath. The longer he kissed her, the more his cock throbbed. He might have guided her hand to his length or pushed her to the bed so he could cover her body with his, but now he feared exerting too much control.

When he pulled away, her lips were lush and her eyes bright with lust.

"How was your day?" he asked in a hushed tone. He could not bring himself to speak louder. There was something about this night that required quiet.

"Hard," she answered, nibbling at her lip—a sign of her anxiety.

He had not expected that answer, given that she had been in the Underworld all day, but perhaps things had not gone well during her visit with Lexa. Before he could ask, she spoke.

"Yours?"

"The same," he said and drew a piece of her hair behind her ear before planting his hand on the bed beside her hip. "Lie with me."

Her eyes were heavy-lidded, her lips parted and swollen.

"You don't have to ask," she whispered.

He disagreed, but there was a part of him that recognized asking might be more about easing his fear than hers.

Now having her permission, he did not hesitate to guide her robe down until she was bare to him. He wanted so much of her at once—her soft moans and her desperate cries. He wanted to kiss her and be inside her.

He wanted to take her slow and then fuck her hard, but his eyes fell to her breasts, her nipples peaked and rosy, and he decided he would begin there.

He bent and took each tip into his mouth, sucking them and her soft skin. Her breaths came slow and deep, her fingers tangling in his hair. At this point, he had no real thoughts, only observations of sensation—the way her nails raked over his scalp, the way her breaths deepened the longer he sucked her, the way she shifted her legs wider as she prepared to accommodate whatever he decided to give—except that she grew impatient and reached for his hand, guiding him to her center and pressing his fingers into her heat.

He groaned at the feel of her arousal.

"So fucking wet," he murmured before his lips crashed against hers and he explored her mouth. He chased her pleasure with his fingers. He liked all parts of sex with Persephone, but this pleased him because he could tell how much she wanted him, and all he could think was how she would feel when he slid his cock inside her—wet, warm, right.

He groaned as Persephone's hands closed around his length and her touch sent a wave of pleasure rippling through him. Her strokes were slow, and when her thumb teased the tip, his whole body began to throb. He could not take it any longer. He had to be inside her.

He left her body, his fingers dripping with her arousal. He planted his hand on her thigh and broke their kiss.

Persephone glared, her eyes like fire, scorching every part of him. She reached for his hand again and brought it back to her center.

He smirked, eyes falling to her lips.

"Do you not trust me to bring you pleasure?"

"Eventually," she said, her tone frustrated, but he liked the look on her.

"Oh, darling," he said and guided her to her back. "How you challenge me."

He moved her to her side so that her back was to him. It was an odd angle, but he wanted her like this because he would watch her writhe as he gave her pleasure. He loomed over her, holding her gaze as his hand glided over her body until he reached the apex of her thighs. There was something about watching the anticipation build within her body that made him feel powerful.

Only he could make her feel this way. Only he would touch her this way.

She widened for him, and he entered her again. Her head fell back, pressing into his arm, her mouth opened, releasing a pleasing moan, and he captured it with his mouth. He moved inside her and kissed her hard, unrelenting as he chased after her pleasure. Beneath him, she couldn't catch her breath. It sounded stuck in her lungs as he built on her ecstasy, and when he tore from her mouth, he whispered near her ear in a fierce and claiming growl, "Is this pleasure?"

Because it pleased him.

He pulled out of her again, and her only answer was a guttural cry, but he did not need her to speak. He knew what he had brought on her. Beneath his gaze, she glowed, ethereal and so fucking beautiful. He needed her so badly it hurt.

He shifted closer, and she drew her legs apart so he could fit himself inside her. He felt as though he were in a different part of her, angled differently, gripping differently, and he thought that maybe Persephone felt the same by the way she moved.

"Is this pleasure?" he teased, his voice quiet and low. She shivered at the sound despite the heat radiating off her body. Together they had grown hot, their bodies slick. He moved inside her, slow at first and then faster and harder, liking the rush it gave him when his balls bounced off her ass.

Fuck, he would chase that.

He dug his fingers into her skin.

"Is this pleasure?" he asked between his teeth, because he felt it acutely and he needed to know she felt the same.

Persephone's hand snaked behind his neck, and as her body jerked beneath his, she managed to speak.

"It is ecstasy."

Their mouths met in a messy kiss. Hades hooked Persephone's leg around his own and used his feet for purchase, increasing his pace. His hand came to rest on her neck, fingers gripping her jaw to hold her in place. He did not want her to look away as he finished this. They ceased to speak, only managing gasps and moans and the occasional *fuck* whispered viciously into the space between them, which hardly had room for anything else.

He knew when Persephone was close. He could feel it in the way she gripped him, the way her body began to shudder. He grit his teeth, keeping his pace as she shattered in his arms, and he followed soon after. His release was draining and never ending, but he stayed buried inside her, coming deep.

It was a possessive thing, but he felt like it marked

her as his, and when he would think about it throughout the day, it was one of few things that brought him true joy.

They lay locked together until they could catch their breath, at which point Hades pressed gentle kisses across her skin, pausing to meet her gaze.

"Are you well?"

Persephone nodded, her face glistening with sweat. She seemed distracted, but he knew she was tired. He could feel it in her body, which had become limp and heavy.

"Yes."

He smiled, a strange relief washing over him. He had always felt it, a moment of fear after having sex with her that he might have gone too far, but with the knowledge of Pirithous looming in the back of his mind, his unease had only grown.

And he hated that he had forgotten, having found himself so caught up in the moment of giving and receiving pleasure.

What if he fucked up and things were never the same again?

Those thoughts stole his high, and he pulled out of Persephone carefully, rolling onto his back. He stared at the ceiling, one hand on his stomach. Beside him, he could feel Persephone watching, and he knew she had something to say as he prepared himself for the worst.

"Has Zeus approved of our marriage?"

That was not what he had expected, and while not as bad as he'd feared, it was still something he was not prepared to talk to her about. In fact, he'd hoped to avoid this altogether. It was not something he wanted her to fixate on or fear so much that she decided not to marry him.

He didn't like the way that last thought made him feel. Like his heart was being torn from his chest.

After a moment, he spoke. "He is aware of our engagement."

"That is not what I asked."

He knew it wasn't, but it was the only answer he wanted to give. He met her gaze, which was steady and dark. She'd lost that bright gleam that had come with her lust. He wanted that back so he did not have to face this.

"He will not deny me."

"But he has not given you his blessing?"

He hated the frustration he felt at her insistence. Who had planted this in her head?

Hecate, if he had to guess.

His mood grew darker.

"No."

He did not like the silence that descended after his answer. He knew she was not pleased with him. Suddenly, he thought about the feeling he'd had after sex. Perhaps he'd been dreading this—having to explain what it really took to marry a god.

"When were you going to tell me?" Though her voice was quiet, he could sense her frustration, but he was frustrated too. This had not been a conversation for anyone else but them, and he should have been given the chance to bring it up on his own.

If given that chance, you'd have never done it, you imbecile. He ground his teeth against Hecate's voice in his head.

Don't you ever fucking leave? he thought.

No, she responded, and her trill laughter echoed in his mind.

"I don't know," he admitted. "When I had no other choice."

"*That* is more than obvious," Persephone said, annoyed.

"I was hoping to avoid it altogether."

"Telling me?" she asked. Her frustration had not ebbed.

There was a part of him that wanted to kiss her, both as a distraction from her anger and from this topic, but he knew he had to face it now that it was before them.

"No, Zeus's approval. He makes a spectacle of it."

"What do you mean?"

He wanted to groan, thinking of all the times his brother had arranged marriages, most of which had failed miserably, all because his oracle predicted some kind of potential that would end his rule over the skies and the earth.

Aphrodite and Hephaestus came to mind first, but there was also Thetis, a water nymph, who both Zeus and Poseidon had once courted until a prophecy foretold that she would give birth to a son more powerful than either of them. It was then that Zeus arranged her marriage to Peleus, and that wedding was a catalyst of the Trojan War.

That was often Zeus's way, though—forsaking the lives of thousands of mortals to protect his throne.

While Hades knew there was no child that could be born of their union, he did fear what the oracle might have to say about the unity of their power. Persephone was life and he was death. They were a cycle that could give and end life, which made them powerful.

How powerful was yet to be seen.

"He will summon us to Olympus for an engagement feast and festivities, and he will drag out his decision for days. I have no desire to be in attendance and no desire to have you suffer through it."

"And when will he do this?"

He knew by the sound of her voice that she was worried, and he hated it.

"In a few weeks, I imagine." He tried to keep his voice light to minimize her fear, but it didn't work because when she spoke again, he heard the emotion in her voice.

"Why wouldn't you tell me? If there is a chance we cannot be together, I have the right to know."

His chest hurt knowing how much this scared her. She'd had to face the guilt of loving him despite her mother's wishes, only to be faced with the fact that Zeus might ruin it all.

He rose onto his elbow so that he could look at her, silent tears gliding down her face. He brushed them away.

"Persephone," he said. "No one will keep us apart—not the Fates, not your mother, and not Zeus."

She swallowed and shook her head. "You are so certain, but even you will not challenge the Fates."

"Oh, darling, but I have told you before—for you, I would destroy this world."

Her gaze was unwavering, and he knew what she was searching for—any hint that he was not being truthful, and when she did not find it, she took a breath.

"Perhaps that is what I fear the most."

Her comment took him back to his conversation

with Hecate. *Since when have you worried over carnage?* she had asked.

Since I decided to marry the Goddess of Spring.

Perhaps he would not have to worry. By the end of this, she might not want him at all.

But right now, that was not the case. He wasn't sure what shifted between them. Perhaps it was part of this desperate feeling that everyone outside this space wanted to tear them apart, but the air grew thick between them, and wordlessly, Persephone drew her legs apart, and Hades shifted so that his body rested against hers.

He was so easily aroused by her that his cock was already hard.

Fuck, it had *been* hard, and only within a few minutes of his last release. He felt so foolish, but he was also desperately in love, and all that really mattered was that Persephone did not mind and felt the same.

He claimed her mouth for the hundredth time tonight and kissed her deep and slow, giving the same attention as he made his way down her body, tongue swirling over her skin and hardened nipples, teasing her hips and inner thighs, before he licked the wetness that had gathered there. He could not really describe how she tasted, sweet but also sharp. Whatever it was, he liked it and wanted more. He buried his face farther into her heat, his eyes meeting hers from where he worked. She writhed in his grasp, her hands all over—pulling at her nipples and rubbing over her clit. She did not seem to have any control over her movements or the sounds coming out of her mouth.

He worked in tandem with them, stroking her with his tongue for every breath and moan she took. When his fingers joined, her hands tangled in his hair and her legs came up to brace his head. He pushed down on her to hold her in place, to drive her to the brink of release, and when she came, she whispered his name and took him into her body once more.

CHAPTER V
HADES

Hades lay awake staring at the ceiling. Persephone was asleep beside him, her head resting just under his arm, her hand flat on his chest. He could feel the weight of her engagement ring against his skin. The metal was cool compared to the warmth of her hand. He wondered if she had grown used to the feel of it on her finger, or was it still new?

He could not wait to wear a ring for her.

And he immediately felt like an idiot for having that thought, no matter how it rang true.

A soft knock drew his attention to the door. Normally, he would instruct whoever was on the other side to enter, but the last thing he wanted to do was disturb Persephone's sleep.

"Fuck," he muttered and glanced at the clock.

It was almost three in the morning.

Something was wrong.

He took a deep breath and then held it as he

disentangled himself from her, hoping she was tired enough to remain asleep. She stirred only slightly as he slipped from her hold but settled quickly. Relieved, he crossed to the door and answered.

"What is it?" he whispered vehemently.

Ilias stood on the other side of the door.

"My Lord, we have a murder," he said.

Hades's brows lowered. "The ophiotaurus?"

It was the first thing that came to mind, considering they expected more deaths to come until the monster was captured.

The satyr shook his head. "This is something else entirely."

Fan-fucking-tastic, Hades thought.

"I'll be a moment," he said and started to close the door.

"Hades," Ilias said, and the god met his gaze. "It's Adonis."

That was the *last* thing he expected to hear.

Adonis was most famous for being Aphrodite's favored. Or, if one wished to be less formal, her fuck boy.

But Hades knew him for a different reason. He'd watched as the mortal forced himself on Persephone in the darkness of Aphrodite's club, La Rose. Later, Hades had gone to Aphrodite to threaten the mortal.

"*Nothing*," he'd said, "*will keep me from shredding Adonis's soul.*"

Since that night, Hades had heard nothing from or about the mortal, so he assumed his threat had been communicated.

Now, it seemed, he was dead.

Well, fuck.

"A moment," Hades said again, and he closed the door.

He sighed and then turned and approached the bed where Persephone slept soundlessly. He watched her for a few seconds—the fluttering of her dark lashes on her cheek, the part of her pink lips, the soft rise and fall of her chest. He bent and pressed a kiss to her forehead.

"I love you," he whispered.

She did not wake, only took a deeper breath and buried her face in the silk sheet she kept bunched near her face.

Hades straightened and crossed to the door, calling up his glamour to cover his naked body. He stepped out into the hallway with Ilias, fully dressed in his usual tailored suit.

"Where are we going?" he asked.

"La Rose," the satyr answered.

Hades and Ilias manifested on the deserted, snow-covered sidewalk outside Aphrodite's club. As it was late and many businesses along this road were closed, there was nothing to illuminate the mirrored exterior of Aphrodite's club, making it look like a cluster of dark crystals jutting from the earth.

"This way," said Ilias, who directed Hades to an alleyway that ran between La Rose and the building beside it. The space was so narrow, the edges of his shoulders grazed the wall on both sides.

As they came around to the back of the building, a few people were gathered. Zofie was among them, but also people in Aphrodite's employ.

Aphrodite herself had yet to arrive.

"Has your goddess been informed?" Hades asked Himeros, who he recognized both as the God of Sexual Desire and a close companion of the Goddess of Love. He appeared very young, as if he were in his early twenties. He had no facial hair to speak of, but he did have a swath of thick, dark hair.

"Eros has gone to inform her," he said.

Himeros and Eros were Aphrodite's closest advisors and were two of the Erotes, a group of gods and goddesses who all represented different elements of love and sex.

Hades wondered how the goddess would react to learning one of her mortal lovers had been murdered. He was never certain of Aphrodite's feelings toward those she favored. He knew she was partial to a few, but her love, whether she wanted to admit it or not, belonged to her husband, Hephaestus.

Still, targeting a favored mortal was like targeting the god who had bestowed it, and when Hades turned and saw Adonis's body, his blood ran cold.

He looked…broken. It was the only way to describe it. His body seemed to have been so badly beaten, he splattered where he lay.

"This was a bold move," said Hades as he stepped closer.

To attack not only someone who had favor but outside their club.

"And no one heard anything?"

"Nothing," said Himeros.

"Is there surveillance?" Hades asked.

"There is, but the lenses are frosted over. It's impossible to see what really happened."

Fucking Demeter and her gods-damned winter storm.

"But from what I can see," the god continued, "he seems to have tried to come to the club after we were closed. When he couldn't get in the front, he came back here. That's when he was attacked."

"Who discovered him?" Hades asked.

"I did," said a new voice: Eros, whose magic felt warm and heady—wrong in this environment. He appeared alongside Aphrodite.

Hades turned and looked at the two, but he could only focus on Aphrodite, whose expression remained disturbingly neutral. He waited for her to change, to realize what happened and rage or perhaps even weep, but she did neither, though her eyes did not waver from the dead mortal.

"By the time I found him, he was already gone."

Hades bent over the body. There were any number of people who might be responsible for this death, but the severity of his wounds was what made Hades so uneasy. This was hate.

He stared for a long moment before reaching toward the body.

"Do not touch him!" Aphrodite said. She took a step forward but no more, held back by Eros.

Hades glanced at the goddess but ignored her and placed his hand fully on the mortal's back. Instantly, black tendrils shot from his body, wrapping around Hades's arm. They continued to climb until Hades was sure of his grip, and when he pulled, he freed Adonis's soul from his body, and then it vanished, transported to the shores of the Styx where Charon would greet him and take him across the river.

"What did you do?" Aphrodite demanded.

"His soul had yet to leave his body," Hades said, straightening, which made everything far more horrific. It wasn't unusual for souls to abandon their body during surprise attacks to escape the brunt of the trauma that would inevitably be inflicted on them. But Adonis hadn't escaped it, which meant his soul was just as battered as his body. It also meant there was nothing they would learn from him in the afterlife—he would be too distressed to help.

A small part of Hades wondered if Adonis's attackers had known that. He found it strange that so much had worked in their favor—the cameras, for instance, and the fact that no one heard this horrific attack happening. It all seemed too orchestrated, like they'd had some kind of divine intervention.

"Apollo!" Hades called, hoping his summons worked.

"Why call on him?" Aphrodite asked.

Hades met her bloodshot gaze. Now he noticed her anger.

"We need to know exactly how he died," said Hades. "I do not trust that this was just a few jealous mortals."

"What else could it be?"

"I don't know," Hades admitted, and he couldn't really explain why he cared so much about figuring this out. He did not like Adonis, but he did like Aphrodite, despite her meddling, and it worried him that someone close to her had been killed. This was a violation.

"What is it?" Apollo yawned, appearing in the cold night dressed only in a floral robe. When he ceased to rub his eyes and glanced at the ground, he lifted a foot. "Eww. What *is* that?"

"A body, Apollo," Hades said flatly.

"Gross," the God of Light said, and yet he approached and bent over it, studying it closely.

"I need you to conduct an autopsy," Hades said. "We need to know how he died."

"Well, I can assure you the fact that he was beaten to a pulp did not help his case."

"Apollo," Hades growled, annoyed by his sarcasm. "This man was one of Aphrodite's favored."

Apollo straightened, and his head snapped toward the Goddess of Love, pale with understanding.

"Oh," he said. "Fuck."

"Yes, fuck," said Hades.

Apollo frowned and turned his attention to the body again. His feet were bare, and he did not seem to mind that he was standing in Adonis's pooled and coagulated blood.

Hades was not certain what the god was doing, but after a few moments, he reached for something near the body and held it up. It looked like the handle of a knife.

"I imagine I'll find quite a few stab wounds."

Hades turned to Aphrodite. It was hard to say how to move forward from here. Did they warn her favored mortals of the attack and risk it leaking to the media? It was one thing for the favored to be murdered—attacks were not unheard of—but it was another thing entirely for it to happen so close to a divine establishment.

"I do not think it would be an exaggeration to say this was likely done by the Impious," said Hades. Whether they were associated with Triad was another story.

Impious did not worship the gods. Some lived quietly in their rejection of cult practices, while others were far more extreme, choosing violent methods as a way to attack the gods. Some had organized under the official banner of Triad, a group that touted a belief in fairness, free will, and freedom despite terrorizing numerous mortals in their quest for said freedom.

Now, they claimed to be peaceful protesters, though Hades believed otherwise. But one thing worked in their favor, and that was the chaos caused by anyone who had forsaken the gods.

"Protect those in your circle, Aphrodite," said Hades. "I think they want your wrath."

"Why would anyone want my wrath?" she asked, her fair fingers curled into fists.

"To illustrate a point."

"What *point*, Hades?"

"That a god's favor truly means nothing," he said.

CHAPTER VI
HADES

Hades saw Persephone off to work, which felt like sending her into Poseidon's ocean. She did not even have an office. She worked out of the Coffee House as if she weren't his fiancée, as if she hadn't caught the interest and attention of every god and mortal in New Greece. The sharks would circle, and the only thing that gave him any peace was that Antoni escorted her and Zofie would shadow her.

Once she was gone, Hades went in search of Thanatos and the farmer he had brought to the Underworld. Despite his harrowing end, he'd transitioned to Asphodel, settling on the outskirts of the meadow that was used for farmland. Several acres were set aside for wheat and barley, grapevines and vegetables, olive and fig trees. Beyond that was a field speckled with cows and goats. Souls wandered about the land, conducting maintenance, gathering food, and feeding and milking the cattle.

Among them was the new farmer, who sat on a stool

milking a dairy cow. He wore what he had died in, a flannel shirt and a pair of overalls.

As they approached, they cast a shadow on the old man, and he paused his milking to turn and look at them.

"Georgios," said Thanatos. "This is Lord Hades."

"Lord Hades," the farmer said, stumbling to his feet and fumbling for his hat. As he swept it off his head, he revealed a layer of wispy hair that barely covered his bald head. "Well, I… What can I do for you?"

Hades was amused by the farmer's stammering.

"It is nice to meet you, Georgios," he said. "I trust you are adjusting?"

"Just like home," the soul said.

It was a lie.

Hades could see it in the squint of his eyes and the way they darkened as he spoke.

"I hope it comes to feel more like it every day," he replied—a sincere wish he had for all who came to reside in his realm.

"Thank you, my lord," said the soul with a tip of his head.

"Georgios," said Hades. "I've come to ask about your death."

The farmer paled. "Well, I don't really recall—"

"Do not think of that night," Hades said. "Think of before. Did anyone come around to your house inquiring after the monster you spotted in your field?"

"Well, yes," Georgios said. "A couple men in nice suits."

Hades nodded. "What did they look like?"

"I don't rightly know how to describe them except to say they didn't belong. That much was evident."

"Because of how they dressed?"

Georgios shook his head. "It was more than that. They were just different. Different like you."

"Different like me?" Hades asked. "What does that mean?"

"Godly, I suppose," Georgios said.

Demigods, perhaps, but Hades wondered who exactly and if they were sent by Theseus.

"And what did they want?"

"Said they were there because they heard I'd seen a monster. I'm not sure how they knew... I'd only told a neighbor, but word gets around in the towns outside Thebes. Anyway, I showed them where it had been. It was easy to spot because the grass was still flattened."

"What did they say?"

"Nothing. They just left," Georgios said.

He was quiet for a moment and then seemed to realize why Hades had inquired after the two men and the monster.

"I suppose you think they came back to kill me?"

"We can't really know for sure...unless you saw them?"

The soul shook his head. "Later that night, I heard a sound outside. I thought that monster had returned, but as I stepped off the porch, I was hit on the head. After that, I remember nothing."

Hades exchanged a look with Thanatos. When he met Georgios's gaze again, he offered his hand.

"I'm sorry to have had to bring this up, Georgios."

The farmer shook his hand. "No need to be sorry," he said. "Perhaps you will manage to do me justice."

"I will," said Hades. "That is a promise."

Hades and Thanatos left the farmer to continue milking his cow. The two gods walked side by side and did not speak until they were far away from any wandering souls.

"Do you suspect he was killed by demigods?" asked Thanatos.

It sounded like it. An actual god would have concealed their appearance. A mortal would have never been described as godly.

"If they did not pull the trigger, they ordered it," Hades said, though who had sent them to the farm was the greater question.

If he had to guess, he'd say Theseus, but he also knew it was dangerous to fixate. There were countless demigods who roamed New Greece unchecked, their powers unknown. Any one of them might have heard about the resurrection of the ophiotaurus and decided to track it.

"Whoever they are," said Thanatos, "I dread the lives they will take."

"Let us hope they take no more."

"Fucking female assassins," Hermes said, appearing a few feet away from Hades and Thanatos. As he approached them, he brushed at his clothes and his arms as if he were dusting himself off. "Well," he said, meeting Hades's gaze, "you weren't wrong about Dionysus."

Hades's brows rose, but he was distracted by a reddish mark on Hermes's skin.

"Did you...get punched?"

"Listen, have you seen maenads fight? They are vicious. I think I'm in love."

Hades chuckled.

"Sounds like you've had an eventful day," said Thanatos with a smirk.

"Why don't you tell us about it?" Hades asked, though he knew he would not need to implore the God of Mischief. He had come to perform a drama.

"I was tracking the ophiotaurus. I'd heard rumors that someone had spotted a large snake outside Sparta, which sounded promising, and it was. I found a trail of blood."

Hades frowned. "How much blood?"

"Not enough to make me think it was struck by a fatal blow, but something definitely hurt it. What, I cannot say, because I was interrupted by three ferocious female...*demons!*"

Dionysus's maenads, Hades presumed.

It wasn't so much a surprise, but Hades wondered if Dionysus did manage to capture the ophiotaurus first, would he tell him?

"And then what?" asked Thanatos.

"I came here," Hermes said. "*You* try to escape. They have *teeth*."

"Most people have teeth," said Hades.

"That is not true, Hades. *Trust me*," Hermes said, and by the look in his eyes, Hades guessed he'd seen some things. "Anyway, I'd go back, but I'm kind of aroused now, and I don't think those ladies are interested in a foursome so..."

Hades sighed.

Thanatos let his head fall into his hand.

"Do you have to be so honest, Hermes?" Hades asked.

Hermes grinned. "It's why you keep me."

Hades rolled his eyes, considering what they should do next. "Was the blood fresh?" he asked.

"No, though I could not tell how old."

That was not as promising as he'd thought. Still, he wondered if he could send Zofie on the hunt. She was formidable and an Amazon—she would not get distracted like Hermes, who was, apparently, a masochist.

His only reservation was taking her away from Persephone.

"You know if you really wanted to find this creature, you could ask Artemis," Hermes suggested.

Hades bristled at her name, despite the fact that what he said was true. There was no greater huntress than the Goddess of the Hunt, but Artemis was not the type to help anyone, save those who worshipped her. If given knowledge of the ophiotaurus, she would likely slay it and burn the entrails herself.

"I'd rather have my dick bitten off," said Hades.

"Try having it gummed."

Hades and Thanatos gave Hermes a horrified look.

"I told you not everyone has teeth," Hermes said with a shrug.

Hades made a mental note to never talk about teeth with Hermes again.

"I'm not asking Artemis to do anything," Hades said. "She will see it as a way to obtain a favor."

It was bad enough that he owed one to her brother, Apollo, who still had Persephone wrapped up in a bargain that called her away from Hades's side whenever the god pleased—a fact that made him bitter.

"Talk to Dionysus," said Hades. "If his maenads get to the ophiotaurus first, I want to know."

"You want *me* to talk to Dionysus?"

Hades raised a brow. "Yes, Hermes. You're officially his keeper."

"Do you know if he's still angry about his fiery balls?"

"I don't, but you can ask him yourself."

"Can it wait?" Hermes asked. "I have to get ready for Sybil's housewarming party, and, by the way, *so do you*."

Fuck. He'd forgotten about that.

"What's a housewarming?" Thanatos asked.

"It is a party where everyone brings wood to light the hearth in a new home," said Hades.

"Yeah," said Hermes. He was already taking a step back, preparing to bolt for the Upperworld. "We'll go with that. Bring *plenty* of wood."

"Hermes," Hades warned. "Talk to Dionysus. *Soon.*"

"What's the exact definition of soon?" Hermes asked.

Hades glared.

Hermes grinned. "See you soon, Daddy Death!"

He vanished, and when he was gone, Hades looked at Thanatos, who asked in a very serious tone, "Which one of us do you think he was calling Daddy Death?"

Hades returned to the palace.

He would have to tell Ilias what he'd learned from the farmer.

There had always been an urgency behind finding the ophiotaurus, but Hades had felt an even greater need to locate it as Demeter's storm in the Upperworld worsened and Persephone began to question whether Zeus would allow their marriage.

There were too many obstacles in his way to having

everything he had ever wanted. The ophiotaurus would make anyone's attempt to overthrow the Olympians far too easy, and Hades would be damned if he lost without a fucking war.

As he meandered through the garden, in no hurry to return to the castle, he felt Persephone's magic blossom.

She was back, which was strange. When she went to the Upperworld for work, she often remained for hours.

He frowned and vanished from the garden, following her magic to the bedchamber where he found her naked. She had yet to turn to him as she bent at the waist, inspecting something on her legs. He was content with this and admired her quietly from a distance, though he let his imagination run wild with other things he would like to do to her in that position.

After a few moments, she straightened, still unaware he had joined her. She turned toward the bathroom and startled.

"Hades!" His name slipped from her mouth on a breathless shout. He liked the way she said his name; it reminded him of how she came with his name on her lips. "You scared me!"

His eyes dropped to her breasts, which she covered with one hand, as if she could stop her racing heart.

"You should have known I would find you once you took your clothes off. It is a sixth sense."

He guided her hand away from her breast and kissed her fingers, which were delicate and strong. He thought about how they threaded through his hair, how her nails grazed his scalp, how they twined around his hair and pulled as she rode him until he came.

I am fucking insatiable, he thought, even as his eyes drifted down her body.

Except that now he noticed her thighs, which were red and swollen. Small pockets of fluid speckled her skin, clear in color but obvious. They were blisters.

"What is this?" he demanded, pressing his palm flat against the fiery skin, which seemed to revolt against his palm. Persephone gripped his other arm, her nails biting into his arm as he tried to heal her flesh—to heal her burns.

What the fuck?

"A woman poured coffee into my lap," Persephone said.

He didn't like the pain that seeped into her voice.

"Poured?" he asked, meeting her gaze.

"If you are asking if it was intentional, the answer is yes."

Intentional.

It was as Hades had feared in the aftermath of Adonis's death, and even before that, when news of his relationship with Persephone hit the media. He had always been afraid someone would target her, aware that at some point, something would happen, and Persephone would realize that she could not exist in the world as she once had—as an unassuming mortal.

She was more than that—a goddess to be certain, but *his*, and that made people angry.

He knelt before her, wrestling with his emotions, which were everywhere all at once. There was a pressure in his head and chest that urged him to explode and seek vengeance, but the guilt kept him anchored at her feet. He should have insisted that she not go out in public;

he should have given her an office at Alexandria Tower sooner.

He channeled this frustration with himself into soothing her wounds and healing her. Once he was certain she was no longer in pain and there was no visible sign of the burns, he let his hands slide to the backs of her thighs and held her, his eyes drifting back to hers from his place on the floor.

"Will you tell me who this woman was?" he asked, and he bent forward, letting his mouth drift over her newly healed skin, content when she offered a pleasing sigh.

"No," she said, bracing her hands on his shoulders, her golden hair curtaining her face.

"I cannot...persuade you?"

She hummed when his tongue darted out to taste as he neared the mound of dark curls between her thighs, catching sight of her clit, which was quickly swelling, begging to be touched and teased.

He groaned at the thought of taking it into his mouth, sucking it gently.

He hardened more and he was certain it was cutting off the blood supply to his brain.

"Perhaps," Persephone said, her breathy reply sending a surge of heat straight to the head of his cock. Hades struggled to remember what he had asked. "But I do not know her name, so all your...persuading would be in vain."

"*Nothing* I do is in vain."

He could take it no longer and shifted, his mouth closing over her clit, lips teasing. Her sigh was heavy and guttural, and he enjoyed the way her fingers moved to his hair and the sweet sting when she pulled too hard.

"Hades—"

He pulled away enough to whisper against her heated flesh, the taste of her on his tongue enough to drive him mad. If she did not let him bring her to release, he would spend all evening thinking about everything they had left unfinished here.

"Don't make me stop," he begged between flicks of his tongue against her.

Another pleasant sigh left her, but when she spoke, her voice was controlled and commanding.

"You have thirty minutes."

It was enough to make him pull away and meet her gaze, and for fuck's sake, she was beautiful and far stronger than him. Her eyes gleamed bright green, as if her glamour was fading, but he knew it was just the power of her arousal, a sign of how much she wanted him. The problem was she could control it, could bide her time before release.

Hades could not.

"Only thirty?"

Her eyes flashed and a playful smirk curled her lips.

"Do you need more?"

His let his hands drift to her ass, squeezing as he grinned.

"Darling, we both know I could make you come in five, but what if I'd like to take my time?"

Her smile warmed, her fingers touching his lips. "Later." Though he could not tell if it was more of a command or a promise. "I have a party to attend, and I still need to make cupcakes."

"Is it not a mortal custom to be fashionably late?" Hadn't he heard that somewhere before? He felt like he was pouting, but this was important—pleasure following the pain.

"Did Hermes tell you that?"

"Is he wrong?"

Her eyes narrowed.

"I will not be late to Sybil's party, Hades. If you wish to please me, then you'll make me come *and* on time."

He offered a light chuckle, letting his chin rest between her thighs as he agreed to her bidding.

"As you wish, my darling," he said and continued his work, teasing her clit until he felt as though it pulsed in his mouth. Then he drew her leg over his shoulder, and she kept her hands on his shoulders for support, widening so he could taste her. He wanted to fuck her with more than just his fingers and tongue; his cock begged to be inside her, especially when she began to grind against his mouth, but she had given him a limit, and if this was where she was going to spend the majority of his time, he would make it good. He would have to get himself off later while she iced fucking cupcakes instead of his dick.

But this was good.

It was enough.

It was her, and that was all that mattered.

When she came against his mouth, he was satisfied with her pleasure, and he rose to his feet and covered her mouth with his own, holding her tight against him, his head spinning at the minuscule amount of friction their closeness brought to his cock.

He pulled away when her hands tried to gain access to him, but their bodies were pressed so close, she could not manage it.

"I promised to make you come and get you to Sybil's on time. If you touch me, I will break that promise."

His words bordered on a threat. He knew what he was capable of at this moment. He also knew he could barely think. One touch from her would seal the fucking deal.

She looked very much like she regretted coaxing that agreement from his lips. She started to open her mouth, but whatever words were poised to come out never left because he kissed her again, his hands framing her head. When he pulled away, he let his forehead rest against hers.

"Go make the fucking cupcakes, Persephone."

He released her and stepped back. She seemed a little dazed, which was far better than how he felt. He could hardly contain himself as she slipped into a new dress. At the door, she turned to look at him.

"Are you…going to join me in the kitchen?"

"In a moment," he said.

She nodded, her eyes darting to his dick, which strained hard against his trousers. It was obvious what he intended to do, and the door barely clicked closed before he had unbuttoned his pants, taken his cock out, and began to jerk himself off.

"Fuck me," he thought as he pumped into his palm, which was nothing at all like Persephone's wet and writhing body, but he was out of options.

He came quickly, messily, but the release was nothing compared to what he actually needed, and as he washed away the evidence of his actions, he wondered if he could make it through this night without fucking her in Sybil's new home.

CHAPTER VII
HADES

Hades let Persephone lead, using her magic to teleport to Sybil's new home since she had been there before. They appeared in front of a green apartment door, in an alcove beneath a set of cement and metal stairs. Hades manifested with just enough room that his head brushed one of the steps overhead.

He shifted forward a little to give himself space, his hands settling on Persephone's waist as he did. She shivered, but it had nothing to do with his touch. It was fucking frigid.

He had not been outside since last night when he'd left the Underworld for La Rose, and while it had been cold, it was evident the temperature had dropped.

He should have waited to jerk off. This cold would have killed his boner faster.

Fucking Demeter. It was as he feared. The weather was getting worse.

Hades felt a surge of power against his palms. It was

warm and came from Persephone. He held her tighter, his head lowering so that his lips were near her ear.

"Are you well?"

When she didn't respond, he frowned, straightening. "Persephone?"

She seemed to realize he was speaking and looked up at him, the back of her head resting against his chest. She looked adorable and felt so small in his grasp. These were his favorite moments, the ones that felt quiet and intimate, and he craved them more and more.

"I am well," she said, but something moved behind her eyes—a darkness he recognized in his own. "I am," she attempted to assure him. "I was just thinking about my mother."

"Do not ruin your evening thinking of her, my darling," he said.

She did not need to know that he had been thinking of her too.

"It is a little hard to ignore her given the weather, Hades."

He reluctantly turned his head toward the sky, dense with cloud cover. He hated that Demeter was on her mind. He knew it was likely because she'd read all the reports in the media about the winter storm being a form of divine punishment, and she likely felt responsible.

Despite knowing very few things about her daughter, Demeter was aware that the way to get to Persephone was through her heart.

She would ensure this storm was devastating to the people of New Greece, and when that happened, would Persephone regret agreeing to marry him?

He wondered if she was thinking about it now.

If she wasn't yet, she soon would be.

He ground his teeth, and Persephone shifted from his grasp to knock on the door, her warmth disappearing with her distance. He didn't like it.

And he liked it even less when a man answered Sybil's door.

Not because he felt like a threat or even appeared to be. It was how he *felt*.

Wrong. Deceptive.

Hades returned his hand to Persephone's waist. He wasn't sure if he should feel relieved or worried when she seemed just as confused by the blond, blue-eyed man.

"Um, I think we might have the wrong—"

"Persephone, right?" the man asked.

Hades stiffened. He did not like the way he said her name. It was too casual, too comfortable.

"Persephone!" Sybil cried, running up behind the man who did not move, forcing the oracle to bow beneath his arm, which was braced against the doorframe as if he were some kind of guard.

Hades also did not like that.

He let Persephone go when Sybil pulled her in for a hug.

"I'm so glad you're here!" she said, and it was impossible not to hear the relief in her voice. Hades cast a dark look at the mortal male who watched them, unmoving.

Had he made Sybil uncomfortable in her own home?

His fingers tightened into fists.

If Sybil did not introduce him soon, Hades would send him to a deserted island somewhere off the coast of New Greece.

"I'm glad you could come too, Hades."

Hades was surprised and met the oracle's gaze.

"I appreciate the invitation," he said sincerely.

He was rarely invited to anything that wasn't his own event.

"Aren't you going to introduce me?" The man standing guard in the doorway had finally moved to cross his arms over his chest as if he were pouting. His voice was grating, and he spoke with a crude entitlement Hades found irritating. He got the feeling the mortal only spoke to draw attention back to himself, and his attention he would have.

The God of the Dead glared.

Did he really need an introduction to death?

Sybil half turned to the man, as if she'd forgotten he was here. She gave them a look as if to apologize for his insolence.

"Persephone, Hades, this is Ben."

"Hi, I'm Sybil's boyfrie—"

"Friend. Ben is a friend," Sybil interrupted him.

Hades exchanged a look with Persephone, who could not hide her bewildered expression.

"Well, soon-to-be boyfriend," Ben amended.

Hades couldn't hide his disgust and glowered—which deepened when Persephone shook the mortal's outstretched hand.

"It's...nice to meet you," she said.

She was far too nice.

The mortal turned to Hades expectantly, offering his hand.

"You do not want to shake my hand, mortal."

First, he would crush it, and then he would force the man to face every fear he'd ever conjured. It would all happen in a split second and drive him to the point of madness.

Hades would enjoy watching it, but he felt like Persephone would disapprove.

The mortal did not like Hades's rebuff. A kernel of anger sparked within his gaze. It almost made Hades laugh, and he wished the mortal would say something about his slight. He would take any reason to banish him from this party, but in the quiet that followed, he seemed to gain some sense and recovered his pleasant—albeit unnerving—facade.

He smiled and then finally moved out of the fucking door.

"Well, shall we go in?"

Hades was not keen on being in such a confined space with this mortal. They were already off to a bad start, but he pressed a hand to Persephone's lower back as they entered the apartment.

He could feel her gaze on him, curious but also observant.

"What?" he asked, voice quiet.

"You promised to behave," she reminded.

"It is not in my nature to appease mortals," he said, especially ones who had a sense of self-importance in the face of actual death.

"But it is in your nature to appease me," she said, and her words drew his attention to her face as they came to the end of the hallway, pausing in a small kitchen with a too-bright fluorescent light overhead.

Still, he held Persephone's gaze and offered her a small smile.

"Alas," he said quietly. "You are my greatest weakness."

She watched him, a wealth of feeling flooding her gaze.

If she looked at him like that too long, he really would fuck her in this house.

"Wine?" Sybil squeezed between them as she came into the kitchen, heading straight for the bar. She obviously knew what everyone would need to get through this night since Ben insisted on staying.

"Please," Persephone said.

"For you, Hades?"

"Whiskey...whatever you have is fine. Neat." He paused, noticing the look Persephone cast his way, but he couldn't tell what prompted her displeasure. "Please?"

Perhaps he should have summoned his own alcohol.

"Neat?" Hades could not help but cringe when he heard the mortal's voice. Perhaps it was because he knew every time the man opened his mouth, he would say something stupid. "Real whiskey drinkers at least add water."

There was a horrible silence in the room that everyone seemed to notice, save Ben. Persephone and Sybil froze, wide-eyed as they waited for Hades to retaliate.

He looked at the mortal, voice dripping with a disdain he felt blacken his heart.

"I add the blood of mortals," he said.

Which was a joke, except that Hades was tempted to test it and have Ben be the first sacrifice.

Fuck, he had never hated someone so much in his life.

"Of course, Hades," Sybil said as if she had not heard Ben or Hades's reply. She chose a bottle from the many cluttering the counter and offered the whole thing. "You'll probably need it."

He smiled at her, as warmly as he could. "Thank you, Sybil," he said, already loosening the cap to drink straight from the bottle.

"So how did you meet Ben?" Persephone asked as Sybil poured her a glass of wine.

Hades considered answering for her—the fucker was a stalker—but before she could even get a word out, Ben spoke.

"We met at Four Olives where I work. It was love at first sight for me."

Persephone made a strange sound as she choked on her wine, though Hades had to admit he was pleased with himself.

He hadn't been wrong.

Sybil gave them both a desperate look. It was evident she had tried to put this mortal where he belonged. The issue was she thought she could make him a friend, but he didn't even belong in that zone.

He belonged in jail.

Or Tartarus.

Hades would take either one.

A knock interrupted the awful silence.

"Thank the gods," Sybil said, darting to the door.

Hades imagined she was eager to fill the house with other people to drown out Ben's annoying voice.

"I know she isn't convinced yet," Ben said when they were alone. "But it's only a matter of time."

"What makes you so sure?" Persephone asked, and while Hades could hear the revulsion in her voice, the mortal did not seem to notice.

Instead, he preened, squaring his shoulders and lifting his head in pride.

Hades was already rolling his eyes.

"I'm an oracle."

"Oh fuck," he said, unamused.

Persephone elbowed him, but it wasn't as if Ben was deterred. He had no ability to sense emotion beyond pride in himself.

Still, Hades could not take much more of this. He needed distance from this fucker who he refused to call by name.

"If you'll excuse me."

He glanced at Persephone as he left the kitchen and wandered into the adjacent living room, sipping from the whiskey Sybil had so kindly given him. His only wish was that he could get drunk because tonight, he needed it.

He could still hear Ben from across the room as he leaned toward Persephone—an action that made Hades want to rip his head off. Hades let himself imagine it, what it would be like and feel like, just to calm down.

"I don't think he likes me," Ben said.

Persephone arched a brow, replying unenthusiastically, "Whatever gave you that idea?"

Hades tuned them out for a moment as he observed Sybil's space. It was cozy but sparse—evident that she was starting over. Despite the fact that they were gathering tonight to celebrate her new chapter, Hades knew none of them were completely happy, well aware that the reason they were all here was because one of them was gone.

Lexa's death had changed everything.

He still felt guilty over how he handled Persephone. He had failed to be there for her through Lexa's time in the hospital, failed to prepare her for a death that he had not realized would be so devastating.

You've been the God of the Underworld so long, you've forgotten what it is really like to be on the brink of losing someone.

But even as she had spoken those words, he had felt like he was losing her.

"Sephy!" Hermes's voice tore through his thoughts, and he turned to see the God of Mischief enter the kitchen, two bottles of alcohol in each hand. He set them down before dragging her against him for a hug. "You smell like Hades…and sex," he declared, which, despite feeling a little guilty, made Hades chuckle.

"Stop being creepy, Hermes!" Persephone seethed.

Amusement ignited the god's eyes as he released her and turned to Ben with intrigue. Hades groaned inwardly. Why did Hermes have to be attracted to literally everyone? He supposed it didn't matter. Once the fucker opened his mouth, Hermes's interest would cease.

"Oh, and who is this?"

"This is Ben. Sybil's…" Persephone hesitated, apparently uncertain of how to describe the stalker. It didn't matter, anyway, because neither one of them was paying attention.

"Hermes, right?" Ben asked.

Hermes looked bright with pride. "So you've heard of me?"

Hades offered a humorless laugh as he took another drink. The comment was absurd—there wasn't a mortal alive who didn't know the God of Mischief.

"Of course," the mortal replied. "Are you still the Messenger of the Gods or do they use email?"

Hades tried to hide his smile as he turned toward the window, pulling back a single curtain that had been tacked to the wall as he listened to Hermes's snappy reply.

"It's *Lord* Hermes to you," he said.

Whatever followed was lost to Hades as he observed the weather. The snow was heavier, and now and then, ice tapped against the window.

The storm was worsening by the hour.

"Well, well, well," Hermes announced, his voice closer than before. "Look who decided to darken the corner—literally."

Hades turned from the window and watched the god approach.

Hermes stabbed his thumb over his shoulder. "Can you believe that mortal?" he asked, then spoke in a mocking tone. "Do the gods use email? Fucker."

Hades found himself chuckling again.

Hermes glared. "Don't pretend like you aren't antiquated too. Weren't you replaced by *murder*?"

"That's...no, Hermes," said Hades.

"I mean, the audacity!"

"You know, true revenge would be to not let him know he's gotten under your skin," said Hades.

"You're only saying that for your benefit."

Hades shrugged and took a drink.

"The fucker thinks he is an oracle. Let him offer false prophecies and find himself at the mercy of Hecate."

Hades was not certain which god the mortal claimed to speak for or if he only claimed to see visions. Either way, Hecate despised anyone who alleged false power.

"Summon her," said Hermes, and then his voice darkened. "I want to see him burn."

Hades did not respond, though he enjoyed thinking about the scene Hecate would make inside Sybil's small apartment if he called for her to punish the false prophet.

"Did you speak with Dionysus?" Hades asked.

"No," said Hermes.

Hades glared.

"You said *soon*, not right this minute," Hermes defended.

Hades continued to stare.

"Fine. I'll go tonight."

His gaze was unwavering.

"If you think I'm leaving this party without playing drinking games, you're fucking insane. Oh wait, you are." Hermes crossed his arms over his chest and looked away. "Why don't *you* go talk to him?"

"Because I have to talk to Apollo," said Hades. "Unless you want the task?"

"Hmm, no. Apollo still hasn't forgiven me for stealing his cattle."

"*Again?*" Hades asked.

"No, just that one time. You know, *when I was a baby*."

"I thought you settled that," said Hades.

If he recalled correctly, it was how Apollo had obtained his first lyre, which he now used as one of his symbols of power.

"We did," said Hermes. "But you know how grudges work."

There was another knock at the door, and this time, Helen entered.

Hades was not as familiar with the young mortal, except for what Persephone had communicated, which was mostly to say that she was beautiful and a hard worker.

"This weather," she said as she entered. "It's almost... unnatural."

"Yes, it's awful," said Persephone.

Hades's chest tightened, noting the worry etched across Persephone's face.

It wasn't going to get any better either. The tap of ice on the window was only increasing.

Leuce and Zofie were the last to arrive. Apparently, the two had decided it was a good idea to live together, though from what Hades had heard from Ilias, it was rather disastrous. Leuce had only just returned to her physical form after being a tree for centuries, and Zofie... Zofie was born and bred to be a warrior. Her instinct was to kill when something did not go her way, which meant she spent a lot of time destroying things for no reason.

Like the vending machines at Alexandria Tower.

They both had a lot to learn about society.

Of the two, Hades expected Leuce to act uncomfortable in his presence. After all, he had been the one to turn her into a tree, but it was Zofie who froze when she spotted him.

"My lord!" she exclaimed and swept into a stiff bow.

"You don't have to do that here, Zofie," Persephone said, though Hades was not opposed. He found it strange that the Amazon insisted on bowing to him but not Persephone, who was technically her mistress, but he knew his goddess would be uncomfortable with that considering they were among...*friends*.

"But...he is the Lord of the Underworld!" Zofie said.

Hermes scoffed. "We're all aware. Look at him—he's the only goth in the room." Hades scowled at the god who offered a sheepish grin and left Hades's side, declaring, "Since everyone's here, let's play a game!"

"What's the game?" Helen asked. "Poker?"

"No!"

The reply came from almost everyone in the room—even Persephone.

Hades glowered.

He recognized he had a reputation when it came to card games, and a loss to him came at a great cost, but he was not interested in a bargain with anyone here—except for, perhaps, the mortal parading as a false oracle. He liked the idea of giving him an impossible challenge, something along the lines of: Stop being a fucking creep.

He would fail spectacularly, and then Hades could rid the world of his soul.

"Let's play Never Have I Ever!"

Hades groaned. He hated this game.

Hermes bounded toward the kitchen and reached over the bar, which was followed by the sound of glass clinking as he managed to gather several bottles of liquor in each hand. "With shots!"

"Okay," Sybil said. "But I don't have shot glasses."

"Then you're all going to have to pick something to gulp," Hermes said, strolling toward the coffee table in the living room and arranging the bottles on the table.

"What's Never Have I Ever?" Zofie asked.

"Exactly what it sounds like. You make a statement about something you've never done, and if anyone has done it, they have to take a shot," said Hermes, which was exactly why Hades hated the game. It was the last thing he wanted to play with Persephone in the room.

He'd done everything in the fucking book because he was *ancient*—things he had never had the opportunity to tell Persephone about.

He considered lying but knew Hermes would call him out.

Fuck me.

He would not forgive Hermes for this.

Everyone gathered around the table in the living room and had to watch as Ben invaded Sybil's personal space just to squeeze beside her on the ground.

"Me first!" Hermes exclaims. "Never have I ever... had sex with Hades."

A warm flush rushed from the top of Hades's head to his toes. Forget summoning Hecate to torture Ben. Hades would summon her for Hermes.

"*Hermes*," Persephone hissed.

Forget Hecate. Perhaps Persephone would execute him on her own. She looked murderous enough.

"What?" Hermes grumbled. "This game is difficult for someone my age. I've done *everything*."

It wasn't until Leuce cleared her throat that Hermes seemed to realize the issue with what he'd said. Persephone wasn't the only person Hades had slept with in this room, and the reminder wasn't a pleasant one—for any of them.

"Oh. *Oh.*"

An awkward silence followed as both Persephone and Leuce took a shot, and while he kept his gaze trained on Persephone, he could feel the strain between them.

Without prompting, Ben went next. "Never have I ever stalked an ex-girlfriend."

Hades could taste the lie, and no one drank because no one here was a sociopath.

"Never have I ever…fallen in love at first sight," said Sybil, and despite the statement being for Ben specifically, the mortal did not seem to notice, or perhaps he didn't care, because he took a shot.

Helen was next. "Never have I ever…had a threesome."

Hades could feel Persephone's gaze burning into him before she even finished her sentence, but he did not wish to look at her as he raised the bottle to his lips to drink. When he did meet her gaze, she looked pale, except for her cheeks, which were turning a warm, rosy red.

It was not as if they hadn't discussed this before—well, not exactly *this*. He'd explained his long life, so his varied sexual partners and experiences were to be expected, but perhaps he should have been more specific.

This was no way to learn about what he'd done, even if it was all in the past.

He was desperate to be beside her, to have his arm around her, to whisper in her ear how much he loved her and no one compared.

But as the game continued, things only got worse.

"Never have I ever…eaten food off someone's naked body," Ben said, and Hades had to drink.

"Never have I ever…had sex in the kitchen," Helen said.

Another drink.

"Never have I ever had sex in public," Sybil said.

Another drink.

Hades *never* thought he would say this, but he was getting tired of drinking. Each time he did, he felt Persephone's energy change and morph into something dark and angry, and it recoiled from his own.

He didn't like it.

"Never have I ever...had sex with a priestess," said Hermes.

"That's a lie," said Hades.

"Is it?" Hermes asked, surprised, and then shrugged. "Hmm. Okay."

Hades did not drink.

Helen continued the game, declaring, "Never have I ever faked an orgasm."

Hades watched in relative horror as Persephone lifted her glass to her perfect lips and drank.

What a fucking lie.

He narrowed his eyes. He was the only person she had ever had sex with, and he knew he had never left her unsatisfied or wanting.

"If that is true," he said, his gaze unwavering, burning into her. He hoped she could feel what he intended to do to her—how he would make her beg for release, how he would shatter her so thoroughly she would feel the aftereffects for days. "I will happily rectify the situation."

"Oh," Hermes hummed. "Someone's getting fucked tonight."

"Shut up, Hermes," Persephone snapped.

"What?" he grumbled. "You're just lucky he didn't carry you away to the Underworld the moment you lifted that glass."

He'd thought about it, but it was far more rewarding to fuck her here where everyone could hear her come.

She had no idea what she'd done.

"Let's play another game," Persephone said quickly.

"But I like this one. It was just getting *good*," said Hermes. "Besides, you know Hades is just making a list of all the ways he wants to f—"

"Enough, Hermes!" Persephone snapped, her frustration boiling over.

She got to her feet and disappeared down the hallway.

Silence followed, and after a moment, Hermes looked up at him.

"Well, are you going after her?"

Hades sighed and set his bottle of whiskey on the corner of the coffee table before straightening his jacket and vanishing from sight.

He appeared in front of her, bracing his hands on either side of her head as she leaned against the bathroom door. Her eyes were closed, and he leaned in, his mouth near her ear.

"You had to know your actions would ignite me," he said.

They crawled under his skin and made him burn alive.

He wanted to fuck her, to feel her come around his cock so hard, she was left with no ability to stand or speak.

"When have I left you wanting?" he asked, his lips grazing the edge of her ear and down the column of her neck. She shivered. "Will you not answer?" He pulled away and lifted his hand to her neck. Her pulse raced beneath his hand.

"I'd really have rather not found out about your sexual exploits via a game in front of my friends," she said.

It wasn't his preference either.

"So you thought it better to reveal that I had not satisfied you in the same manner?"

She averted her gaze and swallowed. He could feel her throat constrict.

He leaned in, his tongue trailing the edge of her ear.

"Shall I leave no doubt in their minds that I can make you come?" he whispered and let his hands smooth up the backs of her thighs, under her dress to her underwear, which he tore in two.

"Hades! We are guests here!"

"Your point?" he asked as he took out his cock and lifted her into his arms, letting her back rest against the door.

"It's rude to have sex in someone's bathroom."

Despite her protests, she let him do as he pleased. He kissed her and ground his hips into hers, his cock resting between her thighs, sliding along her entrance, which was slick with her arousal.

"Fuck," he whispered, or perhaps he didn't say anything aloud at all, but she felt *good*.

He thought he would be able to drag this out, to torture her into begging for him, but he couldn't—not when she was so ready and he could not wait to dive into that heat. He slipped inside her, and a guttural moan escaped from Persephone's mouth, which was open against his.

She was...everything.

He held her tight and thrust into her, unable to

manage much movement, but it was still enough, enough to drive all thought from his mind, enough to make his ears ring, enough to send the blood rushing from his head straight to his cock.

Perspiration broke out across his skin and his breathing grew ragged as he rested his forehead against hers, aware that the door beneath them rocked in its frame. It was so loud, he almost didn't hear the knock, and when Hermes's voice sounded from the other side, he wished he'd not heard anything at all.

"I hate to interrupt whatever's going on in there, but I think you two will want to see this."

"Not now," Hades snapped. He wasn't willing to give this up. He was so close to release—she was so close. He could feel her muscles clenching around him, coaxing him to come.

He let his head fall into the crook of her neck, breathing hard against her skin, when he felt her tongue and teeth against his ear. He stiffened, gripping her tighter.

Fuck, she made this hard.

"Okay, first, it's rude to have sex in other people's bathrooms," Hermes said, his tone taking on a higher pitch, as if he were irritated. "Second, it's about the weather."

Fuck, fuck, fuck Demeter, he thought. How was it that this gods-damned storm was ruining even this moment?

"A moment, Hermes," Hades growled.

"How long is a moment?"

"*Hermes*," Hades seethed, and he hoped the god understood what he didn't say—*ask one more question and I'll burn your balls off.*

"Okay, okay."

Hades took a breath.

Leaving Persephone's body was torture. It was worse when he had to face his engorged cock, glistening with *her*.

"Fuck."

"I'm sorry," she said, and he frowned.

"Why are you apologizing?"

She started to speak but seemed to decide against it.

"I am not upset with you," Hades assured and pressed his mouth to hers. "But your mother will regret the interruption."

That was a promise.

They restored their appearances and left the bathroom. From the hall, they could hear the news reporting on the weather.

"A severe ice storm warning has been issued for the whole of New Greece."

"What's going on?" Persephone asked as she came into the living room. Hades was right behind her.

"It's started to sleet." Helen was at the window, the curtains parted. Persephone joined her there and looked outside, her arms crossed over her chest, a sign of her anxiety. Hades had heard when the ice had first started to fall, but now it came down like rain.

"This is a god," the false oracle began. "A god cursing us!"

Silence filled the room at the mortal's declaration, and while no one would argue the point, it was another to state it in a room with actual gods.

Ben met Hades's gaze.

"Do you deny it?" he challenged.

"It is not wise to jump to conclusions, mortal," Hades gritted out.

He really hated this man.

"I'm not jumping to conclusions. I have foreseen this! The gods will rain terror down upon us. There will be despair and destruction."

Hades glanced at Persephone, who looked pale and uncertain. What Ben said was not outside the realm of possibility, but it was also information anyone could spout so long as they were familiar with the history of Greece.

"Careful with your words, oracle," Hermes warned. His body had grown rigid, and he stood with his shoulders squared and fists clenched. He had taken great offense to Ben's words.

"I am only speaking—"

"What you hear," Sybil interrupted quickly. "Which may or may not be the word of a god, and judging by the fact that you have no patron, I'm guessing you're being fed prophecies from an impious entity. If you had training, you would know that."

An impious entity could be anything—another mortal filling his head with impious thoughts or even a soul trapped on this earth, whispering to him in the dark.

"And what is so bad about an impious entity? Sometimes they are the only truth tellers."

"I think you should leave," said Sybil, though her voice quaked.

Fucking finally, Hades thought.

"You want me to…leave?"

"She didn't stutter," Hermes said, taking a step forward.

"But—"

"You must have forgotten the way out the door." Hermes took another step. "I'll show you out."

"Sybil—"

Oh, fuck. *Enough.*

Hades sent his magic barreling toward the mortal, who vanished from sight.

There was a moment of shock, and everyone looked at Hermes.

"That wasn't me," he said and looked at Hades, who made no move to explain what he'd done, which was what he should have done from the beginning—sent Ben to a deserted island.

"I think we all should go. This storm is only going to get worse the longer we stay." Persephone looked at him. "Hades, I'd like to make sure Helen, Leuce, and Zofie get home safe."

"I'll call Antoni."

The cyclops arrived in minutes, and they filed inside the limo. The sound of sleet was louder in the car and filled the space with a sense of dread.

Hades sat beside Persephone, one arm braced around her while Leuce, Zofie, and Helen sat opposite them.

"Did anyone else really hate that Ben guy?" asked Leuce.

What a ridiculous question, Hades thought. Of course everyone hated him.

"Sybil should keep a blade beneath her bed in case he comes back," said Zofie helpfully.

"*Or* she could just lock her door," Helen suggested.

"Locks can be picked. A blade is better," Zofie insisted, and Hades couldn't disagree. Someone like Ben wasn't going to let a lock get in the way of what he wanted, just like he wouldn't let the word *no* stop him.

Hades was glad for the silence because it let him think, though what he had to do next wasn't exactly exciting. He had to visit Apollo and learn what truly killed Adonis, and he needed to know soon before any other attacks like this took place.

He would much rather return to the Underworld with Persephone and pick up where they left off in the bathroom, but he would have to wait until later, after this task was complete.

She wouldn't be happy.

Antoni dropped off Leuce and Zofie. They watched until the two were safe inside their apartment before leaving and continuing on to Helen's home.

The woman sat quietly for a while, but after a moment, she spoke, not looking at either him or Persephone.

"Do you think Ben is right? That this is the work of the gods?"

Hades felt Persephone's body go rigid against his, and his hold tightened on her.

"We'll find out soon enough," he answered.

They arrived at Helen's, and Antoni helped her out of the car.

"Thank you for the ride," Helen said as she left.

Persephone burrowed closer to him as the cold filled the cabin, and he gladly let her.

Now they were heading home, and Hades began to dread arriving. He was content to be here with Persephone, warm and in the back of his limo.

He felt Persephone look up, and after a moment, she spoke in a quiet voice.

"Does she really think a storm will keep us apart?"

It was that question that made him realize she had no idea how bad this was going to get.

"Have you ever seen snow, Persephone?" he asked.

"From afar."

Hades met her gaze, eyes searching. He could not figure out how to communicate what would inevitably happen.

"What is going through your mind?" she whispered as if she were afraid to find out.

"She will do this until the gods have no choice but to intervene."

"And what happens then?"

Then I destroy the world, he thought.

He chose not to speak, and she did not ask for an answer.

A moment longer and they were close enough to Nevernight. Hades straightened, which also caused Persephone to shift away.

He hated it.

"Antoni, please see that Lady Persephone returns safely to Nevernight."

"What?"

Hades reached for her and kissed her before she could say anything more. His tongue slid into her mouth, and it took everything in his power not to pull her into his lap, to seal their bodies together, to fuck her in the back of this car.

Instead he stayed focused on her mouth, his fingers tangled in her hair, gripping her tight to keep her in place, to keep him in place.

Fuck, how was this always so good?

He tore from her lips, pleased to see her eyes alight. It was her passion and her frustration.

She wanted him.

His lips quirked and he touched her with the tips of his fingers. "Do not fret, my darling. You shall come for me tonight."

Then he vanished before he decided not to leave at all.

CHAPTER VIII
DIONYSUS

Dionysus waited for Ariadne in the common area.

They were heading to the pleasure district, where they would begin their search for Medusa. It was the last location the maenads had been able to trace her to, and beyond that, she seemed to have disappeared.

"That's the fifth time you have checked your watch in the last *minute*," said Naia. "I do not think it will get her here any faster."

Dionysus scowled and glared at the maenad who sat in an oversize chair, crocheting. She wasn't even looking at him.

"She's late," he said.

"And you're never late?" asked Lilaia, who sat opposite Naia, a book propped open in her lap.

"Not when it counts," Dionysus replied.

Both women scoffed and rolled their eyes.

"You should be siding with me," he said. "Ariadne has done nothing but make your lives more difficult since she arrived."

"She might be difficult, but her reasons are not unfounded," said Naia. "You know we all wish her sister was free of her abuser."

"I have promised to help," Dionysus said, frustrated.

"Give her time to trust you, just as you gave us time," Lilaia said. "You know this does not happen overnight."

Her words tightened his throat with guilt, which he felt even more keenly as his frustration grew.

He did not have time to wait for her to trust him. Her uncertainty was dangerous. It made her unpredictable, and it put every one of his maenads in danger.

The sound of heels clicking drew his attention, and he turned to watch as Ariadne stepped out of the shadows wearing a short, black dress that barely grazed her thighs and knee-high boots. She looked like she belonged in his bed—and that was where he would like this outfit to stay.

His cock twitched, growing hard at the thought.

"What are you wearing?" Dionysus demanded.

"A dress. What does it look like?" she said, pulling her jacket closed, but it was far too late for that. He'd already noticed the lace over her breast.

Dionysus opened his mouth, but no words came out. He tried again and stumbled over his words. "You cannot wear that to the pleasure district," he said.

"*You* cannot tell me what to wear," Ariadne said.

"I told you to blend in," Dionysus countered.

"This is blending in!"

"You are not blending!"

She crossed her arms over her chest. "I'm not changing."

"Ariadne," Dionysus said, a hint of warning in his voice.

"Dionysus," she challenged just as steadily. "What is so wrong with this outfit? I have been to the pleasure district before. I know how to dress for it."

"You've been before?" he asked, shock washing over him.

"I'm a detective, you idiot. I work on sex crimes. Of course I've been."

He stood opposite her in silence. He wanted to say something, to stand his ground, because he knew the kind of people who wandered those streets, but all he could manage to say was, "Oh."

Naia and Lilaia giggled quietly.

He glared at them and scowled.

"If we're going to find out anything about Medusa, one of us has to look the part."

"Let's go," he said and started toward the elevator.

Once inside, Dionysus punched the button for the main floor and then leaned against the cool, metal wall opposite Ariadne. She kept her arms over her chest, on the defense. They stared openly at each other, frustration present in the air between them.

This was a mistake.

"What's wrong with the dress?" she asked.

Dionysus could feel the heat rushing to his head, roaring in his ears.

"Do you know how many men will look at you tonight?"

"I imagine quite a few," she said. "Including you."

He swallowed and looked away. "I did not intend to be disrespectful," he said, his voice low and gruff, not because he did not wish to apologize but because he was embarrassed.

"I can protect myself, Dionysus," she said.

Her comment drew his eyes once more, and he could not help letting his gaze drift down her body.

"I am armed."

"In that dress?"

"Yes, in this dress."

He raised a brow.

"You don't believe me," she said.

"That dress barely covers your ass, Ariadne."

"It goes well below my ass, Dionysus. Perhaps you need a lesson in anatomy."

"If you're willing," he said.

She glared and then lifted the hem of her dress.

"This is my gun," she said and bared a brace she'd secured at the height of her thigh. "And this is my ass." She turned and exposed one firm, round cheek.

What the fuck was happening?

"*Ariadne*," Dionysus warned, gripping the bar behind him until his fingers hurt. His dick was hard, and there was no fucking way he would find relief with her dressed like that the entire night. It did not help that he could not stop thinking about how he'd like to punish her. He wanted to smack her ass hard enough to elicit a cry from those full lips and bury his fingers in her wet heat. When she came, he would make her suck those same fingers while he fucked her from behind, his pace set to the sound of her choked cries.

But she was not someone he could ever do that with. She hated him and certainly would not appreciate his dominance.

She lowered her dress and turned to face him again, a smug smile tugging her lips.

"Yes, Dionysus?"

Her gaze skated down his front, catching the bulge of his trousers. Her smile vanished. He waited for her to meet his eyes, and when she did, he spoke in a cool and deliberate tone.

"Do not tease me," he said.

She shuddered as she swallowed and then looked away.

Everything was worse after that.

The elevator ride seemed to last forever, and Dionysus felt like he couldn't breathe, because if he did, he'd only smell Ariadne, and then he would never be rid of this aching in his groin.

"Finally," he scowled when the doors opened, bolting from the small space into his garage where he kept a number of pristine vehicles.

He did not wait for Ariadne to follow; he knew she trailed along after him because those fucking boots clicked as she walked.

"Aren't you a god?" she asked.

"Do you really have to ask that question?" he asked.

"I thought you could teleport," she said.

"In case you haven't noticed, I'm not like other gods," he said.

He liked cars, fast ones, and preferred that method of travel over any other, even teleportation.

"I'm sure that's what you all think," she said.

Dionysus rounded a corner of the garage and approached his favorite ride—a custom black chariot motorcycle. He took the helmet where it hung on the handlebar and held it out to Ariadne.

"Put this on," he said.

"*Put this on?*" she repeated. "I can't ride that!"

"You can," he said and swung his leg over the seat, settling on the bike. "You will."

Ariadne yelled over the roar of the motorcycle as Dionysus started the engine. "I am not dressed for this!"

He shrugged. "I tried to warn you."

She glared at him, and he let her do it for as long as she needed. Finally she relented and approached, slipping onto the back of the motorcycle and pulling on the helmet he had given her.

He glanced back at her.

"Hold on," he said. As he took off, Ariadne's arms tightened around his waist and her thighs pressed in on his, which amused him at first and then quickly became the only thing he could focus on as he left his garage and sped down the streets of New Athens toward the pleasure district.

He leaned forward on his bike and Ariadne leaned with him, her head resting against his back and her hands splayed across his chest. He warmed where she touched him, despite the cold that slammed into his body as he zipped in and out of traffic, heading for the coast.

There was a point, however, as he crested a hill and could look down on the glimmering district, with its red-tinged aura and phallic symbols, that made him feel dread, and it was because he was about to put Ariadne in a situation he did not like. It was not the district itself he minded; it was where they were going within it. It was one thing to choose to engage in prostitution, another to be forced.

Michail, the man they were going to see, forced—men, women, children.

Dionysus and the maenads had been working for years to slowly take down parts of his extensive operation, and part of that involved establishing a relationship with the mortal. By this point, Dionysus knew him pretty well and hated him thoroughly, but if he was going to save the numerous women the mortal had sent across New Greece and to the islands beyond, he would have to endure.

He arrived, parking on the street about a mile from the district, which was located down a sloping hill. Ariadne slipped off the bike and pulled off the helmet, shaking out her hair. Dionysus looked away quickly, still suffering a nearly painful erection from her mere presence.

"What's the plan?" she asked.

"The maenads tell me Medusa lived at Maiden House. We do not know where she's gone, since this brothel owner does not keep physical records of anyone who enters their doors, even their workers."

"That isn't legal," Ariadne said.

"I know," Dionysus said.

Legal sex work was not frowned on within New Athens, and a lot had been done to protect sex workers' rights. Unfortunately, the fight for those rights had led to an increase in sex trafficking and brothels like Maiden House.

Her mouth tightened.

"How did she end up at Maiden House?" Ariadne asked. "Do we know?"

"We think she was pulled off the street."

It wasn't a simple process either. Someone had gotten to know her, gained her trust, and then betrayed her.

Ariadne did not respond, likely because she also knew how this worked.

They made their way into the thick of the district, fusing with the crowd. Dionysus was not so worried about blending in, given he was usually sighted here and a god they heavily worshipped. Every year during Apokries and the Dionysia, he held a celebration in the district's courtyard where people came from all over New Greece to fuck each other in public.

What he was far more aware of was Ariadne, who also knew of those celebrations and the revelry he encouraged.

They came to the courtyard where a golden pillar was erected, carved with erotic scenes. Beneath it was the throne upon which he sat and cast his magic.

"I don't understand," she said. "You use your magic to conduct orgies in this square, and yet outside this, you—"

Dionysus gave her a harsh look, warning her not to finish that sentence. All he needed was this mouthy detective to ruin everything he'd worked hard to establish here.

"Why?"

"Consensual sex is not unwilling. You of all people should know that. Those who come to this square, they want to fuck, and they don't care with who."

"I do not come here to fuck," she said.

"Perhaps you should," he said. "You might be a little more bearable."

She glared at him, her mouth tightening, but her silence did not last long.

"Do you participate?" she asked.

Dionysus looked at her. "Why?"

"I just wondered," she said, looking away quickly.

"I suppose that depends on your definition of *participate*."

"What other definition is there?"

"In reference to the festival, you could be asking me anything. Do I dance? Do I sing? Do I—"

"Do you fuck strangers, Dionysus?" Ariadne snapped, clearly fed up with him.

He smirked in triumph, but it only lasted a moment, because he soon realized just how frustrated she was.

"No," he said finally. "Or at least…not in a long time."

A strange and awkward silence descended between them, and they did not speak until they reached Maiden House, a sleek, two-story building with no windows.

Before they entered, Dionysus turned to Ariadne.

"I need to know if you're going to be okay," he said. "If I…can touch you."

She studied his face. "If it means finding Medusa and getting my sister back, I can do anything."

He gave a sharp nod.

They entered the brothel and were immediately thrust into darkness. Already, Dionysus found himself reaching for Ariadne, his arm snaking around her waist. He pulled her against him, his mouth near her ear.

"As badly as you may want to," he said, "don't open your mouth."

He could just imagine the look she was giving him. He could feel her anger, but he was surprised when she didn't shove him away. She did, however, dig her nails into his arm.

"Dionysus! The god of the hour!" Michail said as he approached, pristine in appearance. He was an older man with thinning hair he kept smoothed back to hide an obvious shining bald spot.

Dionysus shook his hand and offered a one-armed embrace.

"And who is this...lovely creature?" Michail asked.

Dionysus turned to look at Ariadne. He expected to see her scowl at being called a creature, but she'd transformed and plastered a sweet smile on her face.

"This is...Phaedra," he said, immediately regretting the choice of name, especially as he noticed Ariadne's smile falter for a second.

"Phaedra," Michail purred. "Aren't you a beauty? I did not know you hired hetairai, Dionysus."

"I don't," Dionysus said.

"Oh," Michail said. "Then—"

"He doesn't have to pay me," Ariadne said. "I simply...enjoy his company."

Michail smiled. "Lucky you. Come, come. The show is about to begin."

When Michail turned, Dionysus glanced back at Ariadne. He wanted to snap at her, *What did I say?*

But she returned an even harsher look that said, *I know what to do.*

Michail took them into the main part of his club but kept to the outside of the floor until they reached the stairs, which spiraled up to the second-floor balcony where there were several individual boxes. They were multipurpose—occupants could watch the show on the floor below or pay for their own private ones. The inside of the box was luxurious—mostly dark, save for a faux fire that danced within a marble wall. There were two large leather chairs and a table between them.

Dionysus felt a lump form in his chest as Michail took a seat, knowing that Ariadne would have to sit in his lap.

His dick was going to fall off at the end of the night.

He lowered into the chair and looked up at Ariadne, meeting her gaze before he placed his hands on her hips and helped her sit. It was as much a show for Michail as it was practical for him. He'd like to avoid having her experience the hardness of his cock, especially knowing she did not see him that way, but that was near impossible. Her eyes had already fallen to it, and when she sat, her thigh pressed against him, a constant pressure that made his head spin.

Fuck me.

"It's been a few weeks since I saw you last," Michail said.

Dionysus could barely focus on his words as Ariadne drew an arm around his neck, her breast pressing against his chest.

"I had an unfortunate visit from the God of the Dead," he said.

"Oh? Did someone die?" Michail asked.

"No," Dionysus said. "Hades likes to accuse me of things he knows nothing about."

As he spoke, he felt Ariadne's eyes on him, burning a hole through his chest. He wondered if she was just as aware of his presence—of the way his fingers splayed against her skin. Could she feel the heat rising between them?

Michail chuckled around a cigar he'd just placed in his mouth. "I have heard he is here this evening."

For a moment, the God of Wine thought he'd misheard, which was quite possible since Ariadne had begun to trace circles on the back of his neck.

"What?" Dionysus asked, surprised.

"Oh yes," Michail said as he lit the cigar. A burst of sweet spice dispersed through the air. "They tell me he's at Erotas. I wonder who he's visiting."

Dionysus wondered too, because Hades certainly wasn't there for sex.

The door to their box opened, and a young man entered carrying a tray. He was practically naked aside from a bedazzled loincloth. He set a bottle of wine and two glasses on the table between Dionysus and Michail. Dionysus noted there was no third glass for Ariadne, which was typical of Michail. He was not inclined to entertain the women or men brought along by his guests. To him, they existed for pleasure and entertainment only.

Michail did not acknowledge the young man, and he soon left. The mortal leaned forward and poured two glasses.

"Hope you will approve," he said. "This is from my private vineyard."

Dionysus took the glass.

"Would you like to taste?" he asked Ariadne.

He felt it only right to offer, but he was not prepared for what she did with it. She wrapped her hand around his and brought the glass to her lips for a sip—and then she kissed him with the taste of wine on her tongue.

He tried hard not to react, but that only looked like digging his fingers into her skin to keep from pulling her closer and grinding against her. When she pulled away, she let her mouth drift over his jaw to his ear, drawing the cartilage into his mouth.

He ground his teeth and Michail chuckled.

"You clearly have your hands full with her," the mortal said, taking a drag of his cigar. "What can I do for you, Dionysus?"

The question was posed with a note of suspicion Dionysus did not miss.

"Do you not trust that I merely wished to catch up with an old friend?"

Michail laughed. "An old friend to be certain," he said. "But catching up is not within your interests. You've come for something as you always do. Tell me. Perhaps I can help."

"Perhaps you can," Dionysus said. Ariadne had ceased to suck on his ear, which was somehow both disappointing and a relief, but now she toyed with his braids as she leaned against him, and all he could really think was how soft her breasts felt against his chest. He considered that he should probably touch her more, but he could not embrace this role as easily as she could, because despite her consent, it still felt wrong without her interest.

"Why don't you entertain us from afar, darling?" Michail asked.

Dionysus was not sure why the mortal made the request. Perhaps he found that Dionysus was too distracted, or he'd incorrectly inferred that the god did not wish for her to hear.

Perhaps he wished to see her.

"No," Dionysus said quickly, his hands tightening on her hips to hold her in place as if he had the right to possess her. "I like her here just fine."

"I've got this, baby," she said, her lips caressing his as she spoke.

He could not help the low growl that escaped his mouth. She'd fully committed to this role, and he was not sure how to feel about it.

Actually, he was sure he hated it, but that was also ridiculous given they'd agreed on the part she would play.

She pushed off him and straightened.

"You got any music, honey?" she asked Michail.

"I've got anything you need, darling," he said.

Ariadne smiled at the man as he reached for a remote. With the push of a button, their box was suddenly vibrating with a steady beat.

"Will that work, sweetheart?" he asked.

Her smile widened. "Perfect."

Dionysus glared at her, but she did not seem to notice as she walked to the space in front of them where a silver pole glimmered in the firelight. He couldn't take her eyes off her as she shrugged out of her jacket. He hated his curiosity. He wondered what she would do. How thoroughly had she played this game as a detective?

But then she took hold of the pole and swung all the way around it, and he knew by the one smooth move she had done this before. She moved beautifully, naturally, almost as if she considered it an art and not a form of entertainment. He couldn't look away as she arched and swayed. He wanted to be that gods-damned pole, and the only thing that kept him rooted in reality and not slipping off into a fantasy was the thought of Michail sitting beside him and watching Ariadne dance while getting hard; it pissed him off to an extent that surprised even him. His fists were clenched in his lap.

This was a mistake.

"Well, Dionysus?" the mortal inquired.

The god cleared his throat and barely managed to look away from Ariadne.

"I'm looking for a woman. Her name is Gorgo," Dionysus said, giving the name Medusa was thought to be using. "I believe she worked for you for a time?"

"Ah," Michail said. "Yes, beautiful creature."

"Do you know where she's gone?"

"Why are you looking?"

From the corner of his eye, Dionysus could still see Ariadne dancing. He wanted so badly to look. He wanted so badly to tell her to stop. He wanted her so badly.

Fuck him.

He cleared his throat. "She owes me money," he said.

"As if you need more," Michail commented.

"It is the principle," Dionysus said. "As you well know."

"As I well know," Michail said, though somewhat distantly. Dionysus noticed his eyes had wandered to Ariadne again, and he could not help looking either.

Fuck, fuck, fuck.

"Come now, darling," said Michail. "Don't be shy. Show us some skin."

"She's showing enough," Dionysus snapped.

The corners of Michail's lips turned up. "Don't tell me, Dionysus, you've fallen for this hetaira. You of all people know they are *paid* for their companionship."

It was lucky that Dionysus had such a reaction, because Michail hadn't seen the way Ariadne froze or paled at the man's suggestion.

They had to get out of here.

"As she informed you earlier," Dionysus said, "I don't pay."

Michail looked at him for a moment as he took another drag from his cigar. He blew out the smoke and offered the same amused chuckle he'd been giving all night.

"Fine, fine," he said. "Far be it from me to disagree. I've fallen for a whore or two in my life."

Just then, a knock sounded at the door, and the young man from earlier entered.

"Mr. Calimeris," he said. "A moment?"

"You'll excuse me," Michail said and rose from his seat.

Dionysus waited in tense silence until the man had gone. Before Ariadne could speak, he cut her off.

"Phaedra," he snapped so quickly, Ariadne flinched.

He hoped she understood why he was speaking to her in such a manner, but he knew what Michail was doing. He'd been called away for no reason other than he wished to observe them alone. They were being filmed and their voices recorded.

"Come."

She seemed to understand something was wrong, because despite her hesitation, she finally approached.

Dionysus sat forward and spread his legs apart. He wanted her between them because he wanted her close.

"Kneel," he commanded.

She held his gaze and placed her hands on his knees as she lowered before him. It was the most erotic thing he'd ever witnessed—likely because he'd never imagined this woman obeying him so easily.

He twined his hand into her hair and pulled her head back, then bent forward, his mouth near her ear. She gasped, and her hands tightened on his legs.

"Watch your mouth," he said. It was the best warning he could give, fearing if he said too much, Michail would become suspicious of his actions.

Dionysus pulled back to look into her eyes again.

Ariadne took a breath. Despite how good she was at this act, it was a challenge for her to remain in this role.

"Have I not pleased you?"

"Hardly," Dionysus barked, though he did not mean to say it aloud.

She rubbed the palms of her hands along his thighs slowly, deliberately. "What can I do?"

Dionysus just stared at her, his mind completely void of thought—and that, he decided, was why he kissed her, but fuck did he need it. He braced his hand against the back of her head, holding her in place as his mouth collided with hers. There was nothing soft or sweet about how they came together either, both fueled by a desperation that seemed to live within their bones. But as quick as it had started, Ariadne pulled away.

She glared up at him from between his legs, her lips wet from his kiss, her eyes gleaming with a storm of hate and lust.

He started to speak, to say he was sorry, but she pushed off the floor and kissed him again. Her arms wrapped around his neck, her knees settled on either side of his legs as she straddled him in the black chair. His hands moved to her bare ass, and he squeezed her soft skin before slapping his palms against each cheek.

He gripped her again and helped her grind against his length, groaning at the feel of her against him.

"Fuck," he breathed as he kissed up her neck and jaw. "Has anyone ever told you you're perfect?"

"You would be the first," she whispered.

"What a shame," he said, and their mouths clashed again.

Dionysus had never felt so frenzied with anyone before, but Ariadne was a match, and he wanted to burn beneath her.

He moved one hand from her ass to one of her breasts, kneading and rubbing until her nipple was hard and each swipe of his thumb made her moan.

Fuck, he wanted it in his mouth, but just as he went to pull her dress down, someone cleared their throat and the two froze.

"I really hate to interrupt," said Michail, who had returned undetected with two large men. They flanked the mortal, dressed all in black. "But I've learned some very unfortunate news."

"What the fuck is this, Michail?"

"Nothing to do with you, Dionysus," said the mortal. "This is between me and your girl, isn't it, Phaedra? Or perhaps you respond better to Detective Alexiou."

"What?" Dionysus looked from Ariadne to Michail.

"Detective Alexiou works for the Hellenic Police Department," Michail said, clearly under the impression that Dionysus was not aware of Ariadne's background. "She's been roaming our streets undercover for months. We'd been onto her for a few weeks when she vanished. I assumed she ended up at the bottom of the Aegean, but it seems she just found another way to get what she wanted."

"And what's that?" Dionysus asked. He was looking at her now. His hands were on her thighs, right beneath her gun.

She held his gaze.

"I was doing my job," she said. "Looking for missing women."

His chest tightened.

So she'd roamed these streets in search of the women she'd ended up finding at his club. Of course she'd started here. She'd assumed they'd been sold into the sex trade.

"Sorry, darling," said Michail. "You're not as sly as you thought. Now why don't you give my esteemed guest some room?"

Dionysus held Ariadne's gaze. He didn't want to let her go.

"Ariadne." He could not help saying her name.

"I'm sorry," she said and rose.

"Ariadne!"

But as she stood, she drew her gun and shot it twice—one bullet for each man on either side of Michail.

Dionysus rose to his feet.

"What the fuck are you waiting for, Dionysus? Fucking kill her!"

That was the last thing he wanted to do.

Dionysus called on his magic, and thick vines exploded from the floor, curling around Michail's wrists and jerking him to the ground. He landed flat on his face, his arms outstretched.

Dionysus crossed to the man and dragged his head back. His face was red and his nose bled. He gave a pained cry.

"If you lay a hand on her, you will die, Michail," he said. "Now, I asked you a question earlier."

"Fuck you!" Michail groaned, blood and spit flying from his mouth.

Dionysus shoved his head against the floor again. This time when he pulled his head back, it was by what remained of his hair.

"Let's try this again," he said. "The girl, where is she?"

"I don't know," Michail said, seething.

Dionysus prepared to bash his face into the floor again, but the mortal had enough.

"Wait, wait!" he said, breathing ragged. "I...I warned her not to go to the shore."

"You expect me to believe you were some kind of savior?"

"You do not understand her beauty. It's like a siren's call."

Disgust twisted through him at what Michail was implying—that Medusa was too beautiful to exist in this world without worrying about a predator.

"She went to the shore?" Dionysus asked. "And then what, Michail?"

"I don't know! She never came back!" Michail yelled, and then his voice quieted. "But the ocean is Poseidon's realm, and we all know what he does to beautiful things."

Yeah, Dionysus did know.

He broke them.

"Fuck!"

Dionysus slammed Michail's face into the floor again, and this time the mortal did not move.

When Dionysus rose to his feet, he faced Ariadne, who stood still and quiet.

"Put the gun away," he said and then crossed to where she'd discarded her jacket. He snatched it off the floor and placed it around her shoulders, drawing her close. "Let's go," he said.

This time, he didn't care to race through New Athens.

He teleported them both home.

CHAPTER IX
HADES

Hades did not particularly enjoy the pleasure district.

He usually only visited to check in on Madelia Rella, who had come to him in search of coin to establish her first brothel. Madelia was different from others who had reigned in the district, as she'd always been vocal about the rights of sex workers. She promised Hades that if he offered up his power, she would use it for good, and she had, though it had come at a great cost, and that cost was trafficking.

The more rules brothel owners had to follow, the more ways many sought to undermine them. Undocumented sex workers could not be held to the same standards, which meant unsuspecting people were disappearing off the streets and forced into this labor.

It was a vicious cycle, as was all life in the Upperworld.

But Hades had not come for Madelia; he'd come for Apollo, suspecting he would be at Erotas, after having visited the god's apartment in the Crysos District and finding it empty. He wondered why Apollo kept a residence there at all; he was hardly ever there.

Hades appeared in the foyer of Erotas in a plume of dark smoke. As he manifested, a few people screamed, but the madam, Selene, hushed them all. She was an older woman, beautiful and refined. Hades did not know her, but he was aware that she had run this brothel for a long time, and by all accounts, she took care of her workers.

The madam took a step forward and curtsied deep, her hands locked in front of her.

"Lord Hades," she said as she rose. "What can I do for you?"

He admired the fact that the woman could hold his gaze. None of the people gathered behind her did.

"I'm here to see Apollo."

A few giggles broke out behind her.

"Silence!" Madam Selene ordered, glaring at everyone in disfavor. "Imbeciles! Do not mock the God of the Dead."

The room went quiet, and a thick tension grew. Hades could feel the anxiety and fear permeating the air, though he wasn't certain if it was his presence or Madam Selene's disdain that perpetuated it. He had a feeling that part of the reason the madam was able to run this multistoried brothel so effectively was because no one wished to earn her disappointment.

The madam met Hades's gaze.

"Of course. Allow me to escort you to his quarters."

She turned without hesitation, and as she did, her workers parted, pressing themselves against the wall as she and Hades walked past. Once in the hallway, they entered a mirrored elevator. The madam pulled a key ring from the pocket of her long skirt, using it to access Apollo's floor. Hades noticed how tightly she held it in her hands. For all her composure, he made her anxious, and she was right to be.

Hades watched her in the mirror. Her jaw was set, her chin lifted, and her chest rose and fell rapidly.

"Do I make you nervous, Madam Selene?"

"Anyone would be nervous in the presence of such a god," she said.

Hades chuckled, and he looked at his feet as he spoke. "Could it be that you are nervous because you once allowed my fiancée to go to auction?"

Madam Selene jerked her head toward Hades. "She said she wouldn't tell."

"Are you suggesting my future wife, the Queen of the Underworld, is a liar, Madam?"

"No, of course not. I—"

"She didn't tell me," he said. "Apollo did."

The madam took a deep, shuddering breath. "Have you come to kill me, then?"

Hades laughed, but she looked stricken.

"No," he said. "Though I will ask for your penance."

She swallowed. "And what might that be?"

"A favor," he said. "To be collected at a future date."

"I hardly have anything of value to offer, my lord," she said.

"You have your soul," Hades said and met her gaze.

She stared, still and silent, likely waiting for him to steal her soul.

"But I can take that at will," he said. "I'll determine what is valuable, Madam, and trust me when I say, I will collect."

When he met her eyes again, she nodded once.

The elevator doors opened then, and Hades stepped out into Apollo's suite. Unlike his Crysos apartment, this was extravagantly decorated. Everything was patterned, none of it the same—a floral couch, striped pillows, curtains stitched with small diamonds—and all of it was trimmed in gold and dripped with jewels.

This should be a torture chamber, Hades thought. It definitely made him feel mad.

Hades moved into the adjacent room where a spotless tub sat on clawed feet. Beyond that was a massive bed upon which Apollo lay flat on his back, arms and legs spread wide. He wore a robe, but it was open, exposing a very obvious erection, and he was snoring.

Loud.

Hades watched the god for a moment, and then his eyes shifted to an empty bottle of vodka that sat on the table beside the bed. Another lay on the ground.

Fuck.

Apollo was difficult to deal with when he was sober, but drunk?

Hades gave a frustrated sigh, swiped one of the empty bottles off the floor, filled it with water from the tub, and then poured it over Apollo's face.

The god flailed beneath the stream.

"What the fuck!" Apollo sputtered.

Though he was awake, Hades did not stop until the bottle was empty. He let his arm drop to his side as Apollo glared back at him.

"You snore," Hades said.

"I do not snore!" Apollo snapped.

"Yes, you do," Hades said. "I just heard you."

Apollo ignored him and pulled on the hem of his robe with two fingers. "You've ruined my kimono." He pushed off the bed and discarded the robe as he walked bare-ass naked to a wardrobe across the room. He threw open the doors to reveal several kimonos of the same color and pattern.

Hades shook his head. "What the fuck?"

"What, Hades?" the god snapped, taking a robe from one of the hangers and slipping it on as he raged. "It's *fashion*, something you would know little about since the only color in your wardrobe is black, but I suppose that is fitting since it's the color of your soul."

Hades raised a brow. He wasn't so certain this was about fashion as much as it was about what Apollo found comforting, but he did not say that aloud.

"Feeling better?" he asked.

Apollo took a deep breath. "Yes, actually," he said, slamming the wardrobe doors. "No thanks to you. What are you doing here anyway?"

"You were supposed to conduct the autopsy on Adonis," said Hades.

"I *did*," said Apollo. "And he was full of *holes*."

That was no surprise given they'd found a knife handle near Adonis's body.

"Any idea what he was stabbed with?" Hades asked.

"Something curved," Apollo answered, running a hand through his wet hair.

"How do you know?" Hades asked.

"Because when I stuck my finger in the wound, it *curved*, Hades. For fuck's sake. You asked me to do an autopsy. I fucking did it."

Hades wasn't sure what disturbed him more, Apollo's

moodiness or the knowledge that whatever had aided in taking Adonis's life was a curved blade.

It made him think of one blade in particular—his father's scythe.

"What's wrong?" Hades asked.

"What's wrong?" Apollo repeated, whipping around to face the God of the Dead. "I don't know, Hades. Perhaps I am angry because I was waterboarded awake."

Hades rolled his eyes and sighed, but Apollo wasn't finished.

"Or maybe it's because I spent most of my day elbows-deep in a fucking body after being summoned to a fucking crime scene at four in the gods-damned morning."

Hades watched the god as he started to pace.

"Or maybe it's because I haven't fucked anyone in a month, but you would know nothing about that because you get fucked every night, multiple times a night."

"I…do not know what we're talking about anymore, Apollo, but I think you need therapy."

"What I need is everyone to leave me the fuck alone!"

There was silence, and then Hades asked, "Apollo… are you in love?"

"What? No!"

"Who is it this time?"

"Don't make it sound like it means nothing," Apollo said.

That was not Hades's intention, though he had known Apollo for a very long time. He'd had a revolving door of lovers, some willing, most unwilling, and he'd claimed to love them all.

"All right then," Hades said. "What makes this one different?"

"I don't *know*," Apollo said, frustrated. "That's the *problem*. I just want him."

"And what? He doesn't want you?"

The god was silent.

"Apollo?"

"I don't want to find out," he muttered.

"What?"

"I don't want to find out!" he shouted, and his eyes were glassy. "You don't know what this is like, but I have loved *so* many, and they have never loved me back."

"Apollo—"

"I don't want to want this man," he said. "It would be better for both of us."

All Hades had wanted was to know what had killed Adonis. Why was this his life?

"The problem is that you do want him," said Hades. "So what are you going to do about it?"

Apollo blinked. "What do you mean?"

"You want this man, whoever he is—"

"Ajax. His name is…Ajax."

"You want Ajax. So you can either tell him your feelings or you can do nothing, but if you do nothing, you will have to accept that he will eventually find someone else."

"Who is to say that isn't for the best?"

"You cannot compare every lover to Hyacinth, Apollo. That is not fair to you or the lover."

"Would you not compare every lover to Persephone?" he countered.

Hades's jaw tightened, and he glared at Apollo. He wouldn't indulge his temper.

"I remember an Apollo who was willing to *lose* just to *win* the love of his life," said Hades. "And here you are, not even willing to take a risk."

"That Apollo died a long time ago," Apollo said. "To think, you could have been rid of me if you'd just thrown me into Tartarus."

Hades had rejected Apollo's plea to die in the aftermath of Hyacinth's death, and he'd had many reasons for it, one being that granting such a wish would have been seen as taking a life, and the Fates would have demanded a soul, a give-and-take, and there was no telling what they'd have done with a sacrifice as great as Apollo.

"While it is true you annoy the ever living *fuck* out of me," Hades said, "*and* I could *murder* you for the bargain you struck with Persephone…I would miss this."

"Miss what?" Apollo asked, confused.

"This," Hades said, waving a hand at the whole of Apollo, "pathetic…"

"Pathetic?"

"…pitiable…"

"Pitiable?"

"…miserable…"

"*Miserable?*"

"…thing you have going on. It really exudes God of Light."

"Fuck you," Apollo said.

Hades chuckled darkly.

"*You're* the one who asked what was wrong," Apollo muttered.

"I also asked how Adonis died," said Hades. "And all you told me was that he was stabbed with a curved blade."

"Did you miss the part where I said multiple times?" Apollo snapped.

"Show me the body," Hades said. "Show me the wounds."

Apollo offered a sigh that sounded more like a growl, a single word slipping between gritted teeth.

"*Fine.*"

Hades manifested inside one of Apollo's dark, cold temples. This particular one was no longer in use and was located in what was now known as the old agora in New Athens. In ancient times, this had been a lively public space where citizens gathered to celebrate, worship, play games, and demonstrate the arts. Now, in the aftermath of battles and deadly weather, it was mostly in ruins.

Apollo appeared and pushed Hades aside, striding to the corner of the room where a metal table was positioned against the wall.

"Don't you think you should change?" Hades asked, as the god was still wearing his prized kimono. If he had thought water had ruined it, wasn't blood worse?

But Apollo did not seem to care. He latched on to the white, bloodied cloth that covered Adonis's body and pulled it off with a flourish.

Hades had seen a lot of dead bodies—*a lot*—so he was surprised that he was not quite prepared for this.

He approached the body slowly. Now that Adonis was clean, Hades could make out the wide wounds down his torso and along his legs and arms, even his face. Around each laceration, reddish-brown bruises had blossomed, as if he'd been stabbed to the hilt with more force than necessary. It was damage beyond anything Hades could imagine with a normal knife.

Then Hades noticed one wound on his side that did not seem to have stopped bleeding.

Strange.

"Apollo," Hades said. "You are certain there's nothing left in those wounds?"

"I dug in each of them," Apollo said.

"Why is this one bleeding?"

"Dead bodies don't bleed, Hades—" Apollo went silent as he came around the body and stood beside Hades. "I don't think that's blood," said Apollo. The god stepped forward and stuck his finger into the leaking wound.

"Don't you want gloves or something?" Hades asked, cringing at the squishy sound it made.

Apollo said nothing as he fished around. "Ouch! Motherfucker!" he said, pulling out his finger. As he did, he shook his hand, sending a spray of bodily fluids across the room.

Hades shielded his face. "What is it?" he demanded.

Still Apollo did not answer and grabbed a long pair of tweezers. This time, he shoved them into the wound, and after a few seconds, something clanked onto the metal table.

Apollo picked it up and rubbed his thumb over it. "What is it?" he asked.

"It's the tip of a scythe," Hades said. "The tip of Cronos's scythe."

CHAPTER X
HADES

Hades kept the tip of Cronos's scythe.

He hated the feel of it—heavy and hot, as if the metal might burn through the fabric of his pocket and brand his chest. When he returned to his chambers, he reached inside to check it but found the metal was cool to the touch.

He was going to need it when he confronted Poseidon about how it had found its way inside a mortal man and far from his shores.

The blade itself was forged partly from adamant and had been given to his father by Gaia. It had the ability to wound the divine. Cronos had used it to castrate his father, and the blood that had dripped to the earth birthed the Furies, the Goddesses of Vengeance and Retribution.

Once Zeus had rescued Hades and Poseidon from Cronos's bowels, they had taken his scythe, the weapon that had come to symbolize his power and struck fear in other gods, and tossed it deep into the ocean.

Then, Poseidon had been a different person, as they all had been, but it was never too late for regret, especially seeing the chaos his brother was so willing to cause.

Being mortal, Adonis would not have survived a single stab wound, much less the fourteen that had punctured his body. Equally as worrying was the fact that someone was still in possession of the rest of the blade. Being broken did not make it any less powerful.

What if these attackers went after a god? Even a minor one?

What things might spring from their blood?

Mortals likely did not understand the consequences of god killing, but Poseidon was well aware.

A shocking wave of hatred twisted his gut. He could not figure out who exactly he felt it for more—Cronos or Poseidon. Whatever game his brother was playing was dangerous. Something was happening, moving beneath the surface of the world. There were too many weapons that could cause harm to gods—first the ophiotaurus, now the scythe, and Demeter's fucking snowstorm did not help mortal opinion of the gods. What was next?

The more he learned, the more he feared for Persephone.

He looked up, expecting to find Persephone sleeping or even awake and waiting for him, but the bed was empty. He panicked for only a second before managing to relax. He could feel her here in the Underworld, her presence skating across his skin as if she were beside him.

She was near.

He left their room and started his search of the castle, finding her rather quickly in the kitchen. She stood behind the island mixing some kind of batter in a bowl.

She was completely oblivious to his presence, and he liked it that way for now. He could observe her freely, without any sort of mask she might put in place to hide herself.

He should not be surprised to find her baking—she did this often when she could not sleep. She hummed quietly as she sprinkled flour into the bowl and paused now and then to sip from a bottle of his whiskey, which was almost gone.

His brows rose at how easily she seemed to be consuming it, recalling that the last time she'd tried it, she hated it.

He wondered just how drunk she was.

When Persephone finished mixing, she poured her mixture into a pan, and he watched as she smoothed the spatula over the top and then brought it to her lips to lick away what remained.

She hummed her approval, which was Hades's sign to make himself known, because he too wanted to know how it tasted—but on her tongue.

"How does it taste?"

He manifested behind her, so close his cock pressed into her ass. He leaned forward as she turned her head toward his voice and answered.

"Divine."

She turned in the small space he had given her and gathered some of the batter onto her finger.

"Taste," she implored.

Hades took her hand to lick at the batter, and then he closed his mouth over her finger and sucked hard and slow, holding her gaze until he was finished. The way she watched him made him groan, and his hips settled against hers, his gaze dropping to her mouth.

"Exquisite," he said, his voice quiet. "But I have tasted divinity and there is nothing sweeter."

He was trying to decide how to continue what they had started at Sybil's when she turned away from him abruptly. She returned the spatula to the bowl and picked up the brownies. He took a step back as she shifted to the oven. He could feel and see the heat as she opened the door. It seemed to melt the very air.

"Where were you?" she asked as she slid them onto a rack.

"I had business," he said, which he realized was not the best reply, especially when she slammed the oven door.

She turned to him, her gaze more of a glare. "Business? At this hour?"

His business was always at this hour, which was anywhere from the middle of the night to early morning.

"I make bargains with monsters, Persephone," he said. "And you, apparently, bake."

She did not like his answer because she did not come to him like he wanted. He thought of how he'd left her in the limo, desperate and wanting. Perhaps he was stupid to hope that when he came home, she would be waiting to rekindle that same wild desire.

Or perhaps she'd taken care of herself and did not need him, but she did not seem so much sated as she was tired.

"You couldn't sleep?"

"I didn't try," she said.

Hades frowned and then nodded to the bottle on the counter. "Is that my whiskey?"

Hades wasn't sure why she needed to look—she was

well aware of what he was pointing out—but when she did not look at him again, he felt like perhaps it was an excuse to avoid him altogether.

"Was," she answered, and he moved closer, coaxing her gaze to return to his and pressing his mouth to hers. She tasted like chocolate and whiskey, and it truly was *divine*. Her hands fisted into his jacket, and she pulled him closer, sealing their bodies together.

"I ache for you," he growled against her mouth. He let his hands smooth down her back to her ass, squeezing her with one and moving the other between them to tease her hot center. Her breath caught in her throat, and he knew she was already wet for him. Perhaps her desire had not ceased since he'd left, and when he entered her body, she would be drenched and dripping.

Fuck.

His cock tightened at the thought, and he felt like his whole head was going to explode.

He continued to kiss her while he touched her, and though he'd have liked to lift her onto the counter then and taste her, he also recognized that the way this had begun was in the aftermath of that fucking game, and he needed to make a few things clear before they continued.

He moved his hand from between her legs and instead rolled his hips into hers.

"Let's play a game."

"I think I am done with games for the night," she said.

"Just one," he said—urged, really.

He kissed along her jaw and then reached for the batter-covered spatula she'd used earlier.

She looked at it and then at him.

"Never have I ever," he murmured as he smoothed the batter over her chest.

Persephone shivered against him. "Hades—"

"Shh," he said, and when she pressed her lips together in firm frustration, he touched the spatula to her mouth. When she started to lick at it, he pressed it against her lips as if it were a finger to hush her. "Stop. That's for me."

She held his gaze, and he felt her uncertainty and her curiosity. Her lips parted and she waited.

He continued. "Never have I ever wanted anyone but you."

"Never?" she questioned. He didn't think she even realized how skeptical she sounded. "Even before you knew I existed?"

"Yes."

His answer sounded more like a hiss as it slipped between his teeth, but he was closing the distance between them, drawing his tongue over her mouth, sucking her bottom lip between his teeth. She tasted so good, so sweet, so right.

He let his body rest against hers as she found purchase against the counter, his lips teasing along her jaw as he whispered truths against her skin.

"Before you, I only knew loneliness, even in a room full of people—it was an ache, sharp and cold and constant, and I was desperate to fill it."

"And now?" The question was almost a demand, as if she did not care about before anymore, just now, just this moment.

Hades smiled as he continued his exploration of her body, making his way to her chest.

"Now I ache to fill you," he said and licked the batter he'd used to mark her skin. His hands moved to cup her breasts, and he teased her nipples, which strained against the silky fabric of her gown. She took that as an invitation to try to undress him, but he wanted control because he still had questions.

He let his hands fall to her ass again, and he lifted her onto the edge of the counter, spreading her legs wide as he stepped between them.

"Tell me about tonight."

It wasn't a question, and his hands smoothed over her thighs, beneath the hem of her dress. Persephone squirmed beneath his touch. He imagined if he were not wedged between her thighs, she would have them closed and rubbing together just to create some kind of friction to ease her suffering.

"I don't want to talk about tonight," she said in a breathy moan.

She reached for his hand and drew him closer to her entrance, and while he would not give her exactly what she wanted just yet, he would take pleasure in teasing her until she answered his questions.

He circled a finger along her opening, around her clit, but he did not touch it, though he could feel it straining and swollen.

"I do," he said. "You were upset."

Persephone didn't look at him. Her eyes were closed, her brows furrowed in concentration even as she admitted, "I feel…stupid."

Well, that was something at least, even if he did not like that she felt that way.

"Never," he said as he slipped an arm around her

shoulders, his finger dipping into her sweet heat. "Tell me."

Her fingers dug into his biceps.

"I was jealous that you had shared so much with so many before me, and I know you cannot help it and that you have lived so long...but I..."

Her breath caught in her throat and her legs tightened around him as he continued to use his fingers and thumb to pleasure her, but it did not matter. He did not need to hear any more.

He leaned closer to her, his mouth hovering over hers. "I'd have had you from the beginning," he said. "But the Fates are cruel."

"I was only given to punish," she said.

Those words were like a knife to his chest. She was referring to the fact that while the Fates had granted Demeter's wish to have a child, it had come with one consequence—her life would be intertwined with Hades's, one of the gods Demeter hated most.

As much as it seemed to be an insecurity for her, it also was for him.

Still, he refused to think too long on it—to consider that just as their futures had been woven, they could also be unraveled.

"No," he soothed. "You are pleasure. *My* pleasure."

He pressed his mouth to hers, fingers continuing to move inside her slick heat and tease her clit until her legs were so tight around him, he thought she would burst. That was the point he wished to drive her to over and over so that when she finally came, it would leave her in no doubt of his obsession.

He left her body, and she gave a guttural, angry

cry. He liked it. He liked the wetness dripping from his fingers and the way she glared at him as he guided her to her back.

"It is you now, you forever," he said as she lifted her heels onto the edge of the counter, letting her legs fall open. He braced his hands on her thighs, his eyes falling to her exposed, pink center. It was swollen and wet, and he bent to taste her, licking from the bottom to the top, suckling gently on her clit, which felt thick in his mouth.

He fucking loved it. His mouth watered for it, and she bent to his will beneath him, writhing beautifully as if she had never felt him this way before.

When he entered her, she practically suctioned to his fingers, her flesh so swollen.

It wouldn't take long to bring her to release.

She groaned between long bouts of holding her breath, reaching to tangle her fingers in his hair, to hold him tight against her for fear he would stop—and stop he did.

"What are you doing?" she demanded as he pulled her up and off the counter.

She glared up at him as he held her, his fingers biting into her body.

"When I'm finished, the next time we play that damned game, you'll walk away so drunk, I'll have to carry you home."

"So what? You intend to fuck me in all the ways I haven't been fucked tonight?"

Yes, he thought, his cock straining. He wanted to feel her around him—all that swollen heat coaxing come into her body as if she were starved for it.

"Technically, it's morning," he said in a breathless chuckle.

"I have to go to work soon."

"Pity," he said and turned her around and pushed her until her cheek met the granite countertop.

She bent to his will, as malleable as ever, and when he sank into her, she gasped, back bowing beneath him as he pumped into her in short, measured thrusts. He moved his hand from the back of her head and cupped it over her mouth, letting his fingers dive past her lips.

She sucked them hard, and his dick grew taut inside her, his head swimming with nothing but her. Then he pulled her up, her back as close to his front as possible, his thrusts more like grinds.

"I haven't forgotten your earlier claim," he said, his mouth near her ear.

"I lied," she said, her words barely audible, she was so lost in the pleasure of this moment.

"I know, and I intend to discourage such lies," he said, mouth closing over her skin, sucking any part of her that was exposed to him. "I will fuck you to the point that you are desperate for release—over and over again so that when you finally do come, you won't even remember your name."

"You think you'll be able to stop?" she said, breathless, and yet there was a challenge to her voice. "To deprive yourself of the satisfaction of my orgasm?"

He smiled against her. "If it means hearing you beg for me, darling—yes."

He pushed her head toward his and their mouths collided. He felt completely out of control, and he refused to find it. All he wanted was to lose himself in this, in her.

He pulled away and turned her toward him, hooking

her leg over his arm to enter her again, to kiss her again. He didn't really care which position he took her in so long as he was inside her, so long as she was delirious with pleasure. And when her body began to quiver, he lifted her up and pressed her against the wall for support and continued his hungry exploration of her body.

"I love you. I have only ever loved you."

The truth of those words tightened his chest.

"I know," she said, a nearly inaudible reply.

"Do you?"

He was not sure she could ever understand the depth of his feeling, how completely and utterly grateful he was for every moment he had with her.

But then, he also could not pretend to understand her either.

As much as he had hoped, as much as he had wished for a reprieve from this world, a single bright spot in his life, she had too.

"I know," she said vehemently. "I love you. I just want everything. I want more. I want all of you."

"You have it," he said, her declaration urging him on.

His mouth met hers and he held her to him tightly, one hand digging into her flesh, the other pressed to the wall for support as he drove into her, finally ready to make her come, ready to come himself.

But the distinct feel of Hermes's magic entering the Underworld made him stop.

"Fuck!" he snapped with all the venom in the world.

It was the second time the god had interrupted them, and for that, he would pay.

He left Persephone's quivering body, her angry

and anguished cry making his body ache. She thought he only meant to torture her more before he allowed release, but she would understand soon enough.

He had just managed to adjust Persephone's dress and himself when Hermes appeared. And while at first Hades had expected some sort of snide comment about the air smelling like sex and brownies or admonishing their fucking in the kitchen where food was made, Hermes looked completely...desolate.

Fuck. Something horrible had happened.

"Hades, Persephone—Aphrodite has asked for your presence. Immediately."

Hades did not mind going, but Persephone?

He held her closer.

"At this hour?"

"Hades," Hermes almost begged, his face growing paler by the second. "It's...not good."

Hades's heart stuttered in his chest. *Who was it now?* he thought. *Hephaestus?*

"Where?"

"Her home."

CHAPTER XI
HADES

Hades brought Persephone to Aphrodite's home on Lemnos. He was never sure where he might appear when he teleported there—the locations had varied over time, but it all depended on where she or Hephaestus decided to grant access.

Today, it was the God of Fire's study, which surprised him, given that Hephaestus did not even allow Hades direct access to his workshop, but he understood why as soon as they manifested.

Aphrodite sat at the base of a chaise positioned in the center of the room, bent over a woman who lay in an unnatural position. Hades recognized her as Harmonia, though it took him a moment because of how badly she was beaten.

She was the Goddess of Harmony, Aphrodite's sister.

This was exactly what he had feared.

Every inch of her exposed skin was covered in dirt or blood or bruises, and at the top of her head were two blunt bones. They were her horns, and they had been cut from her head.

"Oh my gods." Persephone's voice shook, and she left Hades's side to go to Aphrodite. He squeezed his hands into fists to keep from pulling her back to him, to keep from shielding her from this. In some ways, she needed to know the reality of the world and how it preyed on them just as it did on mortals.

But this was worrying. A second attack and this time a goddess, both connected to Aphrodite.

Hades looked up and into the shadowed room, finding Hephaestus nearby. He was not surprised. He was never far behind when Aphrodite was in trouble, her constant shadow, even if she did not realize it.

"What happened?" he asked.

Hephaestus's eyes gleamed in the dark, a hint of the anger Hades could feel roiling inside him.

"We don't know for certain. We believe she was walking her dog, Opal, when she was attacked and had just enough strength to teleport here. When she arrived, she was not conscious, and we have not been able to rouse her."

It sounded similar to what had happened to Adonis. They'd both been alone when attacked and at night.

"Whoever did this will suffer," Hermes said, his voice shaking with anger.

The problem with what happened here was twofold. Not only was Harmonia a goddess—someone of divine blood—but she was also *kind*.

Persephone's gaze moved from Hermes to Hades.

"Who is she?" she asked.

"My sister," Aphrodite said, her voice was thick

with emotion. She sniffed and then took a breath as she whispered her name. "Harmonia."

"Can you heal her?" Persephone asked him, and her question made his chest ache. She asked because he healed her often, but this was beyond what he could do. Harmonia's injuries were far too numerous.

"No," he said, feeling as though he was disappointing her somehow. Despite all his power, he was not all-powerful. "For this, we will need Apollo."

"I never thought those words would come out of your mouth," said Apollo, who appeared at Hades's summons.

The God of Music had changed. Now he was dressed in armor, as if he were preparing for practicing or training, which wasn't outside the realm of possibility considering the Panhellenic Games were approaching and Apollo oversaw training at the Palaestra of Delphi.

His smug expression soon fell when he caught sight of Harmonia.

"What happened?" he asked, striding forward and wedging himself between Aphrodite and Persephone.

"We do not know," said Hermes.

"That's why we summoned you," Hades said.

Persephone's brows lowered. "I...don't understand. How would Apollo know what happened to Harmonia?"

It was an indication of how little Persephone knew about the gods and their power, and though not completely surprising, it worried Hades. He had years to study their many and varied powers, to learn what to anticipate if they battled—but not Persephone. She took their titles as an indication of their abilities, like many mortals.

"As I heal, I can view memories," Apollo said. "I should be able to tap into her injuries and discover how she received them…and from who."

Despite the pride with which Apollo spoke, the power of viewing memories could be dangerous. There was always the possibility that he would not be able to tell the difference in what he was seeing versus his reality, and if he believed he was being attacked, he could face the same outcome as Harmonia.

Persephone rose to her feet and took a step away. Hades wished she would come to his side. He wanted her near, if only for his own comfort, but she remained, watching Apollo as he placed his hands on Harmonia, gently brushing her hair from her face.

"Sweet Harmonia. Who did this to you?"

Apollo began to glow and so did Harmonia, and it wasn't long before the god began to shake, his body convulsing as he viewed Harmonia's memories.

Persephone couldn't handle it, and she surged forward, pushing him away from the goddess.

"Apollo, stop!"

He fell back, catching himself before he splayed on the floor.

"Are you okay?" Persephone asked.

Apollo's hand was under this nose, stained with crimson, but he looked at her and smiled. "Aw, Seph. You really do care."

Despite the fact that Hades did not like Apollo having a nickname for his lover, he was glad for the comfort he attempted to offer.

Persephone was far too caring for her own good.

"Why isn't she waking up?" Aphrodite's voice was

high-pitched and desperate, her fear radiating through everyone present.

No one wanted Harmonia to die.

"I don't know. I healed her as much as I could," Apollo said. "The rest...is up to her."

Once again, Hades felt Persephone turn to him.

How often would she look to him for guidance? How often would he fail her?

"Hades?"

His name fell off her tongue, an unspoken question hanging in the air between them—would she survive this?

"I do not see her lifeline ending," he said. "The more pressing question is what you saw as you healed her, Apollo."

He was frustrated that the god had yet to tell them what he'd seen in Harmonia's memories, though he knew his anger was misplaced. The god was still recovering from whatever he'd witnessed.

"Nothing," Apollo admitted, rubbing circles over his temple. Then he added in a low and defeated voice, "Nothing that will help us anyway."

"So you couldn't view her memories?" Hermes asked.

"Not much. They were dark and hazy, a trauma response, I think. She's probably trying to suppress them, which means we may not have any more clarity when she wakes. Her attackers wore masks—white ones with gaping mouths."

"But how did they manage to harm her at all?" Aphrodite asked. "Harmonia is the Goddess of Harmony. She should have been able to influence these...*vagrants* and calm them."

"They must have found a way to subdue her power," Hermes said.

Hades swallowed something thick in his throat as they all exchanged uneasy looks.

"But how?" asked Persephone.

"Anything is possible," Apollo replied. "Relics cause problems all the time."

Hades was well aware of the problems they caused.

"Hades?"

Once again, Persephone called to him.

"It could be a relic or perhaps a god eager for power," he said.

What he didn't say was that it could be both. He thought of Poseidon, who had handed a spindle over to the mortal Sisyphus. He could have used it to manipulate the lifelines of mortals, but instead, he chose to kill them.

And now there was a chance Poseidon had given over a scythe.

"Any ideas, Hephaestus?" Hades asked.

Despite shaking his head, Hades thought the god knew otherwise.

"I would need to know more."

"Let her rest, and when she wakes, give her ambrosia and honey," Apollo advised as he rose to his feet.

Persephone also stood, and when Apollo stumbled, she caught his arm to steady him.

"Are you sure you're okay?" she asked.

Her concern for him was misplaced, Hades thought—a point that was driven home when he opened his mouth again.

"Yeah." Apollo smirked. "Stay alert, Seph. I'll summon you soon," he said and vanished.

Hades glared at the space where Apollo had been, still uncomfortable with the bargain he and Persephone continued to maintain. He did not like the idea that Apollo could summon his fiancée when he pleased, especially in this environment, where goddesses were openly being attacked.

He met Persephone's gaze briefly before shifting his attention to Aphrodite.

"Why summon us?"

It was probably obvious to Persephone, but it wasn't obvious to Hades. Aphrodite knew he could not heal or view memories.

Aphrodite straightened and looked at him. He wasn't really prepared to see her face—eyes rimmed in red and swollen. He'd never seen her so distraught, and it made him uncomfortable.

"I summoned Persephone, not you," she said.

They both glared at Hermes.

"What?" he demanded. "You know Hades wouldn't let her come alone!"

"Me?" Persephone asked. "Why?"

Why indeed, Hades thought.

"I would like you to investigate Adonis's and Harmonia's attacks."

"No," Hades said immediately. He would not even entertain the idea. Persephone did not need to be involved. *He* was taking care of it. "You are asking my fiancée to put herself in the path of these mortals who hurt your sister. Why would I say yes?"

"She asked me, not you," Persephone snapped, her gaze just as frustrated. There was a brief pause, and then she turned back to Aphrodite. "Still, why me? Why not ask Helios for assistance?"

Hades was already shaking his head.

"Helios is an asshole," Aphrodite said. "He feels he owes us nothing because he fought for us during the Titanomachy. I'd rather fuck his cows than ask for his assistance. No, he would not give me what I want."

"And what do you want?" Persephone asked.

"Names, Persephone," Aphrodite said. "I want the name of every person who laid a hand on my sister."

But not Adonis? Hades glanced at Hephaestus, wondering if she censored herself because of him.

"I cannot promise you names, Aphrodite. You know I can't."

"You can," she insisted. "But you won't because of him."

Hades ground his teeth. "You are not the Goddess of Divine Retribution, Aphrodite."

"Then promise me you will send Nemesis to enact my revenge."

"I will make no such promise."

If Aphrodite decided to kill someone whose fate did not involve her, she would be punished. How, he could not say, but the Fates would come for her eventually.

"Whoever hurt the mortal and Harmonia has an agenda," Hephaestus said. "Harming those who assaulted them will not lead us to the greater purpose. You might also, inadvertently, prove their cause."

Aphrodite did not like what her husband was saying, but then again, Hades liked it less as he continued to speak.

"If that's the case, I can see the value of Persephone investigating Harmonia's assault. She fits in—as a mortal and a journalist. Given her record of slander against gods, they may even think they can trust her, or at least turn her to their cause. In either case, it would be a better way to understand our enemy, make a plan, and act."

"I would do nothing without your knowledge," Persephone said, holding Hades's gaze. "And I will have Zofie."

"We will discuss the terms."

It wasn't a no, but it wasn't a yes either. Still, he was rewarded with her soft smile, and that felt like conquering the world.

"But for now, you need rest," he said, and then he looked at Hephaestus because he did not trust Aphrodite or Hermes for that matter. "Summon us once Harmonia wakes."

Hades took them to their chambers.

When they arrived, they stood apart but faced each other. Neither of them moved.

He was attempting to process what it meant to involve her in discovering Adonis and Harmonia's attackers. If it was something she could do from the safety of Alexandria Tower, her investigative work could help, but was she ready for this? Because right now, he feared she was about to break, and he wasn't even sure she knew it.

"You will keep me informed of every step you take, every bit of information you glean on this case," he said. "You will teleport to work. If you leave for any reason, I have to know. You will take Zofie *everywhere*." He shifted closer to her, bending over her. "And, Persephone, if I say no…"

He meant it. He could not even verbalize what

consequences he would enact if she disobeyed, but they would be dire, and she would *hate* him.

"Okay," she said, and there was a sincerity in her tone and in her gaze he believed so deeply it hurt his chest.

He exhaled and then brought her forehead to his, hands braced at the base of her head.

"If anything happened to you—"

He couldn't let himself imagine it—her in place of Harmonia.

"Hades, I'm here. I am safe. You will not let anything happen to me."

"But I did," he said.

He'd let Pirithous take her, and he had not known. He'd let him violate her.

What good is being God of the Dead if you can't do anything? she had asked him once in the face of Lexa's death, but he asked himself that now. What good were his powers if he couldn't even protect Persephone?

"Hades—"

"I do not wish to discuss it," he said, releasing her. He took a step back. "You need rest."

He rarely put distance between them, but he needed it right now. He hated how it seemed to stun Persephone. She watched him for a moment as if she thought he would call her back, but instead, he turned to pour a drink and she retreated to the bathroom to shower.

She must think he was rejecting her, but she did not want him right now. At least she wouldn't, not if she knew what he was thinking.

And he was thinking that he would never let her leave the Underworld. He had threatened as much before, but these attacks were too close, and it wasn't as if she hadn't been targeted either. Ilias was still looking for the woman who had poured hot coffee in her lap.

It angered him that his realm was not enough. He could never embody the warm summer sun or the blue skies of the mortal realm, and she would never be content to only rule the dead.

She thrived on purpose, on changing the world.

But she had changed his world, and while there were moments when he felt better for it, there were also moments when he felt more violent than he ever had before, more capable of terrible things.

It was wrong to want to hold her hostage, but he was angry. Aphrodite had drawn her into this world, exposing her to what he had tried so hard to shield her from, and of course she had been willing and ready to help. She took responsibility for *everyone*.

It was a quality he could usually admire except in this manner, when gods were the victims.

"Are you coming to bed?" Persephone's voice drew his attention, quiet and apprehensive.

He didn't like it.

He turned to look at her. She was dressed in a shirt that was too big. It clung to the places on her body that had yet to dry. Her hair was heavy and wet. She had been crying. Her cheeks were a little too pink, her eyes a little too red.

His mouth hardened, and he set his drink on the mantle before crossing to her. He took her face between his hands, letting his fingers brush her skin.

His heart squeezed.

"I will join you shortly," he said quietly, hoping it would ease her anxiety, but more than that, he needed time to work through his frustration. He knew it would only get worse before it got better, and he did not wish for her to be the recipient of his aggression.

She rose onto the tips of her toes to kiss him, but he avoided her mouth and pressed his lips to her forehead. It was not the kiss she wanted or the one he wished to give, but it was all he could manage at this moment. He knew if he had let her, she would have drawn him in to keep him here, and he would have obliged, but he would have fucked her and he would be hard and unforgiving.

He was not sure she could handle that.

Though as she lowered to her feet, he wasn't sure if she could handle his rejection either.

She swallowed hard, and as she turned from him, he felt as though she had ripped out his heart and taken it with her to bed.

CHAPTER XII
HADES

Hades returned to the island of Lemnos, to Hephaestus's forge, which was housed on an adjoining volcanic island. As Hades entered, something crunched beneath his foot. He paused and looked down, finding the floor scattered with pieces of metal and wires. He recognized the guts of what he'd just stepped on.

They were mechanical bees.

Hephaestus had started making the bees in response to Demeter, whose unpredictable mood often affected the earth, which, given the state of the weather, was not presumptuous. It was his way of waging war against ancient magic, and according to Aphrodite, he had been working on it for a while, so why were they now discarded?

Hades proceeded inside, careful of where he stepped. There was more than just the broken bees on the floor. There were chips of wood from shattered shields and broken spears, pieces of armor torn to shreds as if they were nothing more than paper, and a string of animatronic body parts, belonging to both human and animal creations.

Hades rounded the corner and found even more of a mess. Nearly everything in Hephaestus's shop had been destroyed. Even his desk where he worked was split down the center, each half lying on its side, and at the center of it all sat Hephaestus.

Hades said nothing as he approached the god, who made no acknowledgment of his presence. Like his workshop, he was in shambles. His hair was unbound, wavy from always being pulled back, and his hands sat in his lap, palms up and bleeding.

He hadn't even tried to heal himself.

"Are you all right?" Hades asked the God of Fire.

Hephaestus did not respond and did not look at Hades. Hades acknowledged it was a stupid question to ask; the answer was obvious. Still, he felt it necessary.

Hades cast another glance around the room and spotted a short wooden stool in the corner, flipped on its head. He swiped it from the floor and used it to sit at Hephaestus's feet.

It was completely uncomfortable, and yet it was likely the only way he would get the god's attention tonight.

"Tell me what happened."

"There is nothing to tell," said Hephaestus.

"Doesn't look that way to me," Hades said.

A long silence followed. Hades did not prompt Hephaestus again and he did not leave. Eventually, the god spoke.

"We fought," Hephaestus said.

"Is Aphrodite all right?" Hades's voice rose in alarm.

"She's fine, physically at least," Hephaestus said quickly. "I didn't touch her. I've never…touched her."

Hephaestus took a deep breath and then raked his fingers through his hair.

"What happened?" Hades asked again.

"She…accused me of being the reason Harmonia was injured," Hephaestus said. "She said that whatever had been used against Harmonia had to have been one of my creations."

So many relics had been stolen and funneled into the black market it wasn't impossible but that did not make it Hephaestus's fault.

After a moment, the god continued. "I left after she told me how miserable I made her and came here," he said. "The rest you can guess."

Hades had to admit, though he'd always known something seething lingered beneath the surface of Hephaestus's calm and quiet exterior, seeing it in person was another experience entirely. He understood that the god was not proud. If anything, he seemed even more devastated that he had not been able to control his anger.

"Hephaestus, you don't really believe—"

"I believe what she says, Hades," Hephaestus said quickly. "I have nothing else."

Hades did not know what to say.

These two gods had loved each other for most of their immortal lives, and yet they had never managed to learn how to speak the same language.

"She should have left me long ago."

"Do you not know the woman you married?" Hades asked. "If she wanted to leave, she would have."

"Then her only pleasure must be my misery," Hephaestus said.

For the second time tonight, Hades did not have a response, and the hardest part was that he could not disagree with Hephaestus. It truly did seem that Aphrodite enjoyed misery, but not for the reason her husband thought. She chose to pine after him, to love him from afar.

The irony of the Goddess of Love was not lost on him.

"Does she know your anger?" Hades asked.

"No," Hephaestus said. "No, I cannot let her know. What if I...what if I..." He could not seem to finish his sentence.

"Do you think you will ever hurt her?"

"I am not good, Hades," said Hephaestus. "I never have been."

Hades wasn't sure what the god was recalling as he spoke, but whatever the memory, it still haunted him.

"Maybe you aren't," said Hades. "But neither am I, and tonight, another person close to Aphrodite has been attacked. One is already dead."

"If you do not think I am aware..." Hephaestus said, he curled his bloodied hands into fists, his knuckles white, though Hades was not certain which thing fueled his anger—the knowledge that the victim of the first attack was Adonis, Aphrodite's favored and lover, or that it seemed she was being targeted somehow.

"Adonis was stabbed with Cronos's scythe," Hades said, and he pulled out the tip he'd kept in the pocket of his jacket.

He handed it to the god, who ran his thumb over

the metal. It was not smooth, the surface etched with delicate designs.

"First this and now Harmonia's horns," Hades said. "These people have weapons that can wound gods, Hephaestus. It's only a matter of time before they find something that can truly kill us…and given this pattern, who do you think they will come for first?"

Hephaestus met Hades's gaze, his eyes stormy.

"You do not have to remind me of the threat to my wife to convince me to help you, Hades," Hephaestus said and then looked at the adamant tip again. "Who are they? These people you speak of."

"I suspect they are Impious," Hades said. "But in truth, I do not know. Perhaps when Harmonia wakes, she can give us clarity. I'm certain now that they have her horns, they will flaunt their victory publicly."

When favored mortals were killed, it often hit the media, and many Impious were willing to take responsibility for those murders. They saw it as a way to prove that the gods were not as powerful as they claimed and at the very least did not care for their mortal worshippers.

But obtaining a set of horns from the head of Harmonia—the sister of an Olympian—was entirely different. It illustrated just how close an everyday mortal managed to get to a god of relative power.

It demonstrated that the gods had weaknesses.

"And where did this come from?" Hephaestus asked, holding up the end of the blade.

"I suspect Poseidon," Hades said, relatively certain of the source. "There is one other issue at hand that makes the threat against us even more troublesome," said Hades. "The ophiotaurus has been resurrected."

Once again, Hephaestus met Hades's gaze, and his fingers closed over the end of the knife. The god had not yet been born when the Titanomachy took place, but he was well aware of the implication.

"Have you found it?" he asked.

"No."

"When you do, let me kill it," he said.

Hades could not help how he bristled, and the instinct made guilt bleed into his stomach.

"If I kill it," Hephaestus explained, "I can make a weapon from the ashes."

Hades stared. This conversation had taken a sudden turn, and it felt almost treasonous—not to Zeus but to themselves. He already knew the god was experimenting. He'd caught him fashioning a trident out of adamant—an attempt to recreate Poseidon's most powerful weapon.

"It's too dangerous, Hephaestus," Hades said.

"It is no more dangerous than your helm," Hephaestus said. "Or Poseidon's trident or Zeus's lightning bolts."

"Except that those weapons are not prophesied to kill gods," Hades countered.

"I will not pressure you," Hephaestus said. "But the offer stands should it be needed."

Hephaestus extended his hand in an attempt to return the tip of Cronos's scythe. Hades's eyes fell to it. Despite only being a small piece of a whole, it was just as deadly and still contained his father's magic.

His eyes returned to Hephaestus.

"Can you make a blade from that piece?" Hades asked.

"I can," Hephaestus said. "If you wish."

It was not as if Hephaestus had not already begun

forging weapons. The scythe was powerful, and it could wound a god severely, enough to trap them in Tartarus if needed.

"I wish it," Hades said.

Hades thought after his visit to Hephaestus he would feel like he had some control over the violent thing that lived within him, but he didn't. It still raged beneath his skin, threatening to explode.

He felt a lot like he imagined Hephaestus had tonight—completely helpless.

He did not know how to keep it in, how to quell it, but he couldn't let Persephone see this. He couldn't allow her to bear witness to his horror when she had seen so much of her own.

So he did the only thing he knew to do—find Hecate. But when he appeared in her meadow, he could tell she was not home. Her cottage was dark and everything was too still. Normally he would have attempted to sense whether she still remained in the Underworld as she often left for the mortal world to carry out whatever she pleased in the night, but it had not really mattered.

This took him away from the castle.

He paced outside her cottage, attempting to expend some of the electric energy that raced through his veins, and started to consider other options.

Should he go to Tartarus and take his rage out on Pirithous who was partly responsible?

Usually, that would seem like the right thing to do, but for some reason, it did not seem so now.

This anger was different. It was not destructive, but it was terrifying.

And perhaps that was what worried him the most—he usually knew what to do with this feeling, but not this time.

This time, it was different, and he needed Hecate.

"Let me get my calendar," she said. "For I must mark this occasion."

Hades turned toward her as she came out of the darkness surrounding them in the meadow. She wore a cloak and pushed back the hood so he could see her face, though shadowed.

"Hecate," he said. "I—"

"Need me?" she asked, smiling and arching a brow.

Hades opened his mouth, but he wasn't sure what to say.

"I don't suppose you have to say it out loud," she said. "I have already heard your thoughts."

Hades slammed his lips together, but after a moment, he spoke. "I do not know who else to ask."

"Well, I am wise beyond my years," she said. "What troubles you?"

"I thought you could read my mind?"

"Do not be cheeky," she admonished.

Hades narrowed his eyes. He knew she was well aware of how he felt. She only wanted to hear him say it, and if he didn't, there would be no moving past this. After a moment, he sighed heavily and scrubbed his hand over his face.

"I'm angry," he said.

"What's new?"

"This is *different*," he said and paused as he tried to

seek words to make her understand. "I...I can't...make it go away, and nothing I usually do is working."

"What made you feel this way?"

He explained what had occurred tonight—Harmonia's brutal attack and how he suspected it was connected to Adonis, how he feared it would encourage other Impious to start attacking gods publicly, as had happened with Persephone while she worked at the Coffee House.

"Perhaps you are not so much angry as you are afraid," she said. "It is not unusual to not know the difference."

Fear seemed...ridiculous. It was much easier to be angry.

"Easier because it is familiar," said Hecate, once again responding to his thoughts.

Hades curled his fingers into fists.

"If I am afraid, it means...I am...helpless."

It took him a moment to meet Hecate's gaze after his admission. He did not like this...whatever this was.

"It's called being vulnerable," she said. "And of course you hate it. You don't like to feel out of control, though you often are, especially where Persephone is concerned."

"You're not helping," Hades said.

"Give me time," she said. "We've only just begun."

He groaned. What more could he possibly need to say?

"I...don't know what to do," he said.

If he could, he would lock Persephone in the Underworld and risk her wrath to protect her. There was so much above working against them. If she never ventured out, at least she would be safe.

"And she would grow to resent you as she resents her mother," Hecate said.

"I know," he said. "I do not wish to hold her prisoner, but it is the only thing that makes me feel…at peace."

That wasn't completely true. While it took one emotion away, it gave birth to several others—dread and anxiety, mostly.

"Perhaps you just need to feel it," said Hecate. "It is all right to honor fear, to acknowledge that it has a place inside you, even if you are a brooding alpha male."

Hades glared.

"It is not as if you do not have a plan to protect Persephone or to find those responsible for Adonis's and Harmonia's attacks. As far as action is concerned, you have done everything possible."

"But will it be enough?"

"Enough for what?" she asked. "To protect Persephone from further harm or trauma? The only world where that is possible is here in the Underworld, and if she is here, it means she is dead."

Hades felt like he was being suffocated.

"If you are to live life with her, all you can do is be the person she needs in those hard moments, no matter how much it hurts you, and she will do the same for you."

He couldn't look at Hecate, so instead, he stared into the dark wood surrounding her meadow. He knew what she was saying, and after all that he and Persephone had been through, it should be easy to lay his burdens at her feet, but it wasn't.

It felt…unfair. What if he gave her too much?

"Has she ever given you too much?" Hecate asked.

"No," Hades said. "She could never…"

"She feels no different about you, Hades. You must cease thinking that your love is somehow greater than hers just because you have lived longer, yearned longer."

He held his breath as she spoke, feeling as though she were attacking him in some way, and yet he knew what she said was right. He did think that way and often.

A sudden gnawing guilt overtook the fear.

"Persephone has chosen you, and she accepts you in whatever way you choose to offer yourself, but is it fair that she cannot see you struggle when so often you must bear witness to hers?"

"I am protecting her," he said.

"Are you protecting her or yourself?"

Hades was quiet.

"Persephone has grown because at some point, you made her feel safe enough to be vulnerable with you. As a result, she has come to see your side of things and respect your decisions. If you do not offer her the same, can you truly respect her?"

Hades's teeth ground so hard, his jaw hurt, and the pain was spreading to the back of his head.

"If you expect the world to tear you apart, it will."

"Then what do you want me to do?"

"I want you to stop being an idiot," said Hecate, though her voice held no scorn. "I want you to recognize the importance of being vulnerable with Persephone, because apart, you are both powerful, to be sure, but together, you are unstoppable."

Hades returned to his chambers and found Persephone fast asleep. He stared at her for a long moment, watching the soft rise and fall of her chest, the way her lashes fanned across the high points of her cheeks, the slight part of her lips. She was beautiful, and while there was a part of him that wished to wake her, to apologize for how he left earlier, he did not wish to disturb her. She had managed to find peace despite the events of this night, unlike him, and it wasn't fair that they both should suffer.

He drank, sipping slowly, turning over Hecate's words in his mind. He considered how he felt now—exhausted, frustrated, still afraid, the friction in his body surging to the very tip of his cock.

Fuck.

He shifted uncomfortably, his eyes trained on Persephone. He could sit here in the quiet and attempt to pleasure himself, but he knew he needed something harder, rougher.

He needed her body.

It was the only thing that would sate him, but he would not ask that of her—not tonight.

He downed the last of his drink and then undressed. His cock and balls felt heavy between his legs, even as he sat on the edge of the bed. He could not quite bring himself to lie down beside Persephone, too tempted to wake her from slumber.

If he started, he wouldn't stop.

But then he felt her hand on his back.

"Are you well?" she asked.

He looked at her for a moment and then leaned over her, lips hovering over hers. He should kiss her.

He hadn't since they'd come home, but he refrained and instead caressed her cheek.

"I am well," he said, but his eyes were trained on her lips. He wanted to kiss her, and it was probably ridiculous that he refused, but he felt so on edge, so out of control—what if she couldn't handle that? He pulled away and noted the hurt that flashed in Persephone's eyes. "Sleep. I will be here when you wake."

"What if I don't want to sleep?"

She followed him, rising onto her knees and straddling him, nestling against his arousal. He took in a sharp breath, his fingers digging into her skin as he kept her still, unable to handle the movement of her body against his.

"What's wrong? You did not kiss me earlier and you will not lie with me now," she said, searching his eyes. Her arms tightened around him. It was like she was trying to remind him she was here and present, though he was well aware.

"I cannot sleep because I cannot stop my mind."

"I can help you," she said.

She could distract him to be sure, but the thoughts would still be there in the aftermath.

"And...why won't you kiss me?"

He swallowed, dropping his gaze for a moment as he found the words to explain.

"Because there is rage inside my body, and to indulge in you...well, I am not certain what kind of release I would find."

"Are you angry with me?"

"No," he said quickly. "But I am afraid that I have agreed to something that will only hurt you, and already I cannot forgive myself."

"Hades."

She whispered his name and took his face between her hands, eyes searching. He wanted to demand to know what she was looking for so he could tell her that she would never find it, but he knew he was just being difficult and that she would not believe him anyway.

Her mouth hovered over his, her touch like fire against his skin, the slight movement of her body against his driving him mad. He was on the edge, losing his grip on control, but he thought of his conversation with Hecate and considered that perhaps he did not need control here.

In this space, he could exist authentically, and Persephone…she would take it.

As if she knew his thoughts, she whispered to him, her breath caressing his lips.

"Indulge in me. I can handle you."

It was the permission he needed.

He kissed her, widening his mouth against hers as his tongue moved against hers. He groaned, his fingers tightening in her hair.

Fuck, she was sweet.

She preened in his arms, pressing into him, opening wider to receive him. Even her legs moved farther apart, his cock tucked between them, rubbing against her bare, slick heat.

"Fuck," he breathed as he broke from her mouth, drawing her shirt over her head. Naked, he let his hands skim over her body and came back to her breasts, which he held in each hand and lavished with his tongue. He liked the way she moved against him as he took each nipple into his mouth, how she held his head in place until she was ready for him to move on to the next.

With his mouth occupied, he let his hand dive between her legs, fingers teasing her opening. She was so fucking wet. He drew his finger along her opening, using the wetness to stimulate her clit.

He looked up at her just as she threw her head back to moan. Hades kissed her throat, then sucked her skin into his mouth, eliciting a louder cry.

He liked it, wanted more of it.

"Fuck," she breathed as he slid his fingers inside her, stroking her into a frenzy until all she could do was hold on to him as he worked.

"Please," she begged, the word a broken cry.

"Please what?"

It wasn't a question. It was a demand.

Her body answered, vibrating against his as she let him wring come from her body.

He pushed her onto the bed unceremoniously, his cock dripping as he got to his knees.

"Can you handle me?"

She was flushed and deliriously high on pleasure. He imagined she would say yes to anything right now, but it would be enough.

She nodded, her chest rising and falling quickly.

"Yes."

He jerked her toward him, lifting her so that her ass rested against his thighs, and entered her.

Persephone arched on the bed, her breasts bouncing with each of his thrusts. It made him move faster, fill her deeper. She was so gods-damned beautiful, so fucking erotic, and she likely had no idea, but watching her take him like this was a fucking dream.

"Oh, fuck," she cried, writhing.

Her hands were everywhere, gripping him and then her breasts, then tangling in her hair, and with each thrust, he felt the pressure build. He chased it, held it longer, determined to make this last.

Their bodies grew slick, and there came a point when Hades could no longer hold on to her. He bent over her, arms braced on either side of her face as he finished. He could feel his cock pulsing inside her, and he could not hold himself up. His whole body shook.

He landed atop her, his head on her breasts. Persephone did not seem to mind as she wrapped her body around him.

After a long moment of silence, she spoke.

"You're mine," she said, her fingers trailing through his hair, which had come loose during their intercourse. "Of course I can handle you."

Hades lifted himself up so he could meet her gaze. He wasn't sure why he always waited for her to break, to leave, to run when she spoke like this. It didn't make sense. It would never make sense.

But he was so fucking grateful she loved him.

"I never thought I'd thank the Fates for anything they gave me, but you—you were worth all of it."

"All of what?"

"The suffering."

CHAPTER XIII
THESEUS

Theseus stared at a series of photos. They were all pictures of the same man, taken from different angles. His name was Adonis—a famous favored mortal—and he had been beaten to a bloody pulp and stabbed through with Cronos's scythe outside Aphrodite's club, La Rose.

While Theseus had not been directly involved in this attack, he'd managed to plant the seeds that saw it through. He wondered how long before Aphrodite's anger got the best of her, how long before Hades's sense of honor brought him right to his door. Theseus has lived a long time in the shadow of the gods. He knew their strengths and their weaknesses, but he also knew mortals and how to make them afraid.

The start of snow in summer had been his sign to incite chaos. Amid the backdrop of Demeter's storm, which would already inspire anger among the mortals and feature heavily in the media, he knew he could further feed the existing doubt and anger against the gods. And while he was aware that it would hardly hurt them, it would cause division, and at the center of it all were two gods: Hades and Persephone.

He had not expected them to feature as they were, but their love worked in his favor, and it would serve to further divide the gods while he continued to build mistrust among the mortals on earth. He would hardly have to lift a finger—the gods always got in their own way.

Theseus just needed to ensure that as the chaos unfolded, mortals had someone to turn to—someone to worship in place of the Olympians who had reigned for so long.

And that person would be him.

Theseus could sense the vibration of his phone before it rang. He snatched it up, answering before the sound could disturb the silence.

He gave no greeting, only waited for the person on the other end to speak.

"I've found her," said the voice—Perseus, the demigod son of Zeus.

Theseus said nothing and waited for him to continue.

"She's with Dionysus in the pleasure district. They're on the hunt for Medusa."

He was not surprised. He'd heard the rumors about the woman—her beauty first and then her supposed power.

She could turn men into stone.

He had suspected Dionysus of searching for her when he'd bought the Graeae's services, and he'd considered that when he'd had them murdered, he would lose the fastest route to finding her—but there were other ways to locate a scared woman.

Perseus, for example.

A new set of photos came through on his tablet, and he scrolled through him. Ariadne was dressed in a short, black dress and high boots. She looked fuckable. Perhaps she had been fucked.

"Is she fucking him yet?" Theseus asked. He meant to express the question nonchalantly, but a hot blade of jealousy shot through him at the thought. Despite his marriage to her sister, Phaedra, Ariadne belonged to him too. She would always belong to him, even if she found temporary reprieve in the hands of this god.

And when she returned to him—and she *would* because he had her sister—she would pay for straying, for thinking for an instant that she could defeat him.

"Not sure," Perseus replied.

"Keep following her," Theseus said. "She'll lead us to Medusa eventually, and when the time is right, we'll take both."

He hung up the phone and continued looking through the photos, his cock growing harder the longer he did. Before he'd married Phaedra, he had dated Ariadne. He'd liked her more than her sister. She liked to fuck and fuck hard. There was nothing soft about her, but therein lay the problem.

Ariadne would not be controlled, at least not on her own, but through her sister, who was so easily swayed with a few pretty words, she was malleable in his hands.

That made him harder, and he let himself think about what he would do when she did return to him and demand to see her sister.

Perhaps he would agree and let her watch as he fucked Phaedra. Her horror would make him come, and when he did, he'd force his dick into her mouth and fill her throat.

Theseus looked up, sensing movement, and found Phaedra lingering in the doorway. She was dressed in a long silk nightgown and a matching robe that did not even close around her round belly.

The contrast of how she dressed compared to her sister was not lost on him. His wife rarely even wished to undress for sex, but Ariadne, she would roam the house naked, as if it were her natural state.

"Phaedra," he said, locking his tablet as he set it down on his desk. "You should be resting."

"I couldn't sleep," she said, watching him from the door. "You...haven't come to bed."

Despite her modesty, she was beautiful. Her softness made her the perfect bride—a trophy he could parade about in public—and her timidness ensured she would never communicate her doubts or her fears about him.

She was the safe choice.

"You know things have been busy."

"Of course," she said. "I only came to check on you."

He managed a smile because he thought that was what she would most like—some acknowledgment that he cared that she cared.

"I am fine," he said. "Just busy."

Except that she did not act as she usually did with his reassurance—which was to fold. Instead, she lingered.

"Busy with Ariadne?" she said, her voice quiet, and he wondered why, if she feared his response, she said it at all.

Theseus clenched his jaw. This defiance was new.

Phaedra hesitated and then added quietly, almost in a whisper, "I heard you."

Heard me? He was certain he had not said her name.

"Were you listening at my door, Phaedra?" he asked. He worked to control his voice, to keep the anger from seeping into his words.

She knew the consequences of eavesdropping.

"No, I...I promise. I only thought I heard her name as I came down the hall."

She was lying. He had to quell this. He wondered what was making her so brave.

"You thought?" he asked.

She took a deep and audible breath. "I must have misheard."

Theseus stood, and as he approached, Phaedra placed her hand on her stomach. Prior to her pregnancy, he would have silenced her with a kiss or even sex, but since, he'd had no interest in fucking her. It did not matter anyway. He'd used sex to keep her, and now the baby would do that for him.

He liked how she tensed as he approached, though, and that made him hard, which was also helpful, because when she noticed, she would think it was her who made him eager to fuck and not her fear.

He touched her chin.

"What have I said about Ariadne?"

Her eyes were glassy. "Theseus," she whispered, and he hated how she said his name. Perhaps it was because she sounded a lot like her sister, and he thought of how Ariadne once moaned it. "She is my sister—"

"What," he said, silencing her, his voice loud and then tapering off, "did I say?"

Phaedra stared at him and swallowed hard, unable to keep the tears from welling in her eyes.

Theseus stepped as close as he could, her stomach pressing into him. "Oh, Phaedra," he whispered and tilted her head back. She winced as his fingers tightened in her dark hair. "What am I to do with you?"

He kissed her forehead.

He knew how Phaedra worked. She melted at the slightest show of affection, the opposite of her sister. Ariadne did not preen beneath soft touches and sweet words. She wanted everything hard and fast and bruising.

He let his hands fall to her shoulders, his mouth near her ear as he spoke quietly. "I wanted to protect you from this, but I suppose I will have to tell you."

He pulled away and crossed to his desk, picking up the tablet. He handed over the device, showing her the pictures Perseus had sent.

"I have kept my promise to you," he said. "I have kept track of your sister, and despite my attempted interventions, she's turned to prostitution. Just tonight, she was spotted in the pleasure district with the god Dionysus."

He watched Phaedra looking through the photos. After a moment, she whispered, "She doesn't look like herself."

"Oh, darling," he said. "Such is the case with addiction."

Phaedra put the tablet aside and buried her face in her hands. Theseus stepped up behind her, pulling her against him. His arousal pressed into her ass. The only thing keeping it erect was her pain, and he siphoned it, fueling the blood that rushed to the crown of his cock.

"I am sorry," he soothed, letting his head rest in the crook of her neck. "I did not wish to tell you. I thought it was better to protect you and the baby."

"No," she said, her hands falling to his, which he'd placed around her belly. He cringed as her palms touched his, wet from her tears. "I should not have asked. I knew better than to hope she had reached out to see me."

She turned in his arms and rested her head against his chest, for which he was glad. He did not think he could muster the ability to appear remorseful any more tonight, his frustration was too acute.

"I know how hard this is for you," he said. "But you always have me when you have no one else."

He let her cry for a few moments longer but pulled her away when he grew tired.

"You need rest," he said, drawing his finger over her wet cheek.

She nodded numbly, but he only cared that she obeyed.

"I love you, Theseus," she said.

He smiled at her and pressed a soft kiss to her mouth.

"Good night, my love," he said and pushed her off into the hallway. "I will be along soon."

He watched her go until he could no longer see her and then closed the door, wiping his mouth free of her tears.

Fucking disgusting, he thought.

He crossed to his desk and pressed the call button on his intercom. It went straight to his secretary, who he knew to be awake and waiting.

"Now," he said, and as he waited, he unbuttoned his trousers and took out his cock, jerking it up and down, priming it for what was to come.

After a moment, the woman entered. He forgot her name. She was new, recently hired to replace the one who had died.

Her eyes went to his cock. There was no hunger in her gaze. This was her job.

She crossed to him and knelt, her mouth even with his dick.

"What's your name?" he asked.

"Rebecca," she said.

"Your real name?"

"No," she said.

He liked the way she looked at him, with as much spite as Ariadne.

He dug his fingers into her hair.

"I'm going to fuck your mouth," he said. "And you're going to take it. All of it."

She rose a little higher, preparing for their transaction, still defiant, still unafraid, and his chest filled with warmth at the challenge of seeing the light die in her eyes.

CHAPTER XIV
DIONYSUS

When Dionysus and Ariadne manifested in his living room, his arm was still anchored around her waist. Her breasts pressed into his chest, and his cock rested again the bottom of her stomach. He wanted to die, and he did not care what kind of death, real or otherwise. He only needed to be rescued from this fucking torture.

He did not immediately let her go, and she did not immediately pull away, which made him think she was far more unnerved than she appeared. Still, he admired her composure.

"Are you all right?" he asked.

She looked confused by his question, and he wasn't sure why. Perhaps she was surprised he asked.

"I...don't know," she admitted.

He frowned and then drew a stray piece of hair from her cheek. "I didn't know that would happen."

"Which part?" she asked, her eyes dropping to his

lips. "The part where you kissed me or the part where I shot those two men?"

They stared at each other, and all Dionysus could think of was that kiss and more—how she'd climbed into his lap and moved against him, how she'd felt in his hands, so fucking hot and right.

And he knew he was in so much trouble because all he would be able to think about was what might have happened had they not been interrupted and if Ariadne had only responded in kind because she believed it was necessary.

She stepped away and he let her go, hating how empty he felt when she was gone.

She turned in a circle, eyes roaming over his space.

He'd forgotten how much he liked being here, how safe it felt compared to the club, which was always alive, always on.

This space was quiet.

The walls were warm in color, mostly covered by shelves, packed haphazardly with books. There was a simple linen couch and a glass coffee table opposite a fireplace, and on the mantle were more books. The windows were lead-paned but covered with heavy drapes. He rarely opened them, rarely wished to look at the world he saw so often.

"Where are we?" Ariadne asked.

"My home," he said.

"You live here?"

"Yes, I live here," he said. "Surprised?"

"Well, you always seem to be at Bakkheia."

He didn't tell her that it had been a month since he'd been here.

"Why are we here?" she asked, facing him. "Why not go back to the club?"

"I don't want to be there right now," he said.

It was too much—too loud, too bright, too crowded.

She took a breath and shrugged off the jacket he'd draped around her shoulders, then took a seat on the edge of the couch. Dionysus watched her. He could not help it. He wanted to know what she was thinking.

"What happens now?" she asked.

Fuck me. Of course she was thinking about their next move. What were they going to do now that they knew Medusa had last been seen near the ocean, near Poseidon's realm?

"I don't know," he admitted. He needed time to think, time to process. The question was, did they have time?

"Can we trust Michail not to tell anyone who we were looking for?"

"No," said Dionysus.

She stared at him. "Then why didn't you kill him?"

Dionysus raised a brow. "Easy, Detective. I thought you were opposed to killing?"

She glared at him. "It is not as if Michail is a good guy."

He didn't argue because he agreed, but then Dionysus had a hard time believing anyone was good in this world. Everyone was capable of bad things.

"It does not matter if Michail lives or dies," said Dionysus. "People will still hunt Medusa."

"But have they gotten as far as us?" she asked.

"It's hard to say, but I can assure you they have likely not gotten any further."

"Why? What do you mean?"

"Because everyone who's in search of her will either abandon the cause once they discover Poseidon is involved or find themselves at the end of a glorified pitchfork."

"Including you?"

"I admire that you think I could go head-to-head with Poseidon."

"I don't care if you can," she said. "I asked if you will."

"You seem to think everything is simple, a decision that comes down to yes or no," he said, frustration coloring his tone. "If Poseidon does not know of Medusa's importance now, he will once I confront him."

"Then don't confront him," she said.

"How else do you expect us to find her?"

"I'll do it," she said.

"No," he said immediately.

He could not even entertain the idea. Poseidon was a dick. A royal one. Especially to women. There was no way he would put Ariadne through that.

"Poseidon knows nothing about me," Ariadne argued and then shrugged. "To him, I am a mortal woman searching for...my sister."

"Do you think he will care?"

"No," she said. "But perhaps he will care about what I have to offer."

"And what do you have to offer?"

She said nothing and Dionysus took a step toward her.

"What do you have to offer, Ariadne? Information on my operations? On maenads? Will you sacrifice a hundred lives just to save one?"

"You think I would betray you?" she asked.

"Your loyalty is with your sister," he said. "And I do not blame you, but it means I cannot trust you."

She said nothing, but her anger screamed at him.

"So you're giving up?" she said finally.

"I am not giving up!" he snapped. "But I need time to think, and you've made it really fucking hard for me tonight."

Their eyes held and then she looked away, crossing her arms over her chest, as if she wished to distance herself from everything that had happened, including him.

He should not be surprised, and it should feel like nothing, but it didn't.

It felt like rejection, like the sting of a too-sharp blade to the chest. He knew what had happened tonight was only situational and to have feelings about it meant that he'd developed some kind of expectation, and that was ridiculous.

This—whatever existed between them—was far too angry to be anything more than something both of them would regret.

Like tonight.

"There's a room down that hallway where you can sleep," he said. "A bathroom too. I'll…uh… Do you need something to wear?"

He looked at her long enough to see her nod.

"Please," she said, her voice a whisper.

"I'll be back," he said, walking down the adjacent hall to his room.

When he opened the door, he was met by frigid air. He'd been gone so long, he had yet to change the controls to warm his apartment, though he should not have to. It was summer. It was supposed to be sunny and hot. Instead, the snow grew heavier day by day.

He snatched a shirt from his drawer and took it to Ariadne.

"It might be cold in your room," he said. "I'll... adjust the temperature."

She nodded. He hated these bouts of quiet tension that kept rising between them.

"If you need anything, I'll be down here," he said and left, adjusting the temperature before returning to his room.

He shed his clothes and showered. He stayed beneath the spray longer than usual, taking his heavy cock in hand, eager to feel release, to no longer feel the fullness hanging heavy between his legs as he had for what felt like days.

Because it had been days.

It had been *weeks*.

He thought of how Ariadne had looked in that dress, the way she had obeyed when he told her to kneel before him, the way her eyes burned when she looked up at him, and perhaps it had been with hatred, but sometimes he did not know it from passion, and it didn't really matter because it fueled the fantasy.

The potential of what could have been took over, and he imagined holding on to her perfect ass and helping her slide down his cock. She would be warm and wet and tight, and she would ride him like she had known his body forever. When she grew too tired, he would take over, pumping into her until everything in his body locked up and all he could focus on was the pressure in his balls that spread all over his body before he came. There was something about opening his eyes and seeing his hand closed around the crown of his cock, semen seeping between his fingers, that left him completely unsatisfied.

He washed again and stepped out of the shower, feeling no less frustrated than when he entered.

He dried off and wrapped the towel around his waist, muttering to himself as he began to grow hard again.

"Fuck me," he muttered.

"I would, but you aren't really my type."

"Fuck you, Hermes," he said.

He'd sensed the god's magic the moment he'd stepped out of the bathroom. He didn't even turn to look at him as he crossed to his dresser.

"Don't be angry about it," Hermes said.

Dionysus ignored him and dropped the towel, changing into a pair of boxers. When he turned to face the God of Mischief, he looked a little stunned.

"You don't have a type, Hermes," said Dionysus. "You would fuck a rock if you found it pretty enough."

Hermes found his speech again. "Hey, I have standards!"

"Which is why I said pretty," Dionysus mumbled, pulling back the blankets on his bed. He did not care that Hermes was here and likely wanted to talk. He was tired.

"Aren't you the least bit curious about why I am here?"

"No, considering the last time you paid me a visit, I dreamed that my testicles were burning off for a week."

Hermes grinned. "Come on. That was funny."

Dionysus glared.

"What do you want, Hermes?"

Dionysus lay down, still intent on sleeping despite whatever the god had come to say. He propped his hands behind his head and stared at the god, but Hermes looked unnerved and swallowed hard.

"Well, Hades tells me I am your keeper," Hermes said. "So I suppose I am keeping."

"Do you always do what Hades says?" Dionysus asked.

"Only when it's fun."

"And checking up on me is fun?"

"Well, it was when I could set your balls on fire," Hermes said, pausing. Then he raised a brow. "Though I suppose nothing's changed." Hermes laughed and Dionysus's eyes darkened as he glared. Hermes choked and cleared his throat. "Anyway, what I really came to tell you was that Harmonia has been attacked."

Dionysus's brows lowered. "What do you mean?"

"Just as it sounds," Hermes said. "She was beaten, and her horns were cut."

Dionysus sat up. There were several shocking things about this news, including that of all the gods, Harmonia was one of the least threatening, but also that someone had managed to get close enough to harm a god at all.

"Beaten?" he repeated. "By who?"

"We do not exactly know, but you should be aware. It's likely the same people targeting gods who are also looking for the ophiotaurus, which means they have some kind of ability to suppress our powers."

"By people, do you mean the Impious?" he asked. "Or Triad?"

Hermes shrugged. "Possibly. It is too early to make a sound judgment."

"Is there really any doubt?" Dionysus asked.

"Hades prefers evidence before making such a call."

"You would think Hades was your king with the way you hang on his every word."

Hermes narrowed his eyes this time. "Perhaps if you were not so threatened by his leadership, you might see the value in his council."

"What council? At this very moment, his decisions have us facing defeat."

Hades had openly admitted he was the reason the ophiotaurus had been resurrected.

"He had no choice," Hermes defended.

"There is always a choice," Dionysus said, and then he snapped his mouth shut, realizing too late that he sounded like his foster father.

"It sounds as though you have yet to make one," said Hermes.

"I chose a side," Dionysus spat.

"You didn't choose a side. You picked the best route for your revenge."

Hermes sounded like Silenus.

"And?"

Hermes shook his head. "You stand for nothing," he said.

Dionysus ground his teeth.

"It's probably a good thing Hades doesn't trust you," Hermes added. "It doesn't sound like he should." And with that, he left.

Dionysus fell back in bed with a sigh, staring up at the ceiling. The god's words frustrated him, and he found himself wanting to argue that he *did* stand for something. That was the whole reason he began rescuing women, offering them refuge, and training them to defend themselves in ways that meant they would never come to harm again. It was why he had spent years infiltrating the pleasure district and various trafficking circles.

Yes, he wished for revenge against Hera. She had made his life a living hell. She had murdered his mother. He wanted her to suffer.

But that did not negate the fact that he also wished to protect other women as a result.

Unable to sleep, Dionysus rose from bed and headed to the kitchen for a drink, but as he rounded the corner, he found Ariadne. She had yet to notice his approach as she reached over her head for a glass, her shirt rising over her ass as she did.

Fuck me.

"Need help?" he asked.

She gasped and turned to face him.

"How long have you been there?" she asked.

"Not long," he said, approaching her. She did not move, pinned against the counter as he reached over her head for the glass and handed it to her.

"Thank you," she said and then stepped up to the sink to fill it with water.

He watched her for a moment and then grabbed another glass to do the same. They stood side by side sipping water.

"Does Hermes visit you often?"

Dionysus choked his water. "What?" he asked.

"I… You weren't exactly quiet."

Dionysus tilted his head, narrowing his eyes. "What did you hear?"

"Noises," she said. "Voices."

"I didn't fuck Hermes, Ariadne."

"I...okay," she said.

He stood there in stunned silence, staring at her. "How could you think—"

"Can you just drop it?" she asked, frustrated.

He didn't want to drop it. He wanted to know why she thought he would fuck Hermes, especially after he had clearly wanted to fuck her instead.

Silence stretched between them, and Ariadne downed the last of her water.

"I should go to bed," she said and brushed past him, but Dionysus did not want her to leave.

"When did you learn to dance like that?" he asked.

She froze and turned to face him.

"I took lessons," she said, as if it were not impressive or even a surprise.

"So you could do what?" Dionysus asked, assuming she'd done so to add to her skill set. "Work undercover?"

"No, for exercise."

"You learned to strip for exercise?"

"I don't *strip*," she said. "But I do dance. You should try it sometime. It's great cardio."

"Don't tempt me," he muttered and caught a hint of a smile on her face.

He didn't think he'd ever managed to make her smile before.

She took a breath and seemed to shiver with it.

"I wanted to say...I am sorry for earlier." For a moment, he thought she was apologizing for the kiss, but then she added, "I had no idea Michail would recognize me."

"You could not have known."

"I should have," she said. "I should have been a better detective."

"You're perfect, Ariadne," he said.

Her gaze rose to his, eyes widened. He wasn't sure why she looked so surprised; it was the second time he'd told her tonight, which made him think of how he had let himself go in those heady moments after she'd climbed into his lap at the brothel. The urge to talk about it danced under his skin. He wanted to know what it meant, that they had been able to play their roles so well.

He wanted it to mean something.

"Ari—" he began and took a step toward her.

"Good night, Dionysus," she said.

He stared a moment and then managed a ghost of a smile and nodded. "Good night, Ariadne."

He watched her turn and disappear down the hall.

CHAPTER XV
HADES

Hades heard Persephone take a sharp breath, and his head snapped in the direction of the bed where he found her sitting up, looking wide-eyed and confused until she met his gaze and relaxed.

Before he could ask what had startled her, she spoke. "Did you sleep at all?"

"No," he said.

He'd lain beside her for a few hours after they had sex but never drifted off, so he rose and dressed and waited for her to rise. He was eager for her to get ready for work because he wanted to take her to Alexandria Tower and show her the floor he hoped she would agree to use for her work on *The Advocate*. There were enough offices for everyone in her employ, at the moment Helen, Leuce, and Sybil.

He felt ridiculous that he had not offered it before, though there were times when Persephone was so independent, he wasn't sure how or when to help her. She certainly would never ask.

"Nightmare?" he asked, worry twisting deep in his gut.

If she had dreamed of Pirithous, he was sure his actions had triggered her. He had been too much last night.

"No," she said, shaking her head. "I...thought I overslept."

He wasn't sure he believed her, but perhaps that was his own fear speaking.

He finished the last of his drink, leaving his glass behind, and went to her. She held his gaze as he approached. She was like a siren in a sea of black silk—one look, one call, and he bent to her will.

"Why didn't you sleep?" she asked as he caressed her cheek.

"I didn't feel like sleeping," he said.

The longer he lived, the less he needed. It did not help, however, that the majority of the business he conducted happened in the dead of night.

"I thought you would be exhausted." Her eyes flashed and she sounded a little cross.

He smiled, amused. "I didn't say I wasn't tired."

He smoothed his thumb over her bottom lip, and she took it between her teeth and then sucked it into her mouth.

Fuck.

He was trying to be *good*, but he found himself twisting his hand in her hair, dragging her face closer to him, level with his cock. He considered ordering her to take it out, to suck him until he came in her mouth, but something about it didn't seem right, so he just held her there, aching.

She released his thumb and frowned. "Why are you holding back?"

"Oh, darling," he said, voice rumbling. "If you only knew."

"I would like to," she said and dropped her blanket, exposing her breasts.

He wanted to groan—perhaps he did. He didn't really know because his ears were ringing, and he was doing everything in his power not to fuck her again like he did last night.

She had work, and while that usually wouldn't matter to him, it did today.

"I will keep that in mind," he said, his voice quiet and even. He wished she knew how difficult it was to speak each word in the face of her beauty, in the face of her temptation. "For now, I'd like you to get dressed. I have a surprise for you."

"What could be more of a surprise than what's going on in that head of yours?"

He laughed and kissed her nose. "Dress. I will wait for you."

He released her and stepped away, heading for the door.

"You don't have to wait outside," Persephone said, sounding confused by his actions. Obviously, this was unusual for him, but his usual would include following her into the bath to fuck her against the wall.

It was better this way. She could get ready in peace.

He paused at the door and looked back at her, and he hoped she could see how difficult this was for him rather than feeling it was rejection. She would understand later.

"Yes, I do," he said and stepped into the hall.

He waited there like an idiot while she showered, which felt like a completely different type of torture. He found himself leaning his head against the marbled wall to cool his heated face as he thought about her on the other side.

"Are you all right, my lord?"

Hades opened his eyes to find a spirit standing at the end of his hallway. He employed many of them in the Underworld. They were different from souls, as they were not dead, and they had minor power and influence over very specific emotions. Aletheia, who stared at him with wide eyes verging on terror, was the spirit of truth and sincerity. Of all the spirits who resided here, her influence was probably the least threatening.

"I am fine," he told her.

She hesitated as if she did not know what to say and then managed, "May I get you anything?"

A bucket of cold water, he thought. "No, Aletheia."

Her eyes grew even wider when he spoke her name. "Thank you."

The spirit nodded and then wandered off, as pale as a ghost.

Hades considered teleporting to the baths to dunk himself in one of the pools, but instead, he remained and waited until Persephone emerged from their room, dressed in the most complicated outfit he'd ever seen.

Why were there so many layers?

"What?" Persephone asked, clearly feeling self-conscious beneath his gaze.

"I'm trying to assess how long it will take me to undress you."

She arched a brow. "Isn't that why you stepped out of the room?"

"I'm merely planning ahead."

For later...when it wouldn't feel so wrong to take her.

He took her hand and pulled her against him, teleporting to Alexandria Tower. When they arrived, he released Persephone, and she looked around in silence for a few minutes. It wasn't until he heard her clear her throat that he realized this place was making her emotional.

"Why are we at Alexandria Tower?"

He felt a rush of panic and then realized why she was struggling. This place reminded her of Lexa.

Fuck, he should have been more discerning. The least he could have done was prepare her for her return here, but he hadn't thought about it at all. Now he feared she would reject his idea outright. Still, he had to try.

"I would like for you to office here," he said.

It was the perfect place. He owned the building and every business that operated out of it, including the Cypress Foundation, which he hoped to see Persephone become more involved with. Being so close to Katerina would ensure collaboration. What mattered most, though, was that Persephone didn't see it as some kind of prison.

She met his gaze and seemed more surprised than anything. He couldn't tell if that was a good sign or not.

"Is this because of yesterday?"

"That is one reason. It will also be convenient. I'd like your input as we continue the Halcyon Project, and I imagine your work with *The Advocate* will lead to other ideas."

"Are you asking me to work with Katerina?"

"Yes. You are to be queen of my realm and empire. It's only fitting that this foundation begins to benefit your passions as well."

Her silence worried him, and he watched as she made a circle around the room.

"You are opposed?" he asked, unable to help it. He needed to know what she was thinking.

"No," she said quickly and then turned fully to face him. "Thank you. I can't wait to tell Helen and Leuce."

Relief flooded him.

"Selfishly, I will be glad to have you close."

"You rarely work here," Persephone said.

"As of today," he said, stepping closer, "this is my favorite office."

"Lord Hades, I must inform you that I am here to work," she said. Her voice was low, her smell intoxicating, and as she spoke, she looked at his mouth.

"Of course," he said, guiding a strand of her hair behind her ear. "But you will need breaks and lunch, and I look forward to filling that time."

"Isn't the point of a break not to do anything?"

"I didn't say I'd make you work."

He held her close and leaned in to kiss her, but before he could, he felt Katerina approach. She cleared her throat as a way of announcing herself. Hades couldn't decide if he found that annoying or courteous. He released his hold on Persephone, who chose to take a step away from him, which he found irritating.

Perhaps he needed to remind her that they did not have to abide by the same kind of rules as others. He would show as much affection as he wished, which included fucking her in his office.

"My Lady Persephone!" Katerina said, full of her usual sunshine and dressed like it too. She bowed respectfully, and Persephone smiled.

"Katerina, a pleasure," she said.

"I apologize for the intrusion," Katerina said, glancing at him before returning to Persephone. Still, in that one look, he knew whatever Katerina had to tell him wasn't exactly the best news. Fuck. His mind went straight to the prophecy she'd given him at the park—had it changed? "As soon as I heard Hades had arrived, I knew I would have to catch him before he vanished."

"I will be along shortly, Katerina," Hades said.

She looked at him and smiled, but that same brightness didn't touch her eyes, which only made him dread what she had to say more. "Of course," she said and then looked at Persephone. "We're honored to have you here, my lady."

When she left, Persephone looked at Hades.

"What was that about?" she asked. Apparently, Katerina's concerns hadn't escaped Persephone's notice either.

"I will tell you later," he said, after he figured it out.

"Just as you were going to tell me where you had been the other night?" she challenged.

He narrowed his eyes. "I told you I was bargaining with monsters."

"A nonanswer if there ever was one."

He let out a frustrated sigh.

"I do not wish to keep things from you. I just do not know what to burden you with in your grief."

She hesitated and then said, "I am not angry with you. I was joking, mostly."

"Mostly," he said with an incredulous laugh.

She was mostly joking, mostly content, mostly angry. He supposed he had to be okay with that because he was also only telling her mostly everything.

"We'll talk tonight," he said. It was the only thing he could promise for now because he needed to figure out what Katerina had to say, and she needed to work.

He held her gaze a moment longer, his stomach tightening. He'd have liked to kiss her, to do something other than stand here like an idiot. But if he started, he wouldn't stop, so he took a step away and headed down the hallway. He felt her gaze on his back until he turned the corner and found himself in Katerina's office.

"What is it?" he asked as he closed the door.

Katerina glanced around, as if she were anxious to speak. It was not as if anyone could hear them in her office, but the walls were all glass.

"I had a dream about the ophiotaurus," she said.

Hades was quiet for a moment and then asked, "And how do dreams work for you?"

All oracles were different. Dreams were said to be the only peek gods and mortals had into the minds of the Fates. Sometimes their dreams foretold the future exactly as it would unfold; sometimes they were warnings for what might come to pass, but the details were still malleable; sometimes they were simply fears. A good oracle could tell the difference, and since Hades knew Katerina was a good oracle, it likely wasn't just a fear.

"I have never dreamed something that did not come to pass," she answered.

Hades felt like something heavy had settled in the bottom of his stomach.

"Tell me," he said.

She shook her head. "This creature, the ophiotaurus. Its death is the catalyst to a battle that rages for years, and by the end, the world will split in two."

"But what did you see?" he asked.

"Fire in all directions and bodies burning within it," she said. "There was nothing left of this world as we know it, as if...we had gone back to the dawn of the earth."

"Did you recognize any of the bodies?" he asked.

He knew she had because she wasn't giving him the details that mattered, and what mattered was who was in the fire.

"Hades," she whispered, her eyes glassy with tears.

"Did you see Persephone?" he asked.

She shook her head, and it was like he could breathe again, unlike Katerina, who seemed to have frozen. "I saw *you*."

Hades had never considered how it would feel to face his own death, but he imagined this was as close as he would get—a prophetic dream from an oracle who was never wrong.

"Anyone else?" he asked.

She swallowed. "I...I couldn't look beyond you. Perhaps other oracles have had similar dreams."

Hades nodded, his mind scattered.

"So the ophiotaurus is the catalyst to this end?" he asked. "Do you mean to say that whoever slays it has the power to bring about this end?"

"You know how this works, Hades," she said.

She could only give him the words and the visions. It was up to him to figure out what they meant and how to stop them.

He hated this game.

"Fucking Fates!" He lashed out, punching one of the glass walls. It cracked beneath his fist.

To her credit, Katerina did not even flinch, and after a moment, she said in a very quiet tone, "I'll inform Ivy. She can have it fixed by the end of the day."

Hades swallowed hard and nodded. "Thank you for the information, Katerina."

A few tears streamed down her cheeks. She had obviously not liked giving him the news any more than he liked receiving it.

Hades left her office, returning to Persephone's floor. What he needed right now was the comfort of her presence, but a sudden, strange smell filled his senses, halting him in his tracks. It was cooling and almost...medicinal.

It was laurel.

Hades froze.

Fuck.

He hurried down the hall to where he had manifested with Persephone earlier to find her gone and the smell of Apollo's magic lingering in the air.

The God of Music had taken her.

Hades strolled into his office and snatched the phone from its cradle.

"Ivy," he said.

"My lord!" she said cheerfully, oblivious to his frustration. "I did not know you were here!"

"Send Zofie up," he snapped.

"Right away, my lord," she said.

He had summoned Zofie to the tower this morning to act as security, but she had not seemed so necessary since he was near. He supposed he was wrong.

Hades paced in the room outside Persephone's new set of offices, frustrated.

Despite giving her space to work here, he could not protect her from everything, and one of those things was Apollo.

Did the god realize how much danger threatened Persephone?

He should.

After all, he had been the one to perform Adonis's autopsy. He had been the one to experience Harmonia's attack secondhand. He had to understand that whisking her away to play companion at this time was not in her best interest.

While he could follow Apollo's magic and snatch her away from the God of Music, Hades also knew that the two had a bargain, a contract in place that Persephone had to honor.

He hated it.

She should have gotten out when he'd given her the chance, and he could not understand why she hadn't.

When would she learn she could not change people? Apollo would eventually disappoint her just as Hades would, he was certain.

The elevator announced its arrival with an annoying beep, and Hades looked up to see Zofie as the doors opened.

Before she could step onto the floor, Hades spoke.

"Persephone's at the Palaestra of Delphi with Apollo." He knew because he could track the stones in her engagement ring. Each had a unique energy, and he could sense it no matter how far she went. "You must go and keep watch, even if you do not make yourself known to her."

The Amazon's eyes widened. "I...I did not know. I am so—"

"Don't be sorry. Just go," he ordered.

While Hades had hired Zofie to keep Persephone safe, he was starting to think he needed someone who had more than just battle skills. As an Amazon, Zofie had little to no ability to handle magic. He wasn't even sure she realized she was no match for it and would probably die trying to go up against a god.

But that was the loyalty and dedication of an Amazon, even those who had been exiled.

"Of course," she said, hesitating a moment before pressing the button for the bottom floor.

There was an awkward pause, and then Hades spoke.

"Teleport, Zofie," he said.

"Right," she said and then vanished.

Hades sighed, planting his face in his hands.

"Fuck me," he said.

"Totally would," said Hermes, appearing in a flourish of cloudy magic.

Hades let his hands drop and tilted his head. "Why the fanfare?" he said. "You aren't in public."

"I wanted to surprise Persephone," Hermes said. "I don't think she's witnessed my...*effervescence*."

Hades raised a brow, and Hermes looked around.

"Where is Persephone anyway?"

"Your brother just took her," Hades said. "Perhaps you should go get her back."

"Uh, no," Hermes said. "I had to do a lot of atoning when I stole his cattle. Do you think I want to do it again after stealing Persephone?"

"Did you just compare my wife to cattle?"

"Wife?" Hermes asked, waggling his brows. "Already practicing?"

"Fuck off, Hermes," Hades growled.

Hades stalked into his office. Ice had begun to stick to the windows, obscuring his view of New Athens, though at this moment, there wasn't much to see as the city was shrouded in mist and heavy snow.

"Demeter is big mad," Hermes said.

Hades looked at him in confusion. "Big mad?"

"You know, really mad," Hermes explained and then shimmied his head and shoulders as he added, "Mad as fuck."

"Why not just say that instead?"

"Because it isn't *cool*, Hades," Hermes said. "If you're going to fit in, you need to learn the lingo."

"Lingo?"

"The *language*."

Hades chuckled and Hermes narrowed his eyes.

"I hate you," he said, crossing his arms over his chest.

They were both quiet for a moment as they looked out at the world. Hades had expected the weather to worsen, but seeing it in real time brought on a greater sense of dread.

"You know who I hate more than you?" Hermes asked.

"I think I can guess," Hades replied.

Demeter.

"I haven't seen anything like this since ancient times," Hermes said.

Not since the Goddess of Harvest had caused a drought after a Thessalian king burned down a grove of her sacred trees. It took the Olympians months of begging to convince her to stop.

Hades was not among those who pleaded with her, uninterested in rewarding her childish behavior. Though that did give him an idea. Could he draw the goddess out by desecrating something sacred to her?

"I wonder what the others think of it," said Hermes.

By others, he meant the rest of the Olympians.

"I imagine the only two upset at the moment are Athena and Hestia," Hades said. "The others will not care until their worshippers begin to die."

Because fewer worshippers meant less power, and that was when they would come after him and Persephone.

"I doubt you came to watch the weather," said Hades. "Or even to show Persephone your…effervescent magic. So what is it?"

"Do I have to have a reason to visit my best friend?"

"I thought I was your best friend," Hades said dryly.

"Listen, there's plenty of me to go around," Hermes said. "You don't have to fight."

Hades turned his head to look at Hermes.

He sighed. "Fine. Aphrodite sent me to inform Persephone that Harmonia was awake."

"Just Persephone?"

"She specifically said not to involve you," Hermes said, rubbing the back of his head. "I can already feel the consequences of this one."

"Would you rather my wrath or hers?" Hades asked.

"Clearly yours," Hermes said, annoyed, then muttered, "Some friend."

Hades was relieved to hear that Harmonia was awake but not so happy that Aphrodite was trying to exclude him from any conversations she had with Persephone. They had agreed she could look into the attack, but the part he needed from this was open communication, and he did not appreciate the Goddess of Love trying to fuck that up.

"Harmonia is just the beginning," said Hades. "There will be other gods."

Hermes stiffened beside him. "Do you really think they can kill us?"

"I think anything is possible," Hades said. "Mortals have their own magic."

It was technology and science, and combined with the power of the gods, they had the potential to be unstoppable.

Adonis and Harmonia were tests, and with each one, they would hone their attacks. It was only a matter of time before someone died, and for the sake of the world, he hoped it wasn't Aphrodite. If any one of the gods was underestimated in their power, it was Hephaestus. If anything happened to his wife, the world would come to know just how terrible he could be.

CHAPTER XVI
HADES

Hades took a seat behind Persephone's new desk.

It had been two hours since Apollo had taken her, and he was growing impatient, but then he could taste something metallic on the back of his tongue, and Persephone appeared.

She looked...freshly fucked, though he knew that wasn't the case. Her hair was windswept, her cheeks and nose reddened from the cold. Had Apollo kept her outside? In this weather? His irritation grew. She seemed to realize where she was and looked up at him, wide-eyed, and then her expression grew almost shy.

"Hi," she breathed.

"Hi," he replied, still frustrated and unable to really hide it.

Her gaze trailed down his body and then back up, eyes bright and lively. "Are you well?"

"Harmonia is awake," he said.

"How is she?" she asked, breathless.

"We're about to find out," he said, getting to his feet. He rounded her desk and stopped only a few inches from her. The proximity did not help the tension he felt between them; if anything, it only made it burn hotter. "Did you enjoy your time with Apollo?"

"On a numeric scale? I'd give it about a six."

His lips twitched and she frowned when she realized her humor wasn't working.

"I'm sorry you are not pleased."

"I am not displeased with you," he said. "I'd just rather Apollo not cart you off to Delphi during your mother's tantrum and while Adonis and Harmonia's attackers are still out there."

"Did you…follow me?"

He held her gaze for a moment and then reached for her left hand, lifting it between them so her engagement ring was on display. This ring…to him it represented so much more than just a promise of their impending marriage. It symbolized what they had gone through to get to this moment.

It was a testament to his hope and a reminder of all the times he'd lost it.

"These stones—tourmaline and dioptase—give off a unique energy, your energy. As long as you wear this, I can find you anywhere. It wasn't…intentional," Hades said. The stones he put in her ring didn't matter; he could still track them because of his power over precious metals. "I didn't set out to…put a tracker on you."

"I believe you," she said, her voice quiet. She looked up at him through her lashes, that strange shyness returning. "It's…comforting."

It was a comfort to him, especially with everything happening outside this space.

"Come," he said, adding something he never thought would leave his mouth, "Aphrodite is waiting."

They returned to the island of Lemnos, appearing outside a large, modern mansion. The fact that Hades had not been able to get them inside said a lot about how Aphrodite felt today. They were past the point of an emergency and on the path to vengeance, but he would be damned if she attempted it through Persephone.

"Can't we just teleport inside like last time?" Persephone shivered beside him.

"We could," he said. "If we had been invited."

"What do you mean? Didn't Aphrodite let you know Harmonia was awake?"

He didn't want to answer because he didn't feel like he could lie.

"Hades." Persephone's voice was laced with disapproval.

"She sent Hermes for you. He found me instead." He met her gaze as he added, "You won't do this without me."

Her lips flattened and she looked away, but not before he realized what he'd said had hurt her. Fuck.

"Persephone—" he started, her name a desperate plea, but the door opened, and Lucy answered the door. She was one of Hephaestus's creations, a nearly human animatronic who took care of their household.

"Welcome," she said. "My lord and lady are not expecting guests. State your names please."

Hades entered the house.

"Excuse me!" Lucy shouted. "You are entering the private residence of Lord and Lady Hephaestus!"

He had made it halfway down the entrance hall when he heard Persephone speak.

"I am Lady Persephone." Then, with as much disdain as she could muster, she said, "That is Lord Hades."

The God of the Dead turned to her. "Come, Persephone."

She folded her arms over her chest and glared. "You could show some courtesy. You weren't invited, remember?"

He ground his teeth. Gods, why did she have to be so stubborn?

"Lady Persephone!" Lucy exclaimed, her voice bordering on a shriek that was supposed to sound like surprise. "You are most welcome. Please, follow me." She allowed Persephone into the house and made her way toward Hades. As she passed, she turned up her nose. "Lord Hades, you are most unwelcome."

She definitely had characteristics from Aphrodite.

Hades fell into step beside Persephone and took her hand, frustrated when she tried to pull away. Normally, he would let her go, but for some reason, he couldn't this time. He held on, rubbing soft circles into her skin, and she seemed to relax.

Hades did not make a habit of coming into Aphrodite and Hephaestus's home. Mostly, when he visited, he was met by either one outside the house. For two people who rarely seemed to get along, their space seemed to be a perfect balance of their personalities—Aphrodite's luxury and Hephaestus's practicality.

Lucy led them down a bright hallway and into the library, announcing them at the door.

"My Lady Aphrodite, Lady Harmonia—Lady Persephone and Lord Hades are here to see you."

Aphrodite sat beside her sister on a small couch. Harmonia looked far better than yesterday, but that was only because Apollo had managed to heal her cuts and bruises, and she had scrubbed her skin and hair free of dirt. She was still pale, almost gray, like souls when they first entered the Underworld, and her horns...mutilated pieces of bone. They still bore saw marks.

"Thank you, Lucy," Aphrodite said, and Lucy bowed before leaving the room. The goddess's eyes narrowed on Hades. "I see Hermes failed to follow instructions."

"You can thank Apollo for that," Persephone said.

"Persephone and I are doing this together, Aphrodite," Hades said tightly.

Harmonia did not react to their exchange. She kept her hand on her dog, who lay curled up in her lap sleeping.

"Persephone, please, have a seat," Aphrodite said, her voice sickly sweet.

It was fake. Hades hoped Persephone could tell.

"Tea?" Aphrodite continued.

"Yes," Persephone answered, shivering.

Hades frowned. Was she still cold?

"Sugar?"

Hades crossed his arms over his chest, growing impatient with Aphrodite's hospitality. It was a ruse.

"No, thank you."

"Cucumber sandwich?"

"No, thank you," Persephone said again.

There was silence as Persephone sipped her tea, and then Harmonia spoke, her voice soft, barely audible.

"I suppose you are here to speak with me."

"If you are feeling well enough," Persephone said. "We need to know what happened last night."

Harmonia looked between him and Persephone. "Where shall I start?"

"Where were you when you were attacked?" Hades asked.

"I was in Concorida Park," she said.

"In the snow?" Persephone asked.

"I go for a walk there every afternoon with Opal," Harmonia explained. "We took our usual route. I didn't sense anything untoward—no violence or animosity before they attacked."

The fact that Harmonia walked through the park often and took the same route probably meant that someone knew her routine and planned the attack. The snow also ensured few witnesses.

"How did it happen?" Hades continued. "What do you remember first?"

"Something heavy consumed me. Whatever it was took me to the ground. I could not move, and I could not summon my power." She paused for a moment, her hand shaking a little even as it rested atop Opal's fur. "It was easy for them after that. They came out of the woods, masked. What I remember most was the pain in my back. A knee settled on my spine as someone took my horns and sawed them off."

"No one came to your aid?" Persephone asked.

"There was no one," Harmonia said. "Only these people who hate me for being something I cannot help."

Hades felt uncomfortable about his next question, but it had to be asked.

"After they took your horns, what did they do?"

"They kicked and punched and spit on me," she said, her voice just a whisper.

"Did they say anything while they...attacked you?"

"They said all sorts of things...broken things." She swallowed, her mouth quivering. "They used words like whore and bitch and abomination, and they sometimes strung them together into a question, like where is your power now? It was as if they thought I was a goddess of battle, as if I had done some sort of wrong against them. All I could think is that I could have brought them peace, and instead, they brought me agony."

"Is there anything else you remember? Anything that you can recall now that would help us find these people?" He recognized that he seemed aggressive in his questioning and paused to add, "Take your time."

She was quiet for a moment, her brows lowering.

"They used the word *lemming*. They said you and your lemmings are all headed toward destruction when the rebirth begins."

"Lemming," Persephone said and met Hades's gaze. "That is what the woman at the Coffee House called me."

Harmonia touched her broken horns. It was hard to watch, to know that she had been violated in such a horrific way.

"Why do you think they did it?" she asked, her voice thick with tears.

"To prove a point," Hades said.

"What is the point, Hades?" Aphrodite snapped sharply.

"That gods are expendable," he said.

He had no doubt that whoever did this would eventually go to the media or at least use Harmonia's horns as a type of trophy to prove they could get close enough to a god to wound them. Unfortunately, it would inspire others to try what they had once feared.

"And they wanted proof. It won't be long before news of your attack spreads, whether we want it to or not."

"Are you not the god of threats and violence?" Aphrodite asked. "Use your seedy underbelly to get ahead of this."

"You forget, Aphrodite, that we must discover who they are first. By that time, word will have already spread, if not among the masses, among those who wish to see us fall. But we must let it go for now."

"Why? Do you wish for this to happen again? It has already happened twice!" Her eyes were alight with her fury, and she had every right to her anger. One person close to her had been murdered, another seriously injured.

"*Aphrodite*," Persephone snapped, which drew the attention of both the goddess and Hades. She'd spoken her name as a warning, and she looked like a queen doing it—perched on the edge of her chair, back straight, hands folded atop one another, completely unafraid of putting Aphrodite in her place, even in her own home.

Harmonia cleared her throat. "I understand what Lord Hades is saying. Someone is bound to let their knowledge of my ordeal slip, and when they do, you will be ready…won't you, Hades?"

He nodded.

"Yes. We will be ready."

CHAPTER XVII
HADES

They left the island of Lemnos, and as soon as they appeared in the Underworld, Hades took Persephone into his arms and kissed her. She tasted divine and she smelled so sweet, and the longer he kissed her, the more his chest tightened, and the more he wanted to part her perfect thighs and bury himself inside her perfect body. He would take his time and warm her body slowly, pleasing her to the beat of her heart, the sound of her breath, and when he slid inside her, her heat would set his entire body on fire.

Fuck, she would feel so good.

He pulled away to meet her gaze.

"What was that for?"

"You defended me to Aphrodite," he said. "I am thankful."

When she smiled, it warmed his chest, but he recalled her anger just before they'd entered Aphrodite's house and frowned.

"I hurt your feelings."

At his comment, it was like he stole her light. She looked away as if to gather her thoughts and then met his gaze again.

"Do you trust me?"

He was surprised by her question, having no idea that her thoughts had gone in quite that direction.

"Persephone—"

"Whatever you're about to do, stop!" Hecate announced as she appeared in their room. She had one hand outstretched, her palm flat. Her other hand covered her eyes.

"Shall we undress before she opens her eyes?" Hades said, looking down at Persephone.

She smiled.

"The souls are waiting!" Hecate said, dropping her hand. "You two are late!"

"Late for what?" Persephone asked.

"Your engagement party!" Hecate exclaimed and reached for Persephone, pulling her from his side. "Come. We don't have much time to get you ready."

"And me?" Hades asked. "What shall I wear to this party?"

Hecate looked over her shoulder as they headed for the door.

"You only have two outfits, Hades. Choose one."

Hades stared at his closet, which contained exactly what Hecate had said—several of the same two outfits, a black suit for everyday and black robes for special occasions—but even the robes did not seem distinct enough.

He sighed, gritted his teeth, and did the only thing he knew to do—summoned Hermes.

The God of Thieves appeared in a puff of white smoke, except this time, it was far too much. It filled the room in a great cloud, blinding and choking Hades.

"What the fuck, Hermes," he growled between fits of coughing.

He had to close his eyes to keep them from burning as he made his way to the door and pushed it open. The smoke began to dissipate, and Hades came face-to-face with Hermes, who wore a bedazzled, light-blue leotard with the center cut out, exposing part of his chest and stomach. Perhaps the worst part was how it stuck to his privates, outlining his balls and semihard dick.

"Why are you like this?" Hades asked.

"What?" Hermes asked, looking down at his outfit. "You don't like it?"

"I'm not even going to honor that question with a response," Hades said. "I need help. The souls have arranged a surprise engagement party and I...want to look..."

"Less like a goth?" Hermes prompted.

"I want to surprise Persephone," Hades said.

"We could swap outfits," Hermes suggested. "That would *really* surprise her."

Hades glared.

"Fine," Hermes huffed and then stalked over to him. "Stand still!"

He placed a hand on his chin and then made a circle around Hades, assessing him from head to toe.

"What are you looking at?" Hades asked, growing impatient.

"Shh," Hermes ordered, waving his hands back and forth. "You are interrupting my genius."

Hades rolled his eyes.

"I saw that," Hermes snapped. "Do you want my help or not?"

Hades crossed his arms over his chest.

"Put your arms down!"

Hades let out a frustrated breath and put his arms at his sides, fists clenched.

"Unclench your fists!"

"If you tell me what to do one more time, I—"

"Undress!" Hermes declared.

"What?"

"You asked me to dress you for your engagement party," he said. "So undress."

"I didn't ask you to dress me," Hades said. "I asked you to help me choose something to wear."

"And the outfit I chose requires that I dress you."

"Then pick another outfit."

"No."

They stared at each other for a long moment, and then Hades gave a frustrated sigh. It was a common occurrence when he was around Hermes. He straightened and then shoved off his jacket.

"Oh, we're doing it the mortal way," Hermes said, grinning.

Hades paused as he started to unbutton his shirt. He thought using magic would make it seem like he was too eager, but Hermes was making him feel like he was performing a striptease.

"Fuck it," Hades said and snapped his fingers, naked except for a pair of underwear.

"Hmm," said Hermes, and a swath of dark fabric appeared in his hands. "Briefs. Who knew?"

Hades tensed as Hermes draped the fabric over his left shoulder and then proceeded to wrap it around him in the style of a traditional himation, keeping part of his chest exposed.

"I could have done this on my own," Hades commented as Hermes smoothed his hands down the front and back of the garment.

"Probably, but would it have looked as good?" Hermes asked, pushing him toward the mirror, and when Hades saw his reflection, he couldn't disagree. The fabric was the color of the night sky, and the edges were trimmed in silver, as if they'd been dipped in the brightness of the stars.

"Well?" Hermes demanded.

"I...suppose you are right," Hades said, crossing his arms over his chest.

Hermes grinned. "Now, let's do something about that hair."

Hermes spent what felt like an entire hour brushing out his hair, then he tied half of it back, away from his face.

"Drop your glamour," Hermes said.

Hades lifted a brow and met Hermes's stare in the mirror. It wasn't that he minded his true form. It was the order from Hermes that bothered him.

"It's hotter," Hermes added.

Hades rolled his eyes but let his magic fall away.

Mostly, he did not notice the difference in how it felt to carry around an illusion all day, but there were times when it felt particularly nice to shrug off the heaviness of his magic.

Tonight was one of those nights.

As he sat before the mirror in the bathroom in his natural form—tall horns spiraling from his head and eerie blue eyes flashing bright—he almost did not recognize himself. Or rather, he felt as though this form belonged to a god who no longer existed. It was the form he'd been given at birth, the one he'd used as he'd waged wars against the Titans, the one he'd used as he received thousands of colorless souls into the Underworld, the one he'd used when he and the other Olympians had come to earth during the Great War.

It was this visage that people had come to dread. He wondered if there were souls in Asphodel who would see him tonight and remember their fear.

He curled his hand into a fist on the counter.

"You need a crown," Hermes said.

Hades focused on the god, who still loomed in the background, studying him like a painting in a museum. He didn't argue and called on his magic. Shadows broke away from his body and slithered through the air, twining on his head to form a crown of iron spikes. Before it was finished forming, he rose to his feet and turned toward Hermes.

"Thank you," Hades said and then looked the god up and down. "Have fun…doing whatever you're doing."

"It's okay, Hades. You can say it. I look fine as fuck."

The corners of his mouth lifted. "Sure, Hermes."

With that, he teleported to Asphodel, arriving at the very edge of the village.

"Lord Hades!"

He grinned as several of the children broke into a run, colliding with his legs hard. He pretended to stumble, and they giggled at their strength.

"Play with us!" one said—his name was Dion. He pulled on Hades's hand.

"Please, please, please," a couple others chanted.

Hades chuckled and reached to pick up a smaller child who had pushed her way to the front of the crowd and buried her head against him. Her name was Lily.

"What shall we play?" he asked.

The children replied at the same time.

"Hide-and-seek!"

"Blindman's bluff!"

"Ostrakinda!"

Their answers continued, some choosing games that had been played since the ancient times while others chose more modern versions. It reminded him just how long some of these souls had resided here and that, at some point, they would ascend to the Upperworld, to be born to new parents and birthed into new bodies, and they would forget everything they had learned here.

It was strange that the thought of life brought him more grief than death.

"Well," he said. "I suppose it's just a matter of which we shall play first."

The children began to shout again, taking his comment to mean they should tell him which game they wished to begin with, but their voices only faded into the background when he looked up and met Persephone's stunning gaze.

Her divine form inspired nothing but awe because she *glowed*. She was like a fucking star in the sky, burning away the darkness, setting fire to every horror he had ever known.

This, he thought, is her truest form. She was wild, free, and beautiful. Her hair was unbound, curls falling thick and heavy around her shoulders and down her back, crowned with white flora from which her horns seemed to rise. Her gown was pink and airy and gave the illusion that she was simply gliding over the earth.

He swallowed hard and gritted his teeth, hoping to oppress the heat stirring low in his belly. Some of the children seemed to notice Hades was distracted and turned, then bounded toward Persephone.

"Lady Persephone, please play!"

They collided with her and pulled at her hands, and a smile broke out across her face. Hades never really considered that beauty would be the weapon to stop his heart, but here he was, barely breathing. She made it so easy to forget every weight he carried—the ophiotaurus, the attacks on Adonis and Harmonia, the dangerous relics and weapons, the anxiety of Demeter's storm.

"Of course," she said, lifting her eyes to his again and then glancing over her shoulder. "Hecate? Yuri?"

"No," Hecate declined quickly. "But I shall watch and drink wine from the sidelines."

The children were already pulling them to the field, and as they did, Hades came to stand close to Persephone. She turned her head and met his gaze.

"Hi," she said.

"Hi," he replied, grinning.

He wanted to lean into her and kiss her but refrained, turning his attention instead to the crowd of children who had gathered.

"We have a lot of games to play," Hades said. "Which shall we play first?"

He called out the name of each game and let the children decide. They began with hide-and-seek, which excited him at first. Perhaps he could manage to get Persephone alone, but that turned out to be impossible, as each time he went in search of her, she had a child in tow, clinging to her skirts or cradled in her arms.

He was again hopeful when they moved on to blindman's bluff. He would gladly grope at her blindly, but before they even began, she dashed his dream.

"Lord Hades is not allowed to be it," she said.

He tilted his head. "And why is that, Lady Persephone?"

She cocked a brow. "Because you cheat."

"What a wild accusation," he replied, affronted.

"Do you deny it, Lord Hades? That you cheated during hide-and-seek, vanishing from sight just when you were about to be found?"

"It's called using your resources," he replied.

She was not amused.

The last game was ostrakinda, which was played in Ancient Greece; it was basically the most chaotic game of tag to ever exist, but Hades was looking forward to it. They formed two teams, the night led by him and the day led by Persephone, each represented by a shell, which was painted white on one side and black on the other.

Their teams stood opposite one another, and Hades never took his eyes off Persephone, even as one of the children tossed the shell between them.

It landed white side up, meaning night would chase day.

Screaming ensued as the children immediately scattered, but Persephone had yet to move, her eyes riveted to Hades. He wondered what she was thinking because he was wrestling with what he would do when he caught her. He would like to tackle her and teleport them to bed before she even hit the ground, but he had a feeling Hecate would arrive and drag them back to Asphodel.

He'd have to be content with a kiss, even if it just made the evening far more tedious.

He smiled, and something within his gaze must have told Persephone to run because she spun on her heels. He reached for her, barely catching her arm as she whirled out of his grasp and bolted across the field. He wasn't wrong when he'd observed how she seemed to glide over the ground because she did so now, bounding ahead of him like some graceful gazelle, leaving flowers in her wake with every press of her foot to the ground.

He wasn't even sure she realized it, because she never once looked back at him, but he didn't take his eyes off her, which was how he witnessed the sudden change in her. The flowers that had bloomed in her wake vanished as her steps faltered, and she came to a sudden, shocking halt.

Hades slowed to a walk and came up beside her, his hand brushing hers at her side. She didn't look at him, her gaze fixed somewhere on the horizon.

"Are you well?"

She took a shuddering breath.

"I just remembered that Lexa was not here," she said, and when she looked at him, tears welled in her eyes. It hurt his chest to see her like this, so...broken, and in the aftermath of a moment of complete bliss. "How could I have forgotten?"

"Oh, darling," he said and pulled her to him, pressing a kiss to her forehead. He held her close for a moment, uncertain of what to say because he knew there were no words that would bring comfort. This was her grief and her guilt, and the only thing either could do was wait until the feelings ebbed.

He only let her go when she seemed ready to move, and then he took her hand and led her to the picnic area where the souls were gathering to feast. Yuri led them to their blanket at the very front of the field, beneath the eaves of Persephone's grove. He helped her sit, and he fed her and filled her cup with wine, unable or unwilling to take his eyes off her as he watched joy creep back into her expression, and it all seemed to come from watching the souls—his people.

"What are you thinking?" he asked, curious.

She was sitting with her legs crossed and picking apart a roll in her lap. At his question, she seemed to realize what she was doing and set it aside, brushing the crumbs into the grass.

"I was just thinking about becoming queen."

"And are you happy?"

She seemed to be, but he remembered a time when she would have resisted that title.

"Yes, of course," she said and paused. "I was just thinking of how it will be. What we will do together. If, that is, Zeus approves."

Hades stiffened at her final comment, frustrated that she was even thinking about Zeus at all. He supposed it was more that she obviously doubted his promise, that they would marry even if his brother did not approve.

"Just keep planning, darling."

A small smile ghosted across her lips, and she looked away, her gaze trailing over the vast field, to Asphodel and to the castle that loomed in the distance like a dreadful shadow.

"I would like to speak about earlier," he said. "Before we were interrupted, you asked if I trusted you."

She stiffened at his comment, and he noted how she hesitated before she spoke.

"You did not think I'd come to you when Hermes summoned me to Lemnos," she said. "Tell me, truthfully."

He swallowed something thick in his throat, and a feeling of shame washed over him. He let his eyes fall to his hands.

"I did not," he admitted and then quickly met her hurt gaze. "But I was more concerned about Aphrodite. I know what she wants from you. I worry you will try to investigate and identify Adonis and Harmonia's attackers on your own. It isn't because I don't trust you but because I *know* you. You want to make the world safe again, fix what is broken."

"I told you I wouldn't do anything without your knowledge, and I meant it."

Her eyes and tone were fierce. He had often sworn oaths to her, and this felt like one now.

He believed her.

"I am sorry," he said. He felt so wrong for doubting her, worse for letting her think he did not trust her.

She did not say it was okay or even that she accepted his apology. Instead, she used his words against him.

"You once said words had no meaning. Let our actions speak next time."

He nodded once.

For a moment, a strange tension lingered between them. Hades almost felt as though he needed to say something else, to apologize again, but he also knew those words wouldn't matter. It wasn't long before they fell into an easier silence, and Hades shifted onto his back, resting his head in Persephone's lap.

She laughed as he did it but seemed content to thread her fingers through his hair. He liked the feel of it, and it lulled him into a sense of calm.

"Hades." She said his name in a hushed tone, as if she feared he might be sleeping.

"Hmm?" He opened his eyes and met her gaze, not quite prepared for what she said next.

"What did you trade for your ability to have children?"

He wondered what had brought on her curiosity. Had it been their time with the children in Asphodel? The question gave way to more. Was she having second thoughts about their marriage? Had she decided she truly wished to become a mother?

"I gave a mortal woman divinity," he said.

At the time, it had felt powerful, but it was also why Dionysus owed him a favor and had little choice but to bend to his will. The God of Wine had come to him after his mother, Semele, was killed by Zeus, her death ultimately the result of Hera's jealousy. He begged Hades to set her free. Hades wished he could say he had been motivated to go to the Fates purely out of sympathy for the god, but he was more interested in binding Dionysus to do his bidding.

The Fates agreed to grant Semele divinity, but in

exchange, Hades had to give up his ability to have children.

He hadn't even had to think about the trade then. It was the easiest decision he had ever made. He had no great love, only lovers. This, he thought, was a true blessing.

But the Fates had known better.

He should have known better.

Now his head rested in the lap of his truest love, and he couldn't make her a mother.

"Did you love her?" Persephone asked, misunderstanding his reasons completely.

"No. I wish I could claim it was out of love or even compassion, but...I wanted to claim a favor from a god, so I bargained with the Fates."

"And they asked for your...our...children?"

There was something about the word *our* that hurt in ways he could not even express. What future had he sacrificed for them in exchange for the favor of a god who hated him?

He sat up and faced her. "What are you thinking?"

He needed to know if that was something she wanted, because if it was, he would find a way.

"Nothing," she said. "I just...am trying to understand Fate."

"Fate does not make sense. That is why it is so easy to blame."

She held his gaze a moment and then looked away, and he could not help feeling like she was actually trying to decide if she could really do this.

He reached for her, letting his fingers linger on her skin as he spoke.

"If I had known—if I'd been given any inkling—I would have never—"

"It's all right, Hades," she said. "I did not ask to cause you grief."

"You did not cause me grief," he said. "I think back on that moment often, reflecting on the ease with which I gave up something I would come to wish for, but that is the consequence of bargaining with the Fates. Inevitably, you will always desire what they take. One day, I think, you will come to resent me for my actions."

"I do not, and I will not," she said, as if she were insulted he suggested it. "Can you not forgive yourself as easily as you have forgiven me? We have all made mistakes, Hades."

He searched her gaze, uncertain of what he was looking for, but only felt her love and kindness peering back. Despite how hard it had been to handle her trusting view of the world, it was also something he admired about her. She reminded him of the good that existed, no matter how little.

He brought his mouth to hers and guided her to the soft ground. She felt so good beneath him, and his body filled with a delicious heat as her eager hands sought an opening in his robes. He drew in a ragged breath when she found his length, already throbbing with need, and jerked him up and down. Each time her palm smoothed over the head of his cock, he felt light-headed, but he kissed her harder and moved his hips, thrusting into her grasp until she released him and gathered the ridiculous cloud of tulle around her waist and guided him to her heat. Once he was inside, he lowered himself onto his elbows, his face only inches from hers, and began to move.

She shuddered on his first thrust and then moaned on the second. By the third, her head was pressed into the ground, and his mouth was on her neck, scouring her skin.

Fuck, she felt so *good*, and it took everything in him to set a steady pace, to not drive into her as he had last night.

He had been a different person then, someone far more primal and possessive, but this...this felt like a claim of its own, a promise of something far greater than what had already been taken away.

"I will give you the world," he whispered, his mouth hovering over hers.

"I don't need the world," she said. "I just need you."

He kissed her, made love to her, and brought her to release under his sky.

CHAPTER XVIII
DIONYSUS

Dionysus was surprised to find Ariadne awake and sitting in his living room. He expected her to avoid him, though perhaps things had only changed between them from his perspective.

He could not look at her the same way anymore. Before, she had only mildly annoyed him, and while that was, in part, due to his attraction to her, nothing compared to how he felt now. She was fire beneath his skin, and all he thought about was how he felt when she kissed him.

It did not help that she looked so at ease in his home, like she belonged right there, at the center of his life. She sat on the couch with a book in her lap wearing his shirt, her long, bare legs crossed in front of her.

She had even made *coffee*.

She looked up as he came into the room.

"How did you sleep?" he asked.

"Fine," she said. "You?"

"Fine."

He wasn't sure why he sounded so passive-aggressive. Maybe it was because he was lying. Silence followed his reply, and for a moment, all he could do was stare at her.

"Where are you going?" she asked.

Dionysus hesitated. He had not expected her to ask.

"I have a meeting," he said. "You can stay here if you prefer, or I can take you back to Bakkheia."

He should not give her the choice to stay, but selfishly, he liked the idea of coming home to her. It was ridiculous, given he rarely stayed here, but it wasn't as if he'd had a reason to be here before.

Ariadne seemed just as surprised by his offer. "I…I think I'd like to stay here."

Dionysus swallowed, frustrated by the relief he felt at her choice.

"The maenads will guard the house," he said.

Ariadne's eyes hardened. "Is that a warning?"

"It's only a warning if you are planning your escape."

Her mouth tightened. "Have you thought any more about your plan to rescue Medusa from Poseidon?"

The reality was that he had thought about it, and his meeting was actually with the god himself, but he did not want to tell Ariadne that because he did not wish for her to accompany him. The fewer women he could put in Poseidon's path, the better.

"I'm working on it," he said with far more frustration than he intended.

"You're moving too slow," she said.

"Can you just trust me once?" Dionysus snapped. He should have stopped talking then, but he couldn't help himself. He continued. "You're used to shoving your way into situations that don't concern you because you think you have authority, but you have none here. The sooner you realize that, the better."

She slammed her book closed. "You wonder why I don't trust you."

"I don't wonder," he said. "I know."

She shook her head. "You don't respect me. You don't value anything I have to offer."

That was not true, but he dared not say that aloud.

"I could say the same about you," Dionysus said.

She set the book aside and stood. The hem of her shirt barely grazed the tops of her thighs. Whatever anger he felt for her, it also spurred his desire. He clenched his fists.

"Take me to Bakkheia then," she said.

"What difference does it make where you stay?" Dionysus said. "It is not as if you will escape me."

"You're the one who offered the option," she said. "So let me choose."

"You already have," he said, though he was distracted, noticing how the soft material of her shirt clung to her breasts, molding around her hard nipples. When Ariadne noticed, she crossed her arms over her chest.

Dionysus looked away, clearing his throat. He needed to go.

"I'll have the maenads bring you some clothes," he said, vanishing before making an even greater fool of himself.

Dionysus stood beside Silenus at the edge of a pier that extended far into the waters of the Gulf of Poseidon.

Behind them, New Greece was shrouded in mist and heavy clouds, but the snowstorm did not seem to have touched this part of Poseidon's realm.

They had been waiting for an hour with no sign of the God of the Sea. Given their history, Dionysus would not be surprised if he did not show at all.

"It is not as if anyone remembers that war," said Silenus.

"I remember," said Dionysus.

The war Silenus was referring to was a battle Dionysus had waged against Poseidon long ago over a nymph named Beroe, who they had both fallen in love with. Each had appealed to Aphrodite for her love, but the goddess was not swayed by their gifts and instead ordered them to fight, so they did. Dionysus lost quickly. It was one of the most embarrassing and shameful moments of his life and another reason he did not want Ariadne involved where the God of the Sea was concerned.

He did not trust Poseidon and believed that if he laid eyes on her, he would pursue her. Dionysus feared what he might do if that happened. It did not matter that he did not love her. She meant something, even if he could not figure out exactly what.

"So how's the girl?" Silenus asked.

Dionysus ground his teeth. "She's a woman, Silenus. And she's fine."

He could feel his foster father's gaze.

"So you haven't fucked her yet?"

"For fuck's sake, Dad," Dionysus said. "*Shut up.*"

"Can't a father be concerned for his son's well-being?"

"*No*," Dionysus snapped. It was not even that he had been celibate, but since he'd met Ariadne, his desire for other women had ceased.

"Fine," Silenus said. "Fine. I just think it would improve your mood."

Dionysus's stomach twisted. Hadn't he told Ariadne something similar in the pleasure district? Gods, he hated that he sounded like his foster father.

"One more word," Dionysus warned, "and I will push you into the ocean."

Thankfully, the satyr listened, and the sound of the sea filled the silence between them, though Dionysus was not certain he liked it any better because it left him with his thoughts, which only centered around Ariadne.

He was fucking hopeless.

"Looks like Poseidon decided to come after all," said Silenus.

Dionysus looked up to see a white yacht sailing toward them, and his heart raced. It was packed with people, and they were mostly nude, though some wore swimsuits. Music blared as they danced on every available surface. At one time, it was an environment Dionysus would have thrived within—created, even—but that was long ago, and now it only filled him with a sense of dread. It was easy to recall how the madness had felt in these moments, when the liquor was strong and the music pulsing.

It took him a few moments to shake the feeling, but by the time the yacht came to port, he had managed to gain control.

Poseidon's staff extended a ramp from the ship to the pier, and Silenus was all too eager to board.

Dionysus placed a hand on his foster father's shoulder. "No drinking," he warned. "We are not here for your pleasure."

"I know, I know," the satyr said, shaking him off and ascending the plank.

They boarded, and it was like stepping into a massive orgy. Some passengers danced, but most were engaging in varied sexual acts.

"This way," said one of the attendants who had lowered the ramp. He turned and cut through the crowd.

Dionysus followed and dragged his foster father along, not releasing him until they entered the interior part of the yacht. It was just as crowded, but at least his fuckery would be contained.

Inside, the music was muted, the environment far more calm. People lounged about in various positions across the floor and furniture, save for a large circular couch, which was where Poseidon waited. He sat with his arms stretched out across the back.

Unlike other gods who often concealed their true forms, Poseidon rarely wore glamour. Because of this, he seemed to glow, his aura gilded and brilliant. He wore gold cuffs and a gold crown that sat at the base of his striking spiral horns. If Dionysus didn't know better, he would assume Poseidon was just more comfortable in his god form, but the reality was that it made him feel bigger and far more powerful than everyone else in the room.

"Dionysus," Poseidon said, eyes glittering, as if he were already amused by his presence. "Come, sit. Have a nap."

Dionysus ignored him and jumped straight to business. "I've been informed that you may know the whereabouts of a woman I'm searching for," he said.

Poseidon tilted his head to the side, eyes narrowing slightly. "You used to be so fun. What happened?"

"You *know* what happened," Dionysus said.

Poseidon studied him for a moment and then took a breath. "You know what makes men weak, Dionysus?"

Dionysus waited for the god to continue, though he knew he would not like his words.

"Women," Poseidon said, holding up a hand before Dionysus could speak. "Hear me out. Hera has stolen your peace, changed you into this…sullen man. She has made you weak."

Dionysus's fingers curled into fists, his anger roaring to life.

"I'm not interested in your opinions, Poseidon. I've only come to ask if you know a woman by the name of Medusa. She was apparently last seen on your shores, and now she is missing."

"How should I know? So many women come and go," Poseidon said airily.

"A woman is missing. She might be in trouble or worse, and that is all you have to say?" Though he was not surprised, Dionysus was still disgusted.

"I cannot imagine why you care so much about this one woman. Have you not rescued thousands on your little mission to end trafficking? By the way, how is that going?" Poseidon paused, his brows lowering. "Do you ever tell them about your past? When you would strike women with such madness they would fall on your dick blindly?"

"You know nothing of what you speak," Dionysus said, his body vibrating with anger.

"Well, perhaps we remember the past differently."

"This was a mistake," he said.

He should have listened to his gut and not tried to please Ariadne.

"The girl staying at your house," Poseidon said. "Has she fallen on your dick too?"

Dionysus froze.

He wasn't sure why everyone seemed so obsessed with his dick.

"Since when do you care who I fuck?"

"I suppose it's been a while," Poseidon mused. "As it is, I do not care, but my son cares who *she* fucks."

"She does not belong to your son."

"I think we both know that isn't true."

"What are you saying, Poseidon?"

"I'm saying I do not think you wish to go to war over a woman again. It did not end well for you last time."

Last time, Dionysus had had Zeus's help, and given Poseidon's support of Theseus, he did not think the God of the Sky would be so willing to intervene this time.

"I did not come here to discuss Ariadne," said Dionysus.

"Right. You came to see what I knew about Medusa," Poseidon said. "I fucked her and left her. I don't know what happened after. Perhaps she begged Hades to die. Pity, though. If I had known the value of her beautiful head, I'd have cut it off where she lay."

Dionysus glared, his nails biting into his palms.

Poseidon leaned forward, his elbows on his knees, hands clasped. "Tell me you knew. They say she can turn men to stone, but only after her head is separated from her body." He paused and offered a horrible smirk. "Just like a woman, isn't it?" he continued. "To be useful only after she's dead."

CHAPTER XIX
HADES

Hades woke because Persephone jerked beside him.

"Persephone?" he asked, twisting toward her as he sat up.

She writhed, her fingers fisted into the sheets, her back arching.

"Persephone," he said, placing his hand on her belly in an attempt to ease her back onto the bed, but she wrenched away, a low moan on her lips.

He shook her.

"Persephone, wake up."

He didn't know what else to do to draw her from this nightmare, but it seemed to have its claws buried deep, because she would not rouse.

Fuck.

He shifted onto his knees and tried to hold her still.

"Persephone!"

This time, her eyes opened, but she still did not seem to be awake. She thrashed, and he could barely hold her still, his knees shifting close to her body as he straddled her.

"Persephone, it's me! Shh!"

It was when her nails dug into his skin that he knew this was a losing battle, but he did not know how else to wake her, and he would be damned if he left her to face the horror of this nightmare. But as he tried to settle back, her knee came up and hit him square in the face.

Hades fell, catching himself before he landed on his back as Persephone pushed herself away, hitting the headboard as if he'd cornered her.

"Persephone." He started toward her, but she screamed, and all of a sudden, a horrifying tearing sound followed as vines and thorns burst from her skin. He could smell the blood as it mixed with her magic, which he usually found overwhelmingly sweet but now just tasted sour.

He was going to vomit.

"*Persephone.*"

This time when he said her name, it was painful.

He summoned a fire to the hearth, and in that horrible light, he could see the mess she'd made of herself.

His stomach twisted, but it was made worse by her wide-eyed and horrified expression.

She was fully awake now, fully aware of what she'd done, and she broke, sobs racking her body.

"Look at me," Hades ordered. He had not meant to snap at her, and he hated that she had flinched at the sound of his voice, but he was almost hysterical, and it was all he could do to stay calm.

He reached for the thorns protruding from her skin, and as he touched each one, they vanished in a cloud of dark dust. Once they were gone, he focused on healing her gaping wounds, a slow and agonizing process. His body was on fire and his ears rang so loud, he could not hear a thing. He wasn't even sure if Persephone was still crying. The only thing he could do to keep from breaking down himself was grind his teeth until his jaw ached, until the burn in the back of his throat and eyes ceased.

Except it didn't, and even when he was finished, he felt like all he could see was the trauma to her skin. Maybe it was because she was covered in her own blood.

"I will take you to the baths," he said instantly, and then he stood, rubbing his palms on his thighs, thinking at first he would dry them but remembered he was naked and his skin was just as damp. He summoned his robes, hoping it would make him less slippery. "Can I... hold you?"

He felt like he had to ask. He should have been more discerning before and not touched her while she slept. Was he the reason this time was so bad?

Persephone nodded, and as he went to gather her into his arms, he felt like he didn't know how to hold her anymore. Which way would hurt her less, scar her less? But taking her to the baths was better than letting her sit here in a pool of her own blood.

He carried her down the hall and took her to one of the smaller pools where he set her on her feet. He thought she would hurry into the pool, but she did nothing. She just stood there, staring at him. He wanted the blood off her body.

"Can I undress you?"

She nodded numbly, and it made him hesitate to

touch her, but he did, helping her out of her nightgown. He pulled his robes off next.

There was nothing sexual about this. His desire was solely to know that she was well.

Carefully, he brushed a strand of her golden hair over her shoulder, and she closed her eyes as she shivered deep.

He dropped his hand.

"Do you know the difference between my touch and his?"

"When I am awake," she whispered.

So he had made it worse. He felt like his throat might close up, his breath freezing in his lungs.

"Can I touch you now?"

"You don't have to ask," she said.

"I wish to," he said and took her into his arms again. "In case you aren't ready."

This time, it felt a little easier.

He ascended the steps into the pool, and as she moved through the warm water, the blood slowly washed away. She didn't push away from him, so he didn't let her go.

"I don't understand why I dream about him," she said after some time. "Sometimes I think back to that day and remember how afraid I was, and other times I think I should not be so affected. Others—"

"You cannot compare trauma, Persephone," he said, interrupting her, knowing what she would say next—*others have had it worse*. There was no man in the world who would claim such a thing; only women were taught their pain was never enough.

"I just feel like I should have known. I should have never—"

"Persephone."

He couldn't hear her say what she should have known or done. She should have never been put in that situation to begin with. She was the prey and Pirithous the predator.

"How could you have known?" he asked. "Pirithous presented himself as a friend. He played on your kindness and compassion. The only person who was wrong here was Pirithous."

She wouldn't look at him as he spoke, but he knew she had started to cry. It was slow at first, a few tears she tried to brush away, and when she couldn't stop them, she buried her face in her hands.

He didn't know what else to do except hold her. The only time she pulled away was when she managed to collect herself and she scrubbed her face in the pool before they left and returned to their room.

Hades poured them both a glass of whiskey.

"Drink," he said as he handed it to her, and he watched her sip it before downing his own. "Do you wish to sleep?"

He asked because he didn't, and he wouldn't blame her if she never wished to return to their bed again. Right now, he wasn't certain he could.

She glanced at the bed. He had burned away the blood with his magic so that no trace of it remained, though he knew that would not erase the memory. At least that was true for him.

"Come sit with me."

Hades sat by the fire, barely touching her as he guided her into his lap, but once she was settled and she rested against him, he held her tighter.

Her body grew heavier against him and her breath evened, and it was not long before she was asleep. For a long while, he did not move, afraid to disturb her, but then he feared that if she began to dream again, he would only make it worse by holding her.

There was another issue at play, and it was that the longer he relived what had happened tonight, the more violent he felt.

He didn't like to feel this way, especially while he held Persephone so close. He rose to his feet and carried her to bed, laying her down on his side before covering her with the blankets. As he straightened, he summoned Hecate in a whisper.

She appeared, pale in the night.

"What is it?" she asked, worry coloring her tone.

"I need you to stay with Persephone," he said. "Only for a little while."

He told her of the nightmare and her magic, the way fear had made her nearly explode. As he spoke, bile rose in the back of his throat.

"I just…need someone to be here in case she has to face him again."

"Of course," Hecate said. "But where are you going?"

He studied the goddess's face. "Do I really need to say?"

"I suppose not."

Hades left then and arrived at the edge of the Forest of Despair. Opposite him, a weak and dazed Pirithous appeared. As soon as his feet touched the ground, he collapsed.

"Get up," Hades ordered.

The demigod looked up, meeting Hades's gaze, and a guttural cry burst from his mouth.

"No, please," he begged. "Please, my lord."

"Get up," Hades said again. The command was low but it vibrated the very air, a warning that brought Pirithous to his shaky feet, though he continued to plead as he sobbed.

"Please," he said, and it turned into a whisper as he said it over and over again. "Please, please, please."

"Did Persephone beg for you to stop too?" Hades asked.

"*She* would forgive me!" Pirithous insisted through clenched teeth, and the words cut through Hades like a blade.

There were a number of things he wanted to say, but he settled on one as he dropped his glamour, the magic curling away from his body in the form of sharp shadows with only one purpose—to hunt.

"Run," Hades ordered.

"Please, no," Pirithous said as he stumbled back and fell, quickly scrambling to his feet.

Hades ground his teeth.

That fucking word.

His hands curled into fists, and as he did, clawed hands burst from the ground, tipped with sharp nails. They grasped Pirithous's ankles, and he fell into more rotting hands. He struggled against their deep hold and managed to free himself, though they had gouged parts of his flesh.

Still, he ran farther into the forest, and Hades trailed behind.

He would be witness to this—to Pirithous's greatest fears, his living nightmare.

"Did she say that word?" Hades asked aloud, and

though Pirithous struggled a distance ahead, Hades knew his voice echoed through the forest.

The demigod hesitated at the edge of a lake that seemed endless in every direction he turned. It was a reservoir, fed by the rivers Phlegethon and Cocytus, but he did not know that, and taking a step in, he found that the water was thick and it burned. He howled, unable to pull himself free.

Then suddenly, Pirithous was jerked from the edge of the shore and hauled into its center where the water churned violently, burning every inch of his skin. He screamed in one continuous wail until he disappeared beneath the surface of the water.

Hades let him suffer there for a while, then parted the tarlike water until there was a clear path from one side to the other. At the center of it lay Pirithous, body scorched and barely breathing.

With a jerk of his hand, Hades drew the black water from his lungs. The demigod gasped and rolled onto his back, breath coming in wheezing rasps.

"Did you let her go when she begged?" Hades asked as he approached.

Pirithous struggled to rise and managed only to get to his hands and knees, yet he crawled, and when he could move no longer, he collapsed.

Despite his burned flesh, the whites of Pirithous's eyes were still visible, his words a low grind that sounded as if it came from his chest.

At least he could no longer say please.

"Was it worth it?" Hades asked, and when the demigod closed his eyes, Hades's rage tore through him, and he let it overtake him.

He beat Pirithous until his bones were jelly beneath his fists, until he had no stiffness to his body, until each impact felt like punching nothing but the thickened water in the Forest of Despair, and he only stopped because Hecate halted his hand.

"That's enough, Hades," she said.

Their arms shook as they resisted one another, but once Hades met her gaze, he relented and then took a step back, though Hecate did not move, like she didn't trust him not to begin again. But he was drained and there was no fury left to fuel him.

He could feel her eyes on him as he stared at the remains of Pirithous, a broken soul.

"He's never coming back, Hades," she said, and he knew that was true. "And you are needed elsewhere."

He finally met her gaze. "Persephone?"

She shook her head. "Ilias and Zofie came. They have located the woman who attacked Persephone."

Hades returned to Persephone, who woke as he arrived. When she saw him, she froze.

His body still hummed with the violence he'd executed on Pirithous, and he hated that she could feel it.

"You went to Tartarus," she said.

He didn't respond, and she rose to her feet, taking his face into her hands.

"Are you well?" she asked, and he leaned into her touch, holding her bright gaze like it was a beacon for his soul.

"No," he admitted, and they held each other tight,

unwilling to let go. "Ilias and Zofie found the woman who assaulted you," he finally said when he felt more like himself.

"Zofie?" Persephone sounded confused.

"She has been helping Ilias."

"Where is the woman?" she asked.

"She is being held at Iniquity."

"Will you take me to her?"

"I'd rather you sleep," he said.

"I do not want to sleep."

"Even if I stay?"

"There are people out there attacking goddesses," Persephone said. "I'd rather hear what she has to say."

He frowned, his fingers twined in her hair, uncertain if this was too much, too soon. They could wait, confront the woman tomorrow.

"I'm okay, Hades," she assured. "You will be with me."

He only hoped he could be what she needed. It was clear to him that he hadn't been prior to this.

Finally, he relented. "Then we will do as you wish."

Ilias and Zofie had taken the woman to Iniquity, where she sat beneath a stream of yellow light, held in place by venomous snakes. Despite the hatred she exuded, she remained still as stone, too fearful of a venomous bite and imminent death.

Hades wondered then why she'd felt emboldened to attack his lover.

As much as he wanted to take over this encounter, he understood it was not his to control, so he let

Persephone lead, and she did so without fear, stepping close until she edged the light.

"I do not need to tell you why you are here," Persephone said.

"Will you kill me?" the woman asked.

"I am not the Goddess of Retribution," Persephone said.

"You did not answer my question."

"I am not the one being questioned."

The woman's mouth tightened.

"What's your name?" Persephone asked.

The woman lifted her chin and replied, "Lara."

"Lara, why did you attack me in the Coffee House?"

"Because you were there and I wanted you to hurt."

Hades's fists clenched. He wanted to hurt *her*.

"Why?"

The why did not matter; it was the fact that she had.

The snakes reacted to Hades's own anger, hissing violently as they lifted their heads and bared their fangs. Lara closed her eyes and prepared for the bite.

"Not yet," Persephone said, and the snakes stilled. When the woman opened her eyes and met her gaze, Persephone spoke. "I asked you a question."

There was a moment of silence, and then the woman broke. "Because you represent everything that is wrong with this world," she said, tears streaming down her face. "You think you stand for justice because you wrote some angry words in a newspaper, but they mean nothing! Your actions are by far more telling—you, like so many, have merely fallen into the same trap. You are a sheep, corralled by Olympian glamour."

This woman had been hurt by a god. Hades knew it and Persephone knew it.

"What happened to you?" Persephone asked.

"I was raped," she seethed quietly. "By Zeus."

Hades wished he could say he was shocked by her answer, but the fact that he wasn't made him feel disgusted with himself. His brothers had existed in this role for some time, using their power to coerce and force women to do their bidding. And while they had faced some consequences, they were nothing compared to what they deserved, which was imprisonment and torture in Tartarus.

Hades had sworn he would see that through, but victory was a long and tedious road with victims of its own.

"I'm sorry this happened to you," Persephone said and took a step forward.

Hades sent the snakes away.

"*Don't*," Lara hissed. "I do not want your pity."

"I am not offering pity," Persephone said. "But I would like to help you."

"How can you help me?"

Hades wasn't sure they could even if they wanted to. Her hate was rooted deep, and no one could blame her.

"I know you did not do anything to deserve what happened to you," Persephone started, but Lara was already shaking her head.

"Your words mean nothing while gods are still able to *hurt*."

"How would you have Zeus punished?" Hades asked.

Persephone and Lara looked at him, surprised, but Hades waited for her answer.

"I would have him torn apart limb by limb and his body burned," Lara said, her voice shaking with menace. "I would have his soul fracture into millions of pieces until nothing was left but the whisper of his screams echoing in the wind."

"And you think you can bring that justice?" he asked.

She had to know she was not capable of such retribution, so she had to have someone else in mind.

"Not me. Gods," she said. "New ones. It will be a rebirth."

New gods. Rebirth.

Those were words used by Harmonia's attackers too.

"No," Hades said. "It will be a massacre—and it will not be us who dies. It will be you."

"What happened to you was horrible," Persephone said, her hand threading through his. "And you are right that Zeus should be punished. Will you not let us help you?"

"There is no hope for me."

"There is always hope," Persephone said. "It is all we have."

Hades looked down at Persephone. "Ilias, take Miss Sotir to Hemlock Grove. She will be safe there."

The woman stiffened. "So you will imprison me?"

"No," he said. "Hemlock Grove is a safe house. The goddess Hecate runs the facility for abused women and children. She will want to hear your story if you wish to tell her. Beyond that, you may do as you please."

Hades squeezed Persephone's hand as he took her back to the Underworld.

CHAPTER XX
HADES

Hades saw Persephone to work at Alexandria Tower, which was harder than he expected given the night they'd had. It was evident Persephone was exhausted, and though Hades was used to not sleeping, even he felt drained.

He returned to the Underworld and went in search of Hecate, finding her in her cottage.

"Is that blood?" he asked, because whatever was in the jar at the center of her table definitely looked like blood.

"It is," she said simply. "Do you want it?"

"I most definitely do not want a jar of blood, Hecate."

"It's your brother's," she said, her voice taking on an enticing tone.

"My brother?"

"From the castration," she said.

"I see Lara's story filled you with rage," he said.

"As it should you," she said.

It did. The only thing he struggled to forgive was what she'd done to Persephone.

Hades picked up the jar for a closer look, noting that two shriveled testicles also floated in the mixture.

"Hecate," Hades said, setting the jar down again. "What are you going to do with this?"

"Keep it," she said. Her back was still to him as she packed small bags with herbs to make tea.

"As a trophy?" Hades inquired.

"You know the dangers of god blood," she said.

"There's more than blood in that jar, Hecate," he said.

"I'm aware," she said, turning to face him. "They are also dangerous, whether attached to his body or not."

Hades knew the dangers. God blood was also called ichor, and it was poisonous to mortals. If it managed to drop to the earth, it had the potential to create other divine creatures or even divine herbs. Really, the possibilities were endless and unknown.

Testicles had the same power, though they often gave birth to gods or goddesses.

"Here," the goddess said, handing him some tea bags. Hades studied the pouches and then lifted one to his nose to smell.

"What is it?"

"It should help you and Persephone sleep," she said.

Hades frowned and then set the tea aside.

"What's wrong?" Hecate asked.

"Nothing," he said and shoved his hands in his pockets.

"Do not *nothing* me," she said. "Tell me what happened just now in that little brain of yours."

Hades narrowed his eyes on Hecate, arching a brow, but he couldn't maintain the guise of frustration for too long. The burden of Persephone's nightmares was too much.

"I worried over her sleep when I think I should have worried over her nightmares," Hades said. "I do not know what else to do to help her. Pirithous haunts her, and there is no pattern or consistency. Some nights, she wakes me up. Other nights, I'm afraid to sleep for fear I won't be able to help her. But last night, I tried and…"

His voice trailed off and he swallowed, unable to continue.

"You cannot help her confront a nightmare, Hades," Hecate said softly.

He ground his teeth.

"She should not even have to face this," he said. "She should have been safe where she worked."

"I do not disagree," she said. "Such is the world for women in a society dominated by men, even for those of us with great power."

"It must end."

It was all he could think to say.

"As all things must," she said, and then she picked up the tea and handed it back to him. "Perhaps you should speak with Hypnos about Persephone."

Hades stiffened. "Hypnos is an asshole."

He was certainly not at all like his brother, Thanatos.

"He is an asshole to you."

"He's only nice to you because you bring him mushrooms," Hades said.

She crossed her arms and lifted her chin. "Do not critique my methods," she said. "At least I manage to get what I want."

Hades's brows furrowed. "What do you want from Hypnos?"

"Use of the Oneiroi, of course," she said.

The Oneiroi were winged daimons who sometimes invaded dreams. If Hecate was asking for them, she was likely haunting a few unfortunate souls.

Hades just used Hermes for that.

"If you wish to help Persephone, then he is worth a visit," she said. "But do not go without an offering."

Hades sighed and pinched the bridge of his nose hard. This was fucking ridiculous. Hypnos lived in *his* realm. That should be enough of an offering.

"It would be if he actually liked it here," Hecate said.

That was not Hades's fault. Hypnos was the one who agreed to help Hera put Zeus to sleep the last time she tried to overthrow him, which was how he ended up as a resident of the Underworld.

"Do not be so difficult," Hecate said. "Think of Persephone."

"I always think of Persephone."

"Then stop pouting and find the God of Sleep a gift."

Hades rolled his eyes and sighed. "*Fine*. I'll get him a gods-damned gift."

Hecate smiled. "That's a good boy."

Hades didn't even honor her response with a glare and vanished.

Hades stared out the icy window of his office at Iniquity. The snow was falling so heavily, the city was hardly visible. He had come to accept feeling dread every time he came to the Upperworld and witnessed how far this storm had progressed, but today felt different—something was *off*. He could feel it in the air around him, a sense of impending doom.

It was not as if he hadn't had similar feelings, and that was what worried him the most as he studied the world that had become Demeter's battlefield. Something terrible was coming.

"Hades?"

He turned and faced Ilias, who had managed to enter his office without his notice, which was just as unnerving.

He was hardly ever this distracted.

Ilias did not seem comfortable with the fact either, his expression concerned.

"Are you all right?"

Hades did not answer and instead asked, "What do you have on Lara Sotir?"

Despite the fact that the woman claimed to have no association with Triad or another organized divine hate group, Hades was not so certain he believed that. *New gods. A rebirth. Lemming.*

They were words Lara and Harmonia's attackers had used. It could not be a coincidence that they shared a common language. He suspected they were part of the same group or at least consuming the same propaganda. Whatever the case, the goal seemed clear—to overthrow the ruling gods.

It was not unusual for mortals or other gods to plot against the Olympians, but this time seemed different. The world seemed chaotic and unstable. With Demeter's unnatural storm, blatant attacks on the favored and the divine with weapons that could actually wound them, and the god-killing ophiotaurus on the loose, Hades worried over what might be next. Death, certainly, but there were worse things.

Ilias handed Hades a thin file. He opened it to find a picture of Lara Sotir and a man walking down a street in New Athens. A second one showed them entering a hotel.

"The man Lara is with in those photos is a demigod named Kai," Ilias said. "He is the son of Triton and a member of Triad."

It seemed overthrowing the gods was a family affair, as Triton was also the son of Poseidon.

There were two more photos in the file, one of Lara at a recent protest calling for an end to the winter storm and another with Kai.

Hades stared at the demigod. He could see parts of Theseus in his face, not so much in his features but his expression. There was a glint of hatred and haughtiness in his eyes. This was a man who believed he was owed the world, likely to make up for the fact that he lacked the power of his father and grandfather.

It was an entitlement Poseidon possessed as well, and it was clear he continued to pass on the belief.

There was a knock at the door, and Hades met Ilias's gaze before nodding. The satyr crossed the room and answered the door to Theseus.

Hades closed the file.

"Ilias," he said. "Leave us."

The satyr bowed and pushed past Theseus, knocking into his shoulder. The demigod smirked, but Hades was not impressed or surprised. Theseus moved through life unaffected by his impact on others, caring only for himself.

Hades moved behind his desk, wanting something between him and his corrupt nephew.

"You have impeccable timing," Hades said.

"My ears were burning," Theseus replied.

"Then word must have reached you about Harmonia and Adonis."

"There have been rumors. I take it you have assumed my involvement."

"Have you come to deny it?"

"I have," he said, his gaze unwavering. "It was not Triad."

"If not Triad, then Impious all the same."

"I cannot be responsible for all Impious or their impulsive decisions."

"I would not call their decision to kill Adonis and harm Harmonia impulsive. They seem rather organized."

"Perhaps organized but not strategic," said Theseus. "Would you really expect me to coordinate something so sloppy?"

Hades stared. "Is that why you're here? You're insulted that I would assume you are responsible for these attacks because they are not sophisticated enough?"

Theseus shrugged. "You may word it however you wish," he said. "But I did not order those attacks."

"You did not order them, but have you denounced them?"

Theseus did not respond.

"Are you hopeful it will have the desired effect and spur Aphrodite into a rage?"

Theseus glanced out the window and then looked

back at Hades. "I do not think I need her rage to prove the wrath of the gods. Your future mother-in-law is illustrating the point perfectly well."

They stared at one another for a moment, and Hades stiffened, sensing Persephone's magic. In the next second, she appeared behind Theseus, looking almost dazed until her eyes met his and then slid to Theseus.

Hades fought the urge to go to her, to shield her from him. If he'd had his way, Theseus would never have met her.

"Darling," Hades said, his tone both questioning and concerned.

Theseus turned to look at her, and Hades curled his fingers into fists.

"So you are the lovely Lady Persephone," Theseus said, and a shock of rage heated Hades's skin as the demigod looked her up and down.

"Theseus I think you should leave," Hades said, his voice almost quaking, a hint at his fury.

"Of course," the demigod said, nodding at Hades. "I am late for a meeting anyway." As he exited, he stopped in front of Persephone and held out his hand. "Pleased to make your acquaintance, my lady."

She did not move to place her hand in his, and Hades was glad for it. He was not certain what he would have done, and he did not trust any reason why Theseus might want to touch her. Could he clean thoughts, memories, perhaps even dreams with a simple touch? His powers were unknown to Hades.

Theseus dropped his hand and chuckled. "You are probably right to not shake my hand. Have a good day, my lady."

As soon as he left, Hades came out from behind the desk.

"Are you well?" he asked immediately.

Persephone was looking at the door when she turned to meet his gaze. "Do you know that man?"

"As well as I know any enemy," Hades said.

"Enemy?"

He nodded toward the closed door where the demigod had disappeared. "That man is the leader of Triad," he said, but he did not wish to discuss Theseus now. She had obviously left work for a reason, and as soon as she had manifested in his office, he had known something was wrong. He tipped her head back. "Tell me."

"The news," she said. "There's been a horrible accident."

Hades swallowed hard. He had been waiting for this—for Demeter's storm to cause the devastation that would lead Persephone to realize she couldn't continue to be with him.

Was this it? Was this the end?

"Come," he said and took her by the hand. "We will greet them at the gates."

CHAPTER XXI
HADES

The gates were the only entrance by which the dead entered the Underworld. They were large and beautifully detailed with symbols of his realm, crafted by the cyclops who had also given Hades the Helm of Darkness.

They remained closed until Thanatos, Hermes, or another psychopomp led souls to the Underworld, at which point they opened to the Dreaming Tree and beyond to the Styx where Charon waited to ferry them across to the Field of Judgment.

He watched Persephone as she observed their surroundings, which were dark—even the sky overhead. Here, outside the gates, it was always night, and it was within this night that the deities of the Underworld resided.

"What clings to that tree?" Persephone asked, nodding toward the gates and at the tree beyond, which was several feet wide and nearly as tall as the gates. Its branches were thick with foliage and heavy with teardrop-shaped orbs of light.

"Dreams," he replied, looking at her. "Those who enter the Underworld must leave them behind."

Her expression did not change, but he could sense her sadness.

"Must all souls walk through these gates?"

"Yes. It is the journey they must take to accept their death. Believe it or not, it was once more frightening than this."

She looked at him. "I did not mean that it was frightening."

He touched her, drawing his thumb over her lips. "And yet you tremble."

"I tremble because it is cold. Not out of fear. It is very beautiful here, but it is also...overwhelming. I can feel your power here, stronger than anywhere else in the Underworld."

"Perhaps that is because this is the oldest part of the Underworld," he said, summoning a cloak that he draped around her shoulders. "Better?"

"Yes," she said, pulling it closed.

Hades sensed the arrival of Hermes and Thanatos, who appeared, peeling their wings away from their bodies to reveal several souls, all of various ages. It was not so surprising and yet never easy to see the young among the dead.

"Lord Hades, Lady Persephone," Thanatos said, bowing. "We...will return."

"There are more?" There was surprise in Persephone's voice, and the fact that she thought this was all made him feel guilty, as if he had been the one who summoned the storm.

"It's all right, Sephy," Hermes said. "Just focus on making them feel welcome."

He and Thanatos vanished.

A man who stood with his daughter fell to his knees.

"Please. Take me, but do not take my daughter! She is too young!"

"You have arrived at the Gates of the Underworld," Hades said. "I am afraid I cannot change your fate."

He worried over his words, wondered whether they would strike anger in Persephone's heart. For those who lived outside his realm, death was hard to accept, and so were his limitations, given that he was a god.

The man scowled. "You are a liar! You are the God of the Dead! You can change her fate!"

"Lord Hades may be God of the Dead, but he is not the weaver of your thread," Persephone said. "Do not fear, mortal father, and be brave for your daughter. Your existence here will be peaceful."

Then Hades watched as she knelt before the young girl.

"Hi. My name is Persephone. What's your name?"

The girl was shy, but she smiled at Persephone and answered, "Lola."

"Lola, I am glad you are here and with your father too. That is lucky. Would you like to see some magic?"

The girl nodded, and Hades felt a rush of Persephone's power as she manifested a single white flower, which she placed in the girl's hair.

"You are very brave," she said. "Will you be brave for your father too?"

The little girl nodded and went to her dad, taking his hand, and the man seemed to calm.

It wasn't long after that more souls arrived, and despite the growing numbers, Persephone never wavered in her dedication to greet everyone with the same kindness and enthusiasm. Hades marveled at how comfortable she seemed despite how distraught she had been when she'd first come to him about the accident. There was a part of him that knew she was still disturbed, that this experience would leave her changed forever, but she did not let her distress show and carried herself like a queen.

He took her hand as the gates began to open and drew her toward them.

"Welcome to the Underworld."

They led the souls through the gates, and beneath the Dreaming Tree, everything they had hoped and dreamed from their life above was drawn from their mind.

"Think of it as a release," he said, squeezing Persephone's hand. "They will no longer be burdened with regret."

They would be content.

Beyond the tree were the lush banks of the River Styx, and waiting in his ferry boat was Charon, a bright beacon against the dark waters.

He grinned as they approached.

"Welcome, welcome! Come, let's get you all home," Charon said, and he stepped into the crowd, choosing the souls who would be first to board the boat. He stopped at only five. "No more," he said. "I will return."

Persephone looked at Hades, confused. "Why did he not take more?"

"Remember when I said the souls made this journey to accept death? Charon will not take them until they have."

"What if they don't?"

"Most do."

"And?" she persisted. "What about the rest?"

"It is a case-by-case basis. Some are allowed to see how the souls live in Asphodel. If that does not encourage them to adjust, they are sent to Elysium. Some must drink from the Lethe."

"And how often does that happen?"

"It is rare, but inevitably, in times like these, there is always someone who struggles."

Like Lola's father, who remained on the bank of the river.

"Lola," said Charon, extending his hand. "It is time."

"No!" Her father knelt and gathered her into his arms. "She doesn't go alone. She can't."

"She can," said Charon. "It is you who cannot."

"We go together or not at all!"

"What are you afraid of?" Persephone asked.

The man held her gaze, almost comforted by her presence. "I left my wife and son behind."

"And do you not trust, after all that you have seen here, that you will see them again?"

"But—"

"Your wife will have comfort because you are here with Lola, and she will wait to be reunited with you both here in the Underworld. In Asphodel. Do you not wish to make a space for them? To welcome them when they come?"

Her words sent chills down Hades's spine. In all his years as God of the Underworld, he had never convinced a soul to enter Asphodel in this manner. It was kind, compassionate, and thoughtful. It was exactly why he loved her.

As she spoke, the man started to cry, and he kept crying.

Charon and Hades exchanged a look, but Persephone waited patiently until he was finished and announced he was ready.

Charon smiled.

"Then welcome to the Underworld," he said, and the two clambered into the boat. Hades and Persephone followed.

It was a journey Persephone had made once before when she had wandered into the Underworld and fallen into the Styx, though he imagined this was far more pleasant, given that she was safe within Charon's boat, where the souls that swam beneath the surface could not reach her.

He recalled that time with some discomfort.

It was her first visit to the Underworld, the first time he had felt responsible for her, especially when he discovered she had been injured. It was the first time she'd met Hermes—though not the first time he'd tossed the God of Trickery across the Underworld.

It seemed like so long ago.

Persephone looked at him and smiled softly.

"What's wrong?" she asked.

"Nothing," he said. "Just thinking about how beautiful you are."

Beautiful in so many ways.

Her brows rose, as if she were curious or perhaps suspicious of his thoughts, but if she were going to comment, it was lost once Lola spoke.

"Look!"

Persephone's gaze shifted to shore where the other souls waited, and while her attention was no longer on him, he did not take his eyes off her.

Lola and her father were helped onto the pier by Yuri and Ian, welcomed with music and food by the other souls in Asphodel as they made their trek to the Field of Judgment.

Charon's soft laughter drew Hades's gaze. "They certainly shall never forget their entrance into the Underworld."

"Do you think it will overshadow the suddenness of their death?" Persephone asked.

He smiled. "I think your Underworld will more than make up for it, my lady." He bowed, stepped into his boat, and returned across the river.

"Is it still a fate woven by the Fates if it is caused by another god?" Persephone asked.

Hades looked down at her, frowning. He knew she asked because Demeter had been responsible for this, but that did not mean the Fates weren't involved.

"All fates are chosen by the Fates," Hades replied. "Lachesis had probably allotted an amount of time to each of them that ended today, and Atropos chose the wreck as their manner of death. Your mother's storm provided the catalyst."

He knew his words were not comforting. They were just what they were—the reality of fate.

"Let us leave this place. I have something to show you."

Today, Demeter had hurt his lover, his goddess, his future wife, and if she thought for a second he would not repay the favor with fury, she would soon learn.

He brought her closer as he teleported to the Temple of Sangri, to the bottom of the marble steps, untouched by ice or snow.

"Hades...why are we at my mother's temple?"

"Visiting," he said and held her gaze as he kissed her hand.

"I do not wish to visit," she said.

"Your mother wants to fuck with us," he said as he ascended the steps, Persephone following at his side despite her resistance. "Then we shall fuck with her."

"Do you intend to burn her temple to the ground?"

"Oh, darling," Hades said with a smile. "I am far too depraved for that."

As they came to the top of the steps, Hades called on his magic, and the doors of the temple burst open. Priests and priestesses froze in place as they saw him approach, eyes wide with fear, though some looked on with hatred.

"L-lord Hades—" A priest attempted to stop him at the doors, though he shook.

"Leave," he commanded.

"You cannot enter the Temple of Demeter. This is a sacred space!" a priestess aid.

Hades ignored her.

"Leave," he said again, gathering his power, knowing they could feel it lifting the hair on their arms and the backs of their necks. "Or be witness—and complicit—in the desecration of this temple."

They fled, and Hades drew Persephone inside, closing the doors behind them.

He turned to her. "Let me make love to you."

"In my mother's temple? Hades—"

He silenced her with a kiss, knowing it would ignite the desire that simmered between them, and it did. Persephone bent to his will, her body like liquid gold, forming to him like his shadowed magic.

"My mother will be furious," she said as her lips left his, breathless.

"I'm furious," he said, bracing one hand behind her head, the other sliding down, over her ass and under her thigh as he drew her leg over his hip. He kissed her hard and ground into her, a taste of how desperate he was for her. He broke from their kiss and trailed his lips along her jaw. "And you haven't said no," he pointed out as she clung to him tighter.

He released her, needing her to choose. He had asked her to do something in direct defiance of her mother, and while she was no stranger to such behavior, this was different. They were going to fuck in this temple, on scared ground. Demeter had ended lives for such behavior.

But the fact was, she already had ended lives, and she deserved to witness this. She deserved the dishonor.

Persephone said nothing as she drew her hands beneath his jacket and slid it from his shoulders. Hades considered using magic to divest them of their clothes faster, but there was no reason to rush. This was meant to be worship, and as Hades undressed her, he did exactly that, kissing and licking every inch of her exposed skin, even as he knelt to help her out of her skirt.

He stayed there on his knees before her for a moment, burying his head between her legs, teasing her swollen clit, which peeked out from the curls at the apex of her thighs.

He liked the way she inhaled between her teeth, the way she rolled her head from side to side as she let the feel of him against her radiate throughout her body.

He wanted to fill every part of her, own every part of her.

Hades rose to his feet and took her into his arms, carrying her down the aisle of her mother's temple to her altar, which was crowded with cornucopias of fruit and sheaves of wheat. Two large, gold basins full of fire roared on either side. Hades had felt their heat from the doors, but now that they were this close, his body was already damp with sweat.

At the center of those basins, Hades knelt to lay her on the tiled floor. She held his gaze as he shifted between her thighs, his blood hot, his body aching as she widened her legs, exposing her soft, slick center.

His mouth instantly watered, and the head of his cock felt as though it had a heartbeat, desperate to be sheathed within her body.

He bent and ran his tongue along her sex once before pulling away and meeting her gaze.

"You are wet for me," he said, voice rumbling in his chest.

He felt crazed and possessive.

She held his gaze, whispering, "Always."

"Always. Even at the sight of me?"

She nodded, and he wrapped a hand around her knee, kissing her there.

"Do you want to know how I feel when I see you?"

She nodded.

"When I see you, I cannot help but think of you like this. Bare. Beautiful. Drenched."

He kissed up her thigh, letting his tongue taste her. She squirmed beneath his touch as he drew closer and closer to her center, whispering truths against her skin.

"My cock is heavy for you, and I am desperate to fill you."

"Then why am I so empty?"

Her eyes glittered with challenge, and Hades smirked before he let himself indulge in her heat. Her clit was erect, and he drew it into his mouth, sucking softly, circling it with his tongue. Persephone arched against his mouth, and he looked up to see her squeezing her breasts and rolling her nipples between her fingers.

Fuck, she was amazing.

He let his tongue slide along her folds and dip into the wetness gathered along her opening before he entered her with one finger. Her body tightened and relaxed with a guttural moan. He could not help watching her take him. She was shameless and wanton, and his lust for her only burned hotter, deeper, fuller.

He added another finger, stroking her, licking her, teasing her until she came against his mouth, and as her body melted into the floor, he worked his way up, kissing her dampened skin until his lips aligned with hers. She tasted him, her tongue hungrily colliding with his own, her hands reaching for his cock, which strained between them.

Suck me, for fuck's sake, he thought as he groaned, but he was also bold enough to ask.

"Do you wish to take me in your mouth?"

"Always," she said and sat up as he leaned back on his heels.

"That word."

It made his breath catch in his chest. It made his body shudder with need. It made his heart rise with hope.

"What's wrong with that word?"

"Nothing," he said, as he stretched out on the floor where he had just made her come. "It's…perfect."

She stared at him for a moment, her eyes like bright gems. Then she wrapped her fingers around him and licked him from root to tip.

He took a breath to repress a violent shudder.

Despite how many times this had happened, there was a part of him that still could not believe it. He hoped she liked the taste. He hoped she wanted more. She seemed to as her mouth closed over the crown of his cock. She sucked softly, her tongue kneading the top where his come beaded. Then she opened and took him to the back of her throat over and over.

He dragged her from his cock before he came. He sat up, and their mouths crashed together and he pressed her to the ground, shifting onto his knees to slide his arousal over her clit and along her slick opening.

She was hot and his muscles clenched at the feel of her.

"Now, Hades! You *promised*."

He managed a laugh, but she did not realize how hard she made this. Her desperation spoke to his even as he struggled to take his time.

"What did I promise, my darling?" he asked as he let his lips skim along her neck to her ear, but she jerked her head toward his, her mouth grazing his as he pulled back.

"To fill me," she said, her eyes on his lips. Then she met his gaze. "To fuck me."

"That was no promise," he said, nestling the head of his cock against her heat. "It was a vow."

He thrust into her, and her whole body seemed to contract around him. He liked the feel of it, the hold she had over him, but he waited for her muscles to ease before he moved.

"Let me make love to you," he said again, though he felt like every time they had sex, they made love. It wasn't about a hard or fast fuck, a slow or fierce chase to release. It was about how he felt about her.

And he always loved her.

She nodded, just barely, her skin glistening under the firelight.

She was fucking beautiful and full of him, and as he began to move, she responded gloriously like she'd never taken him before. He loved everything about how she moved—the way her fingers dug into his forearms, the way her breasts rose as she lifted her hips to meet his.

Fuck.

He pushed off the ground, resting on his knees as he gripped her thighs, pressing her knees into her chest as he moved. Beneath him, her skin grew rosy, her breath shallow, and her eyes rolled.

Fucking beautiful.

He pulled out and licked the thick fluid dripping from her sex. He had never tasted anything so sweet—not even nectar, not even ambrosia. She would heal every wound. Persephone's fingers tangled in his hair, and he let her drag him up her body. He felt far more frantic the second time he entered her, desperate to feel her tighten and release, desperate for her to come on his cock.

"Come on, darling." His voice was quiet, breathless. He wasn't even sure she was listening, because her body had tightened beneath him, around him, and when she came, he followed, burying himself deep to spill inside her.

He felt like he came forever, likely because he'd held his breath until he was finished, to the point that his chest hurt, but he didn't care.

She was worth it. She was worth everything.

He bent and pressed his forehead to hers as he caught his breath, then kissed her mouth and rolled onto his back. They lay like that for a while, listening to the sounds of the crackling fire.

After a while, Persephone moved, resting her head on his chest. "What is this I hear about a horse rescue?" she asked, her voice sounded thick with sleep.

He raised a brow, though she couldn't see. She could only be talking about the acreage he'd recently purchased in Elis with the hopes of establishing a horse rescue and rehabilitation center. It was a bit of a passion project, though he knew Persephone would appreciate it. He'd planned to tell her by taking her there.

"I was going to tell you by showing you," he said, a little frustrated that someone had ruined something he'd been saving as a surprise. "Who told you?"

"No one told me," she said. "I overheard."

"Hmm."

There were few downsides to having her work at Alexandria Tower, but this was definitely one.

After a moment, she shifted, resting her arms atop his chest to meet his gaze.

"Harmonia visited today."

"Oh?"

"She thinks the weapon used to capture her was a net and that it was made with my mother's magic."

That was interesting information.

"Why would my mother help attack her own people?"

She sounded upset, but Hades was not at all surprised, explaining, "It has happened every time new gods rise to power."

"New gods or new power?"

"Perhaps both," he said. "I suppose we will find out sooner or later."

She said nothing for a long moment, but her silence did not last.

"What was Theseus doing in your office today?"

"Trying to convince me he had nothing to do with your assault and the attack on Adonis or Harmonia."

"And did he?"

"I could not detect a lie," Hades admitted, though he knew Theseus was a sociopath. Lying was like speaking the truth to him.

"But you still think he was responsible?"

"I think his inaction makes him responsible," Hades said. "By now, he must know the names of her attackers, and yet he refused to divulge them."

"Don't you have methods for extracting information?" she asked, and Hades smirked.

"Eager for blood, darling?"

But she did not seem as amused. "I just don't understand what power he has to keep that information."

"The same kind of power any man has with a following," Hades said. "Hubris."

Arrogance.

The downfall of man.

"Is that not a punishable offense in the eyes of a god?"

"Trust, darling," Hades said, curling a few strands of hair around his finger. "By the time Theseus comes to the Underworld, it will be I who escorts him straight to Tartarus."

CHAPTER XXII
HADES

"I cannot believe I am doing this," Hades grumbled as he navigated along a rocky path within the mountainous range of Erebos to reach the cave in which Hypnos lived.

He would have teleported, but he had been warned against that by Hecate.

"*You must show him respect,*" she said. "*You are going to ask him a favor.*"

Hades refrained from saying what he wanted, which was that Hypnos could go fuck himself, because at the same time, he had hope that the God of Sleep could actually help Persephone.

So he continued up the path like a mortal, feet slipping on small rocks, barely fitting between narrow passages until he made it to the mouth of a cave. Water flowed from it, glistening like moonstones, down the side of the mountain from where Hades had come. It fed into the Lethe, the River of Forgetfulness.

He hesitated at the dark entrance, uncertain of

how to proceed, but he was saved from deciding when Hypnos yelled from inside.

"Go away!"

"You don't even know why I'm here," Hades snapped.

"I know you and that's enough," Hypnos said.

Hades let out a low growl and then he spoke through gritted teeth. "I have come to ask for a favor."

"I do not grant favors, even for the God of the Dead!"

"Yet you will commit treason when forced," Hades muttered.

"I heard that!" Hypnos snapped.

Hades sighed. "I have brought you a...*token*," he said, unable to call it a gift. "If you are willing to help Persephone."

There was silence, and after a moment, Hypnos emerged from the darkness of his cave. His hair and lashes were white like Thanatos's, but instead of long locks, his hair was short and coiled close to his head. He was dressed in white and had white wings that fell behind him like a cape, dragging the ground.

"A token, you say?" Hypnos sounded curious, even if his expression remained neutral. "Let me see it."

"Agree to help Persephone," Hades said.

"No," Hypnos said.

This was a mistake. Hades had known that the moment Hecate had suggested it, but he'd had to try. He could hardly handle the dread as night approached, the worry that Pirithous would return again tonight to haunt Persephone's dreams. It did not matter that his soul was gone now. He still lived on in Persephone's mind.

Hades stared at the god for a moment and then turned to leave without a word.

"Wait, wait!" Hypnos called.

Hades paused, but he knew the god hesitated.

"A hint at least, before I agree."

A wave of disgust curled Hades's lips, and he continued walking and did not respond. For him, it was bad enough that he had to give some kind of offering just to secure Hypnos's help.

"Not even you would agree to something before you knew the bargain!"

There was a time when Hypnos would, a time when he was known to be calm and gentle, much like his brother.

Hades turned, fists clenched. He had lost all patience. "I have never asked you for anything in your life," he said.

Hypnos averted his eyes and crossed his arms over his chest as Hades continued.

"But I come to you now because my future wife, my queen, is terrorized every time she closes her eyes, and all you care about is whether the reward is worthy of your time. Have you forgotten what it is like to watch the one you love suffer?"

"At least you can witness her suffering," Hypnos snapped. "I have not seen my wife since I was sentenced to this hell!"

Hypnos's wife was named Pasithea. She was one of the Charites, sometimes called Graces. She had been given to him in marriage by Hera, and while he had been lucky that he had not lost her completely, in the aftermath of his betrayal of Zeus, he was separated from her forever.

"Perhaps that would have changed had you agreed to help me."

"You wish to shame me for refusing you, yet you dangle the promise of my wife before me as if that is not cruel."

"You had a chance at mercy," Hades replied.

Hypnos glared, but Hades had nothing more to say. He had not wanted to present the God of Sleep with a gift at all in exchange for his help, but that did not mean the one he'd chosen did not have great significance.

"Wait," Hypnos said, though it was almost a shout. Hades heard him scrambling and slipping down the rocky path. He ran in front of Hades, arms pushed out as if to stop him. His expression had changed, less angry and far more desperate. "Wait, please. I'll…I'll help. Just please…let me see Pasithea."

Hades studied the god, and after a moment, he extended his hand, palm up, where magic swirled. A crystal bloom formed there, and it glinted, even in the muted darkness.

"Have you tricked me?" Hypnos asked.

Hades picked up the bloom by the stem. The center glowed with warm light, like the rays of dawn spilling over a dark horizon.

"Look into its light," he said, holding it up between them.

Hypnos glanced at him, wary, but did as he said and soon grasped his hand, tightening his fingers around the brittle stem.

"Pasithea," he whispered fervently. His mouth quivered, and his eyes glistened.

"You may look through that flower at any point to see her," Hades said, pulling his hands from beneath Hypnos's so the god could hold the flower himself. He averted his eyes, feeling as though he were intruding on a too-private moment.

After a moment, Hypnos took a breath that drew Hades's attention, and when he met the god's gaze, he had managed to compose himself.

"I will see your Persephone," Hypnos said.

Hades took Hypnos to his castle, to the bedroom he shared with Persephone. He had no idea if that was necessary, but it seemed right that he visited the space where she dreamed.

Within the dark space, Hypnos looked like a bright light, glowing in white robes and gold. He took a few steps forward from where they had manifested, his eyes roving.

"How is it for you," said Hypnos, "when she dreams?"

"She struggles beside me. It's how I know she's facing her attacker again, and when I touch her..." Hades paused a moment, a sour taste entering his mouth as he recalled how her fear had made thorns split her skin. "She doesn't know it's me."

"*Do you know the difference between my touch and his?*" he had asked.

"*When I am awake,*" she had said.

He swallowed hard. He did not think he would ever forget that night or her words.

"Hmm," Hypnos said, scanning the room. "Is it always this dark in here?"

"You live in a *cave*," Hades countered. "Who are you to call this dark?"

The door opened, and Hades turned to see

Persephone enter the room. She startled, her eyes widening as she paused in the entryway, eyes sliding from him to Hypnos, who had twisted to look at her from where he observed the room.

"Hello," she said, though it sounded more like a question. She closed the door. "Am I...interrupting something?"

Hypnos snorted.

"Persephone, this is Hypnos, God of Sleep," Hades said. "He is Thanatos's brother. They are nothing alike."

Hypnos's mouth tightened, and he narrowed his eyes. "She would have figured that out on her own. You didn't have to tell her."

"I didn't want her to have the false impression that you would be as kind."

"I am not unkind," Hypnos said. "But I do not do well in the presence of idiots. You are not an idiot, are you, Lady Persephone?"

Hades stiffened at the question.

"N-no," she said hesitantly, obviously caught off guard by Hypnos's blunt questioning.

Hades sighed, explaining, "I have asked Hypnos here so that he may help you sleep."

"I am sure she's gathered that," Hypnos said.

"And you?" she asked him. "Did you tell him that you do not sleep?"

Hypnos laughed again. "The God of the Dead admitting that he needs help? That is a pipe dream."

Hades glared at Hypnos but worked to bury his frustration as he turned his attention to Persephone.

"This is about you," he said, then turned back to Hypnos. "She hasn't been sleeping, and when she does, she wakes from nightmares. Sometimes covered in sweat, sometimes screaming."

"It's...nothing. They're just nightmares."

"And you're just a glorified gardener," Hypnos replied.

"Hypnos," Hades warned.

"No wonder you live outside the Gates of the Underworld," Persephone muttered.

The god's brows rose and his lips quirked. "For your information, I live outside the gates because I am still a deity of the Upperworld, despite my sentence here."

"Your sentence?"

"It is my punishment to live beneath the world for putting Zeus to sleep," he said.

"*Twice*," Hades said. He could feel Hypnos's glare.

"Twice? You didn't learn the first time?" Persephone asked.

"I learned, but it's hard to ignore a request from the Queen of the Gods. Rejecting Hera means living a hellish life, and nobody wants that, right, Hades?"

Hades glared. It seemed the God of Sleep had heard about the labors Hera had assigned him. He had still never shared the details with Persephone, and he wasn't sure he would. It did not seem necessary now, given that he had secured Hera's support.

"Tell me of these nightmares," said Hypnos. "I need details."

"Why must you hear about them? I told you she was having trouble sleeping. Is that not enough to create a draught?"

"Enough, perhaps, but a draught will not solve the issue. I am older than you, my lord—a primordial deity, remember? Let me do my job." They glared at one another before Hypnos returned his attention to Persephone. "Well? How often do you have them?"

"Not every night," she said.

"Is there a pattern? Do they come after a particularly stressful day?"

"I don't think so. That is part of the reason I do not want to go to sleep. I'm not sure what I'll find on the other side."

"These dreams...did they proceed something traumatic?"

Persephone nodded.

"What?"

"I was kidnapped," she said. "By a demigod. He was obsessed with me and...he wanted to rape me."

"Was he successful?"

Persephone flinched, and Hades wanted to come undone. Black spires shot from the tips of his fingers.

"*Hypnos.*"

"Lord Hades," Hypnos snapped. "One more interruption and I will leave your company."

"It's all right, Hades. I know he is trying to help."

Hypnos smiled pleasantly. "Listen to the woman. She appreciates the art of dream interpretation."

"No, he was not successful, but when I dream, he seems to get closer and closer to...being successful."

Hades felt his chest tighten as she spoke.

"Dreams—nightmares—prepare us to survive," Hypnos said. "They bring our anxieties to life so we may fight them. You are no different, Goddess."

"But I survived," Persephone said.

"Do you believe that you would survive if it

happened again? Not in the same situation—a different one. One where perhaps a more powerful god abducted you."

Persephone did not answer.

"You do not need a draught," Hypnos said. "You need to consider how you will fight in your next dream. Change the ending, and the nightmares will cease."

The god stood then.

"And for the love of all gods and goddesses, go to fucking sleep."

Hypnos vanished.

Persephone looked at him. "Well, he was pleasant."

Hades held her gaze for a moment, then his eyes dropped to a red stain.

"Why is there blood on your shirt?"

Her eyes widened and she looked down at it. "Oh…I was practicing with Hecate," she said.

"Practicing what?"

"Healing."

He frowned. "That is a lot of blood."

"Well…I couldn't exactly heal if I wasn't injured," she said.

Hades narrowed his eyes. "She is having you practice on yourself first?"

"Yes…why is that wrong?"

"You should be practicing on fucking…flowers. Not yourself. What did she have you do?"

"Does it matter? I healed myself. I did it. Besides, I don't have a lot of time. You know what happened to Adonis and saw what happened to Harmonia."

"You think I would let what happened to them happen to you?"

"That is not what I'm saying. I want to be able to protect myself."

He could not help staring at the blood. She crossed her arms over her chest.

"I swear I'm fine," she said. "Kiss me if you think I'm lying."

"I believe you, but I will kiss you anyway," he said and pressed his lips to hers softly, too anxious to kiss her the way he wished, especially after what she'd told Hypnos about her dreams.

When he pulled away, she asked, "Why didn't you tell me I had the ability to heal myself?"

"I figured at some point Hecate would teach you," he said. "Until then, it was my pleasure to heal you."

Her eyes fell to his lips, and warmth curled in the bottom of his stomach.

"What shall we do this evening, darling?" he asked.

She smiled. "I am eager for a game of cards."

CHAPTER XXIII
HADES

***"We play by my rules,"* Persephone said.**

Hades raised a brow as he sat across from her at the table in their bedroom.

"Your rules? How do they differ from the established rules?"

"There are no established rules," she explained. "That's what makes this game so fun."

This sounded like his worst nightmare.

"Just listen," she said when he frowned. "The goal is to collect every card in the deck. Each of us will lay down a card at the same time. If the cards add up to ten or you lay down a ten, you slap the deck."

"You...*slap* the deck?" he repeated, confused.

"Yes."

"Why?"

"Because that is how you claim the cards."

He tried not to laugh. This sounded ridiculous, but he wasn't opposed to slapping.

"Go on."

"Outside the rule of tens, there is a rule for face cards," she said, and Hades started to think that maybe he shouldn't have wished for rules. These were confusing.

"Depending on the face card you draw, you have a certain number of chances to get another face card, or the player who laid down the first face card takes all the cards."

He didn't understand anything she said, but he nodded as if he did.

"And last, if you slap at the wrong time, then you have to put two cards at the bottom of the pile."

"Right. Of course. What is this game called again?"

"Egyptian Ratscrew."

Did she just say *ratscrew*? Was that even a real word?

"*Why?*"

She hesitated and then frowned. "I–I don't know. It just is."

"Well, this should be fun," he said drily. "Let's get to the important part—stakes. What do you wish for if you obtain this…whole deck of cards first?"

This was his favorite part of any game. It was what made playing worth it.

She was quiet as she considered, tapping her lips with her finger, which held his attention, making the bottom of his stomach twist and turn with need.

"I would like a weekend," she said at last. "Alone. With you."

"You are wagering for something I would gladly give—and have, many times."

"Not a weekend sequestered to your bedchamber," she said, and Hades felt as defensive as she sounded.

"A weekend...on an island or in the mountains or in a cabin. A...*vacation*."

He liked that.

"You aren't giving me a very good reason to win," he joked.

"And you? What do you wish for?"

"A fantasy," he said. "Fulfilled."

He did not hesitate because he had been thinking about this for a while.

"A...fantasy?" Persephone asked, confused at first, so he clarified.

"A sexual one."

"Of course," she said breathlessly. "Can I ask what this sexual fantasy entails?"

"No," he said, though that was only because he hadn't quite decided on which one he would ask her to explore...if she was willing. "Do you accept?"

"I accept."

Her quick reply made his heart beat faster, and he was suddenly struggling with his blood rushing to his cock. He liked her eagerness but liked more that she trusted him enough to say yes.

Persephone divided the deck and dealt each half.

Her first card was a two of spades, and he placed a queen of clubs.

"That means I have three chances to get another face card."

He just agreed because he had no clue what was happening, but he figured the longer they played and she explained, the clearer the rules would become...that was if he was able to focus beyond his throbbing length.

She made it harder because she sat opposite him,

flushed and aroused. He could tell by the way she kept crossing and uncrossing her legs.

Her next card was a king.

"Now you have four chances to get a face card."

He was pretty sure she was making this all up as she went along. *A face card*, he thought, attempting to recall what those were—a jack, queen, or king. The first was a five of diamonds, the next a three of clubs, the third a jack of hearts, which meant it was now her turn.

Except that she immediately placed a jack on the pile.

"Now you have one chance to draw a face card."

What he drew was a ten of spades.

Hades wasn't sure what overcame him, but as soon as he saw, he slammed his hand down on the table. Persephone jumped at the sound and stared at him, wide-eyed.

"What? You said to slap."

"That wasn't a slap. That was more like a *collision*."

His eyes darkened. "I just really want to win."

"I thought you were intrigued by my wager."

"Yes, but I can make your wager come true at any point."

"And you do not think I can make your fantasy come true at any point?"

"Can you?"

He knew she could, but the question was if he would be willing to ask outside a wager, though now that he knew she was receptive, it would be easier. It wasn't that he was embarrassed. It was more that he did not wish to scare her or make her uncomfortable, especially given that her nightmares about Pirithous were only worsening.

He held her gaze, and the air between them thickened. He liked the way she looked at him, like she wanted to fuck him raw.

"Shall we continue?" he asked.

He had no issue continuing after she came around his cock.

Persephone cleared her throat and her eyes dropped to the cards.

The longer they played, the more uncomfortable he became, wishing to relieve this tension pulsing between his legs. Soon, Hades was down to one card, and Persephone's victory seemed imminent, but she underestimated his wish to win.

"Do not look so smug, darling. I will come back with this card."

She rolled her eyes, but when he laid the card down, it was a ten, and he slapped the deck and claimed the cards.

Persephone sat back, her shock quickly turning to frustration.

"You cheated!"

He smirked. "A loser's claim."

"Careful, my lord—you may have won, but I am responsible for the experience. You want it to be good, don't you?"

She was responsible for his experience, but he would like anything so long as it was with her. She followed him as he stood and loosened his cuff links.

"Ten seconds," he said.

"What?" she asked, confused.

"You have ten seconds to hide," he said. "Then I will seek you out."

"Your fantasy is hide-and-seek?" she asked.

"No. My fantasy is the chase. I am going to hunt you, and when I find you, I will bury myself so far inside you, the only thing you'll be able to say is my name."

She tilted her head to the side. "Will you use magic?"

"Oh, this will be much more fun, with magic, darling."

"But this is your realm," she protested. "You will know everywhere I go."

"Are you telling me you don't wish to be caught?"

She smiled wickedly and, without another word, vanished.

He remained in his room, counting to the throbbing of his cock, and when he reached ten, he followed after her.

He found her in the garden outside his palace, hiding beneath a willow. She looked wild and beautiful, her eyes burning with lust and delight as she pressed into the trunk of the tree. Her gaze raked his body, tracing every hard part of him. He felt it like a physical caress.

"I've thought of you all day," he said darkly. Her eyes gleamed as she pushed away from the tree, luring him deeper into the garden. He followed, eager for his prize. "The way you taste, the feel of my cock slipping inside you, the way you moan as I fuck you."

She turned toward him as she reached the garden wall, and he trapped her beneath him, leaning close.

"I want to fuck you so hard, your screams reach the ears of the living," he said, leaning over her. As he spoke, their lips brushed, then he felt Persephone's tongue caress his mouth.

"Why don't you?"

He growled low in his throat at her teasing, aware that he had asked for this torture.

She gathered her magic, and he considered stopping her from teleporting, but he had not had enough of this yet. He wanted to see what she would do.

Except he had not been prepared for her to arrive at the center of Asphodel, amid crowds and crowds of souls. By the time he arrived, the children had already swarmed, pulling on her hands and the end of her skirt.

When he appeared, they turned their attention to him.

"Hades!" they cried and rushed him.

Well, this was embarrassing.

He caught the youngest child at the waist, letting him soar into the air as he shrieked with laughter.

"Hades, play with us!" they cried.

"I'm afraid I have made a promise to Lady Persephone I must keep," he explained as he set the child on his feet. "But I will make a promise to you now—Lady Persephone and I will return to play as soon as possible."

He met her gaze and could not quite place her expression. She looked stunned. After a moment, she swallowed and managed to smile at the children.

"We shall visit soon," she said before she vanished.

Hades followed quickly, reaching for her magic to direct where she appeared—in the Asphodel fields.

As soon as they arrived, he took her into his arms and kissed her almost violently, his body shaking with such keen desire, he could hardly contain himself as he lapped at her mouth with his tongue. Fuck, she was amazing, and she tasted like spring.

He was surprised when she pulled away. They stared

at one another for a moment, breathing hard, and then he took a step forward. When she did not take one back or leave, he reached for the front of her dress and pulled her to him again.

She did not protest as he tore the fabric or when he took her breasts into his hands and sucked them into his mouth until she clung to him and ground against him.

"Surrender," he whispered as he kissed up her neck.

He could take her in this field among the asphodel, but as he met her gaze, she offered the faintest smile.

"No," she said in the headiest whisper.

Then she was gone again, and he groaned in frustration as he followed, determined that wherever she ended up would be the place he took her—he didn't care who watched. He could not maintain this any longer, and then he appeared before her as she sat on his throne, and he almost knelt at her feet.

She was a fucking dream.

"My queen," he said and took a step toward her.

"Halt!"

He had not expected her command, so he obeyed despite the way it bristled through him. He watched her, breathing hard, frustrated beyond all reason. He wanted to defy her so badly, but he also wanted to see what she was capable of.

"Undress."

His gaze was steady. "For someone who doesn't like titles, you sure are commanding."

She lifted a brow. "Must I repeat myself?"

He smirked, but as he began to call on his magic, she stopped him.

"Not with magic. The mortal way. Slowly."

He swallowed hard and licked his lips. "As you wish."

He rarely did this, but with the way Persephone was looking at him, he thought he might need to do it more often. Her gaze was unwavering as he shed his clothes, slowly exposing himself to her burning gaze.

"And your hair. Take it down."

He watched her shudder as he shook out his unbound hair. He thought he was finished, but she gave one more order.

"Drop your glamour."

"I will if you will," he challenged.

She hesitated, though he wasn't sure why. Perhaps she just had not expected him to bargain. Then she released her magic, and he could not quite describe the awe of watching her transform. He felt like he rarely saw her like this, and though he loved her in any form, there was something about seeing her as she was made that left him reeling.

He took his time appreciating her, his eyes roaming her body—from her horns to her bare feet. He would never tire of looking at her.

When he met her gaze again, her eyes were dark and hooded. He dropped his glamour, his magic peeling away from his body like shadows only to disappear into the darkness.

She rose, and each step toward him only wound him tighter.

"Don't move," she said, her voice hushed.

He took in a low and harsh breath as she placed her hand on his chest and explored him until her hand wrapped around his cock. He thought he might explode then, just from the sheer anticipation of her touch. She stroked him until come beaded at his head and then gathered it on the tip of her finger, only to lick it away as she looked up at him.

He ground his teeth.

He wanted to kiss her and taste himself on her tongue.

Then she took a step back and returned to his throne, reclining before she spoke. "Come."

Fucking finally.

He smirked. "Only for you."

He was on her in an instant, his hands tangled in what remained of her dress, and when she was completely naked, he picked her up. She needed no coaxing, her legs instantly winding around his waist, and he guided his cock inside her.

They groaned together, mouths open and touching.

"I was beginning to think all you wanted to do was stare," he said, breathless as he ground against her.

"I wanted you," she breathed. "I wanted to fuck the moment we were alone."

"And instead of fucking, you asked for a game. Why?"

"I like foreplay," she said, and all he could offer was a choked laugh.

Her teeth grazed his ear, and he inhaled between his teeth, mouth colliding with hers. Her body grew slick beneath his hands, and it was almost hard to hold on to her, but she gripped him hard.

"I hate waiting for you," she said.

"Then find me," he said.

"You are busy."

"Dreaming about being inside you." It was true—every minute of every day.

She managed a breathy laugh.

"I love that laugh," he said, dragging his lips along her jaw and to her mouth.

"I love you."

Hades pulled away and met her gaze, then he sat, holding her against him.

"Say it again."

Her eyes softened and her fingers threaded through his hair.

"I love you, Hades."

He grinned. He was so in love with her.

"I love you," he said as she moved against him harder and faster, meeting her movement with equal vigor. "You are perfection. You are my lover. You are my queen."

She came around him and he followed, and they collapsed against his throne, spent.

"Why is this the first time I am hearing about your fantasies?" she asked as he kissed her head.

He didn't really know what to say. "How do I verbalize such a thing?"

She held his gaze. "I suppose you just…tell me what you want. Is that not what you would want from me?"

"Yes," he said, intrigued by the thought of desires. "So tell me, what is your fantasy?"

Her eyes widened and then her brows furrowed. "I…do not think I have one."

"You'll forgive me if I do not believe you," he said.

"No, I won't. It is in your nature to detect lies."

He chuckled. "But what will it take? To learn of your fantasies?"

It took her a long moment to speak. He knew she

had an answer; it was on the tip of her tongue, building tension between them.

"One day...I want you...to restrain me."

He'd expected something different—maybe exhibitionism. Given her experiences with Pirithous, he'd thought restraints something that would be off-limits. He had a feeling that was something they were both going to have to work toward.

"I will always do as you ask."

They were quiet, and she rested her head against his chest. After a moment, she spoke. "And you? What other fantasies live in that head of yours?"

His arms tightened around her slick body, his arousal growing long and thick inside her again.

"Darling, every time I fuck you, it's a fantasy."

CHAPTER XXIV
THESEUS

***"So,"** Theseus said, looking over a plume of yellow flowers* at the woman who sat across from him. "You wish to learn about Triad?"

She had introduced herself as Cassandra, but he knew her real name was Helen. She was an aspiring journalist, a student at New Athens University, and she worked for Persephone Rossi.

She was still unaware that he knew everything about her, still pretending to be interested in joining his organization, just as she had last week when she'd arrived at a rally.

Normally, he would not indulge this behavior, but he was an opportunist and he saw her potential.

He knew what she truly wanted.

She was ambitious and constantly on the hunt for the pathway that would propel her to the top. She was no more interested in him than he was in her, beyond what they could do for each other, only at this point, she still believed she had the upper hand, that she would be solely responsible for breaking a story about the greatest threat to Olympian rule.

He admired her confidence, but he hated her ignorance.

She was holding a knife and fork, cutting into a steak she had ordered. Her movements were careful, graceful even—she was trying to impress him.

She hadn't yet.

"I think I'm more interested in how *you* view it," she said. Her voice took on a heady note, and as she stared at him, her eyes dropped to his lips.

He found her seduction boring and predictable. Her fatal flaw was thinking that her beauty was enough to sway him. Phaedra was beautiful, and so was her sister. He could fuck beauty all day. It changed nothing, gave him nothing.

It was only pleasurable if he could hurt them, and it made his cock hard just thinking about it.

"I do not wish to sway your opinion," he said. "Let our actions speak."

"Your actions seem terroristic."

"That is a matter of perspective," he said. "I would argue that Olympus is responsible for terrorism."

She glanced to her left and right, likely anxious about what he'd said.

He smirked. "Does that make you uncomfortable?"

"Well, it is blasphemy," she said.

"I suppose it is," he replied. "If you worship the gods."

"Worship or not, they are real," she argued. "The consequences of heresy are dire."

"No more dire than a deadly snowstorm," he replied. "If I die spouting truths about the gods, then so be it."

She was silent as she reached for her glass and then sat back in her chair. It was an action he had not expected. It exuded comfort.

"Do you want to know what I think?" she asked, sipping her wine.

He didn't, but he had to admit, he was curious about the sudden change in her posture and her strange and sudden confidence.

He waited. He would not implore her.

"I don't think you care what happens to the people of New Greece, but I think you need their worship."

His gaze did not waver from her face.

"And what do you think of that?" he asked, his eyes darkening.

"Everyone wants to be worshipped."

"Do you?" he asked.

He was eager for her answer. He expected something generic—a comment along the lines of *what woman doesn't wish to be worshipped?*

Instead, she said, "I could be feared for all I care. I just want power."

There was a glint in her eyes he had not seen before, a darkness he wanted to prod.

After a moment, he stood.

"Come with me," he said, and though she stiffened, she took his extended hand.

Once his fingers closed around hers, he teleported.

When they appeared, it was in the shadows of a large warehouse, on a balcony that overlooked a crowded floor.

Theseus called this the Forum.

Those in attendance were there by invitation only and chosen based on their grievances with the gods—those whose prayers had been rejected.

"Where are we?" Helen asked.

"You are safe," he said.

She turned her head but did not look at him. "I was not asking if I was safe."

"That's all you need to know."

Theseus placed his hand on the small of Helen's back and guided her toward the rail. He caged her within his arms, pressing her against it, his erection settling against her ass. Her back ached, her shoulder blades biting into his chest.

A man stood at the head of the crowd facing six demigods who sat, half shrouded in darkness.

"I have begged Apollo," he said as he made his case. "I have laid golden honey and hyacinths at his altar, but my prayers have gone unheard."

"Unheard or unanswered?" The question was posed by Okeanos. He was the twin brother of Sandros, both sons of Zeus.

"Unanswered!" someone shouted. Others roared in agreement.

That was the beauty of a crowd of followers—it took one leader to incense them, to shift the energy and inspire anger.

"Who are they?" Helen asked, her voice quiet, nearly inaudible over the noise below, which echoed all around them.

"They are agents of their people," he said, speaking near her ear. "Within Triad, they are called high lords, demigods, descendants of the gods."

The man who had at first spoken with a quiet disposition was now riled. His voice rose to a shout.

"Listen," Theseus said, directing her attention below again.

"I have lit candles and picked laurel leaves, I have carved symbols into stones that have basked in the sun, all in the name of a god who ignores my pleas!"

The crowd roared in anger and began to chant, "Death to Apollo!"

"Have mercy on me, my lords!" the man petitioned. "I only wish to be well so that I may continue to support my wife and daughter."

A demigod stood and took two soft steps into the light, and the room grew quiet. He was large and warriorlike. Despite this, he had the gift of healing.

Theseus felt Helen take a breath.

"Who is that?" she asked.

"Machaon," he said. "Technically the second. He is a descendant of the demigod Asclepius."

"Apollo's son?"

"The very one," he said.

As Machaon approached, the man began to shake.

"Do not be uneasy," said Machaon, and he placed his hand on the man's head. "I will heal you of this blight."

The man shook more, and then his knees gave out.

It was not evident what exactly the demigod was doing, but Theseus could feel his power just as he felt all divine influence. Machaon's power was gentle, like the soft caress of a wave against the shore.

The man collapsed forward, but Machaon caught him and held him upright. The man's head fell back, eyes closed.

Theseus felt Helen lean forward, her body tight with anticipation.

"Is he alive?" she whispered.

Then the man's eyes blinked open, and the room broke out into cheers.

"Rise, my friend," Machaon said. "You are healed."

He helped the man to his feet, and he was consumed by the crowd as he was celebrated and Machaon's name was chanted in worship, feeding his power.

Theseus could feel it too.

"The gods withhold," he said, his lips grazing her ear as he spoke. "We give. The gods hinder," he said, hiking her skirt up. "We assist. The gods destroy," he said, touching her between her legs. "We mend."

She moaned as his fingers slid through her heat. It was all he needed to know, that she was wet enough for his cock.

He pushed her forward, pulling one hand behind her back.

He let his hand smooth over her ass and then spanked her before kicking her feet apart and shoving inside her.

"Yes, fuck!"

She gasped and met him thrust for thrust, as if she yearned for something harder and darker.

He twisted her hair around his hand and pulled. She cried out but followed his command, arching her back as he moved, keeping one hand planted on the rail. She did not move to kiss him, did not try to be anything more than a vessel, and when he felt his balls tighten and a rush surge up his cock, he pulled out, his come spraying across her ass and down the backs of her thighs.

He restored his appearance as she turned to face him, her eyes darkened with lust.

"I'll write the story you wish to tell," said Helen. "But I want a ride to the top."

"Your boss is the future wife of Hades," he said.

She raised a brow. "If Persephone will not agree to publish my story, I will go elsewhere."

He took a step closer, letting his thumb brush over her lips. He licked his own as he did.

"Next time, I will come in this mouth," he said and then took a step away. Before he left her, he paused. "Be sure your words sow the seeds of war...*Helen*."

The Forum was empty, save for him and six high lords.

He was waiting for the arrival of a group of Impious who had taken to calling themselves god killers. Normally, he was not opposed to isolated acts of violence by the Impious, but he drew the line when they became boastful. And these particular men could not stop talking about how they had dehorned a goddess.

"Where are they?" Theseus asked no one in particular, certain one of them would answer.

"On their way," Damian answered. He was the son of Thetis, a goddess of water.

Theseus bit back his frustration.

A tension had been building in his body since Helen's departure, and it had nothing to do with lust or a desire to fuck.

This was a different need—a violent one.

The doors opened, and five men entered.

The one in the middle, who was large and bearded, carried in each of his hands a long, white horn.

"My lord," he said and bowed low for Theseus. "I have come to lay offerings at your feet."

The man set the horns on the ground, and Theseus stared at them.

"Well, are you not pleased?" the man asked, his voice booming. "Are they not what you asked for?"

Theseus did not speak, but he bent to take one of the horns in his hand, testing it. They were rough and light.

Then he slammed it into the man's chest.

"I am pleased," Theseus said as blood burst from the man's mouth.

"What the fuck!" one of the men shouted.

Another man vomited.

Theseus jerked the horn free, and the man groaned and then fell to his knees.

The other four men scrambled, screaming as they sought an exit from the warehouse. Two were struck with bolts of electricity by the twins. Another began to convulse and turned to ash as if he were burning from the inside out. The last began to gurgle and spewed water before he spun and fell onto his back, drowning.

"But unfortunately, I cannot have you live to tell the tale," Theseus said when they were all dead.

CHAPTER XXV
HADES

Hades teleported to his office at Alexandria Tower.

He was anxious, and given that he planned to meet with Zeus today about his future with Persephone, it was no surprise. His hope was that he could convince his brother to agree to the marriage without his usual demands. Perhaps he would even agree that it was best that they marry in secret given Demeter's obvious disapproval.

It was a lot to hope for, but when it came to Persephone, he preferred to dream.

He hadn't expected to find her in his office when he arrived. She stood before the floor-to-ceiling windows, eyes focused on the street below. He thought perhaps she was worrying over the weather—over her mother, which meant she was likely thinking about all the lives she had taken.

His chest felt tight.

In the aftermath of that horrific crash, he had felt

certain Persephone would leave, and it would not be because she wanted to but because she felt like she had to. But instead, she'd remained by his side and greeted souls as they entered the Underworld as if she were already his wife—as if she were already queen.

He closed in behind her and placed his palms flat on the glass, trapping her between him and the window. He let his nose drift up the column of her neck, lips trailing along, leaving light kisses. He recalled the first time she had visited here, the first time he had seen her in this room and how much he had wanted to fuck her on his desk.

"*It will be the most productive thing that happens here*," he had said, and that remained true.

"Careful," Persephone said, though her voice was quiet and a little breathless. "Ivy will scold you for smudging the glass."

"Do you think she will have an opinion if I fuck you against it?" he asked, letting his teeth graze her ear. She turned to face him, and he was troubled by her expression. He'd expected to see her eyes ignited with a dark passion, but instead, she looked...distressed.

Perhaps Demeter had done something more.

"What's wrong?" he asked, letting his hands fall to his sides.

"I had Helen escorted off the property today," she explained, her voice quaking. "I..." She paused, letting her gaze break from his. "She wanted to write an article about Triad, which I supported if she could find actual sources, but I guess in the process, they managed to bring her to their side."

"What do you mean?"

"She met with me today and explained what she wanted to write about. She told me that Triad was... good. That they are like the gods, but they protect their people, as if we do not."

Hades was not surprised. He knew how Triad recruited members, and he knew their use of magic always seemed to override fate, so it was not surprising that they had managed to snare Helen in that web.

"They can be very convincing," Hades said. "It is unfortunate. Mortals who fall into their trap only see an isolated event—a moment of healing where these demigods have seemingly defied fate. They do not see the fallout."

"What is the fallout?" she asked.

He shrugged. "It depends on the anger of the Fates, but usually, they face an end worse than the one that was chosen for them."

She was quiet for a moment. "I feel like this is my fault. If I'd never—"

"You could not have known, Persephone," Hades said. "If Helen was so easily swayed to join Triad, her loyalties were never very strong."

Persephone frowned.

Hades touched her chin, tilting her head back so she would meet his gaze.

"She threatened you," she said. Her fists clenched, and there was a shift in her power. It was angry and seething. "Do you think Triad will...target you?"

"I imagine so," he said.

She blanched, and he was a little surprised by her shock. He frowned.

"Are you afraid for me?"

She glared at him. "Yes. Yes, you idiot. *Look* at what those people did to Harmonia!"

"Persephone—"

She was quick to stop him.

"Hades. Do not diminish my fear of losing you. It's just as valid."

Something warm invaded his chest at her words, and his features softened. "I'm sorry."

He had never thought twice about whether Triad would target him. He knew they would. He was one of the three most powerful gods among the Olympians. If they wished to come into power, they would have to defeat him. Up until the resurrection of the ophiotaurus, he had not considered it a possibility, though things were very different now, especially in the aftermath of Katerina's dream.

"I know you are powerful, but…I cannot help thinking that Triad is trying to bring about another Titanomachy."

Hades's gut twisted. He had known this for a while, but to hear Persephone speak it was another thing entirely. It made him think again of Katerina's vision.

Hades did not wish to give power to this dream, but he could not help wondering how much of it was true. If the ophiotaurus was slain, would they face a hundred-year war? Hades was not certain he could bear the burden of that future, not when his past had been fraught with the same horror.

It wasn't what he wanted—not for him and not for Persephone.

Hades cupped Persephone's face between his hands.

"I cannot promise we will not have war a thousand

times over during our lifetime, but I will promise that I will never leave you willingly."

"Can you promise to never leave at all?"

He gave her a soft smile. It was all he could really offer, because in the back of his mind, he was imagining that burning battlefield and his corpse among the flames. He held her gaze, and when she started to frown, he kissed her, pulling her against him. She was warm and her hands eager as they closed over his cock, which was hard between them.

Hades pressed into her, a groan escaping his mouth as his lips left hers to explore her skin. He wanted to take her against the window, the desk, on every surface of this room, and while he'd once promised to shield them from prying eyes, he considered that perhaps he should allow the world to watch their passion unfold.

It was never-ending. It was fire in his veins.

He gripped her ass, ready to lift her when she pushed against his chest. Reluctantly, he pulled away.

"Let me have this," she said.

He lifted his brows, curious. "What do you want?"

Her hands slid down his arms and she laced her fingers through his, leading him to his desk, where she guided him to sit. His eyes darkened as she used his thighs for support to lower herself to the floor before him, as if she were about to pray.

To worship.

Fuck.

His muscles tightened instinctively, and he held his breath as she unbuttoned his pants, seeking his arousal, which ached for her soft touch, her wet mouth. She said nothing as she took him into her hand, jerking him from root to tip. She held his gaze, eyes like emeralds, their light dancing with a lust he could feel in the bottom of his stomach.

He could not help watching her mouth as she moved her hand up and down his shaft, and he dug his fingers into the arms of his chair to keep from taking control. He wanted to feel her tongue on him, wanted the warmth of her mouth to close in around him, wanted to hit the back of her throat as he thrust into her.

She must have sensed his turmoil because she smiled and then drew her tongue over the head of his cock. His body clenched under her control, and when he sighed, it sounded more like a groan.

"Yes," he whispered. "This. I dream of this."

He liked her control because he had none. He had no thoughts save for the awareness that his cock was in her wet and warm mouth, that he was vibrating with pleasure, that his body was throbbing.

He could not figure out which part he liked more—the feel of her or watching this intimate worship.

She was glorious.

He made an effort to breathe through the pleasure, wanting to see how far she was willing to let him go.

"Lord Hades."

Ivy stood in the doorway. She sounded startled, and he thought perhaps she realized what was happening at his feet, but she lingered rather than retreating, which only irritated him more.

It was impossible to concentrate on anything she was saying because Persephone had not paused in her work. Her tongue slid over his head, trailed along every ridge, lapped at his come, which beaded incessantly. She used it to moisten her lips, to gently suck him, all while her hands jerked him and teased his balls.

Gods.

Fuck him.

He had to gain some kind of control, so he twisted his fingers in her hair. It was as if she were challenging him—could he hold himself together in Ivy's presence while she so diligently worked to make him come?

"Why are you sitting?" Ivy asked.

"I'm working," he gritted out, though to be fair, he never used this desk. He never used this office. This was the most he had been here in years, and it had everything to do with his newest tenant, who was currently positioned between his legs.

"There's nothing on your desk," Ivy observed.

"It's...*coming*," he said with less control than he wanted, but there was a pressure building on the base of his cock, and it was pulsing.

Ivy remained oblivious.

"Right, well, when you have a moment—"

"Leave, Ivy," he snapped suddenly.

The dryad went silent, her eyes widened, and instead of fleeing, she froze.

"*Now*," he gritted out.

She left quickly, and Hades braced his other hand behind Persephone's head, and when she looked up at him, he felt a rush of heat ignite his body. This was one of the most erotic experiences of his life, looking down at this woman who he loved, his cock swollen and filling her mouth.

"Take all of me."

She nodded and braced her hands behind his thighs,

widening her mouth as he leaned back and let his hips surge forward. The head of his cock hit the back of her throat, and she gagged but held on tighter.

"Yes, like that."

He continued making slow, steady work of the passage of her throat, feeling her gulp and gasp around him, and when he came, she swallowed him whole.

When they were finished, she rested her head on his lap, and he smoothed her hair. His body felt light, almost weightless.

"Are you well?"

"Yes," she said quietly. "Tired."

Her lips were wet and deliciously swollen.

"Tonight, I will make you come just as hard."

"In your mouth or around your cock?"

She posed the question with a raised brow, and Hades felt his cock twitch.

"Both."

He adjusted himself, needing to leave soon. He rose to his feet and brought her with him.

"I know you are having a hard day. I hate to leave, but I came to tell you I will be meeting with Zeus."

"Why?" she asked warily. The air between them was suddenly heavy with dread.

"I think you know. I hope to secure Zeus's approval for our marriage."

"Will you confront him about Lara?"

"Hecate already has," he said, guessing she had yet to see the jar of blood the goddess had collected from the god. "It will take a good two years before his balls grow back."

"She...*castrated* him?"

She definitely hadn't seen it, then.

"Yes, and if I know Hecate, it was bloody and painful."

"What good is his punishment if he can just regenerate?"

"It is a power that cannot be taken away, I am afraid. But at least, for a little while, he will be…less…of a problem."

Though Hades had to admit that he dreaded this confrontation more, knowing his brother would not be in a good mood given his current state.

"Unless he denies our marriage," she said, and he liked the threat in her voice.

"There is that."

Silence stretched between them, and he knew she was troubled. He had not given her much comfort when it came to Helen, and he had only added to her worry by telling her about Zeus, but this was important. He had to at least attempt to play this game.

He brought his forehead to hers and spoke.

"Trust, darling, I will let no one—not king or god or mortal—stand in the way of making you my wife."

Hades teleported to Mount Olympus, to his brother's gilded estate, which rose higher than any other. Over the years, Hades had made a habit of avoiding the home of the gods, though he had his own palace there. His reluctance to spend time with the other Olympians had been interpreted by the media as rejection, and they enjoyed writing dramatic headlines that made it seem as though he had been banished from Olympus for his dour mood.

But Hades had been the one to reject Olympus even when his brother ordered him to appear.

The skies were not his realm, and the opulence left him feeling uncomfortable, especially in times such as these, when the world below their feet suffered. In some ways, Hades could not blame those who were swayed by Triad. They were right to feel abandoned by the gods. Even now, few Olympians remained on earth, and those who did were unwilling to challenge Demeter.

He entered Zeus's estate, which was grand and everything gold, even the floor at his feet, but what gave him pause was Hera, who stood at the end of the staircase. She watched him, her head slightly tilted, her disdain evident.

"Why are you here?"

"I have come to speak with your husband. Perhaps you should join us," he said. "It is about Persephone."

He could feel her resentment, but she had trapped herself within this bargain, and she would have to see it through unless she wished for Zeus to know about her association with Theseus. Though Hades knew his leverage over the Goddess of Marriage was limited. It was only a matter of time before Theseus was ready to move against the Olympians, before whatever plan he had concocted with Hera and likely his father, Poseidon, was exposed.

But that was why Hades needed to secure Persephone's hand in marriage as quickly as possible.

"I'd rather sit on a tack," Hera said.

"Perhaps you should. From what I hear, Zeus will be out of commission for at least two years."

Unlike her husband, who was notorious for his

infidelity, Hera had not once strayed. Hades did not know why she remained so loyal.

Hera's mouth hardened. "He will not let you marry her."

"It is your job to sway him," said Hades.

"Even if I speak on your behalf, he will only listen to his oracle."

"I did not ask," Hades said.

They glared at one another, and then she took a step down.

"He's this way," she said, and she led him into an adjoining room that was just as large and extravagant as the entrance. She crossed in front of Zeus where he lounged near a large set of windows.

"Your brother is here," she said.

Zeus did not look his way, fixated on two swans floating idly on the lake. He sat with his legs spread wide, naked, save for a robe that hung open. A large bag of ice sat in his lap.

"In pain, Brother?" Hades asked.

It was likely not the best way to open their conversation, with a reminder of what Hecate had done to his balls, but it was more than deserved.

Hera, who lingered behind Zeus's chair, glared at him.

"Have you come to witness my shame?" Zeus asked.

"I hope you are referring to the acts that got you here and not the fact that you have no balls."

His brother was quiet, which was unusual, and Hades began to wonder exactly what Hecate had put him through.

There were few gods Zeus feared, but the Goddess of Witchcraft was one.

After a moment, Zeus asked, "Why have you come?"

"I have asked Persephone to marry me," Hades said.

"The whole world is aware," said Hera, placing her hand on Zeus's shoulder. "And if they were not before, Demeter's storm will remind them."

Hades narrowed his eyes, uncertain of her intentions.

"Are you saying you do not approve, Hera?" he asked, the words slipping from between his teeth—a threat, barely veiled by his anger.

"It is not for me to approve," she replied. "That is the job of my husband."

Her words disgusted him, mostly because he knew she resented them. Everyone knew that Hera's role as the Goddess of Marriage had been essentially overshadowed by Zeus's approval. In the aftermath of her last attempt to overthrow him, he ceased to trust any unions she might approve of.

This was all a game.

Zeus reached for Hera's hand, covering it with his own. Hades could only stare. He was used to his brother's boisterous laugh, his booming voice, his unbearable ribbing, and yet Zeus remained unnervingly quiet.

Hades was not used to this subdued god, but he recognized him. He was the version of his brother that might have done great things. The one who had rescued him and Poseidon from the belly of their father, the one who had secured alliances and defeated the Titans.

"You once wished me happiness," Hades said.

"I did," Zeus said. "But as I recall it, you also never told me who it was that had gained your affection."

"That *never* bothered you," Hades countered. "You know what the Fates have said."

"The Fates have given you a lover, not a wife," Zeus replied.

Hades's hands fisted, and he hated the truth of those words.

"Now, my dear, do not be so hard on Hades," Hera said and bent so her head was near his. Hades wondered if she could only stand to be beside him now because he was a eunuch. "He is very much in love with the daughter of Demeter."

Hades seethed.

Zeus looked at his wife. Their noses brushed but their lips did not touch.

"Will you deny me?" Hades asked.

"I am saying that if you are to marry, it will be because I have given you that gift."

"So you want to make this about power?"

He knew in some measure that would be the case. It was why Zeus consulted his oracle before arranging marriages, but Hades had never thought it would look like *this*.

"It is always about power," said Zeus. "Your first mistake was thinking it never was."

Hades returned to the Underworld in a foul mood—even fouler when he found Hermes in his bedroom with Persephone. He was holding up two short dresses, neither possessing enough fabric to cover her completely.

"You should wear this. Hades won't like it, but you'll blend in," the god was saying.

"What's going on?" Hades asked.

Persephone whirled, eyes wide, but when she saw him, she frowned.

"Are you okay?" She took a step forward and then halted. "What happened with Zeus?"

"Nothing," he snapped. "What's happening here?"

"I...um...Hermes was..."

"Sephy has to go to a sex club," said Hermes.

"That's *not* what's happening," Persephone snapped, glaring at the god.

"Well, not yet," Hermes said. "She has to ask you first."

"Hermes, shut up," they said in unison.

The god slammed his mouth closed. "Fine. I'll be in the closet."

When they were alone, Persephone turned to him and spoke. "After Helen was asked to leave, Sybil, Leuce, and Zofie went through her things. We found a date, time, and an address for Club Aphrodisia. We think she might be attending a meeting of some kind associated with Triad."

"And you want to go?"

"We all do. Zofie, Sybil, Leuce, Hermes," she said. "This is personal, Hades."

"It might be personal, but that does not mean you can be stupid," he said.

Persephone's mouth hardened.

From inside the closet, Hermes groaned. "Oof. What an idiot."

"We may have a chance to learn what they are planning," Persephone said. "Do you not want to prevent another attack?"

"Of course," Hades said. "But that does not mean I want you there. Hermes can go."

She stared at him, but her expression was not so much angry as it was hurt, and he didn't like it.

"Why don't you trust me?"

"Persephone, it isn't you I do not trust. It's—"

"Everyone else. I know," she said, frustrated. "I want to respect your perspective, but I need you to also respect mine."

Hades studied her in the silence, grinding his teeth. There was a part of him that wanted to say it did not matter, that the danger outweighed any reason she might have for going, but he knew that wasn't fair.

He worked to keep the frustration from his voice as he asked, "What is your perspective?"

"I don't want to be a passive god or decoration at your side. I have my own battles I wish to fight. Helen betrayed me. I want to know the extent."

Hades understood, but it was hard to *let* her, and perhaps that was where he had failed. She was not one of his subjects or souls. She was not in his employ. She was his future wife. He had sworn to treat her as an equal, and he realized that fear got in the way.

"This is more than just a wish to help, Hades," she said, her voice quiet. "You have to let me stand for something."

He reached for her, brushing his thumb along her cheek.

"Hermes is going?" he asked.

She nodded.

"He has already agreed to swear an oath to protect me...if that would make you feel better."

Nothing about this will make me feel better, he wanted to say, but he kept those words to himself, knowing they were no good here.

"I think the other dress, Sephy," Hermes said, stepping out of the closet. He wore one of the outfits he'd held earlier. It was a short black dress with strings of pearls holding the sides and bodice together. "This one's a little too...fuck me, if you get my meaning."

Hades ground his teeth.

"Hermes..." Persephone groaned.

Hades took a step toward the god. "You agreed to swear an oath?" he asked.

Hermes's expression grew serious. He nodded, tense. "I did."

Hermes knew the gravity of such a promise. It was not something offered to placate, though Persephone had used it in that manner. An oath such as this meant the god was bound to protect Persephone for eternity. It went beyond a single moment.

"Swear it," Hades said. "Swear you will protect her at all costs, even if it means an end to your own life."

"Hades," Persephone said, a note of horror in her voice, but he did not look at her.

"I swear it," Hermes said.

"You know the consequences if you fail?"

He nodded once, and then Hades let his gaze drop to his outfit.

"Black is not your color."

Hermes arched a brow. "Since when did you become the fashion police?"

"I had a...decent teacher," Hades replied.

"*Decent*?" Hermes scoffed, but whatever he was going to say next was cut off by a knock at the door.

They all turned in the direction of the sound.

"Come in," Persephone said.

The door cracked open, and Ilias entered the room, hesitating when he saw the three.

"Sorry to interrupt...whatever this is," he said. "Hades, you're needed."

He could sense the satyr's urgency, and he dreaded whatever waited for him.

He turned to Persephone and took her into his arms, cradling her head between his hands.

"I love you," he said and kissed her hard on the mouth, and as his lips moved against hers, a new sense of unease overtook him. It fueled the way he kissed her and felt a little like goodbye.

He did not like it, and when he pulled away, she looked just as troubled, but she held his gaze and whispered breathlessly, "I love you."

Hades took a step back, leveled a final warning look at Hermes, and stepped outside his chamber with Ilias.

"What is it?" he asked.

CHAPTER XXVI
DIONYSUS

Dionysus knocked on Ariadne's door.
Since he'd returned from his visit with Poseidon, she had not come out of her room. He hadn't even tried to get her attention last night, wanting to give her space.

He was frustrated with himself. When she'd called him out for not respecting her or valuing her, he hadn't protested. He'd just accused her of the same thing.

In addition to that, he wasn't sure he could tell her about his visit with Poseidon.

It had unnerved him more than he thought it would, not only because of what he had learned about Medusa but because of what the God of the Sea had said about Ariadne. He wondered why Theseus was so obsessed with her. What did she have that he wanted? Perhaps it was merely that she knew his secrets and she had escaped.

Whatever it was, it worried Dionysus the more he thought about it, and it made him anxious that he had involved her at all in this quest for Medusa.

Medusa's fate was another horrifying revelation. What sort of curse had befallen her? To only become a weapon in death?

"Ariadne?" he called. "Are you awake?"

He waited for her reply, but he heard nothing from the other side of the door, which made him uneasy.

"I'm sorry about yesterday. I didn't mean to make you feel like I don't respect or value you. I…" He hesitated. "I think you're…great."

He paused and still heard nothing.

Then he pressed his ear against the door and listened hard. Even if she was just ignoring him, he should hear *something*.

"Ariadne," he said and tried the door. It was locked. He banged on the door again. "Ari, answer the fucking door!"

His heart started to beat harder in his chest the longer the silence progressed.

"I'm coming in," he said, ramming his body into the door. He burst through to find an empty room.

He stood there for a moment, gaze sweeping the familiar but empty space. He crossed to the bed and threw the blankets off, but she wasn't beneath. He checked the bathroom and the closet, but each were empty.

She was gone.

"Fuck!"

Dionysus paced the length of Hades's office at Nevernight.

He raged. His body was shaking. He had not felt this kind of hysteria in a long while. He knew where Ariadne had gone—to confront Poseidon about Medusa. She had threatened to go herself; she'd told him he was moving too slow.

Fuck.

"You were supposed to watch her!" he had roared at the maenads he had posted outside his home.

They glared back at him, just as angry.

"We did," snapped Makaria.

"Then why is she gone?"

"Perhaps she is more skilled than we thought," said Chora.

He should have checked on her sooner, but he had wanted to give her privacy and space.

Fuck privacy. Fuck space.

He whirled toward Hades when he appeared and gave him no time to ask questions.

"Ariadne has gone to confront Poseidon," he said. "She thinks he has Medusa."

"Does he?" Hades asked.

"Does it matter?" Dionysus snapped.

Hades narrowed his eyes.

"No, he doesn't have Medusa," Dionysus said, frustrated. "I would go to her, but I cannot teleport to his realm without being invited. I need your help."

Hades was one of the three who had control over all realms.

"Are you certain she has gone to him?"

"Yes," Dionysus hissed. "Hades, he will hurt her."

Whatever the God of the Dead saw in his eyes, he must have believed.

"Fucking Fates," he said as he called up his magic.

They teleported to the Gulf of Poseidon, where Dionysus had come earlier to wait for the God of the

Sea. The weather was stormy—the clouds overhead were low and thick, the wind was strong, and the waves were large, crashing against the dock. He shielded his eyes as the rain beat down on him, feeling solid and painful.

Poseidon's yacht was some distance from shore, rising and falling with the waves.

"Do you have a plan?" Hades shouted over the storm.

"No," Dionysus said. As if he'd had time to think any of this through.

Hades's mouth hardened, and he sighed, teleporting again.

This time, they appeared on the yacht, only to find Poseidon already standing, holding Ariadne as a shield. Her wrists were tied in front of her. One of his hands was around her neck, the other pressed into her stomach. She looked furious and afraid, and Dionysus feared what the god had done to her up until this point.

"This is low, even for you, Poseidon," Hades said.

"Would you forsake me divine justice, Brother?"

Poseidon's face was pressed against Ariadne's as he spoke, though she tried to pull away.

"Divine justice?" Dionysus demanded. "For what offense?"

"The mortal accused me of abducting a woman."

"It was a question," she spat. "And it wasn't outside the realm of possibility, given your track record."

Poseidon squeezed her neck harder, tilting her head back farther.

"The mouth on this thing," he said. "Have you not taught her to hold her tongue?"

"Not everyone abuses women like you, Poseidon," said Hades.

"And now I am being accused of another crime," Poseidon said.

"It's not an accusation if it's true." The words slipped through Ariadne's teeth.

Poseidon gripped her mouth and turned her head toward him. Dionysus started forward, but Hades stopped him. They glared at one another, but Hades's gaze was also a warning. If they moved too soon against Poseidon in his own realm, Ariadne would be caught in the cross fire.

"I will teach you to be silent," Poseidon hissed.

"If you wish to dole out justice, then I will too, if you harm her," said Dionysus.

Poseidon released her face, his eyes returning to Dionysus. He chuckled. "So eager to be valiant," he said. "And all for pussy you haven't even tasted."

The yacht rocked violently. Dionysus struggled to stay on his feet, though Poseidon seemed unaffected by the sudden jolt.

"Don't worry. I'll tell you if she's sweet."

Ariadne's gaze was locked with Dionysus's. He shook, desperate to go to her.

"Don't look so glum," Poseidon told her. "I'll let Dionysus join if it will make you more comfortable."

His hand smoothed down her stomach to her hip.

"Do not touch her," Dionysus barked.

"What's the matter? Threesomes not really your thing anymore?" Poseidon asked with a chuckle. "You really have changed, and for the worse, if you ask me."

Hades's magic manifested like tendrils of smoke, one snaking around Poseidon's neck and yanking him back. The sudden move forced him to loosen his hold on Ariadne. She bolted for Dionysus.

"No!" Poseidon growled, and suddenly the yacht pitched again. Ariadne fell to her knees and rolled, crashing into the wall. Dionysus rushed for her, but as he did, the windows shattered, glass rained down on them, and water began to pour into the boat as it was tossed about on the sea.

"All this for a mortal who called you a name?" Hades's voice carried over the storm.

"I could say the same to you," Poseidon said.

Dionysus could tell when Hades struck Poseidon with another blow because the fury of the storm lessened. Still, he stayed focused on Ariadne, and she crawled toward him.

When they reached each other, they were on their knees, and he took her face between his hands.

"Are you all right?"

She nodded, and Dionysus helped her to her feet, though it was almost impossible to stay upright with the way the yacht heaved.

They fell again, and as Dionysus hit the floor, he saw Hades looming over Poseidon, his hand on his head. Beneath his touch, Poseidon trembled. His teeth were bared, the veins in his neck strained, and then he managed to summon his trident, breaking whatever hold Hades had.

Poseidon rose and swung at Hades, who vanished, reappearing some distance away, but Poseidon followed. While they charged each other, Dionysus reached for Ariadne again, but as he did, her eyes rolled into the back of her head, and she went limp in his arms. Her body convulsed as water poured from her mouth.

"No!" he growled. "Hades!"

But when he looked to the brothers, Hades had ceased to fight. He seemed to be frozen, stricken by Poseidon somehow.

"You are here fighting for a woman who does not even belong to you while yours suffers at the hands of my sons."

Poseidon's voice reverberated throughout the cabin despite the roar of the storm. Dionysus did not know what the god meant, but he'd clearly gotten to Hades because his chest heaved and his body trembled.

Then he vanished.

Dionysus did not know what had happened, but he was now alone and facing Poseidon. He rose to his feet and summoned his thyrsus—a fennel-tipped staff—though he knew he was facing a god in his own realm, one of the three, and that his power was no match.

Still he charged and was thrown back. He crashed through the wall and was nearly swept into the sea, but he managed to grab hold of the rail of the ship.

The rain pelted him, and the ship rocked beneath him, but he managed to crawl his way back on deck. When he returned, he found Ariadne within Poseidon's grasp again. He had her bent over a table, her legs spread, his hips pressed into her ass.

"I wouldn't have made you watch," he said. "I was satisfied that you would be tortured by merely the thought of my dick inside her, but then you brought Hades into my realm, and for that, you too must be punished."

Dionysus's anger burned, and his eyes locked with Ariadne's, which glistened with tears. He had no power here, save one, and the only thing he could think to say before his magic hit her was, "Forgive me."

He knew when the madness struck her because her eyes changed. They took on a crazed and feral look. She let out a sudden, horrifying shriek and found the strength to rear back suddenly, throwing her head into Poseidon's face. The blow struck home with a loud crack, and the god released her, stumbling back. She whirled on Poseidon and began to claw at his body. Her fingers dug into his skin as if he were nothing but clay, and before he could stop her, she had ripped chunks of his flesh away from each arm.

It was horrifying. It was the nature of Dionysus's magic.

Despite her frenzy, Ariadne was very much aware of what she was doing, though she had no control. There was no way she could ever forgive him for this, and he did not blame her, but he'd had no other choice.

A scream tore from Poseidon's mouth, and Dionysus bolted forward, trapping Ariadne's arms beneath his own as he held her against him, her bloodied hands still holding Poseidon's flesh. She growled unnaturally and lurched as he dragged her back, still overcome with madness. If he let her go, she would try to tear the god limb from limb, and while Dionysus would not mind witnessing that, it was only a matter of time before Poseidon gained the upper hand.

Dionysus's only advantage here was that he'd managed to surprise the god, but this was still Poseidon's realm.

The God of the Sea seethed, eyes flashing with malice. He looked at each of his bleeding, mangled arms. His breath came quickly between clenched teeth. The yacht pitched on the sea.

Dionysus struggled to hold Ariadne at bay. Still under

his spell, she thirsted for Poseidon's blood because it was the first she had tasted, and she would not rest until one of them was dead.

"If she manages to survive the sea, I will hunt her down and tear her to pieces in front of you," Poseidon said. As he spoke, the flesh on his arms regenerated, and though he was whole, he was still covered in blood. "And you will be forced to eat each one, each slice of skin, each hot organ, and with each bite, you will know that it would have been easier to let me fuck her in front of you."

And then Dionysus heard a crack, and the entire ship was taken under. Water filled the room with such force, the only thing he was conscious of was the way it stole his breath before everything went dark.

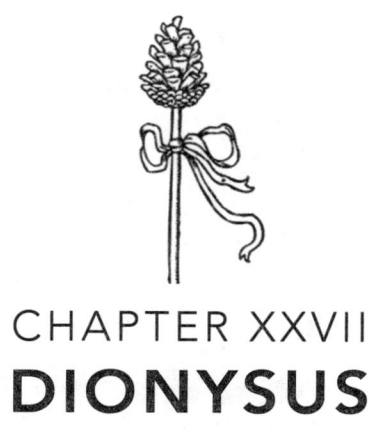

CHAPTER XXVII
DIONYSUS

Dionysus's head hurt.

He squeezed his eyes shut against the pain that radiated at his temples, tensing his whole body. His mouth was dry, his tongue swollen, and there was a roaring sound that filled his ears. He did not wish to awaken fully, but the longer he lay there and the more he surfaced to consciousness, the more he remembered about how he had come to be in this state.

Poseidon.

Ariadne.

He realized the roaring in his ears was the sea, and he forced his eyes open, blinking rapidly at the bright blue sky, realizing how the hot sun burned his skin.

He turned his head, and for a moment, his vision swam, but then everything came into sharp and sudden focus when he saw Ariadne lying some distance from him, half in water, half on land, and unmoving.

"No," he croaked, scrambling to his feet, slipping on

the sand as he rushed to her. "Fuck!" He fell to his knees beside her. The water surrounding her was tinged with scarlet. "Ari!"

He rolled her into his arms and cupped her face, brushing the sand from her cheek. She was too pale; even her lips were colorless. He checked for a pulse, pressing two fingers against the hollow area beneath her windpipe. A sluggish beat thrummed against his touch.

He placed a hand over her chest and closed his eyes, calling the water in her lungs, and after a moment, it spilled from her mouth. Yet there was still no movement, no sign of consciousness.

"Fuck," he cursed again, noticing a large gash on her thigh, and while he could heal it, he had no idea how long she had bled or what kind of infection might have set in while they lay unconscious on shore.

He pulled her close and then looked up to find an old man staring down at them from atop a hill of white rock. He had wild white hair and a matching beard, and his skin was dark and bronzed as if he had spent his whole life beneath the sun. He wore only a white sash around his hips, and it seemed as wispy as sea-foam.

He was divine, Dionysus was sure of it, but he did not know who exactly he was. There were numerous sea gods.

"Please," Dionysus called to him. "Please help us, I beg of you."

Though the old man stared directly at him, he turned and walked out of sight.

"No, please!" Dionysus gathered Ariadne into his arms and scaled the rocky hill, squinting against the brightness of the rocks, which reflected the sun's rays.

From time to time, he was blinded by the light, and he slipped, falling hard to one knee. He knelt there for a moment, his gaze dropping to Ariadne's face. Her lashes were long and fanned across her cheeks, which were turning rosy from the heat. While she was beautiful, he was desperate to look into her eyes once more. He couldn't imagine never feeling her gaze on him again.

He wouldn't.

He got to his feet. His knee stung, and he could tell there was blood, but it healed quickly. He tried to hold her closer to his chest, attempting to shield her face from the sun. As he came to the top of the white rocks, he saw the old man standing at the base of the hill as if he were waiting for them.

His heart rose a little, though he was not sure he should have hope.

"Will you help us?" Dionysus asked.

"I have helped you," said the man. "I dragged you from the sea."

Dionysus swallowed but his throat was dry and scratchy. "Then I am in your debt," he said. "Please—"

The man turned again, his bare back burning red from the heat, glistening with sweat.

"Please," Dionysus shouted. "I will remain in your debt if you will help us a little while longer. I need refuge—"

The man kept walking, disappearing down a sandy path overgrown with bright green flora.

"Wait!" Dionysus followed the man, who seemed to move like a ghost. He caught only a glimpse of him as he made his way down the shady path.

He was not sure how long he walked, but the terrain

shifted as they neared the mountainous center of the island. The air became wetter, the ground mossy and rockier as it inclined steadily upward until he rounded a corner and found the man standing outside a small cottage that had been built into the side of the earthy wall.

Dionysus stared at the man.

"You say you are in my debt," said the man.

"Whatever you wish," Dionysus said.

"There is a cyclops who resides here and eats my sheep," the man said. "Kill him."

"After she is better," Dionysus said. "I will see my debt through."

The man gave no other demands or acknowledgments, and before Dionysus could say more or even ask where they were, he vanished.

Alone, Dionysus carried Ariadne into the cottage.

He was surprised to find that the floor was covered in sheepskin rugs. There was also a cot and a small clay fireplace. A few pots and a kettle were stacked beside it.

It would be enough.

He lay Ariadne on the cot and covered her with one of the blankets. He smoothed her hair away from her face, letting his hand linger on her forehead, which was warm to the touch. Then he brushed his fingers over her heated cheeks.

This was fever.

He frowned and pulled the blanket back to look at the wound on her thigh. He would need to clean it before he could heal it.

He was still in Poseidon's territory, stranded in the middle of the sea, and while he could not teleport, he could call on his magic. The only danger was that the more he used, the more he faced the risk of drawing the god to them.

He spent a few more moments caressing Ariadne's skin, reluctantly pulling away.

"I'll be back," he said.

He didn't think she heard him at all, but it made him feel better to speak to her as if she could.

He left the cottage in search of firewood, herbs, and clean water.

Dionysus was familiar with the art of healing. He had been taught by Rhea, the mother goddess, who had cured him of Hera's madness. The only thing that worked against him on this island was that he was not familiar with the environment. He had no idea where to find supplies or even if the wild would have what he needed.

He gathered wood first and then set water from the ocean to boil, offsetting the lid so he could collect the desalinated water. He checked on Ariadne before he left again to search for herbs, which was a far more tedious task. There was a variety he could use for fever—elderflowers, yarrow, echinacea, willow bark. The issue was finding one of them on this island wilderness.

It took him a while, but he finally located lemon balm and aloe, which he would use to disinfect her wound. By the time he returned to the cottage, anxiety tore at his chest, worsening when he checked on Ariadne, whose fever had spiked. Her skin was on fire.

He drew the blankets from her body and set about drying the lemon balm leaves over the fire and boiling the clean water he'd made. He studied the wound on her leg. It was a jagged cut that ran the length of her thigh, and the skin around it was red and angry. He guessed that she must have hit some kind of rock after they'd been swept out to sea.

Dionysus was disturbed that he could not recall what happened in the immediate aftermath of Poseidon's yacht capsizing. He remembered holding on to Ariadne while she raged with madness, but at some point, he had lost consciousness, and so, it seemed, had she.

They were lucky they had managed to stay together.

He thought of Poseidon's final words to him and his threat against Ariadne. He would be careful with how he used his magic and hope they could make it out of Poseidon's realm before he realized either of them was alive.

Before he could clean her wound, he stripped her of her clothing, which was dry and stiff from salt water. There was nothing sexual about the process, and he hated having to do it without her knowledge.

When she was bare, he used hot water to clean her wound and then added a layer of aloe, leaving it uncovered. He would wait until tomorrow to heal it to ensure it was free of infection.

When the lemon balm leaves had dried, he crushed and boiled them to make a tea, and when it was cool enough, he propped Ariadne's head into the crook of his elbow and brought the minty drink to her mouth.

"Come on, Ari," he coaxed as he poured it into her mouth. He wasn't sure how much actually made it down her throat, but it would have to do.

By the time he finished medicating her, night had fallen outside the cottage.

He washed her salt-encrusted clothes and lay them by the fire to dry. While he worked, he could hear thunder in the distance—there was another storm raging at sea, and as it hit land, it roared around the cottage, causing it to creak and groan.

Though he grew tired, he remained beside Ariadne, too afraid to leave her alone even if it was to sleep.

For a while, he did not speak, just stared at her face as color slowly crept back in. Finally, he spoke.

"You make me feel insane," he said. "Like I'm struck with madness. I never thought I would want to feel that way again...but it's different with you."

He fell quiet and then he scrubbed his hand over his face, feeling ridiculous for having said that aloud, but at least she had not heard him.

―――

"Dionysus."

He turned his head toward the soft sound of his name. Fingers twined into his braids, and lips trailed along his jaw.

"Ariadne?" he murmured, though he recognized her scent, the heat of her touch.

"Dionysus," she said his name again, and it shivered across his skin. He wanted to capture her lips against his and taste her like he had that night in the pleasure district.

"Ari," he whispered, and her hold on him tightened.

"Dionysus!" she barked, and he opened his eyes to find her staring at him.

He blinked, realizing he had fallen asleep with his head on her cot.

"You're awake," he said, straightening, rubbing at a sore spot on his neck.

"Where are we?" she asked.

"I'm not certain," he said. "But if I had to guess, an island somewhere in the Mediterranean Sea."

She frowned and then shifted beneath the blankets, drawing in a harsh breath between her teeth.

"Careful," he said as she shoved the blankets aside to look at her leg. "I haven't fully healed you yet."

He rose onto his knees and placed one hand on her hip, the other just below her knee to keep her still.

"Why not?" she hissed.

"I can't heal an infected wound, Ariadne," he snapped.

It took a few more moments for her to relax, and once she did, they both seemed to realize she was naked. He lifted his hands and then quickly covered her again.

"I'll get you more medicine," he mumbled, rising from his place on the floor. He crossed to the fireplace and ladled more of the tea into a cup before returning to her and helping her sit up. "It's lemon balm," he explained as he placed the cup to her lips.

She held her hands against his as she drank and groaned in disgust as the tea touched her tongue.

"I know it isn't the best," he soothed. "But it will take the pain away."

When she'd had enough, he helped her lie back down, and an awkward silence filled the cottage.

"Do you...remember what happened?" he asked after a moment.

It took her some time to respond and when she did, her voice was a whisper. "Mostly."

Again they were quiet.

"Did he hurt you before we got to you?" He had to ask. He needed to know.

"Not really," she answered.

It bothered him that her answer wasn't a definitive no. He wanted to ask what Poseidon had done, but he also did not want to press. Last night had been traumatic enough.

"I'm sorry," she whispered.

Dionysus looked at her, but she was staring at the ceiling, a single tear trailing down the side of her face.

Her apology carried the weight of her regret, and it shuddered through him. It wasn't until she spoke the words that he realized he hadn't wanted to hear it because he did not deserve it. She'd had to face a horror that went well beyond simple consequences.

"Why are you sorry?"

"I should not have left to go to Poseidon on my own," she said.

He was quiet. Then he said, "I went to him the day before. I didn't tell you because I thought you were still angry with me and I..." He let his voice trail off. He hadn't wanted to disturb her, but it didn't matter anymore. What was done was done. Now, they had to move forward. "Poseidon does not have Medusa. I'm not sure where she is, but the worst part about her situation is that her power is only active after she's dead."

Ariadne met his gaze. "What?"

He had nothing more to say.

"Perhaps it's best if she stays missing," Ariadne said after a moment.

Dionysus did not disagree at this point.

Neither of them spoke for several minutes, and Ariadne had gone so quiet, he thought she had fallen asleep.

"I blame myself for what has happened to my sister," she said, her voice soft. She wasn't looking at him anymore; her gaze had returned to the ceiling.

"Why?" Dionysus asked, confused.

"Because I introduced them," she said. "Theseus was...with me first."

Dionysus bristled, surprised by just how hot his jealousy burned.

"Why didn't you tell me?" he asked, though that felt like a stupid question. She didn't have to.

"Because I'm ashamed," she answered, her voice thick with emotion.

Her words cut through him, and he shifted closer, hovering over her.

"Ari," he whispered, letting his fingers trail along her cheek. "You have nothing to be ashamed of."

"I don't care that he never loved me," she said. "But I hate that he does not love my sister and that she is so devoted to him. She deserves more. She deserves everything."

Dionysus studied her, and after a moment, he asked, "And what do you deserve?"

She was quiet.

"Ari?"

"Nothing," she said, looking at him.

He frowned and started to speak, but Ariadne pressed her fingers to his mouth and shook her head. Tears welled in her eyes and her mouth quivered. After a moment, she managed to speak in a quiet whisper, "Good night, Dionysus."

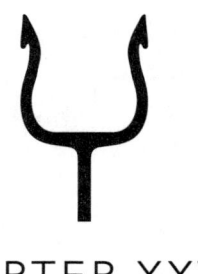

CHAPTER XXVIII
HADES

There was a roiling in Hades's stomach and an ache in the back of his throat. Poseidon had known Persephone's location; he'd taunted him with images of her broken and beaten body. *"You are here fighting for a woman who does not even belong to you while yours suffers at the hands of my sons,"* he'd said.

Hades had left.

There was no thought behind what fate he might leave Dionysus and Ariadne to face because he could not shake his fear, and after what had befallen Adonis and Harmonia, he had to know Persephone was okay.

Except that when he appeared in the basement of Club Aphrodisia, he found a bloodbath. Hephaestus was there holding Aphrodite by the shoulders. The Goddess of Love clutched a human heart in her hands. There were bodies strewn about, limbs misshapen and chests gaping. Then there was Persephone, who sat on her knees amid the carnage, the center of a circle of bodies.

None of them were lucky enough to escape her magic—Persephone included.

Her body was torn. It was the only way to describe it. It was the same horror he had witnessed the night she'd mistaken him for Pirithous. She was bent slightly, and as she breathed, her chest rattled.

Hades felt panic claw up his throat, and his heart wasn't beating right.

When she met his gaze, she opened her mouth and blood poured from it. She seemed surprised and a little confused. Then she swayed and Hades caught her, gathered her into his arms, and took her away.

Hades's hands shook.

They had never shaken before this moment. Perhaps this was the shock of everything settling deep into his bones now that he had gotten Persephone to safety. She lay in bed across the room, motionless but breathing. Though he had managed to heal her, he wasn't sure he could look at her without seeing her the other way—bloodied, broken, *dying*.

A shadow fell over him, and he recognized Hecate's magic. The goddess folded a towel around each of his hands, cleaning away the blood, though it was long dried. She was saying something, but he could not make out the words because the ringing in his ears was too loud.

The goddess knelt in front of him, a blur of color. He frowned, brows furrowed, unable to focus on any part of her.

Then he felt her hands on either side of his face and a rush of her magic.

"Hades?"

His eyes roamed her face until he was able to focus on her gaze.

"Hecate?" he said, and she offered him a small smile. "I'm here."

He stared at her a moment longer, and then his attention turned to Persephone.

"She is well, Hades."

He knew she meant to comfort him, but her words only brought anger and guilt. He should never have allowed her to go to Club Aphrodisia. He should never have entrusted her care to anyone save himself.

"You would have only encouraged resentment," Hecate said, reading his thoughts.

"I'd rather she resent me every day of our life if it meant never having to see her like that again."

"Careful of your words, Hades. Resentment is just as fatal a wound."

Hades ground his teeth. "Is it any more fatal than what I see when I look at her?"

"Magic can heal a wound to the flesh," she said. "But it cannot heal a wound to the soul."

"You do not have to remind me. I've had enough blows of my own."

"Then you should never want the same for Persephone."

Perhaps he would feel differently in a day or two, but right now he was tempted to never let her leave this island.

"What you should want is for her to learn to control her power," Hecate said, rising to her feet. "She would have been fine had she channeled it correctly."

"Is that not your job?" Hades asked curtly.

Hecate narrowed her eyes. "Careful, God of the Dead. I have little patience for your hubris."

Hades let his head fall into his hands, and he scrubbed his face.

"I'm sorry, Hecate."

She placed a hand on his head. "I know."

They were silent, and then Hades sensed Hermes's magic.

Anger coiled inside him, tightening his muscles, curling his fingers into fists. Shadows darkened the room as his hold on his glamour slipped, and when Hecate stepped out of his way, he met Hermes's gaze.

The god looked haunted, and angry lines were etched on his face. His white shirt was covered in blood.

"Before you begin," Hermes said, knowing what was to come, "you should know that Tyche is dead."

Those words made Hades straighten, and Hecate took an audible breath.

It was not news he had expected, but it gave context to the massacre he had stepped into and explained why Aphrodite had been present—to seek revenge on those who had hurt her sister.

"How?" Hecate asked.

"We do not know," Hermes said. "I...took her to Apollo."

"You left her," Hades said, his voice darkening. He took a step toward the god.

"Persephone ordered me," Hermes said.

"*I* ordered you to protect *her*," Hades said. His voice rose and black spikes shot from the tips of his fingers. "You swore an *oath*."

"I know," Hermes said, voice quiet, a shamed whisper as his eyes dropped to his feet. "I failed."

Hades reached him and placed a hand on his face, tilting his head back so their gazes met. His thumb settled just beneath Hermes's eye, the sharp tip of a spike drawing blood.

"*I* failed," Hades said.

Hermes flinched, those words far more painful than any wound Hades might inflict, and yet they were not enough. This type of magic required a physical debt, a daily reminder of the oath that was broken.

Hades braced his other hand against Hermes's head.

"I will never forget this night," Hades said. "And neither will you."

Then he jabbed his thumb into Hermes's face. The god screamed and jerked away, but Hades held him steady, dragging the spike down his cheek and over his lip before shoving him away.

Hermes stumbled back, his hand shaking as he held it to his bleeding face.

A normal wound to a god would have already healed, but this one would take time, and even then, it would scar. It was the price of breaking an oath.

"Do not worry," Hades said. "That will be the last oath you ever have to make."

Hades would never trust him with one again.

Hermes glared, eyes glistening, but he did not say a word as he vanished from sight.

Hades sat on the balcony just outside the room where Persephone lay sleeping. He remained awake, knowing his dreams would be no better than his reality—he would still relive what haunted him now.

There was a part of him that wanted to acknowledge the sheer terror of Persephone's magic, but he also knew she would not see the lives she took as power, though they had made the choice to attack her, to bargain with their lives, and all for a cause that saw another goddess dead.

He certainly had not expected Tyche to become the next victim, though she was as close to one of the Fates as any goddess could be, given her control over fortune. Perhaps that was why she was targeted. Triad and their followers—official or otherwise—had an obsession with free will, and powers like Tyche's threatened that because she could grant prosperity and abundance just as easily as she could take it away. Perhaps they blamed her for Demeter's storm.

Though Hades also knew it was futile to assign a reason to Tyche's death. Why she was chosen did not matter. It mattered only that she had died.

He knew when Persephone woke because he could hear the rustling of the sheets and the patter of her feet as she made her way to the balcony.

The closer she came, the more he tensed. As much as he wished to look at her, he was also afraid. Even now, all he could picture was her bloodied body. He feared never seeing her the same again.

"Hades."

Her voice was quiet, her presence warm. He could not help letting her coax his gaze, though even he felt the hardness of it.

"Are you well?"

She posed the question with a hint of hesitance, likely because she knew the answer.

"No," he said, dropping his gaze again. He could not maintain it, staring into her lively eyes, which conveyed a desperation to comfort him, though he knew what she would say. It was what they all said when he had faced her loss—*I'm here. I am well. She is here. She is well.* Her body screamed it, and he ached for her warmth.

His hands tightened, one around the glass he was holding.

He had forgotten about it but was glad for the distraction and swallowed a mouthful of whiskey, frowning when it tasted like ash.

Persephone neared and took the glass from him.

"Hades," she said again, and he closed his eyes as her voice shuddered through him. He waited to feel like he had some sort of control over his emotions before finally meeting her gaze.

"I love you," she said.

He ground his teeth against the feeling clawing up the back of his throat, burning the backs of his eyes. It was the first time he'd let himself think of the possibility of never hearing her voice again.

It was the first time he understood her desperation to keep Lexa alive. It did not matter that he was the God of the Dead and that she would come to reside in his realm forever. What mattered was that she was warm and well and whole, that her heart could beat in tandem with his, that she could go between their worlds, because that was what made her happiest.

She shifted toward him, and he leaned back as she settled in his lap and took his face between her hands. Her eyes were searching, observing.

"Will you tell me how you're feeling?"

He gripped the arms of the chair.

"I don't know that there is anything to say."

She was quiet, her hands still framing his face. "Are you angry with me?"

Her question made his chest ache. He hated that the consequences of his behavior left her feeling like she had done something wrong.

"I am angry with myself for letting you go, for trusting another to take care of you."

"I ordered Hermes—"

"He swore an *oath*."

He felt her tense.

"Hades, I hurt myself. I failed. I couldn't heal."

It did not matter. Hermes had been bound by magic to protect her. If Hades had been there, perhaps he could have helped her heal faster.

She leaned closer, tilting his head higher.

"I'm okay," she whispered. "I'm here."

"Barely."

Her words were no comfort. She had not been awake to know the struggle.

She slid from his lap and backed away. He recognized the look in her eyes because he felt the same pain.

"I don't know what to do," she said.

"You can stop," he said. "You can decide not to get involved. You can stop trying to change people's minds and save a world. Let people make their decisions and face the consequences. It is how the world worked before you, and it is how the world will continue."

She glared.

"This is different, Hades, and you know it. This is

a group of people who have managed to capture and subdue gods."

"I know exactly what it is!" he snapped, rising to his feet. "I have lived through it before, and I can protect you from it."

"I didn't ask you to protect me from it."

"I can't lose you," he said, planting his hands on the balcony behind her, trapping her against him. "I almost did, do you know that? Because I couldn't fucking get my mind right to heal you. I have held men and women and children to me as they bled like you bled. I have had my face sprayed with their blood. I have had them beg for their life—a life I could not extend or heal or gift because I cannot fight their fate. But you—you did not beg for life. You were not even desperate for it. You were at peace."

"Because I was thinking about you," she seethed, and Hades went cold. "I wasn't thinking about life or death or anything but how much I loved you, and I wanted to say it, but I couldn't…"

His throat felt full and his mouth quivered. He drew her against him and buried his head in the crook of her neck, hiding his face as he shook and shed tears. He hated this feeling that racked his body, hated that he had not been able to remain composed for her, but this had been too much. Too great a wound.

He drew comfort from her, and when he was calm, he straightened, still holding her close.

Persephone stared up at him, then pressed a hand to his cheek.

"Will you take me to bed?"

His stomach twisted, and he shifted close, leaning into her hips.

"I will take you here," he said, and her mouth opened against his, his tongue taking advantage of her own, her body bowing to his hands, ready and willing. He groaned as he pulled away, grazing her bottom lip with his teeth. "And then I will take you on the bed and then in the shower and on the beach. I will take you on every surface of this house and every inch of this island."

He dragged her by the hips as he returned to the chair, and she dropped the sheet she'd used to cover herself. As she returned to straddling him, he touched her breasts and sucked her nipples into his mouth. He liked the way her breath shallowed, the way her body rocked against him as he touched her. She sought his skin just as hungrily, parting his robes to sweep her hands along his chest and over his stomach, grinding her slick heat over him.

There was a moment when he wondered if he should do this, indulge in her so fully, but she had asked, and feeling her against him, warm and wet, reminded him that she was well.

He smoothed his hands over her ass and let his fingers part her flesh. She was hot and swollen, and she rocked against him, keeping a steady pace as she used him for her own pleasure. He knew she was finding release when her muscles tightened and her thighs squeezed around his, and then she pulled free of him suddenly and reached for his cock, sliding down his length until she was fully sheathed.

Fuck, she is brilliant, he thought as he leaned back to watch her ride him—her breasts bouncing, her body vibrating, her hands reaching behind her to tease his balls. When she grew tired, he took hold of her hips, alternating between helping her grind against him and thrusting into her. Now and then, he rose to kiss her, to let his mouth explore her skin, until he felt Persephone's body tense around him—every muscle and every limb.

When she came, it shuddered through her so hard it brought him to release.

He held her as she sagged against him, though he felt just as spent.

"Are you tired?" she asked, sitting back.

He wasn't tired, not in the way she meant. "I have never felt more alive," he said.

That answer seemed to please her because she kissed him, and when she stopped, she burrowed against him.

"Where are we?" She sounded sleepy and his hold on her tightened.

"We are on the island of Lampri. Our island."

"Our?"

"I've had it, but I rarely come. After I found you in the club, I did not wish to go to the Underworld. I did not wish to be anywhere but alone. So I came here."

Bringing up the club again shifted the energy between them; it grew heavy with grief and regret. Then she asked the question he had dreaded.

"Do you know if Tyche survived?"

"No," he answered. "She did not."

She asked about Sybil, Leuce, and Zofie.

"They are safe."

"And Hermes?" she asked.

Hades's response was to carry her to the shower.

Later, she asked, "How many people did I kill?"

He'd hoped she would wait longer to ask.

"What do you remember?"

"Hades—"

"Will it help to know?"

It would haunt her, but if she insisted, he would tell her. "Think on it. I say this as a god who knows the answer."

He took her down to the beach where they walked along the shore. He watched her run from the waves and laugh when the water rushed over her feet. Her ease made him happy. Hadn't she wished for a vacation? A weekend spent away from the Underworld with him? He supposed he'd granted her wish, even if it had been out of his own need for distance—a need to regain some kind of control. He thought coming here would give him a sense of peace, but he had yet to feel it. The reality was, outside this isolated island, a bitter snowstorm still raged, the ophiotaurus was still unaccounted for, and Tyche was dead.

The world was in shambles, and it felt as though he and Persephone were at the very center, each on different sides of a chasm that would tear them apart.

"How long has it been since you have visited the ocean?"

"For fun?" He felt the need to clarify because there had been plenty of visits for very unsavory reasons, no thanks to his brother. "I hardly know."

"Then we will make this memorable."

He wanted to say that this was already memorable, but she wrapped her arms around his neck and jumped to secure her legs around his waist.

"I love you," she said, and Hades kissed her until all thoughts of the outside world were gone and the only thing he could focus on was the way she felt against him and how badly he wanted to be inside her again.

"I want to show you something," he said as he pulled away.

"Is it your cock?"

Her directness made him chuckle.

"Don't worry, my darling. I'll give you what you want but not here."

He set her on her feet and took her hand, guiding her into the surrounding flora to a grotto where the water gleamed beneath a stream of sunlight.

He watched Persephone to gauge her reaction.

"Do you like it?"

"It is beautiful."

He grinned and undressed, diving into the pool. When he surfaced, Persephone still stood on the bank, watching him.

"Will you join me?"

She didn't hesitate, which made him think she'd waited so he could watch her undress—and he did so, gladly. As she entered the water, he pulled her to him and kissed her again.

"I will build temples in honor of our love," he said, lips brushing along her jaw, down her neck, along her shoulder. "I will worship you until the end of the world. There is nothing I wouldn't sacrifice for you. Do you understand that?"

"Yes," she answered, holding his gaze, but there was a part of him that knew she could not even guess the lengths he would go to for her, and yet she made her own promise.

"I will give you everything you ever wanted, even things you thought you would live without."

She was the only thing he'd ever thought he would live without, and yet she was here.

He claimed her lips in a deep kiss, holding her tightly to him until he was ready to pull her from the water, and when he did, he backed her into the wall roughly. Her eyes did not waver from his, did not communicate a hint of fear or unease.

He took pride in maintaining balance within their relationship, never wishing to be too domineering, but right now, he wanted that.

He wanted to command her and watch her obey.

"There is something dark that lives inside me. You have seen it. You recognize it now, don't you?"

She held his gaze as she nodded.

"It wants you in ways that would scare you."

He wanted so many things—to blindfold her, to bind her. He wanted her submission.

"Tell me."

"That part of me wants you praying for my cock. Writhing beneath me as I pound into you. Begging for my come to fill you."

Her eyes were so dark, they were ringed only with a thin circle of green.

"How do you prefer to receive prayer, my lord?"

His head rushed and he almost forgot to answer, so distracted by the way she looked and the words she'd spoken, so willing to please.

"On your knees."

She lowered to one, then the other slowly, and when her face was level with his cock, he gathered her hair into his hands.

"Suck me," he said.

Her breath was already warm on his cock, filling him with a heightened sense of anticipation. Even though he was expecting it, he still took a steady breath when she licked him. She was careful as she worked, her kisses numerous, her tongue teasing. When her mouth closed over the tip, she sucked him gently, and he groaned as his cock spasmed against her tongue. She was warm and wet, and now and then, she looked up at him as if to gauge how he was receiving her.

Fuck.

It was the most relaxed he'd ever felt, even though his body was completely on edge, his muscles continuing to tighten, building toward release.

She took him deeper and faster, and his grip on her hair tightened.

Then she opened her mouth wider and took him to the back of her throat, and if he hadn't been balls deep in her, it would have brought him to his knees.

She was all over him—the crown of his cock in her throat, his shaft in her mouth, the root in her hand.

It was everything. It was exquisite. He wanted to come but he also wanted to fuck her.

He took her face into his hands and pulled her from his cock, hauling her to her feet. He took her mouth in a possessive kiss while she jerked him in her hand and guided him to between her legs.

"Hades—"

He lifted her, slamming against the wall far more roughly than he intended. She didn't seem to care or even notice as his flesh parted hers and a strangled cry left her open mouth. He groaned, his chest feeling tight, the tension in his body climbing with each thrust.

"I want to feel your release," Persephone said, her fingers biting into his shoulders, her hips grinding into his. "I want your come inside me."

Perspiration broke out across his skin the faster and harder he moved, spurred by her words.

"I want to feel it drip down my thighs," she moaned, legs tightening around him as she neared release. "I want to be so full of you, I only taste you for days."

She grew rigid and her muscles clamped down around him as she came. It seemed to last forever, her body unable to stop shuddering. He ploughed through, pumping into her hard, chasing her orgasm with his own. His balls tightened, and the pressure in the base of his cock surged to the tip, and when he came, it felt just as explosive as her own.

His legs shook as he held her supple body, but he peeled them away from the wall and teleported, returning to the bedroom, where he knelt between her legs and took her against his mouth. She was swollen, still hot, and completely drenched with their mixed come, but he knew he could bring her release again, and when he found that sweet spot—the one where her fingers dug into his scalp, where her legs squeezed him, where her hips arched harder into his face—he held on and took her over the edge.

After, he lay beside her, and it was the first time in a long while that he fell asleep.

When he woke, Persephone was gone.

He rose from bed and found her on the balcony, looking out over the dark sea.

As he watched her profile, he knew she was troubled, and he could guess why. They had left New Athens to find refuge on an island in the middle of chaos, and Persephone felt guilty.

"Why do you frown?"

She jumped and turned to face him. She looked warm and rosy, her lips still swollen from his kiss, and she gazed at him possessively.

"You know we cannot stay here," she said. "Not with what we left behind."

He wished her possessiveness would override her guilt.

"One more night," he bargained.

"What if that's too late?"

It was a little childish, to indulge in his desires when there were so many threats, but he had never run before. He had been present for every challenge, even those that did not belong to him. At least here, he could protect the person he valued most.

He crossed to her and held her face between his hands.

"Can I not convince you to stay here? You would be safe, and I would return to you every free moment."

"Hades, you know I won't. What kind of queen would I be if I abandoned my people?"

"You are Queen of the Dead, not Queen of the Living."

Though he could not deny that this was what he loved about her—she cared about everyone, even when they did not deserve it.

No one deserved her, not even him.

"The living eventually become ours, Hades. What good are we if we desert them in life?"

He took a breath and then rested his forehead against hers, almost mournfully.

"I wish that you were as selfish as me."

"You are not selfish. You would leave me here to help them, remember?"

To please her.

He would do anything to please her.

He pulled back enough to hold her gaze and then kissed her. He would take advantage of every spare moment until they returned. His hands slid beneath her robe, over her soft skin to the space between her thighs where her curls were damp with need.

"Hades."

He could not discern her tone, if she was warning him or inviting him, but she did not pull away.

"If not another night, then at least another hour."

She sealed their agreement as her arms slid around his neck and he lifted her to the edge of the balcony, wedged between her thighs, pushing them wider. Her flesh felt swollen from their earlier coupling, but she was still wet, still needy.

"You were wrong," he said as he pulled out of her heat, her arousal thick on his finger. He took it into his mouth to taste her. "I am selfish."

"Only an hour," she said, eyes darkening as she widened for him.

He wasn't sure if she was reminding him or herself.

Hades smirked, his hand on his arousal. He pumped his fist up and down, preparing to enter her again, but the excitement that had engorged his flesh and made him pulse with need was doused the instant he felt Hermes's magic.

"Fuck."

He pulled Persephone off the edge of the balcony

just as the god appeared only a couple of steps away. He did not even give them the courtesy of distance.

"Hermes," Hades growled.

"I'd love to join you," Hermes said. "Another time, perhaps."

Hades hoped his glare communicated the violence he was imagining inflicting on the god, which went beyond the pain of the scar he now bore as a sign of their broken oath.

"Hermes, what happened to your face?" Persephone asked.

Hades's mouth tightened. He hadn't expected to feel anything when Persephone finally bore witness to the fallout, but the concern in her voice made him feel guilty.

To Hermes's credit, he didn't joke. He just smiled softly and said, "I broke an oath."

"What do you want, Hermes?" Hades asked, growing impatient. "We were about to return."

"How long is 'about to'?"

"Hermes—" Hades warned.

"Zeus has summoned both of you to Olympus," Hermes explained. "He has called Council. They wish to discuss your separation."

"Our separation?" Persephone asked, surprised. She looked from Hades to Hermes. "Are there not more pressing issues? Like Triad murdering a goddess and attacking another?"

There were certainly more important things, but Zeus was of the mindset that Triad was not a threat to Olympians.

Demeter's storm, on the other hand, was.

The longer it continued and the more fatalities, the more mortals began to question whether they should worship the Olympians. Less worship meant a change in strength—in power.

"I only gave you one reason Zeus called Council," Hermes said. "That does not mean we will not discuss other concerns."

"I will be along shortly, Hermes."

Hermes nodded, his gaze hard, softening as it slid to Persephone.

"See you later, Sephy," he said and vanished.

It didn't take long for Persephone to turn on Hades. "Did you do that to Hermes's face?"

"You ask and yet you know," he replied, frustrated.

"You didn't have—"

"I did." He did not mean to snap, but this was not something to argue about. He and Hermes had entered into a divine agreement that had divine consequences. "His punishment could have been worse. Some of our laws are sacred, Persephone, and before you feel guilt for what happened to Hermes's face, remember that he knew the consequences even if you did not."

She sagged beneath the weight of his reprimand, and that felt worse than her anger over Hermes's face.

"I didn't know."

Gods. He never got this right.

He pulled her close, holding her tightly. They should not be arguing or hurting each other right now. Zeus had just summoned him to Council to discuss their future, something he'd feared for a long time. If anything, they should be enjoying these final few moments before all hell broke loose.

"I'm sorry. I meant to comfort you."

"I know. It must be *trying*...to constantly have to teach me."

"I never tire of teaching," he said. "My frustration comes from another place."

"Perhaps I can help...if you told me more," she said.

Telling her more meant he would have to handle his fear of being too much for her—too angry, too vengeful, too cruel.

"I worry my words will come out wrong and that you will find my motives barbaric."

"I'm sorry," she said. "I think I gave you this fear when we met."

"No. It was there before you, but it only mattered when I met you."

She studied him quietly and then offered, "I understand Hermes's punishment. I am comforted."

He appreciated her words, even if he was hesitant to accept them.

He kissed her forehead, wishing they'd had the hour they promised—more so now given what they would face.

He pulled back.

"Would you like to accompany me to Council?"

"You are serious?" she asked, surprised and a little suspicious.

"I have conditions," he said, and she arched a brow as if to say *of course*. "But if the Olympians are to discuss us, it is only fair you are present."

She looked so grateful he felt guilty for ever having excluded her before, but she needed to hear this because it would make her angry, and he needed her fury.

"Come. We must prepare," he said, and they left the island for the Underworld.

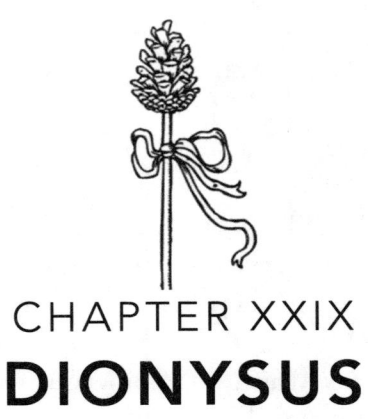

CHAPTER XXIX
DIONYSUS

Dionysus had left the cottage to retrieve more water from the ocean and find something that would suit for breakfast. When he returned, Ariadne was sitting up with her legs hanging over the edge of the cot.

"How are you feeling?" he asked.

"Better," she said, holding his gaze. Her eyes were warm, and they made his blood stir.

He cleared his throat and held up the basket he carried. "I hope you like figs," he said. "Because that's about all there is to eat."

"Figs are fine," she said as he set the basket by her feet and knelt before her.

The move felt intimate, more so because she held his gaze the entire time.

"Let me see your leg," Dionysus said.

He expected her to resist, but she drew the blanket back and let him see her wound, which was far less angry today. He drew his hand beneath her thigh and let the other hover over it, using his magic to heal and mend the cut until no sign of it existed.

"If you are able to use your magic to heal me," she said as he dropped his hands from her, "are we not able to teleport off this island?"

"I am not able to teleport within Poseidon's realm," he said.

Only the three could teleport to and from realms without permission. The only exception was Hermes.

"Even if I could get us off this island," he said, rising to his feet, "I must fulfill a debt before we leave."

"A debt?"

"An old man pulled us from the sea and led me to this cottage. In exchange, I agreed to kill a cyclops."

He was pretty sure the old man was a god, but who exactly he did not know.

Ariadne's eyes widened. "Why?"

He answered honestly. "Because I was willing to do anything to keep you alive."

A heavy silence stretched between them as he crossed to the hearth where he had laid her clothes to dry. They weren't in the best condition, but they were better than nothing. He gathered them and brought them to her.

"Get dressed," he said.

"Why?"

"You're more than welcome to stay naked," he said. "I will surely enjoy watching you traipse across this island."

She glared, and he was relieved that the tension that had been building between them suddenly felt familiar again.

"What if I don't want to watch you kill a cyclops?"

"Then you can close your eyes," he said. "But you aren't staying here."

"I can—"

"Don't tell me you can take care of yourself," he snapped. "We're on an island we know nothing about in the middle of Poseidon's territory. He was willing to rape you in front of me. He threatened to tear you to pieces and feed you to me. I'm not letting you out of my sight."

She did not argue, and to his surprise, she did not wait for him to turn away. She pushed the blankets away and stood completely naked and changed. He watched, transfixed, eyes scouring her perfect body. She was beautiful, and his mouth watered at the thought of tasting her.

She didn't even seem to notice he was staring. He was certain if she had, she would have snapped at him or turned away. As it happened, he managed to tear his gaze away and focus instead on deflating his growing erection while he packed food and water.

His efforts were in vain, however, and he only became more aware of his thickening arousal as they left the old man's cottage and began their search for sheep.

"Where are we going?" Ariadne asked.

They had been walking at a steady incline for about an hour, and she was lagging.

"Up," he replied.

Her silence worried him, and he paused to look behind him in time to see a fig flying toward his face.

Dionysus caught it and narrowed his eyes. "It's not nice to throw things."

"I wasn't trying to be nice," she hissed.

He sighed and then descended to her. He drew the water skin from around his neck and handed it to her.

"We need the height so we can see where we're at," he said as she took a drink from the bottle.

"You want to go all the way up this mountain just to see where we're at?"

"Do you have a better idea?"

"Yes. How about we just stay on flat land?"

Dionysus stared. "Are you afraid of heights?"

"No," she snapped.

He smiled. "You are."

"I am not!"

"Are too."

"Shut up!"

Dionysus laughed and she pushed him. He wasn't prepared for the shove, and it sent him to the ground. Ariadne must not have expected him to actually fall either, because she lost her footing and landed on top of him.

She leaned over him, her lips inches from his, her hands planted on his chest.

"Stop laughing," she said, but he already had.

He was solely focused on where their bodies met, where his cock swelled between her thighs.

Their gazes held, and then her eyes dropped to his lips and she said his name, a quiet and fervent whisper.

He wasn't sure who moved first, but their lips slammed together, and he groaned as their tongues clashed again. Fuck, he was starved for this—for her. He had never had enough. She was in his blood, filling his veins, an addiction so keen, he craved it.

He rolled, pinning her beneath him, grinding his hips into hers.

"Yes," she gasped into his mouth, and his body felt alive and electric.

He could not believe this was happening.

And then, all of a sudden, a terrible wail tore them apart.

Dionysus rolled off Ariadne, his gaze going to the sky where something white and round soared through the air. At first, Dionysus thought it was a rock, but...it was screaming.

"Is that...a fucking *sheep*?" Ariadne asked.

They exchanged a look, and then a booming sound filled the air and the ground began to shake. Far above the canopy, they saw the cyclops, who seemed to be running after the sheep.

"Guess he likes to play with his food," said Dionysus, looking at Ariadne, who rolled her eyes. "What?"

She didn't say anything but started down the mountainside.

"Where are you going?"

"Well, we don't need to go up anymore, do we?"

He vehemently disagreed, but that was mostly because he was still hard and his only source of relief was practically running away from him.

Stupid fucking sheep.

"You don't even know where you're going," Dionysus called to Ariadne, who walked several paces ahead.

He got the impression that she was running from more than just the height of the mountain. She was running from what had happened between them, from how quickly things had escalated.

She was running from him.

"I'm taking you to your cyclops," she said.

He smirked. He had let her lead for the last hour. Once she'd come to the bottom of the mountainous terrain, she'd started in the direction of the cyclops and the sheep. The issue was that the cyclops was huge, and his strides were miles, not feet.

"You think the cyclops will still be there when we make it out of this forest?"

"I'm not sure that's my problem, given you're the one with the debt."

"Considering you're the reason I have a debt, I think it is your problem."

He didn't really mean those words, and he could tell they hurt her because her steps faltered for the first time since they'd left the mountain.

"I... That isn't what I meant," Dionysus said.

He did not want Ariadne thinking that what had happened to her on Poseidon's yacht was her fault. She shouldn't have had to worry that Poseidon would assault her, but now, because the world valued his power and had for so long, she would never be safe from him.

"I think we both know what you meant," she said.

"I didn't—" He paused, frustrated. "Why do I always fuck up?"

She hesitated a step.

"What do you mean?" she asked.

"Look at where we are," he said, gesturing to his surroundings. "All because I promised you we would find Medusa and it turns out, it's probably best if we don't find her at all. I should have just continued helping

Hades look for the ophiotaurus. It would have been another way to Theseus."

Ariadne paused and turned to face him, a line of trees just behind her. "That ophio...what?"

"The ophiotaurus," he explained. "It's a half-bull, half snake creature that will likely be our downfall. So everything I have done will be in vain anyway."

"Has it been found?" she asked. "The ophiotaurus?"

"Not yet," he said. That he knew of, at least.

"Then nothing has been in vain," she said.

They stared at one another for a moment and his chest felt funny, eased by her words. She turned from him and stepped through the trees and screamed.

"Ari!"

Dionysus scrambled after her and was surprised when the ground gave way beneath his feet. He fell forward and rolled down the side of a shallow ravine. He came to a stop and groaned as he hit a large rock. Nearby, Ariadne sat up, holding her arm to her chest.

When the pain in Dionysus's side had subsided, he met her gaze.

"Are you all right?"

"I think I...hurt my arm."

Dionysus paled and crossed to her, kneeling in front of her. He took her hand in his and felt along her wrist and forearm. Though she winced, it didn't seem broken. He let his power radiate through her, knowing she'd fallen just as hard as he had and would likely be sore.

"You know what might have prevented this?" he said, glancing at her as he worked.

"Fuck off, Dionysus," she said, rolling her eyes.

He chuckled and helped her to her feet. He took

in their surroundings, realizing that they were in fact standing on the edge of a cliff that dropped down into a massive canyon. In the valley below, amid green rolling hills, several sheep grazed.

"Well," Ariadne said. "I found you sheep."

CHAPTER XXX
HADES

Hades left the island of Lampri with Persephone in his arms and took her to his armory, which was located far below his palace. It was full of ancient and modern weapons, shields, and armor. It was also where he kept the Helm of Darkness, one of three great weapons made by the cyclops Brontes and his two brothers, Steropes and Arges. Unlike Zeus's lightning bolt and Poseidon's trident, which could wound, Hades's helm's magic was far more subtle but no less powerful.

"Is this..."

"An arsenal," Hades said.

He watched Persephone as she scanned the room, eyes fixating on the very center where his armor was on display. She approached it, letting her fingers drift across the helm, which sat at the base.

"How long has it been since you wore this?"

"A while."

Since the Titanomachy and the Gigantomachy—the battles against the Titans and the Giants.

"I do not need it unless I am fighting gods," he explained, knowing she had likely thought of the most recent battle that involved the Olympians: the Great War.

"Or against a weapon that can kill you," Persephone said pointedly.

He reached around her and picked up his helmet.

"This is the Helm of Darkness. It grants its wearer the ability to become invisible," he said, and though it granted other abilities, only one power was relevant at the moment. "It was made for me by the cyclopes during the Titanomachy."

"Why do you need this helm? One of your powers is invisibility."

"Invisibility is a power I gained over time as I became stronger." As he had gained more and more worshippers. Then he smirked. "Outside of that, I prefer to protect my head during battle."

She was not amused as she took the helm into her hands, studying it closely. He knew she was focused on the marks that scored its surface—one for every blow he'd taken.

"I want you to wear this while at Council."

She looked at him, surprised. "Why?"

"Council is for Olympians, and I am not eager to introduce you to either of my brothers, especially under these circumstances. You will not like everything that is said."

And the helm would ensure she remained undetected while she listened.

"Are you worried my mouth will sabotage our engagement?"

He smiled at her arched comment.

"Oh, darling, I have faith your mouth will only improve it."

They stared at each other, and then her gaze dropped to his cock. She raised a brow.

"Are you going to Council naked, my lord? If so, I insist on watching."

"If you keep staring at me like that, we will not go to Council at all," he said, though he knew this visit was necessary, as much as he hated it.

He summoned his glamour and dressed them both.

"Ready?" he asked.

She did not speak, but she took his hand, and they left the Underworld for Olympus, appearing in the shadows, which vibrated with raised voices.

"This storm must end, Zeus!" Hestia said. "My cult begs for relief."

"I am not eager to see the storm go," said Zeus. "The mortals have grown too bold and need to be taught a lesson. Perhaps freezing to death will remind them who rules their world."

Persephone's head snapped toward Hades, her eyes narrowed in frustration. He recognized the problematic nature of Zeus's words. They were the root of every mortal's frustration with the gods.

He pressed a finger to his lips, signaling her to be quiet as he took the helm from her and secured it over her head. It was too large and did not fit properly, but the magic would work, and that was all that mattered. He kissed her fingers and then left her in the shadows.

He teleported.

"You will be reminding them of nothing save their hatred for you—for all of us," Hades said as he appeared in the middle of the arc of Olympian thrones and strolled toward his own beside Zeus.

"Hades." Zeus's voice rumbled like thunder.

It did not seem like his mood had improved since their visit, and considering this meeting had been called to discuss Hades's relationship with Persephone, that was not a good sign.

"From what I understand, Hades," said Ares, who lounged on his own throne, "the storm is your fault. Couldn't keep your dick out of Demeter's daughter."

"Shut up, Ares," Hermes snapped.

"Why should he?" Artemis asked. "He speaks the truth."

"You could have fucked a million other women, but you chose to stay with one," said Ares, a slant of amusement in his voice. "And the daughter of a goddess who hates you more than she loves humanity."

"That pussy must be gold," Poseidon said.

Spikes shot out of the tips of Hades's fingers, and he dug them into the arms of his throne. He spoke, his voice low and threatening. "I will personally cut the thread of any god who dares to speak another word about Persephone."

"You wouldn't dare," Hera said, as if she thought his threat were empty. "The consequences of killing a god outside of the Fates' will are dire. You could lose your dear goddess."

Hades tapped the ends of his clawed fingers against his iron throne, leveling his gaze at the Goddess of Marriage.

He did not speak, but his challenge was clear—*Try it and I will end this world*.

The silence that followed was tense and only eased when Athena spoke. "The fact remains that the snowstorm is causing great harm."

"Then we must discuss solutions to ending Demeter's rage," said Hades.

"Nothing will convince her to end her assault except the separation of you from her daughter," said Hera.

"*That* is out of the question."

"Does the girl even wish to be with you? Is it not true you trapped her in a contract to force her to spend time with you?"

He wanted to incinerate the goddess with his gaze. His sister-in-law had grown bold. Perhaps she needed to be reminded that he knew of her alliance with Theseus, but before he could speak, Hermes interrupted.

"She is a woman and she loves Hades. I have seen it."

"So we should sacrifice the lives of thousands for the true love of two gods?" Artemis's voice dripped with disdain. "Ridiculous."

The goddess shared a lot with her twin, Apollo, including the tragic loss of a great love. For Artemis, it was the princess Iphigenia, who had been sacrificed in her name during the Trojan War.

"I did not come here so that Council could discuss my love life," Hades said.

"No, but unfortunately for you, your love life is wreaking havoc upon the world."

"So is your dick," Hades countered, though that was likely a sore subject given that he had no balls. "And no one's ever called Council about that."

"Speaking of dicks and the problems they cause," Hermes jumped in. "Is no one going to speak about the trouble your offspring are causing? Tyche is dead. Someone is attacking us...succeeding in killing us...and you want to bicker about Hades's love life?"

"We'll have nothing to worry about if Demeter's storm continues," Artemis snapped. "Mortals will be frozen to the ground. It will be Pompeii all over again."

"You think Demeter's wrath is the worst that could happen?" Hades asked, his voice shaking the very air in the room. "You do not know mine."

He recognized that declaring war on his fellow Olympians was not the smartest move given that they needed to be united against Triad, but if they insisted on tearing him away from Persephone, he would handle the consequences as they came.

Then he felt Persephone's magic like a hint of sun streaming from the spring sky.

Fuck, he thought as she stepped into view from the shadows surrounding their thrones. She had dropped her glamour and stood in her true form, radiating beauty like wildflowers in a field. She said his name and held his gaze, offering a small apologetic smile.

It was likely she could feel his magic. It surrounded hers, waiting in the wings to whisk her away if anything went wrong.

"Well, well, well," Zeus said, leaning forward on his throne. Hades bit down on the inside of his cheek, a hot wave of anger curling in his stomach. "Demeter's daughter."

"I am," she said, casting her gaze to the right and then to the left.

"You have caused a lot of problems," Zeus said.

Her eyes flashed, and Hades found her obvious frustration amusing.

"I think you mean my mother has caused a lot of problems," she said. "And yet you seem intent upon punishing Hades."

Zeus sat back and shrugged. "I merely seek to solve a problem in the simplest way possible."

"That might be true if Demeter were only responsible for a storm, but I have reason to believe she is working with the demigods."

"What reasons?"

"I was there the night Tyche died. My mother was there. I felt her magic."

"Perhaps she was there to retrieve you," Hera said, waving her hand in the air as if to dismiss her accusation. Hades imagined that was what she'd hoped for too, given that she had every reason to want Triad to succeed. "As is her right by Divine law. She is your mother."

"Since we are basing our decisions on archaic laws, then I must disagree," Persephone said.

Hades's lips curled.

"On what grounds?" Hera countered.

"Hades and I fuck," Persephone said flatly. "By Divine law, we are married."

Hermes's choked on a laugh. Hades eyed him before returning his attention to Persephone, whose eyes were trained on Zeus. He didn't like it, knowing his brother enjoyed her attention and the fact that she had to appeal to him.

"It was my mother's magic that kept Tyche restrained," she said again.

"Is this true, Hermes?" Zeus asked.

"Persephone would never lie," the god replied.

"Triad is a true enemy," Persephone said quickly. "You have reason to fear them."

Hades was not surprised when a few Olympians laughed.

"Did you not just hear what I said?" Persephone asked, exasperated.

"Harmonia and Tyche are goddesses, yes, but they are not Olympians," said Poseidon.

"I'm sure the Titans thought the same of you. Besides, Demeter *is* an Olympian."

"She would not be the first who attempted—and failed—to overthrow me," said Zeus, who glanced toward Hera.

"This is different," Persephone said. "You have a world ready to shift their alliance to a group of people they believe are more mortal than god, and my mother's storm will force the decision."

"So we return to the real issue," Hera said. "You."

"If you return me to my mother, I will become a real issue," Persephone said. "I will be the reason for your misery, for your despair, for your ruination. I promise you will taste my venom."

Hades sat rigid and ready. His magic caressed Persephone's, a darkness ready to consume her light.

After a moment, Zeus spoke.

"You speak on what we will not do, but what would you have us do? When the world suffers beneath a storm of your mother's creation?"

"Were you not ready to watch the world suffer minutes ago?" Persephone asked, and Hades cringed, though he loved her more for calling his brother out.

The challenge was maintaining his favor, though he hated that they even needed it.

"Are you suggesting we allow it to continue?" Hestia asked.

"I'm suggesting you punish the source of the storm," Persephone said.

"You forget. No one has been able to locate Demeter."

"Is there no god here who is all-seeing?"

There was laughter.

"You speak of Helios," said Artemis. "He will not help us. He will not help you, because you love Hades and Hades stole his cattle."

He had yet to regret that choice even if it would help them now.

Persephone's gaze did not waver from Zeus.

"Are you not King of Gods? Is Helios not here by your grace?"

"Helios is the God of the Sun," Hera said. "His role is important—more important than a minor goddess's obsessive love."

"If he were so great, could he not melt the snowstorm that ravages the earth?"

"Enough!" Zeus snapped. Hades's magic inched closer. "You have given us much to consider, goddess. We will search for Demeter—all of us. If she is in league with Triad, let her admit it and face punishment. Until that point, however, I will defer judgment on your wedding to Hades a little while longer."

Hades's eyes shifted to Hera, who glared back at him. In reality, Hades had no hope that this meant Zeus would allow their marriage. He had merely offered this concession to impress Persephone.

"Thank you, Lord Zeus," she said.

Hades hated those words on her tongue.

Then Zeus stood and cast his gaze around the room. "On this night, we will say goodbye to Tyche."

Then he vanished.

Hera followed, but not before casting her murderous gaze on Persephone.

"See you later, Sephy!" Hermes said.

When they were alone, Hades left his throne and approached Persephone, who had already begun to explain herself.

"I'm sorry. I know you asked that I stay hidden, but I couldn't. Not when they wished—"

He kissed her hard before pulling away.

"You were wonderful," he said. "Truly."

"I thought they would take me from you," she said, quietly.

"Never," he whispered, speaking it against her skin like an affirmation, and perhaps if he said it enough, it would come true.

Hades's arms tightened around Persephone as soon as Hephaestus lit the pyre upon which Tyche lay. Her energy was dark, almost chaotic. He was not certain what she was thinking, but if he had to guess, she blamed herself for Tyche's end. It was not fair, given she had no control over her mother's actions, but that was the nature of a narcissist.

Demeter had taught Persephone that she was at fault for her mother's poor decisions.

"Tyche's death was not your fault," he said. He felt the need to say it aloud.

Persephone did not speak and he knew it was because she did not believe him. In the quiet, the fire popped and sizzled, and the smell of lavender and burning flesh filled the air.

"Where do gods go when they die?" Persephone asked.

"They come to me, powerless," he said. "And I give them a role in the Underworld."

"What kind of role?"

"It depends on what challenged them in their life as a god. Tyche, though, she always wanted to be a mother. So I will gift her with the Children's Garden."

"Will we be able to speak with her? About the way she died?"

"Not immediately," he answered. "But within the week."

Though Hades worried by then, it might be too late.

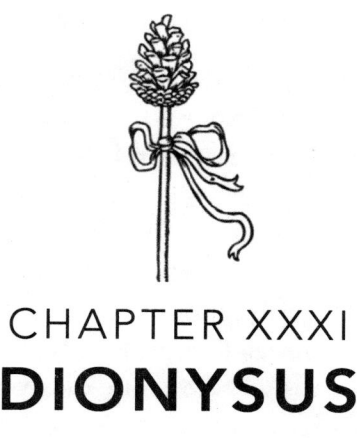

CHAPTER XXXI
DIONYSUS

Dionysus and Ariadne found a narrow path down the side of the cliff, but their progress was slow because Ariadne was afraid of heights, though she still refused to admit it.

"I'll carry you," Dionysus said.

"No. What if you fall?"

"I'm not going to fall. I'm a fucking god," he said, annoyed.

"As if that's somehow impressive," she snapped.

"I fucking *healed* you!"

"And yet we're still stranded on an island in the middle of the ocean because you can't compete with Poseidon's power."

He ground his teeth, wishing her words didn't sting. He knew his abilities did not compare to the God of the Sea, and he had thought often over the last two days that none of this would have happened had he had more power—had he been better.

Her words seemed to bother her just as much as they

had him, because her shoulders fell and she let her hands drop from the wall, shuffling toward him. He watched her approach, feeling heat creep into his body the closer she came.

"I'm sorry," she said.

He wanted to say something sarcastic, to draw her anger to the surface again, because that was more comfortable, but instead, he touched her cheek, brushing his fingers across her skin. She didn't pull away.

"I think you're hungry," he said.

She nodded and then let her head fall against his chest. She didn't fight him as he swept her into his arms. He carried her until he found an opening in the rocky wall—a shallow cave where they could rest for the night.

He left to gather wood for a fire. When he returned, they sat beside one another on a large log he'd dragged from the back of the cave and ate figs. Dionysus did not hate the fruit, but they reminded him of sex, and given that he sat in close proximity to the woman he'd desperately desired over the last month, eating them was torture. Their pulp was sweet like honey, their juice a fine syrup.

He glanced at Ariadne, who was sucking her fingers clean, and thought about how she probably tasted just like this, but then she spoke, and his thoughts came crashing down under the weight of his past.

"How long did you live with madness?" she asked.

Dionysus looked down at his half-eaten fig.

"A long time," he said, which was not a very good answer, but in truth, he did not know. "Long enough to wander the world...long enough to do horrible things."

Hera had known what she was doing when she had inflicted such a punishment. He'd been completely aware of the horror he caused but unable to stop it. He had wandered from country to country, body high and mind euphoric, dancing and drinking, dragging along followers who were just as crazed. Anyone who stood in his way or questioned his divinity faced his bitter wrath. He'd sentenced men to be torn to pieces by their daughters, punished them by killing their sons. He had driven people mad to the point of death.

"It was awful," she said.

Her words twisted in his gut, and suddenly, he had no appetite. He sat the fruit aside.

"I did not want to do it," he said, but he had not known what else to do. It seemed like the better alternative given the threat Poseidon posed.

"I don't blame you," she said, though he wasn't sure he believed that or if it would remain true. "I'm sorry you had to live like that for so long."

He said nothing, preferring not to indulge in this line of conversation. It took his mind to places he preferred to keep buried.

They were quiet, and the only sound was the fire crackling as it burned before them, casting shadows on the wall.

"Why did you become a detective?" he asked.

"I wanted to help people," she said.

"And now?" he glanced at her, but she was staring into the fire.

"I guess I just found out how hard it is."

It was strange to hear her say that—to acknowledge that it was hard to help people who did not want it, especially given that she felt responsible for her sister and was determined to rescue her from Theseus.

"It isn't fair," Dionysus said at length.

"What isn't fair?"

"That Theseus had you," he said, and while he spoke honestly, he couldn't look at her. "He didn't deserve you. He still doesn't, and yet he takes up so much space in your head."

He would give anything to replace him—to fill her mind every minute of every day.

"I'm sorry," he muttered and hesitated. "You should rest. I will watch over you while you sleep."

"I do not wish to sleep," she said, and there was a heat to her voice that drew his attention. They stared at each other, and the air between them felt thick and heavy. It always did, but this was somehow different, sharper. He could taste her desire.

He swallowed hard.

"Then what do you wish to do?"

He knew what he wanted—had wanted since the moment he met her—but that yearning did not prepare him for what she did next.

She leaned in and kissed him once, her lips barely brushing his. It was a chaste kiss, and he knew she was capable of more—he had experienced it before. When she went to pull back, he followed, anchoring his hand behind her head as his mouth collided with hers. She did not pull away, and he kissed her hard, channeling every ounce of frustration she'd built within him since the beginning.

This, he thought, *is how badly I want you.*

When he broke away from her, it was because he knew he would take this too far, but it was somehow harder to face her now, her eyes dark and her lips gleaming.

"I want you," she said.

Dionysus started to speak but no words came out. He tried again. "Are you sure you didn't hit your head when you fell earlier?"

"I'm of sound mind, Dionysus," she said, her voice taking on a frustrated edge. "I'm asking you to have sex with me. Are you saying you don't want me?"

"No," he said quickly. "That is not what I am saying at all. Fuck, Ari. I just want you to be sure."

She held his gaze. "I asked for it. I want it."

He swallowed hard. He wasn't sure why he was having such a hard time with this. It was everything he had dreamed about since he'd met her.

"Why me?"

She seemed to think the answer was obvious because she frowned and shook her head a little.

"Because you'll take care of me. Because…you have taken care of me."

Dionysus did not know what to say. There was a part of him that could not believe this was happening, no matter how much he'd desired it, no matter how many times he'd fantasized about it, no matter how often she'd aroused him just by being…her.

She rose to her feet and pulled her shirt over her head, baring her beautiful, full breasts. Her pants followed, and for a few glorious moments, she stood completely naked before him, the firelight and shadow dancing over her skin.

His cock thickened and throbbed.

She placed her hands on his shoulders as she lowered into his lap.

"Touch me," she whispered, guiding his hands to her breasts.

He obeyed her, squeezing her soft flesh, letting his fingers trace lightly over her nipples until they peaked, then he drew them into his mouth. All the while, she ground against his length, careful and slow. Each thrust made his head rush, and when he lifted his mouth to hers, he timed the thrust of his tongue with her body's movement.

"You are glorious," he said, tearing away from her mouth. "Up."

He was so used to her arguing that he expected resistance, but in this, she obeyed, and as she rose, his face was level with her center. Her curls were dark and he could smell her sex. It made his mouth water.

He let his hands slide down over her ass and met her gaze as he kissed along one thigh and then the other before guiding her to brace one of her feet on the log where he still sat. He rubbed his fingers along her opening, her skin like silk, hot and warm, and when he buried his head between her thighs and gathered her moisture against his tongue, she tasted just like the fucking fig—honeyed and sweet.

She breathed in tandem with his strokes, her fingers tightening in his hair as he directed most of his attention to a single point inside her while Ariadne rubbed her clit. He pulled his head back to watch her expression as they both worked together, moving at an equal pace to chase her release.

She clenched around his fingers hard and her hands clamped down on his shoulders as her whole body shuddered. Dionysus released her and rose to his feet, capturing her mouth against his, pulling her hard against him, ready to feel her heat on his cock. He lifted her into his arms and carried her to the wall, unwilling to take her on the hard ground of the cave.

It wasn't how he'd ever imagined this, but he would never miss the chance to know her in this way.

He pressed her back into the smoothest part of the wall as he kissed her, and when he pulled back, her eyes smoldered like embers. He could feel the impact of her gaze like a blow to the chest. He wanted her to look at him like this every fucking day.

"Undress," she said, pulling at his shirt.

He let her slide down his body and obeyed, and as he removed his shirt, she went for the button of his pants, kneeling before him as she pushed them down his legs. She didn't wait for him to step out of them before her hand closed over his cock and her mouth was on him.

He took a breath and then groaned, bracing one hand against the wall, twining the other in her hair.

She concentrated on the tip of his cock while she fisted his length, gently squeezing until he thought he would explode. He pulled her to her feet, slamming his mouth against hers as he took her into his arms again. He shifted her so that her shoulder blades met the wall. His cock was between her thighs, nestled against her heat. It made the bottom of his stomach knot with anticipation.

"Where do you want me to come?"

It wasn't the most romantic question, but it was important all the same, and he'd rather know now before he was too lost in her to think.

Her lips hovered near his as she answered, "Inside me."

The only way to describe how he felt was giddy, like he'd never fucking done this before, but he hadn't, not with her, and this mattered in ways he couldn't explain. He managed to lift her enough to settle the head of his arousal against her opening, and then he gripped her ass, spreading her as she slid down his length. They both groaned, and Ariadne's head rolled back against the wall as he moved her and his hips.

"Gods, you are perfect," he said, leaning forward to press a kiss to her mouth, then her jaw, then her chest. She felt so *good* and her muscles clenched around him like a hand jerking him off. He could not ask for more. He could not ask for better.

She was all there was, the center of his universe, and the more she responded to his body, the more powerful he felt.

"Fuck," Ariadne moaned, her voice vibrating with his thrusts. "You feel so good."

"Is it what you imagined?" he asked.

"Yes," she breathed, one of her hands moving to her breasts, and he marveled at how she touched herself. "Gods, yes, yes, yes."

Her voice went higher and her body tightened around him, and then she released all at once, suddenly heavier in his hands. But he did not care as he held her, driving his hips forward toward his own release, and when he came, he let his head fall into the crook of her neck, his legs shaking.

He couldn't move for a long moment, fearful he might fall and take her with him, and when he finally set her on her feet, he felt cold, the heat they'd shared suddenly gone. As he stared down at her, he realized he didn't know what to do now that they were finished.

Did he kiss her?

"Are you okay?" he asked instead.

"Yes," she said, her voice quiet.

He hesitated.

Fuck, why was this so hard?

"Let me get your clothes," he mumbled and shuffled away to retrieve her shirt and her pants.

"Thank you," she whispered as he handed them to her.

They dressed in silence and then sat beside each other in front of the fire just as they had before they'd fucked. He could still feel her on his skin, smell her sex in the air. He was hyperaware of how she felt beside him, both close but also so distant.

"Do you regret it?" he asked suddenly.

Her eyes widened and she met his gaze. "No. Do you?"

"No," he said. "I never will."

Dionysus woke with one arm hooked around Ariadne's stomach. The other was under her head and numb. After they'd had sex, they sat in a strained and awkward quiet. He had meant it when he'd told her he would never regret what happened between them, and while she'd said no in the aftermath, today was a new day, and it was possible she might see everything that had transpired between them in a different light.

Even with these doubts, he marveled at her beauty, hardly able to comprehend that he had woken up to her.

When she stirred, dread crept into his chest, roiling in his stomach as he tried to prepare himself for her rejection, but when she opened her eyes, she didn't roll from his grasp but turned to face him. He found he was just as confused as he was last night after they'd had sex. He no longer knew what to do with his hands, though he was highly aware of where they lay, splayed across her lower stomach.

"Good morning," he said.

She smirked, her eyes dropping to his lips. "Good morning."

He felt like that was enough of an invitation and kissed her, his lips brushing hers softly. He had every intention of letting that be enough, but he had not accounted for her enthusiasm, which was like a hot claw curling into his stomach.

Her mouth widened and he took her deeper, tongues clashing. She pulled on his shirt, luring him on top of her, and he gladly obliged, his hips settling against hers, and as they descended further into this mad passion, his thoughts went wild—they were going to fuck again.

This was more than he'd ever imagined.

A sudden, sharp bleating tore them apart.

Dionysus wasn't sure what it was about the sound, but it had sent his heart into a complete panic, and when he looked up from Ariadne, he saw a sheep at the entrance of the cave, its narrow pupils unnervingly focused on them.

Ariadne giggled.

"Go away," Dionysus said, throwing a small pebble in its direction. The sheep offered another wavering cry.

"Don't hurt him!" Ariadne said, pushing against Dionysus's chest as she sat up.

He wanted to groan, knowing there was no reclaiming what might have been now that they had been interrupted.

"He's lucky it's just a pebble," Dionysus said. That was twice now he had been cockblocked by a fucking sheep.

He hated this island.

He fell onto his back and stared up at the cavernous ceiling while Ariadne inched closer to the animal. It was lucky Ariadne was nice, because if Dionysus had gotten near it first, he would have tossed it across the island like the cyclops had done yesterday.

As he worked through his frustration, the cave, which was full of morning light, darkened. He turned his head in time to see a large eye block the opening, and then a giant hand shoved its way into the mountain's side.

"Ariadne!" Dionysus shouted as she screamed, enveloped by the cyclops's fingers. As the monster tore her away, parts of the cave came with it, and the ground shook beneath his feet. Dionysus summoned his thyrsus and dodged falling rock, racing toward the edge of the cave, catapulting through the air to rescue Ariadne, but the cyclops's other hand closed around him. Trapped beneath his fingers, Dionysus thrust the sharp end of his thyrsus into the cyclops's palm. The monster screamed and then slung him away.

He flew through the air and hit the earth, moving through each layer as if it wasn't a solid thing beneath his body. When he finally came to a stop and managed to climb out of the hole his body had made, Ariadne and the cyclops were gone.

CHAPTER XXXII
HADES

Okeanos sat in a chair opposite a mirror.

He was still and restrained, head leaning back, chest gaping from where Aphrodite had stolen his heart. From what Hades knew, she still had it in her possession, though he had not seen her or Hephaestus since that night at Club Aphrodisia.

"What's the mirror for?" Hermes asked.

Hades met Hermes's gaze in the reflection. "So Okeanos can watch his torture."

"Kinky," Hermes said and then turned to look at the demigod. "I hope you tear him to pieces."

Hades glanced at the god and raised a brow. "And you said I was a psychopath."

"He ripped Tyche's horns from her head," Hermes said.

Hades narrowed his eyes.

"Wake," he commanded, and the man took a gasping breath, though his chest rattled where his heart should be. He looked around, confused, until his eyes settled on his reflection in the mirror, as Hades expected it would. Then his gaze moved to Hermes, then to Hades.

"Release me!" Okeanos demanded.

Hermes chuckled. "Listen to him. He thinks he can command you."

"How dare you," Okeanos seethed. "I am the son of Zeus!"

"So am I," said Hermes. "It's nothing to brag about, trust me."

"You wish to overthrow my brother, and yet you use his name as if that will protect you," Hades said. "The hypocrisy."

"You are one to speak, God of *Death*," Okeanos seethed.

Hades dealt a blow to the demigod's pristine face, the bones giving way beneath the punch. His head snapped back, and blood poured from his ruined nose.

"That," Hades said, shaking the blood off his hand, "is not my title. You would do well to remember, given that you are in my realm."

Okeanos smiled despite the blood, despite his ruined face. "Is that all you've got?" he asked. "A measly punch to the face?"

Hermes cast Hades an annoyed look. Hades knew what he was thinking—*I told you to tear him limb from limb*.

Hades was not so certain he wouldn't by the end of this.

"Go ahead," said the demigod. "Do your worst."

"The audacity," said Hermes.

"I believe the word you are looking for is hubris,"

said Okeanos. "Isn't that what you Olympians like to punish? The so-called fatal flaw of humanity?"

Gods rarely needed to punish hubris. The consequences came about on their own, as they clearly had with Okeanos, yet he seemed oblivious to that fact.

"Why Tyche?" Hades asked.

Okeanos shrugged. "It seemed like the thing to do."

"You ritualized the death of a goddess who caused you no harm," Hades said, his voice shaking.

"There are always casualties in war, Hades."

"As you well know," Hades said pointedly.

For all his arrogance, Okeanos seemed to forget that he too was dead.

"Well, perhaps neither of us would have been here had you not fucked the wrong woman."

Hades punched Okeanos again. This time, his teeth bite into Hades's skin. The cuts healed as quickly as they were formed.

"He's fucking with you, Hades," Hermes said.

"You don't even know how much you are to blame." The demigod laughed, though it sounded more like a wheeze.

Hades lifted his fist again, but before he could strike Okeanos, Hermes caught his arm and met his gaze.

"Allow me," he said and turned toward the demigod. "It seems you've forgotten our strength. Let me remind you."

Okeanos smirked.

"Give me your best, trickster."

"I'll do more than that...*brother*," said Hermes, and with a wave of his hand, the chair disappeared from beneath Okeanos, and before he could fall to the floor,

Hermes caught his arm and twisted it behind his back until the bone cracked, sending him to his knees.

The demigod screamed, huffing through his teeth, but still he managed to speak. "You may have strength," he said. "But we have weapons."

"So we have heard," Hades replied. "Why don't you tell us more?"

Okeanos shook his head, breathing raggedly.

"Oh, don't stop talking now," Hermes said, jerking his broken arm back farther. "You were just getting to the good part."

Okeanos's roar of pain echoed throughout the room, making Hades's ears ring. It was a while before it dissolved into sobs.

"Nothing to say?" Hermes asked, and just as he was about to wrench the demigod's arm again, he spoke.

"No! No! Wait!" Okeanos shouted into the floor. "Please. Please. Please."

"Since you said please," Hermes said.

"There's a warehouse in the Lake District. The weapons are made there. The attacks…they were tests to see if they would work."

"Are you saying they were…practice?"

Hermes spoke deliberately, his anger barely restrained.

"The goal was always to lure an Olympian," Okeanos admitted.

"*Which* Olympian?"

"At first…Aphrodite," Okeanos choked out.

Hermes and Hades exchanged a glance. "Why?"

"Because Demeter ordered it. It was her price in exchange for the use of her magic."

Hades had suspected Demeter was helping supply

weapons to Triad, but he had not expected her to have ordered the attacks on Adonis and Harmonia. Now that he considered it, though, it was not all that surprising. Aphrodite was the only reason Hades had approached Persephone that evening at Nevernight. Her challenge—make someone fall in love with you—was why he'd drawn the Goddess of Spring into a bargain that saw her visiting the Underworld nearly every day.

Hades frowned. What Okeanos said was true—he really was to blame.

"Then why Tyche?" Hermes asked, holding his arm tighter.

"I don't know," Okeanos moaned. "But Demeter's war is with the Fates."

"Well, that was easy," said Hermes.

Then he jerked on Okeanos's arm, tearing it from his body as if it were nothing but paper. While the demigod writhed, Hermes tossed the limb aside, and it landed with a wet thud on the floor in front of Hades.

He met Hermes's gaze, whose face was spattered with blood, and spoke over the demigod's guttural cries. "Do what you wish with him," Hades said. "But I want that warehouse destroyed, and while you're at it…burn that club to the ground."

"You got it," said Hermes as he took Okeanos's other arm in hand, but before he could tear it from his body, Hades left.

Hades disrobed and climbed into bed beside Persephone. He lay on his side, watching her sleep, thinking about what Okeanos had said. The news that Demeter had been behind the attacks on Adonis, Harmonia, and Tyche would likely devastate Persephone.

It was one thing to suspect her mother's involvement, another to have it confirmed.

There were times when Hades wondered how someone could possess this kind of hatred for anyone, but Demeter continued to maintain it for him, and all because the Fates had woven his destiny with Persephone's. Something he considered a gift was Demeter's greatest curse.

Persephone stirred, and Hades's heart raced as she faced him. He recognized how often he had taken this for granted, and he never would again. There was a part of him that was angry he could not simply live in the knowledge that she would be beside him forever.

"You're awake," he said, his voice quiet.

She smiled, as if she were amused. "Yes. Have you slept?"

"I have been awake for a while," he said, though he had not slept at all. He reached between them and brushed her lips with the tips of his fingers. "It is a blessing to watch you sleep."

She shifted closer, and he wrapped his arms around her as she laid her head on his chest.

"Did Tyche make it across the river?" she asked.

"Yes, Hecate was there to greet her. They are very good friends."

They were silent for a moment, resting in each other's warmth. He would have liked to stay like this forever, buried beneath Persephone's weight, but he knew they were running out of time. The attacks on the Divine were escalating, and Persephone was still not able to control her power. He thought of what Hecate had said in the aftermath of the club. *She would have been fine had she channeled it correctly.*

"I would like to train with you today," he said.

"I would like that."

Hades frowned, doubtful. "I don't think you will."

He had no intention of making this fun. When she faced him, it would be as if they were enemies on the battlefield.

She would not even know him.

Persephone pulled away to look at him.

"Why do you say that?"

He studied her for a moment, then his eyes fell to her lips.

"Just remember that I love you."

She shifted on top of him, sliding down his length until she had consumed him. There were no words as they moved together, nothing spoken beyond their quickening breaths. He lost himself in her, knowing that when he surfaced, things might not be the same again.

Persephone's gaze touched every part of him. Hades could feel it tracing over his body, burning his soul. It would make this harder for her, worse for him. He could already see uncertainty moving behind her eyes. She did not know what to make of his flat affect. He had never been indifferent to her, but they had entered a space where teaching her meant showing her a harsher power—the terrible truth of the gods.

She was afraid to hurt people.

She could not be afraid to hurt the Divine.

"I will not watch you bleed again," he said. It was an oath to her, a promise to himself.

"Teach me."

She thought she knew what she was asking, just as she had the night they'd met in his club.

"*I haven't taught you how to play,*" he'd said.

"*Then teach me,*" she'd replied.

Those words had sealed their fate.

They were responsible for every high and every low he had experienced in his life.

But not even Hades could have guessed that it would lead to this very moment, when he stood opposite his lover, his future wife and queen, with the intention of becoming her enemy.

He hated it, how it made him feel wrong and lent a darkness to his magic he might not use otherwise, but that was what Persephone needed to experience.

Whatever Persephone saw in his expression made her frown.

"You love me," she said, though he could not tell if she was asking or reminding herself.

"I do," he said, his guilt as heavy as his magic, which blanketed the air, silencing the Underworld.

Persephone looked around warily, her anxiety spiking her own power. Yet it was not enough, and he mourned that she had not put up enough of a barrier to withstand the wraiths he had summoned.

They formed from shadow, starved for souls, and hunted anything with one—even goddesses. They barreled toward Persephone, nearly imperceptible until they hit, jolting her. It was hard to watch her take the blow, her body moving unnaturally as the wraiths passed through. She fell to the ground, gasping for air.

"Shadow-wraiths are death and shadow magic," he said. "They are attempting to reap your soul."

Persephone met his gaze. "Are you...trying to kill me?"

He gave a hollow laugh. There was a part of him that could not believe he was doing this and that she was asking him to.

"Shadow-wraiths cannot claim your soul unless your thread has been cut, but they can make you violently ill."

Slowly, she rose to her feet.

"If you were fighting any other Olympian—any enemy—they would have never let you up."

"How do I fight when I do not know what power you will use against me?"

"You will never know," he said.

It was how they would have to fight the demigods—blindly.

The point was to be prepared for anything.

The hand of a corpse burst from the ground beneath her. Persephone screamed as it took hold of her ankle, yanking her to the ground, dragging her down into its pit, intent on burying her alive.

"Hades!"

He hated how she screamed, hated more how she cried for him, how he had to watch her fingers dig into the dirt as she tried to escape his magic.

He was also frustrated.

She relied on him because he was present when she needed to rely on herself. She was intelligent and capable; she had power raging inside her, power that had turned his own magic against him, and yet she acted like a mortal caught in a spiderweb.

Finally she did something.

She twisted onto her back and tried to claw at the hand, but Hades's magic was defensive, and as soon as she touched it, spikes shot from the shadowy skin. A cry tore from her mouth, but she swallowed it, and he felt her anger rising.

Yes, darling. That's it.

Her magic flared, and a thorn burst from her palm. She shoved it into the hand, and it released her. Though she was free of one challenge, he sent another her way. Another wraith flew toward her.

Her body bent back as it passed through her, and Hades felt like her screams were stealing his soul, piece by piece.

He swallowed the bile that had risen in the back of his throat as he approached her, chest heaving as she tried to catch her breath.

"Better," he said. "But you gave me your back."

He stood over, wanting so badly to take her into his arms, to tell her he would protect her from all this, but the truth was, he couldn't. He had already proven that, so she had to learn.

Her hands shook and she curled them both into fists. He vanished as her magic roared to life and brambles sprouted from the earth around her. It was her attempt at fighting him back, and it had failed.

She got to her hands and knees, glaring at him, her cheeks tearstained.

"Your hand gave away your intentions. Summon your magic with your mind—without movement."

"I thought you said you would teach me," she seethed, and it almost felt like she was saying *I thought you loved me.*

Hades took a painful breath. "I am teaching you. This is what will become of you if you face a god in battle. You must be prepared for anything, for everything."

She looked miserable, and he felt responsible as she stared down at her hands.

"Up, Persephone. No other god would have waited."

Her eyes met his, different this time—different even from the night she'd nearly destroyed his realm. That look was the pain of betrayal. This was fury.

As she got to her feet, the ground began to shake, and the earth rose. Hades dispatched his shadows, and he watched both shocked and amazed as they bent to her will, slowing and sliding up her arm, seeping into her skin.

She shuddered for only a moment before her palm uncurled, and her fingers were tipped with black claws.

"Good," he said.

Persephone's eyes shifted to him, and she smiled, but it was short-lived before her knees hit the ground. She threw back her head, convulsing as Hades fed her illusions he had crafted from her greatest fears.

This was torture.

He knew that, but it was also warfare, and he was not the only god capable of it. She would have to learn how to perceive the difference, but as he watched her fears unfold, he knew she was already lost—she believed this was reality.

Perhaps he should not have started with Demeter, whose harsh expression filled even him with dread.

"Mother—" Persephone choked, her panic so real, Hades could feel it gripping his lungs, stealing his own breath.

"Kore," Demeter said, the name Persephone hated most coming out like a curse. She tried to rise, but Demeter was on her, yanking her from the ground. "I knew this day would come. You will be mine. Forever."

"But the Fates—"

"Have unraveled your destiny."

Hades's stomach twisted. It was one of his greatest fears too.

Demeter teleported with Persephone, which only added legitimacy to the illusion, because the scent of her magic permeated the air. Hades watched as Persephone found herself back in the glass greenhouse—her first prison.

She raged inside, kicking and screaming, spewing hatred at her mother, who only regarded her in mocking amusement.

She went silent when everything went dark as she was forced to watch the lives of her friends play out in her absence. The worst of the visions was when Leuce returned to him as a lover. He could barely watch as Persephone's expression turned to horror. Her fingers curled into fists, her chest heaved, her eyes watered—and then she screamed.

She screamed so loud, she shook.

"*Persephone*," he said, but her reality had already shifted, and when Hades witnessed it, he could taste something metallic in the back of his throat.

They were on a burning battlefield, and he lay at Persephone's feet, speared by her magic.

It reminded him of Katerina's vision, the one that would come true if the ophiotaurus was slain.

"Hades," Persephone said, her voice shaking. She fell to her knees beside him as if she had been struck.

"I thought...I thought I'd never see you again," he whispered, and he lifted a trembling hand to her face.

She pressed his palm flat against her cheek. "I'm here," she whispered and closed her eyes against his touch, until his hand fell away. "Hades!"

"Hmm?"

"Stay with me," she begged through her tears, taking his face between her hands.

"I cannot," he said.

"What do you mean you can't? You can heal yourself. Heal!"

"Persephone," he whispered. "It's over."

"No," she said, her mouth quivering.

"Persephone, look at me," he said, desperate for her to see, to hear his final words. "You were my only love—my heart and my soul. My world began and ended with you, my sun, stars, and sky. I will never forget you but I will forgive you."

"Forgive me?"

It was then she realized what Hades already knew—that she had raged against him and destroyed the Underworld. She had destroyed him.

Was this why she refused to harness her magic? Because she feared this potential? This reality?

Hades had to be honest. He feared this too, and it only got worse as Persephone tried to undo her magic, as she begged Hades to stay.

"No, please. Hades, I didn't mean—"

"I know," he said slowly. "I love you."

"Don't," she begged. "You said you wouldn't leave. You *promised*."

Persephone's screams rang in his ears as her visions went dark. Her body went still and then she fell.

Hades hurried to catch her and held her close. She was not out long when her eyes blinked open and met his, glistening as they filled with tears.

"You did well."

She covered her mouth and then her eyes as she sobbed, her body shaking in his arms.

"It's okay," he soothed. "I'm here."

But she only seemed to cry harder. He hated that he could not calm her, and he felt worse when she pulled away and got to her feet.

"Persephone—"

"That was cruel," she said, standing over him. "Whatever that was, it was cruel."

"It was necessary. You must learn—"

"You could have warned me. Do you even know what I saw?"

She acted as if it was easy for him to witness too.

"What if the roles had been reversed?"

"They have been reversed," he snapped. They'd been *real* for him.

She blanched, looking horrified. "Was that some kind of punishment?"

"Persephone—" That had not been his intention. Fuck. He reached for her, but she took a step away.

"Don't." She put her hands up. "I need time. Alone."

"I don't want you to go," he said.

"I don't think it's your choice," she said.

She took a deep, shaky breath, as if she were gathering the courage to go, and when she did, Hades let out his own frustrated cry.

CHAPTER XXXIII
DIONYSUS

Dionysus found himself walking up the fucking mountain again, and though he was faster without Ariadne, he'd have much rather had her slowing him down.

Gods fucking dammit.

He was angry, but worst of all, he was worried.

Dionysus did not know much about cyclopes beyond their role in ancient times. Then they'd been great craftsmen and had helped the Olympians in the battle against the Titans. While he knew some remained in their employ, they did not all appear to have evolved the same, as evident by this one, which roamed this island eating sheep. And if it ate sheep, it surely ate humans.

As Dionysus came to the top of the mountain, he looked out on the island, which was far vaster than he expected; the terrain varied from deep canyons to rolling hills. Despite how huge the cyclops was, Dionysus caught no sight or sound of the monster. It was as if it'd disappeared.

That only served to make his anxiety worse, and he felt a familiar and dreadful shuddering deep in his bones. He ground his teeth and fisted his hands against it, unwilling to let the madness take root. If it did, he would be useless, and it was likely that more than just the cyclops would die in his quest to rescue Ariadne.

He took deep breaths until the feeling subsided, though the fact that it had come about so quickly unnerved him. But for now, at least he was in control.

He tore down the mountain, retracing his steps to the cottage where he'd healed Ariadne, then to the shore where he'd met the old man.

"Hello!" he bellowed. "I need you, old man! The cyclops has taken her!"

He paced the shore, catching a glimpse of something in his periphery. He startled and turned to find the strange god standing on the rocks, the same as he had been before.

"Where the fuck do you come from?" Dionysus demanded.

"I saved your life once," the old man said. "What more could you want from me?"

"The cyclops has taken my—" Dionysus hesitated, uncertain of what he intended to say. "The cyclops has taken Ariadne, and I do not know where. I have climbed that gods-forsaken mountain. I have looked across this fucking island. Where has he taken her?"

"To his lair, I imagine."

Dionysus took a step, his hands shaking.

"*Where*?" he asked through gritted teeth.

"Across the way," replied the man. "On the other side of the strait."

Dionysus turned to where the old man had nodded, and far in the distance, with an ocean between, was something that resembled a set of islands, but they were barely visible on the horizon.

Dionysus whirled. "Did you not think this information valuable enough to share when you asked me to kill him to begin with?"

"Nothing is as valuable as your life," replied the man.

Dionysus took another seething step. "And I am this close to taking yours!" He turned toward the shore and started toward the sea.

"I would not do that if I were you," the old man warned.

Dionysus glared. "How else am I supposed to get to the fucking island?"

"It would be better if you waited for the cyclops to return."

"Did you miss the part where he has her?"

The old man stared, and then he looked off toward the island again. "There are only two ways to the island—through the wandering rocks between which the sea is violent, or through the strait where Charybdis and Scylla reside. Take either and you will surely die."

Dionysus was more than familiar with the two sea monsters the old man had mentioned, given that he was in the habit of collecting them. Charybdis was a deadly whirlpool that could destroy ships in an instant. Scylla was a six-headed monster with three rows of deadly, sharp teeth. They lived opposite one another so that any who passed through their realm and attempted to avoid one hit the other.

"Thanks for the vote of confidence," Dionysus muttered as he waded into the ocean.

He tried in vain to run against the current until he could propel himself forward with his arms and legs. At first, he moved along at a steady pace, but the water felt heavy and his arms burned. It became harder to keep his head above water, and the salt stung his nose and the back of his throat. The more his arms and legs burned, the less certain he was that he was actually moving forward, though nothing was fast enough while Ariadne's fate was unknown.

He gave a frustrated cry and rolled onto his back, floating atop the surface, and though the sun reddened every inch of his exposed skin, he remained there until he felt like he could move again.

As he neared the strait, he could feel the current of the ocean change and knew that Charybdis was active, churning the sea with all her might. He made a wider arc, hoping to avoid the pull, aware that doing so would bring him closer to Scylla, though if he was going to take on the two monsters, he'd prefer the one he could stab over the one that might drown him.

As he entered the strait, he remained close to the cliff wall, grasping the rocks to keep from slipping away into Charybdis's whirling depth, which was visible on the surface, a stormy vortex of foaming water and ocean sand. As the water raged, it pulled roughly at his skin. If Charybdis did not take him, she might surely skin him alive.

He was so focused on avoiding the pull of the current, he forgot to look up until a pebble struck his face, and as he turned his gaze skyward, he came face-to-face with six heads racing toward him.

"Fuck!"

He moved at the last second, narrowly missing the teeth of one of the six heads. The heads plunged into the ocean below, and as they pulled back, five of them roared in a high-pitched wail, while one of them clutched a dolphin between its horrible teeth. Jealous, the two heads on either side hissed and nipped, and soon they were fighting, Pieces of dolphin flesh rained down on him as they engaged in combat, while the other three heads were trained on him.

Dionysus summoned his thyrsus just as the heads descended on him again. This time, he shoved the sharp tip of his staff through one head as its mouth came down around him. It reared back screaming and then fell into the water, limp. The other five heads shrieked and came for Dionysus at once.

"Fuck!"

He climbed onto the neck of the head that had gone limp and raced across it, chased by the others, teeth bared. He turned quickly, jumping atop the slippery head of another before quickly scrambling onto another when its whole head was bitten by its partner.

This thing is stupid, Dionysus thought as he shoved the end of his thyrsus into it, ducking when two other heads raced toward him and crashed into each other. The impact jarred him, and he slipped, falling into the ocean below where he was swept into Charybdis's current, and though he paddled fiercely against it, it drew him under. Water filled his nose and mouth, and he grasped desperately at anything within reach, which was nothing save the solid weight of the water on him. But as Charybdis churned, he was brought closer to the other side of the strait, so close that his body rammed into the rocks, breaking skin.

Before he could try to dig his fingers into the rocks, he was whisked away again. The water fought him, taking him under, but he managed to position his arm so the next time he came closer to the wall, he rammed his thyrsus into it. With it lodged in place, he held on as the water raged around him. Opposite him, the remaining heads of Scylla screamed, though while Charybdis churned, he was safe.

Scylla retreated up the rock to her cave, dragging two of her limp heads behind.

Dionysus was not certain how long he clung to the end of his thyrsus, but he could sense when the current around him slowed, and soon Charybdis ceased her assault. When it was done, he felt weak, and swimming out of the strait felt impossible, though he made it. And when he saw the cyclops's island ahead, he felt a sense of relief.

He propelled himself forward, thinking only of Ariadne—of the way she tasted and how she kissed, of the feel of her body, inside and out.

He had not had her long enough to lose her forever.

The thought kept him moving, and when he could touch the sea floor, he dug his feet in and tried to run. Staggering to the shore, he fell to his knees, landed facedown on the beach, and lost consciousness.

A strangled cry startled him awake.

He rolled over and back onto his ass, summoning his thyrsus, only to come face-to-face with a sheep.

"*Where* did you come from?" he snapped.

The sheep bleated loudly, and Dionysus cringed at the sound.

His head hurt and the sun was making it worse. He squinted against it and then took in his surroundings. The cyclops's island was vast and wooded, rising into high mountainous slopes.

If the cyclops was among them, he wouldn't even be able to tell.

"Baa!" The sheep's sudden cry made him jump.

"Gods, will you stop *doing* that?"

He glared at the sheep, but it continued to scream at him.

"What do you want?" he snapped, rising to his feet.

The sheep backed away and started to turn, bleating as it did.

"I'm not following you," Dionysus said.

The sheep seemed to glare at him, which left him feeling uneasy. It reminded him of Ariadne's frustration.

Fuck. What if she was turned into a sheep?

What if this sheep was Ariadne?

You're a fucking idiot, he scolded himself.

But he found himself taking a step toward the sheep, which offered another wavering cry and started toward the dense green forest ahead.

Dionysus followed, feeling ridiculous but also hoping the animal might lead him to others and eventually the cyclops.

The terrain was thick and varied, the ground covered in vines that tangled around his feet. After tripping once, he was over it and used his magic to untangle a clear path as he followed the sheep. It was not long before they came to a quiet river, which the sheep seemed to follow up and into the more mountainous part of the island.

At some point, the sheep stopped and turned to look at him. "Baa!" it yelled.

Gods, he hated that sound, but the creature was looking up at a towering cave where several sheep had been herded.

His heart raced. This had to be where the cyclops lived.

Dionysus scrambled across the river and scaled the steep incline to the cave where the cyclops's flock was gathered. The ground was littered with bones, and his stomach churned as he fought the urge to call out to Ariadne, not knowing what lingered in the cave. Most of it seemed to be well lit, given that part of its roof had fallen away, allowing sunlight inside. The entrance sloped down, and at the base, there was a lake, green in color.

The sheep gathered near it, their bleating cries echoing inside the cave, making him cringe, though he hoped it was enough to drown out his footsteps as he crept through the shadowy parts of the cave, scanning the mossy rocks for any sign of Ariadne.

Suddenly, he spotted a hand sticking out from the darkness.

"Ari!"

Her name slipped from his mouth, a cry he could not contain. He raced to her, and his hand had barely touched hers when she was yanked away.

Dionysus's eyes widened, and he looked up into a pair of red-tinged eyes.

"What the fuck?" he said and summoned his thyrsus. The weapon seemed to trigger the creature in the shadows, because its eyes flashed and then it bellowed, lurching toward him and out of the shadows.

Dionysus was face-to-face with the ophiotaurus. Its shoulders were hunched, neck curved, hoofs pawing at the ground.

He took a step back and it lurched forward, farther into the light. He noticed the rest of its body, which went from that of a bull to a serpent tail, curled protectively around Ariadne, who was not conscious.

"Ari," Dionysus said again and started toward her, but the ophiotaurus roared, and he froze. "Easy," Dionysus said, holding up his hands. "I came to rescue her."

The ophiotaurus stared, still rigid.

"Were you protecting her?"

The creature huffed a few times, and Dionysus took the opportunity to inch toward her. The ophiotaurus kept its spotted and striped tail around her.

He didn't take his eyes off the creature until he had knelt beside Ariadne. He wanted to take her into his arms, to make sure she was okay, but he knew if he moved too fast, the ophiotaurus would react.

Instead, he stroked her face and muttered her name, and her eyes fluttered open.

For a moment, she looked confused, but when she recognized him, relief flashed in her eyes, and she smiled, though it vanished quickly, and the ophiotaurus emitted a low, hollow sound as a shadow passed over him.

Something was wrong.

He stilled and turned in time to see the cyclops's hand barreling toward him.

"Stranger," said the cyclops. His voice was loud and made Dionysus's ears ring. The cyclops's fingers closed around him tightly, stealing his breath as he lifted him to his narrowed eye. "Have you come to steal my sheep?"

"No," said Dionysus, struggling in his grasp. His hands were trapped too close to his body to summon his thyrsus. Even if he could, he'd have no room to use it. "I have not come to steal your sheep."

"Then you have come to kill me," the cyclops said, voice rising in rage.

"Are those your only visitors?" Dionysus asked. "Those who wish to steal your sheep and those who wish to kill you?"

"Visitor?" the cyclops asked. "I do not know that word. I know thief. I know murderer."

"Then allow me to teach you a new one," said Dionysus.

"I also know trick, stranger," said the cyclops. "Is this one?"

"No," said Dionysus. "But if it would please you, I will make an offering of good faith."

"What sort of offering, stranger?"

"My very best wine," he said.

"I do not know wine," said the cyclops.

"Then you shall know today," said Dionysus. "Let me down and I shall share my drink with you."

"No tricks?" said the cyclops, wary but curious.

"None," Dionysus promised.

The cyclops glared at him for a few moments, long enough to make Dionysus think he might choose to crush him instead, but then he set him on his feet.

Dionysus took the opportunity to glance in the direction of Ariadne and the ophiotaurus, but he could not see them, thoroughly hidden in the darkness of the cave.

He took a few careful steps toward the pool in the cave.

"Do you drink this water?"

"Drink, wash, bathe," said the cyclops.

Dionysus tried not to look disgusted as he summoned his magic and turned the still water into a deep, red wine.

He turned toward the cyclops. "Drink, friend."

The cyclops looked at him warily but eventually dipped his cupped hand into the wine and brought it to his lips. He paused a moment, as if testing the flavor on his tongue, and then he seemed to purr, pleased. "It is good," he said, and then he shoved his face into the wine and drained the whole lake.

The cyclops sat amid his sheep as Dionysus waited for the wine to take root, trying his best not to glance too often at the darkness where Ariadne and the ophiotaurus still hid.

"What is your name, stranger?"

"Oh, I am no one," said Dionysus, unwilling to offer up his name, though he was a god.

"No one?" the cyclops said. "I am Polyphemus."

"A pleasure," Dionysus said.

"How did you come to my island?" the cyclops asked.

"I was stranded here," said Dionysus. "I am afraid I do not know where I am."

"This is Thrinacia," Polyphemus said. "You will have to know if you are ever to visit again."

Dionysus smiled. At least he had some idea of where they were now.

"Would you like more wine?" Dionysus asked.

"But there is not water for you to turn into wine," said Polyphemus.

"I do not need water to make wine," said Dionysus,

and suddenly, the lake was full again, and Polyphemus downed another batch.

This time, when it was gone, Dionysus refilled it without question.

"That is quite a trick," said Polyphemus, blinking slow and swaying.

"I suppose it was a trick," said Dionysus.

"I think...I think I have been poisoned," said the cyclops, slurring, and then he swooned and crashed to the ground, unconscious.

As soon as he was down, Dionysus scrambled to his feet, and Ariadne darted from the shadows, throwing her arms around him.

"Dionysus," she whispered, and his name had never sounded so good.

He kissed her, holding her face between his hands. "Are you okay?"

"I'm fine," she said, holding his gaze. "You came for me."

"Of course," he said.

The ophiotaurus huffed, drawing their attention. Ariadne pulled Dionysus closer to the creature.

"This is Bully," she said. "He's a friend."

"Bully?" Dionysus asked. *A friend*?

"That's his name," she said.

"You named the ophiotaurus?"

"Well, I had to call him *something*," she said. "He kept me safe."

He smiled at her and shook his head a little. "Fuck, Ari. I didn't know what to think. I—"

"It's all right, Dionysus," she said, her eyes searching his, and then he kissed her again.

He was too relieved to think twice about it, too grateful she was okay to feel awkward or uncertain.

"How sweet," said a voice, and then the ophiotaurus roared.

They whirled to find Theseus standing a few paces from them with two men, who had restrained the ophiotaurus. Bully was pushed onto his back so his soft belly was exposed.

Before Ariadne could scream, Theseus plunged his knife into the creature's stomach to the hilt and then dragged it down.

"No!" Ariadne shrieked, jerking in his arms as Dionysus held her, unwilling to let her go.

The ophiotaurus's bellow turned into a low and keen cry before it was silent.

With the creature slain, Theseus turned to them, blood spattered across his front, while the two men who accompanied him fished inside the ophiotaurus for its intestines.

"Fuck you!" Ariadne spat, tears tracking down her face.

Dionysus held her against him, his arms crossed over her chest.

"Now this I never expected," Theseus said. "Bonding with a monster other than Dionysus."

"You're the monster!" she seethed.

Theseus placed a hand over his heart. "Oh, how you wound me, Ariadne, and after I have taken such care of your sister."

"Don't let him provoke you, Ari."

"Is it Ari now?" Theseus asked, his eyes shifting to Dionysus. "Did you call her that before or after you fucked?"

Dionysus glared. He did not know if the demigod was only assuming, but his fixation on Ariadne was evident. This was more than jealousy. It was obsession.

Theseus's men finished with the ophiotaurus, and they each approached and flanked him with handfuls of intestines.

"It is too bad, *Ari*, that you cannot see my potential even as I hold it in my hands."

"You aren't holding anything," she said.

Dionysus chuckled, but Theseus glared, and his lip curled into a snarl, then he held up his bloodied knife.

"Oh, look. You were wrong."

Theseus appeared in front of them and drove his knife toward Ariadne. Dionysus blocked the blow with his arm, though the blade lodged in his flesh. At the same time, he summoned his thyrsus and shoved it into the demigod's stomach. Theseus's eyes widened. Dionysus wrenched free from Theseus, who stumbled back, holding his hand to his stomach where he bled.

"If you hurt her, I will kill you," said Dionysus.

"Get in line," Theseus replied, and when he smiled, his teeth were bloody.

It seemed that Theseus was slow to heal. What a grave weakness. He was clearly very much aware of that fact too, because he decided against attacking again, and instead, he and his two men vanished, taking the ophiotaurus's intestines with him.

When they were alone, Dionysus released Ariadne, who raced to the creature, lowering to her knees. A horrible cry tore from her throat as she extended a shaking hand to pet the creature, and the only thing Dionysus knew to do was hold her too.

"I hate him," Ariadne said on a shuddering breath.

"I know."

He wasn't sure how long they sat there, but the sudden flare of Hermes's magic straightened his spine. He knew it because it had haunted his dreams a time or two—and as it surrounded them, they were pulled from the cave and deposited on the hard and pristine floor of Hades's office at Nevernight.

"I never thought I would see the day you knelt at my feet," said Hades.

Dionysus ignored Hades's comment while he stood and helped Ariadne up. She wiped at her face with her hands, trying to recover from the horror they'd experienced in the cave.

When he did look at the god, Hades's expression was a strange mix of confused frustration.

"Perhaps you should try kneeling too," Dionysus said. "You'll have to get used to the pose. Theseus has slain the ophiotaurus."

CHAPTER XXXIV
HADES

Hades sat on the couch staring into the fire, and while he should be thinking about what he would do now that the ophiotaurus had been slain, he could only think about Persephone. It wasn't even the way they'd parted that weighed heavily on his mind; it was their future, which would likely not exist once Zeus discovered everything he'd been hiding. How long until his brother discovered not only that the ophiotaurus had been killed but that Hades was also responsible for its resurrection because he'd killed one of Zeus's closest friends and servants, Briareus?

How long until Zeus not only forbade his marriage but wed Persephone to someone else?

He recognized his concerns were selfish, and if it were Persephone, she would worry over humanity, but humanity rebuilt itself even in the aftermath of the most destructive battles.

There would be nothing to rebuild if he lost her.

There was a knock at his door.

He looked up to see Ilias enter his office.

"I thought you might want to see today's headline," he said, handing Hades a copy of the *New Athens News*. A bold, black banner ran across the top of the page, a screaming insult:

Meet Theseus, the Demigod Leader of Triad

It seemed Helen had made good on her threat against Persephone. Hades scanned the article, his jaw slowly tightening the more he read her biased words. The issue was that mortals would not see her favoritism; they would see a man who was half human, someone who could understand and fight for them.

They would see their reality reflected in Theseus's words.

"Why not let the gods speak for themselves? I knew it wouldn't take long for one—or many—to execute their wrath upon the world."

Perhaps that was what made this so damning—the fact that he wasn't wrong.

If anything was going to turn mortals away from the gods, it would be their own actions, and right now the greatest threat was Demeter's storm.

"His timing is commendable," Hades said, tossing the paper into the fire.

"I imagine he is feeling pretty powerful right about now," said Ilias.

Hades imagined he did, so what could they do to remind him of his insignificance? After a moment, he rose to his feet and turned toward the satyr. Usually, he would give him some kind of direction or order, but given the circumstances, he had no idea how to proceed.

He truly felt like he had no control.

Hades manifested in Hecate's meadow. He was there for only a moment when he felt the goddess's magic blast toward him. While it took him by surprise, he managed to teleport before the blow struck, except that she was one step ahead, and as soon as he appeared, her power hit him square in the chest.

The force sent him flying backward. He felt the ground give way at his feet as he dug his heels in to stop himself from crashing into the mountainous walls of the Underworld.

Even as he came to a halt, he sensed Hecate's approach. The problem was, he could not see her, but her magic crackled in the air, raising the hair on his arms.

"I'm not sure what I did," Hades growled. "But you could try talking to me before going to battle."

"Perhaps you should have considered doing the same before you put Persephone through such torture," she said. Her voice came from all around, as if there were hundreds of Hecates surrounding him.

"I *know*," he said, frustrated. "I am an idiot."

"You are more than that," she replied, appearing before him, arms crossed.

"Are you done?" he asked.

"Maybe," she said, sounding uncertain.

Hades glared. "You know, I was feeling horrible about it even before I came to you. Now I somehow feel worse."

"As you should. What were you thinking?" she demanded.

"What do you mean what was I thinking? I was training her! And don't critique my methods. You're the one who stabbed her just so you could teach her to heal."

"I *prepared* her," said the goddess. "Was it kind? No. But you may have undone all the progress we have made!"

"What progress?" he seethed. "She nearly tore herself apart."

"She is afraid she will destroy the world with her magic, and you brought that to life for her."

Hades averted his eyes, frustrated with himself. "I don't know what else to do, Hecate. We are headed for darker times, and she is not learning fast enough."

"You cannot force this, Hades, just because you are afraid."

He ground his teeth.

"The best thing you can be for her is a safe space. You are where she heals from trauma, not where it seethes."

"Do you really think that's still true?"

"Yes," Hecate said. "So go apologize to your queen."

Hades had promised never to use invisibility to spy on Persephone, but this did not feel so much like spying as it was waiting. He hadn't intended to hide at all, but Ivy had warned him she wasn't in a great mood—and then she'd thrown her tablet against the wall. Now Leuce was here, *chatting* about nothing when he had things to do.

Gods, he was so *frustrated*.

Finally, the nymph left, and he made a move before anyone else could interrupt. But for some reason, when he stood opposite her, he suddenly did not know what to say. His mouth was dry, his words gone.

Maybe it was because of the way she looked at him, hesitant and haunted, or maybe it was the way the room felt, awkward and thick with an unfamiliar tension.

"Do you need something?" she asked.

Need something? As if he had come to ask for a cup of sugar. He reached behind him and turned the lock into place.

"We need to talk."

Persephone stared at him for a moment and then pushed away from her desk, folding her arms over her chest. "Talk."

He held her gaze as he approached and lowered to his knees before her. He watched her chest rise sharply as he placed his hands on her knees.

"I am sorry. I went too far."

It was almost like she could not handle the impact of his apology, because she lowered her gaze from his, staring at her fingers, which she twisted nervously.

"You never told me you had the power to summon fears," she said.

"Was there ever a time to speak of it?"

She said nothing, though he still felt like he had failed her in some way. It wasn't the first time she had asked him to share more of himself, but some things just seemed to come with time. Perhaps they were both impatient for forever.

"If you will let me, I'd like to train you differently. I'll leave the magic to Hecate, and instead, I will help you study the powers of the gods."

He would begin with himself, though the thought was uncomfortable, but he felt like it was the only way he could atone, given that he had used powers against her she did not know he had.

"You would do that?"

"I would do anything if it meant protecting you," he

said. "And since you will not agree to being locked away in the Underworld, this is the alternative."

She gave him a small smile, and he wanted more.

"I'm sorry I left," she said.

"I do not blame you," he said, even if he hadn't liked it. "It is not very different from what I did when I took you to Lampri. Sometimes, it's very hard to exist in the place where you experience terror."

She let her gaze fall, licking her lips.

"Are you angry with me?" he asked, leaning closer.

"No," she said, looking at him. "I know what you were trying to do."

His chest felt tight. "I would like to tell you that I will protect you from everyone and everything...and I would. I would keep you safe forever within the walls of my realm, but I know what you wish is to protect yourself."

"Thank you."

This time, he smiled. He wanted to kiss her, but she did not lean into him. Instead, her gaze shifted to her desk.

"I assume you have already read this," she said.

"Ilias sent it this morning," Hades said. "Theseus is playing with fire, and he knows it."

"Do you think Zeus will act?"

"I do not know," he said, frowning. There was a part of him that hoped he wouldn't, given that Theseus had killed the ophiotaurus. "I do not think my brother sees Triad as a threat. He does, however, see your mother's association as dangerous, which is why he shifted his focus to her."

"What will become of her if Zeus can find her?"

"If she ceases her attack upon the Upperworld? Probably nothing."

"You mean she will get away with the murder of Tyche?"

Given that Zeus seemed to believe in survival of the fittest, he likely believed Tyche just wasn't powerful enough.

"She must be punished, Hades."

"She will be. Eventually."

"Not only in Tartarus, Hades," she insisted, leaning forward her in chair.

"In time, Persephone," he said, covering her hands with his own. "No one—not the gods, certainly not me—will keep you from retribution."

That was a promise he could keep.

They stared at one another for a moment, and then he rose to his feet.

"Come," he said, bringing her with him.

She hesitated. "Where are we going?"

"I just wanted to kiss you," he said, claiming her lips with his. He felt relief pour over him now that she was in his arms again.

He called on his magic and teleported them to the site where Halcyon was being built. She had only seen models and sketches of the future rehabilitation center, but he had never brought her here in person.

There had been a lot of progress on the project, even with the snow, and as she pulled away from him, he heard her breath catch.

"Oh."

"I cannot wait for you to see it in the spring," Hades said. "You will love the gardens."

They were only plans now, but they would be extensive.

"I love it all. I love it now." Then she looked at him. "I love you."

He smiled at her and kissed her again, then led her inside. It was far easier to visualize what it would look like when it was finished because most of the walls were up, though there was still so much work to do.

He took her into each section of the facility.

"My hope is it feels less like a hospital and more like…a place where people can really heal," he said. He frowned at himself because he wasn't sure if those were exactly the right words, but it was important to him that when they were ready to receive patients, it wasn't a place that felt sterile and inflexible. He associated those things with judgment, not acceptance or even hope.

"It will be everything it needs to be, Hades," Persephone said, and her assurance eased the anxiety he'd started to feel over the whole thing. He felt a little ridiculous, but he was personally invested in the success of this project. It had been inspired by her, and for some reason, if it was not everything he intended, he would feel like he failed.

He was getting used to that feeling, and he didn't like it.

He took her upstairs, which were just hollow wood that creaked beneath their feet, bringing her into a large room that had floor-to-ceiling windows making up most of the walls, just like his office in Alexandria Tower. The purpose was to give her a view of the gardens—specifically Lexa's garden—but it also overlooked the woods surrounding the property and New Athens's dreary and misty skyline.

He hung back near the entrance and watched her cross the room to stare out at the landscape. She took a breath, as if it brought her peace.

"What room is this?"

"Your office," he said.

She whirled to face him.

"Mine? But I—"

"I have an office at every business I own. Why shouldn't you?" he said, his lips curling. "And even if you do not work here often, we'll put it to use."

She laughed and her eyes were so bright, they burned in this muted weather. She looked beautiful, and for a moment, all he could think about was how he was grateful she could continue to look at him like this—like she loved him no matter what would come. And more would come. In some ways, this felt silly—the planning, knowing that Theseus had killed the ophiotaurus, knowing that Zeus had yet to approve their marriage, that Demeter's storm still raged.

And yet he still hoped.

She shivered and brought her arms over her chest to try and contain it. He hadn't noticed the cold.

"We should return," he said.

Except she didn't move, and he didn't call his magic.

Persephone licked her lips, and his eyes fell there as she whispered his name.

He was on her the next second, and as he kissed her, he pressed her into the unfinished wall, his hips grinding into hers. He was highly aware that he was insatiable, his desire for her never-ending. His need for sex went beyond anything that was normal, and he used it for everything—to avoid, to process, to heal—but Persephone was no different.

"I need you," he groaned as his mouth left hers to trail down the column of her neck, his hands smoothing down her back to her ass. Persephone was already fumbling with the buttons on his shirt, and for a moment, he considered stripping them both with his magic, but there was something alluring about being undressed by her, and he wanted that today.

Hades had a second of warning before he smelled laurel, and then Apollo appeared and snapped at them.

"Stop that!"

"Go away, Apollo," Hades barked.

He was not in the mood to be interrupted or to have Persephone pulled away from him because of their ridiculous bargain.

"Hades," Persephone said, a note of reprimand in her voice.

She was far more modest than him and was never inclined to continue what they'd started with an audience. Hades, while possessive, had no shame. He could fuck her in a crowded room—that was what illusion was for.

"No can do, Lord of the Underworld," Apollo said. "We have an event."

Hades pulled away with a frustrated sigh.

"What do you mean we have an event?" Persephone asked. Hades wanted to know the same.

"Today's the first of the Panhellenic Games," Apollo said.

Hades had definitely forgotten that, though to be fair, he had been very distracted and not at all with anything pleasant.

"That isn't until tonight," she said.

"So? I need you now."

"For what?" Persephone countered.

Hades watched the exchange, looking between the two. He felt like he was moderating an argument between two siblings.

"Does it matter?" Apollo asked. "We have a—"

"Don't." Hades said. "She asked you a question, Apollo. Answer it."

Apollo's mouth tightened, and he crossed his arms as if he were pouting. "I fucked up. I need your help," he said, glaring at Hades as if to ask if he was happy now.

The answer was no.

"You needed help and yet you wish to command it from her?" Hades said.

"Hades—" Persephone tried, but he wasn't interested in her defense.

"He demands your attention, Persephone, has your friendship only because of a bargain, and when you needed him before all those Olympians, he was silent."

It was probably that last thing that frustrated him the most. The one person who had defended them the most was Hermes, and that was even in the aftermath of his broken oath. Where had Apollo been?

"That's enough, Hades," Persephone said. "Apollo is my friend, bargain or not. I will speak to him about what bothers me."

He stared at her, wishing she would do it right now, because he'd really like to witness her reprimanding Apollo, but he knew she wouldn't.

He swallowed his frustration and then kissed her, his tongue pushing past her lips and into her mouth. He gripped her face, her jaw widening to accommodate the deep thrusts of his tongue, and when he pulled away, her face was flushed.

She swallowed, holding his gaze, and he hoped that all she thought about while she was with Apollo was what he'd interrupted.

"I will join you at the games later." Then he vanished.

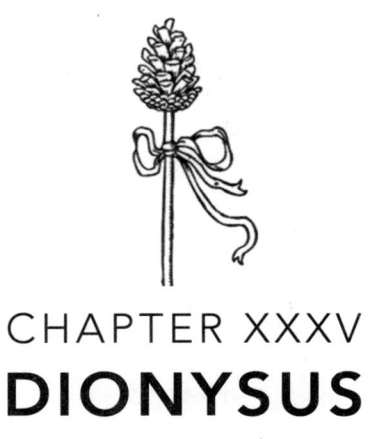

CHAPTER XXXV
DIONYSUS

Dionysus sat in his usual place in his darkened suite at Bakkheia. It was crowded with people who were drinking and dancing and fucking. He usually watched the revelry or at least was far more present for it—it was essentially how he received worship—but today, he was distracted.

He could not think of anything beyond what had happened over the last few days—his confrontation with Poseidon and everything that had occurred on that island, from fucking Ariadne to the death of the ophiotaurus. He was also very much aware that he had left the cyclops he'd promised to murder alive, albeit with a severe hangover.

He wondered what consequences would come from not fulfilling that debt.

"Are you ever going to tell me what happened on that island?" Silenus asked.

"There's nothing to tell," Dionysus replied.

Nothing he *wanted* to tell.

"It changed you," his foster father said. "You're different, and I'm not sure how."

"I'm not sure how either," Dionysus said, which was true.

He had never wanted to face off with Poseidon, but doing so had left him feeling incapable of protecting Ariadne and very aware of the inferiority of his powers.

"Dionysus," said a sensual voice, and his attention was brought to the present as a woman with dark hair and eyes knelt before him, hands on his knees. "You seem on edge. Can I not ease you?"

Normally, he would indulge her, but as her palms slid up his thighs, he stopped her and leaned forward. Just as he did, the door to his suite opened, and Ariadne stepped inside. Her eyes went right to him and the woman at his feet.

His throat tightened. He could just imagine how this looked.

"Ari—" he said as she approached.

"Don't get up," she said, and he wondered which of them she was talking to. "I need to talk to you."

"Of course," he said, his eyes falling to the woman. "*Go.*"

When he looked at Ariadne, her gaze was hard.

"It wasn't what you think," he said.

"Do you know what I think?" she countered.

Dionysus started to respond, but Silenus interrupted. "You must be Ariadne," he said, leaning over the arm of his chair into Dionysus as he extended his hand. "I am Silenus, Dionysus's father."

"Adopted father," Dionysus felt the need to clarify.

Ariadne took his hand, though she didn't seem completely comfortable.

"Aye, I can see why my son is smitten," Silenus said.

Dionysus shoved him back into his own chair. "*Shut up*," he seethed and then looked at Ariadne again.

"I want to go back to the island," she said.

"What?" That was not what he expected to hear.

"I want to bury Bully," she said.

"Ari, it isn't safe."

"It's not right to just leave him there to rot," she said. "He deserved better than that."

"Did you ignore the part where he is in a cave with a fucking monster?"

"A monster you were supposed to kill," she pointed out.

Dionysus shook his head. "I am not going to have this conversation with you. We aren't going back to that island just so you can fulfill your misguided sense of duty to this creature."

"If you won't take me, I'll ask Hades."

Dionysus ground his teeth. "Out!" he commanded, and suddenly, everyone gathered in his suite stopped drinking and dancing and fucking. As if they were under some spell, they filed out of the room—except for Silenus.

"What about me?" he asked.

Dionysus glared, and his father sighed.

"*Fine.*"

Once they were alone, Dionysus rose to his feet. To Ariadne's credit, she didn't back down.

"Do you think Hades will bend to your childish will?" he asked.

"It isn't childish to want to give someone a proper burial," she said.

"It is when you wish to go back to an island that nearly took both of our lives," he said. "Why go back? Are you hoping to see Theseus?"

She slapped him, and it stung.

"*How dare you*," she seethed, her voice trembling.

They glared at each other, the silence strained, and then Dionysus broke, taking her mouth against his in a hot kiss. One of his hands cupped the back of her head, the other pressing into the small of her back.

Gods, she felt so good.

He had feared returning from the island would mean pretending nothing had happened between them. He had tried, but repressing his desire felt like trying not to breathe.

Ariadne responded to his touch just as enthusiastically, hands sliding up his chest and around his neck. She pressed into him, her breasts soft against his chest. He groaned at the contact.

"I want to be inside you again," he said, and then someone cleared their throat.

They tore away from each other to find Hermes.

"Well, that was entertaining," the god said.

Dionysus pressed his fingers into the bridge of his nose. "Oh, fuck me."

"We've had this discussion, Dionysus."

"What do you want, Hermes?" he demanded.

"Hades has summoned you," Hermes said. "He wants to discuss the ophiotaurus."

Dionysus exchanged a look with Ariadne.

"I can give you a few moments," said the god. "You know, to recover."

"We're fine," Ariadne said.

"I think you're speaking for yourself," said Hermes, and then his eyes slid to Dionysus—and down to his raging erection.

"Fuck off, Hermes," Dionysus said. "Let's go."

"Oh, I'm not taking you," Hermes said. "I have an event, but there's a car waiting for you downstairs. Say hello to Antoni for me."

Antoni took them to Iniquity, where they found Hades sitting at a table in the private, members-only bar. He sat with a glass of whiskey, two fingers full. In one hand, something gold gleamed—a coin, an obol, the currency of the dead. Ilias sat nearby and nodded at their approach.

Hades did not look up until they were seated. He seemed distracted.

"I need you to tell me everything that happened on the island."

"Everything?" Ariadne asked.

Hades looked at her and then at Dionysus. "When Theseus arrived," he clarified. "Though it sounds like you both had quite a time."

"There's nothing to tell," said Dionysus. "Theseus found us on Thrinacia, he slayed the ophiotaurus, and he has the intestines. I imagine he has already burned them."

Theseus was not one to hesitate. He'd demonstrated as much with how quickly he'd stabbed the ophiotaurus.

"What happens when he burns them?" Ariadne asked.

They all exchanged a look.

"We don't exactly know," said Hades. "That's the problem."

"What does the prophecy say?" Dionysus asked.

The last thing he remembered about this was that Hades was going to verify that the creature had still reincarnated with a prophecy.

"If a person slays the creature and burns its entrails, then victory is assured against the gods." Hades repeated the words carefully, as if he was trying to deduce the meaning as he spoke.

"That's a terrible prophecy," said Dionysus.

"I liked Hermes's version better," said Ilias.

"I'm not sure what you expected," said Hades. "Prophecies are rarely straightforward, and when they are, the stakes are far higher."

Dionysus understood what Hades was saying—at least there was ambiguity here. There were instances in the past when prophecy had been so specific, there was no avoiding the inevitable fate, no matter how mortals tried.

"Something with a little more context would have been nice," Ilias said. "Which gods does the prophecy refer to?"

"Perhaps all of us," said Dionysus. "Or maybe just a few. I think we should be relieved the prophecy isn't specific. There is power in knowing what to expect. We can work with that against Theseus." Dionysus glanced at Ariadne. "Theseus is arrogant enough to believe that the prophecy means he will conquer the gods. It will make him feel invincible when he is not."

Hades's brows lowered. "What do you mean?"

"At the island, I stabbed him with my thyrsus. He did not heal quickly, not like you or I. It is a weakness."

"You mean this whole time, we could have just stabbed him?" asked Ilias.

"It's more complicated than that and you know it," said Hades. "He's endeared himself to the public. If he dies by our hands, we risk losing worship."

"Okay, so we can't assassinate him publicly," said Ilias. "Where do we start?"

Everyone's eyes turned to Ariadne, who paled. She did not need them to speak to know what they were asking—they needed to know everything about Theseus.

"No," she said, her voice even. "You cannot ask that of me. He will kill my sister."

"I told you we will rescue her," said Dionysus.

"With what?" she countered. "You said that's why we needed Medusa, or did you just say that so you could add another weapon to your collection?"

Dionysus flinched at her anger and her accusation.

"Trust us when we say rescuing Phaedra will be our first priority," said Hades. "But we cannot do anything without information, even plan her escape."

She shook her head. "He will know I told you."

"In the end, does it matter if Phaedra is safe?"

"It matters because she will go back."

There was a long and stark silence. Dionysus wanted to say the most unhelpful thing, which was that perhaps then she did not need rescuing. They had put Ariadne in a difficult situation, but she was fighting her own losing battle.

"Are you saying you will not help us?" Dionysus asked.

"Aren't you all gods?" she asked. "Can you not figure it out?"

Dionysus didn't look at her. He couldn't pretend to understand her reasoning, just as he couldn't pretend to understand the trauma that kept her from helping.

He took a breath. "I'll assign the maenads to spy," he said. "They can gather intel on those who are involved, their weapons, their hideouts."

They were going to need to know as much as possible to formulate their plans.

Hades nodded. "The battle's already begun," he said. "Now we must prepare for war."

CHAPTER XXXVI
HADES

Hades was not surprised that Ariadne would not help them actively plan against Theseus. She had been under his spell for a long time and knew what he was capable of. Clearly, she had come to see one too many of his threats realized.

After she left with Dionysus, he sat with Ilias.

"Those two fucked," the satyr said.

"Finally," said Hades, downing his whiskey in one swallow. "Did Hermes give you an update on the warehouse and the club?"

"Yes," Ilias said. "It went up in flames last night."

It was good to know, considering Hades expected retaliation from Theseus.

"I don't know if I made the right decision," he said. He knew that warehouse in the Lake District wasn't the only place Theseus was storing weapons. He wasn't that stupid, though he hoped it had made a dent in his arsenal all the same.

"I don't know that there are right or wrong decision where we are headed," said Ilias. "There are just decisions and their consequences."

Hades supposed that was right.

Then he noticed how the satyr's eyes shifted from him and widened. He sat up in his chair.

"Hades, the news."

But he had already turned to see the headline flash across the screen:

Explosion and Shots Fired at Talaria Stadium.

Here was Theseus's retribution.

Hades appeared in the middle of the chaos of Talaria Stadium.

The magic of the gods hung heavy in the air as they fought amid the sounds of horrified screams, clashing metal, and gunshots.

"Persephone!" Apollo screamed as a bullet struck her shoulder.

She staggered, and as she fell, Hades caught her, sweeping her up into his arms as she gave a guttural cry.

"I've got you," he said and immediately took her to the Underworld, leaving the mayhem at the stadium to the other Olympians.

Fucking Fates.

How many times was this going to happen?

He set her on the bed, only having enough patience to help her out of her jacket. Once it was off, he tore her dress to reach and inspect her wound.

"Wh-what are you doing?" she said, the words slipping between her gritted teeth.

"I need to see if the bullet left your body," Hades said. When he looked at her back, there was an exit wound.

"Let me heal it," she said.

"Persephone—"

"I have to try," she argued. "Hades—"

He forced himself to step back, though he wanted to do it himself. He was faster and it would make him feel better. Of all the times she wanted practice, why now?

"Do it, Persephone," he barked. He had not intended to sound so hostile. This couldn't be any easier for her. She was the one who was hurt, but he couldn't help panicking.

She took deep breaths and then closed her eyes. He watched her wound for any signs that her magic was working, growing frustrated the longer she just lay there bleeding.

"*Now*," he said, impatient, but he saw her magic at work as the wound began to close.

"I did it," she said with a smile when she opened her eyes.

"You did," he said, though he wanted to double-check just in case. And then he wanted to return and help his fellow Olympians kill those who had attacked the stadium. He would leave their bodies a mangled mess for all to see as a warning to anyone who might think to participate or continue these horrible assaults.

"What are you thinking?" Persephone asked, drawing his attention.

"Nothing you wish to know," he said softly. "Let's clean you up."

He took her into the bathroom, carrying her though

he knew she could walk perfectly well. When they had undressed, he kissed her and touched her shoulder to ensure it was fully healed.

She pulled away, looking at the now-smooth skin.

"Was I not good enough?" she asked.

"Of course you are good enough, Persephone," he said. He had not intended to make her feel any less. "I am overprotective and fearful for you, and perhaps selfishly, I wish to remove anything that reminds me of my failure to protect you."

"Hades, you did not fail," she said.

"We will agree to disagree," he said.

"If I am enough, then you are enough," she insisted.

He hoped one day he would believe that.

Her hands moved over his chest and around his neck.

"I am sorry," she said. "I never wanted to see you suffer again, not like you did in the days following Tyche's death."

"You have nothing to be sorry for," he said and kissed her.

They showered together, hands smoothing over soapy skin until both of them felt flushed and wanting, but Hades could not bring himself to act on his desires—too much had occurred tonight. Instead, he relied on words and told her he loved her.

"I love you," she said, voice quiet. "More than anything."

Tears welled in her eyes, and as they trailed down her face, he whispered her name and gathered her into his arms. He carried her from the shower to the fire, sitting with her nestled against his chest.

"All those people...gone," she whispered.

Mass death was never easy, and they'd had a lot of it in a short amount of time.

"You will not be able to console everyone who makes their way to the gates unexpectedly, Persephone. Those deaths are far too numerous. Take comfort. The souls of Asphodel are there, and they will represent you well."

"They represent you too, Hades," she reminded him and grew quiet for a moment before asking, "What about the attackers who died tonight?"

"They await punishment in Tartarus." He paused, holding her gaze. "Do you wish to go?"

She offered him a small smile. It wasn't humorous, more an acknowledgment that he had changed.

"Yes," she said. "I wish to go."

Hades took Persephone to Tartarus, to his den of monsters. Some of the creatures here were dead while others were living and merely prisoners, but that did not change their usefulness when it came to torture.

Persephone looked around, rubbing her hands up and down her arms. The magic was heavy here, different, and it hung in the air like a winter chill, suppressing the power of the monsters within.

Now and then, the faint echo of a growl, shriek, or scream echoed outside the dungeon.

"There are monsters here," Hades explained.

"What...kind of monsters?" she asked.

"Many," he said, raising his brows a little. "Some are here because they were slain. Some are here because they were captured. Come."

He led her through the gates and into the dungeon, down the darkened walkway, past shadowed cells. All the while, the animal-like sounds of the monsters grew louder, cut through with a horrible wail.

"The harpies," Hades said. They were half-human, half-bird creatures who were often insatiable in their hunger for food and were used in punishments to starve mortals. "Aello, Ocypete, and Celaeno—they get restless, especially when the world is chaos."

"Why?"

"Because they sense evil and wish to punish."

They continued, passing cells occupied by chimeras, griffins, sirens, and the Sphinx. Persephone did not pause long before any of the bays and remained close to Hades as they made their way to the very end of the cell, which was barred by a massive gate.

"What is this?" Persephone asked.

"That is a hydra," Hades said. "Its blood, venom, and breath are poisonous."

He had been responsible for its death when Hera had forced him to fight the creature during her notorious Fight Night. It had not been easy. It had seven heads that grew back even after they were cut off. He'd only managed to defeat it with fire, and in the end, it had become a resident of the Underworld.

"And the mortals in the pool?" she asked. "What did they do?"

Hades's eyes dropped to the men and women at the hydra's feet. They were all sitting in a pool of black venom that dripped from the creature's fangs, their bodies covered in horrible sores and burns as it ate away at their bodies slowly.

"They are the terrorists who attacked the stadium."

"Is this their punishment?"

"No. Think of this as their holding cell."

She was quiet and then looked up at him.

"And how will you punish them?" she asked.

"Perhaps...you would like to decide?"

He was a little hesitant to hand over the task, uncertain of how she might feel about torture. She'd been hesitant when it came to Pirithous. She'd asked him if it *helped*. He still wasn't sure, but it was fair to say that in the moment, vengeance felt good.

Her gaze returned to the souls.

"I wish for them to exist in a constant state of fear and panic. To experience what they inflicted upon others. They will exist, for eternity, in the Forest of Despair."

"So you shall have it," he said, and then he offered his hand. As her fingers settled into his, the souls beneath the hydra vanished. "Let me show you something," he said, taking her to the library, which contained a basin that acted as both an accurate map of the Underworld and a portal. "Show the Forest of Despair," he said, and the water changed to show the souls that had sat in the hydra's venom and their punishment in the forest.

The reality of the forest was that it became whatever one feared.

When Persephone had entered it, she had found Hades in Leuce's embrace. When Hades entered it, he saw nothing.

Persephone watched for a while and then turned away, stepping down from the basin. "I have seen enough."

Hades followed and reached for her hand, worried

that he had gone too far in showing her the horrors of the forest even if she knew them.

"Are you well?" he asked.

"I am...satisfied," she said. "Let's go to bed."

He did not argue, and they made their way back to their bedchamber, but he couldn't help noticing the shift in her energy. It was dark and sensual, and he wanted to taste it on her tongue.

Hades hung back as they entered their room, and he watched as Persephone walked ahead. She slid out of her robes and faced him. His eyes roamed her body—from her full breasts, over her stomach, to the curls at the apex of her thighs. When he met her gaze again, her stare was dark and carnal.

She wanted to fuck.

"Persephone."

"Hades," she said.

"You've been through a lot. Are you sure you want this tonight?" He never thought those words would come out of his mouth. It wasn't as if this wasn't their usual way, but he wanted her to be sure. Today had been harrowing, full of emotions and experiences neither of them had processed.

"It's all I want."

He didn't argue further and closed the distance between them, bringing his lips to hers. She opened for him, and it was easy to become lost in everything that she was—soft and warm and eager. He thought that perhaps this was what he loved most, her obvious desire. He felt it so often for her, and he loved when she could not be contained.

Her hands dipped beneath his robes, and he helped

her remove them so he could feel her skin against his, liking the way his rigid cock felt against her coarse curls. He couldn't wait to bury himself inside her, to feel her clench around him as she came. It was that feeling he was addicted to—that release he was chasing.

She kissed down his chest and stomach until she knelt before him. Taking the base of his erection into her hand, she let her lips close over the tip where his come beaded.

"Is this okay?" she asked, looking up at him from the floor.

It was almost comical to him that she would ask, given that he wanted nothing more than to watch her take him into her mouth.

"More than," he said and was rewarded with the touch of her tongue again. She took her time, kissing along his shaft, drawing her tongue over every ridge she could find, and then she took him to the back of her throat, swallowing around the crown of his cock.

He threw his head back, gritting his teeth, muscles tensing, his body on the very edge of release, but he wasn't ready for this to be over.

As he came down from that first intense high, he looked at her, her lips still wrapped around his cock.

"You don't know the things I wish to do to you."

The thing about her mouth, about her magic, about her, was that it made him want everything with her—things that went beyond anything he'd considered doing with anyone before.

She rose to her feet, holding his gaze.

"Show me," she whispered.

He wanted to groan. Fuck. She was *perfect*.

His hand slid behind her neck, and he gripped her there. As he kissed her hard on the mouth, he guided her back to the bed and lay her at its center. He hovered over her, her body trapped between his thighs as he continued to kiss her, his tongue lapping at hers. The longer he kissed her, the more she writhed beneath him, arching against him just to feel the friction between their hips.

She was making this harder, and he was trying to make this last longer.

His fingers clamped down on her wrists, and he drew them over her head before she could reach for him, before she undid every reason he'd had for bringing her to this bed in the first place, and called on his magic to restrain her.

When she felt the brush of his magic, she pulled away and looked up at his bindings.

"Is this okay?" he asked, his voice quiet.

He couldn't tell by her expression, and that made him uneasy, but one word from her and he would take them away immediately. It was only something he wished to explore with her, not something he needed.

She nodded and he took that chance to appreciate the way she looked. She was art and he wanted to make her feel like that beneath his hands. This was a type of embrace, a way for her to truly feel how he saw her—as the center of the universe.

"I will make you writhe," he said, stretching out over her body. "I will make you scream. I will make you come so hard, you will feel it for days."

He kissed her mouth and then down her body, starting with her breasts. He took each hard peak into his mouth, teasing with this tongue and grazing with his teeth. Beneath him, she squirmed, and he wondered how wet she would be when he finally reached her center. He could feel her heat, and as her hips ground against him, her slick center moved over his knee.

It made him far more eager for the descent.

But even as he hovered between her thighs, he still took his time, holding her gaze as he kissed every part of her. Her body was flushed from frustration, likely because if her arms weren't pinned over her head, her fingers would be tangled in his hair, and she would pull him against her heat.

He spread her thighs until her legs were flat against the bed and dragged his tongue along her wet heat. Her body arched against the bed, her hands fisting in the restraints.

"Hades," she moaned, and he pressed into her deeper, tongue caught between the walls of her silken flesh, his fingers teasing her erect clit.

He held her harder as she began to move against him, chasing her release. She was on the edge—he could feel it in the way her body strained, the way her muscles tightened. It made his blood rush to the head of his cock, which lay heavy and rigid against his own stomach.

"Hades!"

It was the way she said his name this time that alerted him that something was wrong. He drew back as her heels dug into the bed and she yanked against the bindings. Her eyes were open and wide, but it was like she wasn't seeing anything—not in this present moment anyway.

Fuck. He wished he'd never had this idea.

He banished the bindings quickly, wishing he'd done so sooner.

Fuck.

"Persephone." He tried to reach for her, but she lashed out, and her hand came down on his cheek, full of thorns. The pain was biting, and blood dripped between them onto her skin. She seemed to be awake now, her face pale and her horror evident. She started to reach for him but realized her hands were still full of thorns.

She burst into tears, holding her hands away from her body.

For a few brief seconds, he was too stunned to move, too confused by what had happened. He was trying to remember exactly when things had gone wrong. How had they gone so wrong? He'd thought she was enjoying this. Was it possible she never had?

Finally, he moved and pulled her to him, though he wasn't sure he was what she needed or wanted. He'd been too self-concerned to even realize that she was suffering.

"I did not know," Hades said. "I did not know. I'm sorry. I love you."

But there came a point when even he couldn't speak.

CHAPTER XXXVII
HADES

"I don't see why I need to be here," said Apollo.

Hades had summoned him to the island of Lemnos.

He had come to discuss weapons with Hephaestus, and he needed to know what Apollo had found during his examination of Tyche. This was necessary given their eventual movement against Theseus, but he also did not think he could face Persephone so soon. He was still reeling from how quickly everything had escalated from something so erotic and right to an utter nightmare.

He felt embarrassed but mostly completely horrified that he'd managed to trigger her so badly, and at a time when they'd been most intimate.

Perhaps worst of all, he didn't know how to handle what had happened. An apology did not seem like enough, and the thought of pushing her too far again was agonizing. In some ways, he'd prided himself on knowing how her body responded to his, and yet last night, he'd been wrong.

"You are quiet," said Aphrodite as she walked them to Hephaestus's workshop.

He wasn't sure why she felt the need to play escort, but he thought it might be so she could catch a glimpse of Hephaestus.

"He's always quiet," said Apollo. "Unless he's reprimanding you for taking his lover away to fulfill a bargain."

"Shut up, Apollo," Hades said. "I...didn't sleep."

"Are you worried Zeus will deny you your marriage?" she asked.

"I was," he said. "But now I am more worried Persephone won't make it to the altar."

He didn't look at Aphrodite or Apollo as he spoke. They'd both borne witness to her attacks. Aphrodite had been there that night at the club, so lost in her own need for vengeance, she hadn't helped Persephone either.

"Are you...angry with me?" Aphrodite asked after a long pause.

"Hermes swore an oath to protect her," Hades replied.

"That is not what I asked," she said.

He didn't answer. There was no need. Would he have been indebted to Aphrodite had she saved Persephone? Yes, but perhaps it was better that he wasn't.

To Hades's surprise, Aphrodite did not leave once they were at the doors of Hephaestus's workshop. Instead, she followed them inside.

The God of Fire was at his forge. He stood before the fire, his hair knotted on top of his head, bare-chested and sweaty as he removed a piece of metal from the fire. He turned to lay it on the anvil, intent on hammering, but he caught sight of Aphrodite, who had walked ahead into the shop.

Hephaestus's eyes locked on her and darkened, and his whole body went rigid. Hades wondered if Aphrodite would interpret his reaction as anger or frustration at her intrusion, though he saw it as something else—obvious desire.

"Are you in need?" Hephaestus asked her.

"Whoa," said Apollo under his breath. "It's hot in here."

"No," she answered. She had her arms behind her back as she leaned against one of his tables. "Hades and Apollo are here to see you."

Hephaestus's gaze shifted. He hadn't even realized anyone else had accompanied his goddess into his workshop, he was so consumed by her.

"Hades...Apollo," Hephaestus said, tossing the piece of metal he'd been working into the quench tank nearby. "What can I do for you?"

"We must discuss weapons," Hades said. "My first concern is the net."

He hesitated to bring it up because he knew Aphrodite had accused Hephaestus of being responsible for Harmonia's attack, believing that only his magic was strong enough to capture a god. The problem was, she wasn't wrong.

He had built an unbreakable net, and all the gods knew it existed, including Demeter.

"I think we can agree that the net used to restrain Harmonia and Tyche was likely modeled after your own."

Hephaestus did not speak, and the tension in his forge grew heavy.

"So how does one escape it?" Apollo asked and then looked pointedly at the Goddess of Love. "Aphrodite?"

Hephaestus's posture was rigid, and Aphrodite narrowed her eyes.

"You don't," she said and then looked at her husband. "You must be set free."

"Is there no weapon you could forge to cut it?"

"Nothing is impossible," Hephaestus replied. "But I would need to know how they forged their net."

Hades exchanged a look with Apollo. He wasn't so certain that information would be easy to come by. He wished Ariadne had been willing to help with Theseus. He was certain she knew his operations, and if not how things were being created, she knew who was doing it.

"Then that leaves the weapon used to kill Tyche," he said and looked toward Apollo.

"At first, I thought she had been stabbed by Cronos's scythe, but her wounds had a different shape. More like an arrow, but a simple arrow would not have killed a god."

"What makes Cronos's scythe dangerous?" Aphrodite asked.

"It's made of adamant," said Hephaestus. "But adamant only wounds. It will not kill us. Whatever Tyche was stabbed with had to be…laced with something. A poison."

Or venom, Hades thought.

"Heracles had arrows poisoned with hydra blood," said Hades.

Before the hydra had come to reside in the Underworld, it had been in Hera's possession. He wondered how much of its venom Theseus had sourced before Hades killed it.

"Well," said Hephaestus. "It seems you did not need me at all."

"That isn't true," said Hades. "I need armor."

"You have armor," Hephaestus said.

"Not for me," Hades said. "For Persephone."

Hades returned to the Underworld, though he felt anxious facing Persephone. He wasn't exactly sure what he would say when he saw her. Would either of them be ready to talk about what happened? He didn't think he could verbalize anything beyond an apology, which seemed useless here. He couldn't even promise it would never happen again, because he had no fucking clue how to prevent it. Maybe the only thing to say was that he would do better, but that did not feel like enough either.

His heart beat strangely in his chest. It was not hard or fast but irregular, and it only grew worse when he found Persephone in the library, sitting in her usual place, a book in hand. She seemed to sense him almost instantly and looked up when he entered the room. Beneath her gaze, he felt trapped—unable to retreat or even move forward. Maybe it had something to do with the fact that she looked haunted, and he knew he was responsible.

They sat in strained silence for a moment, and he scrambled for words, but none of them seemed right. Finally, Persephone spoke.

"I spoke to Tyche today," she said. "She thinks that the reason she could not heal herself was because the Fates cut her thread."

"The Fates did not cut her thread," he said simply.

The Fates had never cut a god's thread, save Pan. Even those trapped in Tartarus were not dead, just imprisoned.

"What are you saying?"

"That Triad has managed to find a weapon that can kill the gods," he said.

"You know what it is, don't you?"

"Not for certain," he said, hesitant to say until they had an actual arrow in hand, but it was a good lead.

"Tell me."

"You met the hydra," he said. "It has been in many battles in the past, lost many heads—though it just regenerates. The heads are priceless because their venom is used as a poison. I think Tyche was taken down by a new version of Hephaestus's net and stabbed with a hydra-poisoned arrow—a relic to be specific."

"A poisoned arrow?"

"It was the biological warfare of ancient Greece. I have worked for years to pull relics like them out of circulation, but there are many and whole networks dedicated to the practice of sourcing and selling them. I would not be surprised if Triad has managed to get their hands on a few."

"I thought you said gods couldn't die unless they were thrown into Tartarus and torn apart by the Titans."

"Usually, but the venom of the hydra is potent, even to gods. It slows our healing, and likely, if a god is stabbed too many times…"

"They die."

Hades nodded. "I believe Adonis was also killed with a relic." He was hesitant to admit this information, given that he had it for so long, but he added, "With my father's scythe."

"What makes you so certain?"

He should tell her that they'd found a piece of the

blade inside Adonis's body, but Hades was not eager for anyone to know that he'd handed it over to Hephaestus so he could forge a new blade. It wasn't that he thought Persephone would tell. It was that he didn't trust anyone not to pry the information from her mind.

"Because his soul was shattered."

"Why didn't you tell me?"

"I suppose I had to get to a place where I could tell you. Seeing a shattered soul is not easy. Carrying it to Elysium is even harder."

His eyes dropped to her book, uncomfortable with this conversation, though it was better than the alternative.

"What were you reading?"

She looked down at the book as if she'd forgotten it was there.

"Oh, I was looking up information on the Titanomachy."

"Why?"

"Because...I think my mother has bigger goals than separating us."

Hades already knew that, but even he had to admit he couldn't quite understand her motive. It seemed to have moved beyond her initial wish of separating him from Persephone, and it appeared she preferred to end the world.

CHAPTER XXXVIII
HADES

Hades split his day between Inequity and Nevernight. It had been a long while since he had time to focus on day-to-day matters—there were bargains to strike and deals to be made. After all these years in this role, Hades knew there was one constant in the world, and it was the predictable desires of gods and mortals. No matter the threat of war, they would always seek love, wealth, and power.

He was no different.

He had spent his life yearning for love, aware of its absence like a sharp thorn in his side. He used to think it was a selfish desire, but it was the only thing that made any of this tolerable. It was the only thing that would carry him through his war.

While he planned for it daily—and had done so for a long time—he had not had the time to sit long and dwell on what it would mean to return to the fold. Perhaps that was best, because when he did think too long on it, he remembered the heaviness of his armor, the way it trapped heat and burned him alive. He remembered the wet sound of bodies being speared and smashed and the smell of fire and festering death. He remembered blood—the color and consistency as it pooled and dried—and he remembered the day he no longer noticed its scent, so used to how it permeated the air.

War was inevitable when great power was at stake; it was inevitable when great love was at stake too. In the end, he would face it, and he would fight for Persephone while she fought for the world.

"You look terrible."

Hades turned to see Hecate standing in the doorway of his Nevernight office.

"I feel terrible," he said.

He hadn't gone to bed, even after Persephone had asked. He'd upset her and she'd gone to the queen's suite to sleep, which meant he hadn't seen her when she'd risen for work either, and her absence weighed on him.

He should have conceded; he should have gone to her. He had essentially punished her for his own failures. He wasn't sure why he thought space and distance were best. Only a few days ago, he had hated those words.

"Good," Hecate said. "I need you."

Hades's brows rose. "For what?"

"I've made a suit," she said. "I need to see you in it so I can decide if I like it."

"Is it black?" he asked.

"No, it's yellow," she replied.

Hades sneered.

"Of course it's black," she said. "Why would I ever attempt to dress your dark soul in anything else?"

"If it's black, why do I have to try it on? You know how it will look."

"On second thought, I am certain I will like the suit. It's you I take issue with."

Hades smirked and rose to his feet. "Fine, Hecate. Work your magic."

"Stop fidgeting!" Hecate commanded, speaking around the pins in her mouth. She was on her knees messing with the hem of his jacket.

Hades couldn't help it. He had expected this suit to look like all the others he wore daily, but once it was on, he realized it did not even resemble his usual wardrobe. That wasn't why he was fidgeting, though. It was because trying it on made him realize that he was really getting married.

"Is this silk?" he asked.

"It's wool," Hecate hissed. "If you do not stop moving, I will freeze you in place."

"Wool?" he asked. "Why is it shiny?"

"Because it's *soft*."

He chuckled. "Why are you so frustrated?"

"I do not know if you are aware, Hades, but your very presence is frustrating."

"Can't you use your magic to tailor this? It would be easier."

"Easier, yes," she said. "But this project is special to me, and I prefer to hand stitch."

Hades swallowed hard. As much as he joked, he was very grateful for Hecate.

"There," she said, rising to her feet and stepping back to observe her work.

"It's perfect, Hecate," Hades said as he stared in the mirror. "I don't know how I could ever thank you enough."

"You can thank me by actually getting married," she said. "I have written a speech."

"You know it isn't a matter of wanting."

"You're going to do whatever you want," she said. "You always have, no matter the consequences. The important part is that Persephone will need your magic for what is to come."

That was the real reason Zeus wanted a say in their marriage and why he would consult the oracle about their marriage. What would come from the union of life and death? They were the beginning and the end, the dawn and the night. They were never-ending, and their magic would be too.

"What is to come, Hecate?" Hades asked, arching a brow.

She was the triple goddess, able to view the past, present, and future, but even with that great power, Hades never inquired. He just trusted that Hecate would guide him, and she did, but now that she had acknowledged the threat and the unknown, he had to ask.

"You know what is coming," she said and met his gaze. "You feel it in your bones. It is why, as much as you wish to fight for Persephone, you keep pushing her away."

He considered her words.

It was true there was a part of him that he was trying to keep buried—a part of him that felt too deeply.

"It will not serve you to be cold in this war, Hades," she said. "This is a battle best waged with passion."

The goddess stared a moment longer and then dropped her gaze to his suit.

"I like it...but it's missing something—a boutonniere on the breast. What flower, Hades?"

She stepped aside so he could look in the mirror, but he didn't need to. He knew which to choose, and he touched the pocket, where a red, star-shaped polyanthus unfurled. It was the flower he'd worn when he first met Persephone, the one she'd let wither beneath her touch.

"Perfect," said Hecate.

After Hecate's interruption, Hades finished a few more mundane tasks before heading into the gardens. He wandered until he came to the Asphodel Fields where he was met by Cerberus, Typhon, and Orthrus. The three had been busy, given so many souls had made their entrance to the Underworld, and they seemed to vibrate with pent-up energy.

"Eager to play, boys?" he asked.

Hades did not order Cerberus to drop his red ball, and when he went to reach for it, the Doberman dug his teeth in and yanked against Hades's grasp. Since he was locked in a game of tug-of-war with one, Typhon and Orthrus began to grow restless, barking at them as they fought over the ball.

Hades waited until Cerberus had put enough tension on the ball and let go. Unprepared, Cerberus dropped the ball. Typhon and Orthrus pounced, but as they did, they kicked the ball away, and it rolled to Hades's feet.

The three charged, ramming into him. He stumbled

back and fell into the grass, and still none of them had managed to obtain the ball.

"Sit!" Hades commanded, and the three instantly listened.

He got to his feet and picked up the ball, their eyes following his every move, muscles tensing as they prepared to launch themselves across the Underworld for the sake of this red toy. He didn't blame them—it was their one reprieve from their duties.

"Stay," he said and tossed the ball, which went soaring through the sky and disappeared somewhere in Persephone's meadow.

None of them moved, except Orthrus, who had the least control over his excitement when it was time to play.

"Go—"

The word was barely out of his mouth before the three bolted for the grove. Hades chuckled, watching them practically fly through the grass, leaving a flattened trail as they went. Sometimes it was hard to remember that these three were in fact scary monsters.

As he watched them race for the grove, he noticed something different about it. The trees, which were usually full and a muted silvery green, were skeletal and sparse, as if his magic had been drained from that part of the Underworld.

Strange.

He teleported, and it was like he'd arrived at a battleground. Stretches of land were disturbed by deep fissures and chasms. Clusters of thorns shot from the ground, tangling into trees so thickly, it was hard to tell where one began and the other ended, though most of them were gone, just piles of ash that swirled and blew in the wind.

He could feel Hecate's magic, but he could also feel Persephone's.

It seemed they'd had quite the training session.

As he stood there, he watched as Typhon pounced on the red ball, bright against the gray backdrop that Persephone's grove had become.

Hades took his time restoring it, calling up his glamour to make the trees grow taller, their foliage thicker, covering the ashy ground with a carpet of periwinkle and white phlox—the same flowers he'd helped Persephone grow here when he'd taught her how to channel energy for her magic. Those memories gave way to far more passionate ones—the ones where she'd taken him into her body beneath these trees and on this ground. He wanted more of that.

When he was finished, he left the grove, returning to the fields. Typhon still had the ball and refused to relinquish it, and the dogs ran in circles around his feet. Their excitement made him laugh, and he followed their movements, even as Cerberus tore away, followed by Typhon, then Orthrus, to greet Persephone.

She stole his breath as she approached, wreathed in an aura of moonlight. She looked wild and her energy was raw. It scraped against him, not uncomfortable but inflaming.

She seemed to hesitate as she held his gaze and stopped a few paces away. It felt like a chasm had opened up between them. He wanted her closer.

"I haven't seen you all day," she said.

"It was a busy day. As was yours. I saw the grove."

"You do not sound impressed."

"I am, but to say I am surprised would be a lie. I know your capabilities."

Hades watched as Persephone drew her bottom lip between her teeth in the silence that followed. He wanted her mouth against his—on every part of him.

"Did you come to say good night?" he asked.

She took a breath. "Will you not come to bed with me?"

It wasn't that he didn't want to. It was that they still had so much left unacknowledged. He swallowed hard.

"I will join you shortly."

He wasn't sure what he expected, but she didn't leave and instead seemed to grow frustrated.

"I want to talk about the other night."

Hades's chest tightened as he considered whether he was ready to face this.

"I did not mean to hurt you," he said, unable to meet her gaze. He cleared his throat when the words came out in a rasp.

"I know," she whispered.

"I was so lost in my desire, in what I wished to do with you, I didn't see what was happening. I pushed you too far. It will never happen again."

There was a beat of silence.

"What if that's what I want?" Hades's eyes snapped to hers, and she continued, "I want to try so many things with you, but I am afraid you will not want me."

He was taken aback by those words.

"Persephone—"

"I know it isn't true, but I cannot help how I think, and I thought it was better to say what was on my mind than keep it to myself. I don't want to stop learning with you."

He closed the distance between them and cradled her face, tilting her head back so he could look at her. She seemed so fragile within his grasp and yet so fierce.

"I will always want you," he said, his voice quiet. He pressed a kiss to her forehead.

She braced her hands on his forearms as if she wanted to hold him in place. "I know you hurt for me, but I need you."

"I am here."

Her hands slid down to his, and she guided them to her breasts.

"Touch me," she said. "We can go slow."

He swallowed thickly. A rush of dizzying heat went straight to his head, and his cock grew thick and heavy between them. He touched her, letting his head rest against hers as her nipples grew harder beneath his touch.

"What else?"

"Kiss me," she said, breathless.

He tried to go slow, to kiss her sweetly, their mouths locked in a delicate exchange, but fuck, it was hard. She was so soft and receptive, and each sweep of her tongue made him harder and more aware of the fact that he wanted her warmth fisting his cock.

He shifted closer, one hand anchoring against the back of her head. He bent her back, kissed her harder, faster, losing himself to the desperate tangle in the pit of his stomach, until he froze and pulled away.

"I'm sorry. I did not ask if that was okay."

"It's okay," she said, her eyes bright and present. "I'm okay."

She led this time, and her mouth was hot and demanding. He liked when she took control, and in this instance, it made him feel less like he would fuck this up.

Her hands tangled in his hair as she pulled him closer, then skimmed down his body until they rested on his cock. He pressed against her, grinding his teeth against the friction of her body.

"Touch me," he said.

She spent a few moments rubbing him through his clothes before unbuttoning his pants and taking his flesh into her hand.

Gods, it felt good.

He kissed her harder, consumed by the feel of his cock in her hand. It was like all sensation in his body came from this one place, and she had all the control—she could bend him and break him, and he would let her.

"Kneel," she said, and the breathless order sent both of them to their knees.

Persephone urged him onto his back and crawled up his body, her slick heat settling over his arousal as she straddled him.

His hands splayed across her thighs, digging into her skin as she lifted herself and guided him inside her. He could barely contain himself, and as she slid down, he thrust his hips upward. Their bodies slammed together, moving the same or at different times. It didn't matter so long as they were inside each other, so long as they were drowning in this ecstasy that moved through their bodies like blood.

"Yes," he hissed. "Fuck."

He sat up, gripping her with one hand while the

other moved between them so he could stroke her clit. Her body wound so tight that when she came, she shuddered around him, and it was enough to coax him to release. He groaned and fell back, bringing her with him as he continued to thrust deeply into her. After, they lay there for a while, quiet and content, until Persephone rose to her feet, legs shaking.

"Are you well?" he asked, holding on to her as she steadied herself.

"Yes," she said with a smile, laughing a little. "Very."

He stood and dressed and then took her hand.

"Are you ready for bed, my darling?"

"As long as you are coming too," she said, arching a brow.

He smiled. "Of course."

They cut through the garden, and he was pleased with the easy silence between them, though as they continued toward the palace, he thought more on what she'd said in the field—about wanting more and fearing he would not want her.

"What is it?" she asked as his steps slowed.

"When you said you wanted to...*try*...things with me. What things, exactly?"

He liked that she still blushed.

"What are you willing to teach?"

"Anything," he breathed. "Everything."

She studied him, tilting her head as if considering what to do next. "Perhaps we should begin where we failed. With...bondage."

There was something about this that felt completely unreal, like every fucking fantasy he'd ever had was coming true in this tempting form.

He'd never had any doubt that she was made for him, but she proved it every day.

"Are you sure?" he asked, brushing a stray piece of hair from her face.

"I will tell you when I feel afraid."

He was glad they could begin again, even if it meant standing on the ruins of trauma. He drew her closer, his hand on the back of her neck, his forehead against hers.

"You hold my heart in your hands, Persephone."

"And your cock too, apparently," said Hermes, amused.

Hades tore away from Persephone, growling Hermes's name, but his frustration quickly turned to dread when he saw what the god was wearing—gold robes.

"I thought interrupting now was probably better than a few minutes ago," Hermes explained.

"You were watching?" Persephone asked, cringing noticeably.

"To be fair," said Hermes, "you were having sex in the middle of the Underworld."

"And I have thrown you just as far," Hades said. "Need a reminder?"

"Ah, no. If you are going to be angry at anyone, be angry at Zeus. He sent me."

"Why?" Persephone asked, apprehension already seeping into her voice.

"He's called for a feast," Hermes said.

"A feast?" She looked at Hades, and he ground his teeth. "Tonight?"

"Yes. In…exactly an hour," Hermes said, looking at his wrist, which conveniently bore no watch.

"And we must be in attendance?"

"Well, I didn't just watch you have sex for nothing," Hermes replied.

Hades was already thinking through how he would punish the god for that.

"Why must we attend? And why at such short notice?" she asked.

Hades knew why—because this was meant to be their engagement feast. A misnomer if there ever was one, given that at the end of the event, Zeus would decide whether they could wed.

"He did not say, but perhaps he has finally decided to bless your union." Hermes chuckled. "I mean, why would he call for a banquet if he was going to say no?"

"Have you met my brother?" Hades asked.

"Unfortunately, yes. He's my father," Hermes said, and then he clapped his hands, rubbing them together—eager for drama, no doubt. "Well, I'll see you two soon."

Hermes left, and Persephone turned to Hades.

"Do you think it is true? That he is summoning us to bless our marriage?"

Bless was a generous word.

"I will not venture to guess," he said.

She frowned and paused a moment before asking, "What do I wear?"

He almost laughed, but considering they were about to present together at an Olympian feast for the first time, the way they dressed needed to make a statement, to convey they were already united even if Zeus said no.

"Let me dress you."

She narrowed her eyes, suspicious. "Do you really think that is wise?"

"Yes." He hooked an arm around her waist, bringing

her flush against him. "For one, it will not take long, which means we have approximately fifty-nine minutes for anything you may desire."

"Anything?" she asked, rising higher on the tips of her toes.

"Yes," he whispered, his blood roaring to life beneath her stare.

"Then I desire," she said, voice quiet and breathy, "a bath."

Hades laughed, grinning wide, and it felt good to laugh given the evening they were about to have.

"Coming up, my queen."

CHAPTER XXXIX
HADES

Hades took his time admiring Persephone.
When it came to dressing himself, he preferred simplicity, and while he'd applied the same concept to the gown he'd manifested for Persephone, on her, it was magnificent. There was something regal about the way it draped over her body. She wore it like a queen.

"Drop your glamour," he said, the words a low command.

She did not hesitate, and he felt a rush as her magic slipped away. He liked watching her transform, as he imagined she did him. They so rarely existed in this state together, it felt sinful and almost erotic.

"Just one more thing," he said, and as he lifted his hands, a crown of iron grew between them.

"Are you making a statement, my lord?" she asked as he placed it on her head.

"I thought that was obvious," he said.

"That I belong to you?" she asked with a pointed stare.

"No," he said, tilting her head back. "That we belong to each other."

He pressed his lips to hers in a tame kiss, conveying nothing of the desire raging beneath his skin. Seeing her like this was a dream.

"You are beautiful, my darling," he said, his voice quiet, admiring.

She was quiet too, studying his face, and he grew worried when he couldn't quite place her expression.

He touched her cheek softly. "Are you well?"

"Yes. Perfect," she said and offered him a smile, though he knew it wasn't completely genuine. She likely dreaded facing the Olympians, and he could not blame her. It took a lot to interact with them, to keep up with their mind games. Tonight would be trying for him, worse for her. "Are you ready?"

"I am never ready for Olympus," he said. "Do not leave my side."

Hades took her to the courtyard of Olympus, where Tyche's funeral had been held. Far above them, atop the mountain, was the Temple of the Sun, where music and a cacophony of chatter already proved to be both lively and exhausting.

He wondered if Helios would join the festivities, given that the temple was usually where he resided during the night after he returned from his journey through the sky. Hades dreaded the thought but knew the God of the Sun would likely be there. It did not matter that he hated Hades—gods would congregate anywhere there was sure to be wine, ambrosia, and drama.

"I am assuming that is our destination?" Persephone asked.

"Unfortunately," Hades replied.

He would have teleported, but he was in no hurry to reach their destination. Besides, if they walked, Persephone could see more of Olympus rather than Olympians, and that would benefit them both.

They made their ascent, and while he had no particular interest in the home of the gods, he enjoyed watching Persephone appreciate its beauty. It wasn't as though he didn't recognize its splendor. It just wasn't something he valued—a kingdom at the height of the world that only served to remind mortals of what they could not have. At least within his realm, there was always one truth—everything came to an end.

They arrived at the Temple of the Sun.

He had tried to prepare himself for this, but he hadn't had enough time, and it was far worse than he imagined. There were too many people, and they were all crowded on the porch of the temple, talking all at once.

He hated it.

Until it was silent, and every pair of eyes turned to them.

He hated that more.

Beside him, Persephone squeezed his hand, and when he looked down at her, she was smiling. She looked…enchanting.

"It seems I am not the only one who can't help staring at you, my love," she said quietly. "I think the whole room is enthralled."

He grinned. "Oh, my darling. They are staring at you."

He could sense the fear rising in the room as they made their way onto the floor, the crowd splitting to accommodate their presence. Those gathered here were minor gods, the favored, nymphs, satyrs, and other servants of the Olympians. Like mortals, they all had their own opinions of him. Some were indifferent; most were afraid.

"Sephy!"

Persephone released Hades's hand as she turned to see Hermes barreling through the crowd. He was wearing a bright yellow suit. It was embroidered with flowers.

It was probably the ugliest thing Hades had ever seen.

"You look stunning!" Hermes told her. He held her hands aloft, inspecting her gown.

"Thank you, Hermes, but I should warn you—you are complimenting Hades's handiwork. He made the dress."

There were a few gasps from the crowd and a wave of murmurs.

No one had stopped watching or listening to them since their arrival.

"Of course he did, and in his favorite color," Hermes mused.

"Actually, Hermes," Hades said, "black is not my favorite color."

Another round of whispers. He felt like he was having a conversation with a crowd.

"Then what is it?" someone shouted.

Hades smirked as he answered, "Red."

"Red?" another demanded. "Why red?"

He looked down at Persephone, his hand splayed across her waist. "I think I began to favor the color when Persephone wore it at the Olympian Gala."

There were a few sighs, but one voice carried over the crowd.

"Who would have thought my brother to be so sentimental?" Poseidon said with a humorless laugh.

Hades had not seen his brother since he'd taken Dionysus to his yacht to rescue Ariadne. He stood across the room with Amphitrite on his arm, and Hades wondered if Poseidon's wife knew about that encounter and the horrible things he'd threatened.

"Ignore him," Hermes said. "He's had too much ambrosia."

"Do not make excuses for him," Hades said. "Poseidon is always an ass."

"Brother!" Zeus boomed, and Hades took a deep breath as he prepared to face him. Zeus pushed through the crowd until he reached them, slapping Hades on the back. He seemed jolly and exaggerated. He was either drunk or his balls had started to grow back. "And gorgeous Persephone. So glad you could make it."

"I was under the impression we did not have a choice," she said.

Zeus's laughter burst from deep in his throat. "You're rubbing off on her, Brother," he said and elbowed Hades in the side. There was an angry glint in his eye, as if he did not like Persephone's tone, but Hades did not care, because he loved it. "Why wouldn't you come?" Zeus continued. "This is your engagement feast after all!"

"Then that must mean we have your blessing," Persephone said and then added pointedly, "to marry."

Zeus's laugh was dull, though he tried to hide it behind a boisterous tone. "That is not for me to decide, dear. It is my oracle who will decide."

"*Don't* call me dear," Persephone said.

"It is only a word," he replied, tone devoid of any humor. "I mean no offense."

"I don't care what you intended," Persephone said. "The word offends me."

The silence around them was deafening. As much as Hades was enjoying this exchange, he also shifted closer to Persephone. He knew Zeus's anger well, and nothing triggered it more than defiance, but his brother only burst into peals of annoying laughter.

"Hades, your plaything is far too sensitive."

Hades wasn't sure which word triggered him more—*plaything* or *sensitive*—but it didn't really matter. This was his queen, and Zeus had disrespected her.

Hades's hand shot out, and he gripped Zeus by the neck. "What did you call my fiancée?" Hades spoke between his teeth.

Zeus's eyes were as dark as stormy skies, flashing with the threat of his power. This was likely not the best move, given that Hades wished for his brother's blessing, but he would not let this slight pass.

"Careful, Hades. I still rule your fate."

Zeus determined whether he would marry, and even that was up for debate. Hades was not above defying Zeus, even if it meant the possibility of facing divine retribution.

"Wrong, Brother," Hades said, his voice quiet and harsh. "Apologize." He squeezed enough to feel the god swallow against his palm.

"Persephone," Zeus said, his voice rough and low. "Forgive me."

She said nothing, but Hades released him.

His brother's eyes remained trained on him, but Zeus

smiled and laughed, throwing his arms into the air as he exclaimed, "Let us feast!"

They filed into the banquet hall with the crowd where several round tables were spread across the large room. Hades would have liked to believe that making it to this part of the night meant they were closer to the end and Zeus would make his decision soon, but he knew this was just the beginning. They would have to make it through this tedious dinner and the festivities that followed. It was possible, given Hades's earlier behavior, that Zeus would delay his decision another day, but Zeus had deserved the very public shaming.

"It appears we will not be sitting together," Persephone said, glancing at him.

"How so?"

She nodded toward the front of the room where one long table was elevated above the rest.

"I am not an Olympian."

"Being one is overrated," he replied. "I shall sit with you. Wherever you'd like."

"Won't that make Zeus angry?"

"Yes."

"Do you want to marry me?" Persephone asked, looking up at him.

"Darling, I will marry you despite what Zeus says."

She was quiet for a moment as they navigated around the tables.

"What does he do when he does not bless a marriage?"

"He arranges a marriage for the woman," he said, but that would not happen here.

Hades steered Persephone to a table on the other side of the room against the wall. He preferred something as far away from people as possible and with a view of the entrance. He pulled out her chair, and as she sat, he pushed it in before seating himself.

Persephone smiled at the man and woman sitting across from them, who did not even try to hide their terror.

"Hi," she greeted. "I'm—"

"Persephone," the man said. "We know who you are."

"Yes." She hesitated, and Hades admired her for trying to make polite conversation. "What are your names?"

"That is Thales, and that is Callista," Hades said. "They are children of Apeliotes."

"Apeliotes?"

"The God of the Southeast Wind," Hades explained.

There was a god for *every* type of wind.

"Y-you know us?" Callista asked.

Maybe I chose the wrong table, he thought. "Of course."

"Hades, what are you doing?" Aphrodite asked, halting at their table. Hephaestus stood in her shadow.

"Sitting," Hades said.

"But you are at the wrong table," she pointed out, as if he did not know.

"As long as I am with Persephone, I am right," he said.

Aphrodite frowned, and Hades wondered why she cared at all about where he sat.

"How is Harmonia, Aphrodite?" Persephone asked.

"Fine, I suppose," Aphrodite answered. "She has been spending much of her time with your friend Sybil."

"I think they have become very good friends."

Aphrodite smirked, eyes glinting. "*Friends.* Have you forgotten I am the Goddess of Love?"

Persephone said nothing, and Aphrodite turned to Hephaestus, who took her offered hand and led her to the Olympians table.

"Do you think Aphrodite is…opposed to Harmonia's choice of partner?"

"Do you mean is she opposed because Sybil is a woman? No. Aphrodite believes love is love. If Aphrodite is upset, it is because Harmonia's relationship means she has less time for her."

She was quiet for a moment, and he noticed that her gaze wandered back to the goddess.

"Do you think Aphrodite and Hephaestus will ever reconcile?"

"We can all only hope. They are both completely unbearable."

Persephone elbowed him, but Hades felt like he had been dealing with the saga of their marriage since its inception. He wasn't at all sure what exactly went wrong, but whatever had occurred had happened the night of their wedding, and neither of them had ever been the same.

Dinner finally appeared once Zeus decided to join them. It was usual of the god to make them wait; he liked to remind everyone of his importance anytime he had the opportunity.

Hades reached for a silver pitcher on the table.

"Ambrosia?" he offered.

"Straight?" Persephone asked, sounding surprised.

"Just a little," he said as he poured her a small amount

and then filled his glass. Like any alcohol, it required developing a certain level of tolerance—his was high. "What?" he asked, noticing Persephone's stare.

"You are an alcoholic," she said.

She wasn't technically wrong, but it wasn't as if alcohol had any effect on him.

"Functioning," he replied, watching as Persephone took a sip from her glass, as she licked her lips. "Do you like it?" He leaned closer, thinking about kissing her so he could taste it on her tongue, but he didn't.

She met his gaze, and her answer came out on a breath. "Yes."

Callista cleared her throat. The interruption irritated him, and Hades would have ignored it, but Persephone was far more courteous than him.

"So how did you two meet?"

A snort drew Hades's attention, and he looked to see Hermes approaching with his plate and silverware. "You sit before gods and that is the question you choose to ask?" Hermes said.

"Hermes, what are you doing?" Persephone asked.

"I missed you," he said as he sat beside her.

More movement from the Olympian table caught Hades's attention as he watched Apollo leave to sit by a man he could only assume was Ajax—the one he'd agonized over when he'd come to inquire about Adonis's autopsy. Artemis looked both confused and irritated, her mouth set tight, while Zeus glowered. Neither of them liked watching Olympians abandoning their places above the crowd.

"I think you started a movement, Hades," said Persephone.

He met her gaze, smiling at her expression, which seemed to be a mix of amusement and soft admiration.

"I have a question," Thales said, interrupting, and Hades cast his gaze on the minor god. "How will I die?"

"Horribly," Hades replied without pause. He would not normally be so direct, but the response felt deserved given the question.

"Hades!" Persephone scolded.

He felt her elbow nudge him again. This time, he caught it and slid his hand down her arm, threading his fingers with hers.

"Is—is that true?" Thales stuttered.

"He is just kidding," Persephone assured Thales, giving Hades a pointed look. "*Aren't* you, Hades?"

"No," he said.

Hermes choked on a laugh, but a silly question deserved the right answer, though he considered adding that perhaps it would change. It was possible the Fates would not like that he had told Thales of their plans. It wasn't as if he knew the details, just that it would not be pleasant.

A few minutes of blissful silence followed until Zeus pushed back his chair, letting it scrape on the floor loudly to draw attention, and then clanking his glass until Hades wanted to break his teeth.

As Zeus wanted, all eyes were now on him.

"We are gathered to celebrate my brother Hades," Zeus exclaimed. "Who has found a beautiful *maiden* he wishes to marry, Persephone—Goddess of Spring, daughter of *dread* Demeter. Tonight, we celebrate love and those who have found it. May we all be so lucky, and, Hades—" Zeus lifted his glass, and all eyes turned to their table. "May the oracle bless your union."

Zeus's statement served as both a reminder to Hades and Persephone that he was in control but also communicated to those gathered that if he denied their marriage, it was the fault of the oracle and not his.

Reluctantly, Hades lifted his glass to his brother. It was more of a way to emphasize his promise of vengeance than an acknowledgment of what Zeus had said.

As Hades brought his drink to his lips, Persephone turned to him, and the smile on her face drew his attention, tightening his chest. He set the drink aside in favor of her mouth and kissed her.

The mild applause that started at the end of Zeus's toast turned voracious and cheerful. Hermes whistled.

When Hades pulled back, Persephone gave a breathless laugh. "Careful, Lord Hades," she said quietly. "Or you'll lose your vicious reputation."

He wasn't certain about that, but he smiled anyway.

The rest of the dinner passed in relative quiet, and they retired to the porch where Apollo specifically had taken it upon himself to play his lyre. It was likely he desired praise for his skill while also impressing his newest conquest.

"Shall we dance?" Hades asked, turning to Persephone.

"I would like nothing more," she answered.

Hades led her to an open spot at the center of the crowded floor, drawing her close with no intention of trying to conceal his erection, which had roared to life when he'd kissed her at dinner.

"Aroused, my love?" Persephone asked, her voice husky, her eyes heavy-lidded. Perhaps it was the ambrosia that made her so bold.

"Always, my darling," he replied lightly.

When she reached between them to grip him, he knew she was definitely under the influence of ambrosia.

"What are you doing?" he asked, his voice a hum in his chest.

"I don't think I need to explain myself," she said.

"Are you trying to provoke me in front of these Olympians?"

"Provoke you?" she questioned on a breathless laugh. "I would *never*."

He drew her closer and considered how long he would be able to take this teasing, but Persephone was making it *very* hard.

"I am just trying to please you," Persephone said quietly, her gaze unwavering.

"You please me," he said and claimed her mouth in a hard kiss that only grew more demanding as she continued to move her hand against his rigid cock, and there came a point where he had no desire to hold back.

"Enough," he hissed as he tore from her mouth, and though he'd caught the attention of the whole room, he cloaked them in glamour as he gripped her ass and drew her up his body.

"Hades!" she gasped. "Everyone can see!"

"Smoke and mirrors," he said and teleported.

He chose not to leave Olympus, given that Zeus may still summon them to consult the oracle, and teleported to his own estate on the mountain, which typically remained abandoned.

"Not so interested in exhibitionism?" Persephone asked.

"I cannot focus on you the way I wish and maintain

the illusion," he said, which was partly true. The other reason was because his brothers could see through it, but he did not want to talk about them.

He leveraged her against the wall and shifted his fingers so they could drift along her opening where she was hot and wet—a temptation that made his cock twitch.

Persephone's cry caught in her throat. She held him tighter, her breasts pressing into his chest.

"So wet," he said between his teeth. "I could drink from you, but for now, I'll settle with tasting."

He freed his fingers from her sex and sucked them into his mouth before kissing her again—first her mouth and then her jaw, even her breasts, though he had to tease them through the fabric of her dress. She was lively beneath his touch, bending and arching every part of her body, all while her hands sought his skin.

"Hades, I want you inside me," she said, her skin flushed, her eyes bright. "You once told me to dress for sex. Why can't you?"

He laughed. "Perhaps if you were not so eager, darling, finding my flesh would be much easier."

He reached between them, unclasping his robes, and they slipped from his body like shadows. When he managed to slide inside her, they both groaned. Hades's mouth was open against hers, and his tongue darted out to taste hers, his fingers biting into her skin as he held her. His head was so full of dizzying pleasure, he could barely think beyond the feel of it.

"I love you," he said, a little breathless.

"I love you too," she said, her smile genuine.

He thrust his hips, grinding into her, groaning as his balls tightened.

"You feel so good," he said, letting his head fall into the crook of her neck, a thin layer of sweat breaking out over his whole body. "Come for me," he said. "So that I may bathe in your warmth."

Usually, he would try to draw this out—to bring her to the edge and retreat, building up her desire until she demanded to come—but this time, he felt an urgency in his own body that seemed to demand a quick release.

He reached between them, rubbing Persephone's engorged clit. Her legs tightened around him, pulling him closer even as she arched away, body pressing into the wall as she shook with her orgasm.

"Yes, my darling," Hades growled, pumping harder into her spasming muscles until he came too.

Slowly, he lowered Persephone to her feet, smoothing her wild hair.

"Are you well?" he asked, still breathless.

"Yes, of course," she said with a small laugh. "And you?"

"I am well," he said.

More than well.

He kissed her forehead and dressed while Persephone looked around the room.

"Where are we?" she asked.

"These are my accommodations," he said.

"You have a house on Olympus?"

"Yes, though I rarely come here." Which was why he couldn't really call this a home.

"How many houses do you have?"

He thought for a moment, listing them in his mind. His palace in the Underworld, his home on the island of Lampri, the one here on Olympus, and another in Olympia. He had another in Thesprotia and one in Elis.

"Six... I think."

"You... *think?*"

"I don't use them all."

Persephone crossed her arms over her chest, raising her brows. "Anything else you want to tell me?"

"At this very moment?" he asked, the corners of his lips lifting. "No."

"Who manages your estate?" she asked.

"Ilias."

Ilias did *everything*.

"Perhaps I should ask him about your empire."

"You could, but he would tell you nothing."

"I am certain I could persuade him."

"Careful, darling, I'm not opposed to castrating anyone you decide to tease."

"Jealous?"

"Yes," he said, unashamed. "Very."

There was a knock at the door. Since Hades was near, he opened it, though he already knew it was Hermes.

"Dinner wasn't satisfying enough?" Hermes asked.

"Shut up, Hermes," Hades said.

The god grinned, but it soon disappeared as he spoke. "I was sent to retrieve you."

Hades had not considered how he would feel when the time finally came to hear the oracle, but suddenly, he was filled with dread.

"We were just on our way," Hades said.

"*Sure*, and I am a law-abiding citizen."

Hades rolled his eyes.

They left his estate, walking back to the temple, which was so close, he could still hear the music and merry-making. The irony of this feast was that it had nothing to do with celebrating them, not like the celebration the souls in Asphodel had organized for them. This one was about tradition and control.

"Why do I get the feeling Zeus does not want Hades and I to wed?" Persephone asked Hermes, and Hades thought perhaps she was seeking some kind of reassurance.

"Probably because he's a creep and would rather have you himself," said Hermes.

"I am not opposed to murdering a god," Hades said. "Fuck the Fates."

"Calm down, Hades," Hermes said. "I'm just pointing out the obvious. Don't worry, Sephy. Let's just see what the oracle says."

Hades's stomach twisted sharply, but he had to admit he was glad this was almost over. At least then he could decide on his next move. Either way, he would marry Persephone. What mattered was what would come after.

Hades took Persephone's hand as they returned, meeting Zeus just outside the temple. He stood in a slice of golden light that streamed from the arched opening behind him.

"Now that you have decided to rejoin us, perhaps you are ready to hear what the oracle will say about your marriage."

"I am very eager," said Persephone sweetly, though her gaze was hard.

"Then follow me, Lady Persephone," Zeus rumbled.

They left the temple area and made their way through a courtyard of statues, down a narrow path to Zeus's temple. It was a round structure with oak doors, and inside was a basin of oil that he would use to summon Pyrrha, his oracle.

Hades had been through this before, but as a member of what Zeus liked to call his council, though whether he actually listened was debatable. Tonight his council included Hera and Poseidon, neither of whom were favorable choices, though this was where Hera's word mattered most. Would she support Hades as she had agreed?

Persephone hesitated, and Zeus swept his hand before him.

"My council," he said as a way of introducing them.

"I thought the oracle was your council," she said.

"The oracle speaks of the future, yes," he said. "But I have lived a long life, and I am aware that the threads of that future are ever-changing. My wife and brother know that too."

Hades swallowed thickly. He only hoped Zeus applied the same thoughtful consideration to his own situation.

Zeus took a torch from the wall, and as he turned toward the basin, he spoke. "A drop of your blood, if you will."

Hades still held Persephone's hand, and together they approached. He went first as a way of showing her what to do, pressing his finger into the sharp needle protruding from the edge of the basin. He held his hand out until a single bead of his blood dropped into the oil.

Persephone followed his example, her blood mixing with his.

"Hades," she whispered as he took her finger into his mouth to heal.

"I do not wish to see you bleed."

He had said it before. Need he say it again?

"It was only a drop."

He said nothing and guided her away from the basin as Zeus lit the oil.

The fire burned hotly, the flame tinged with green, and the smoke was thick and billowy, emptying via an opening at the height of the domed ceiling. It wasn't long before the oracle appeared, an old woman wreathed in flame.

"Pyrrha," Zeus said. "Give us the prophecy of Hades and Persephone."

"Hades and Persephone," the oracle repeated, as if testing their names on her tongue. "A powerful union—a marriage that will produce a god more powerful than Zeus himself."

Hades stood in quiet and confused shock, scrambling to both recall and memorize every word the oracle had spoken. In truth, he wasn't sure what he had expected the oracle to say, but he knew as soon as he heard her message they were doomed.

Zeus was not likely to allow anyone to wed with his reign at stake.

"Zeus," Hades warned, his body going rigid, his magic on edge—but so were Zeus's and Hera's and Poseidon's.

"Hades."

"You will not take her from me," he said.

"I am king, Hades. Perhaps you need reminding."

"If that is your wish," said Hades, "I am more than happy to be the end of your reign."

There was silence as Hades's threat hung in the air. They all knew it wasn't empty.

"Are you pregnant?" Hera asked suddenly.

"Excuse me?" Persephone asked, but Hades did not flinch. He knew that was impossible.

"Need I repeat myself?" Hera asked.

"That question is not appropriate," Persephone snapped.

"And yet it is important when considering the prophecy," Hera replied.

"Why is that?"

"The prophecy states that your marriage will produce a god more powerful than Zeus," said Hera. "A child born of this union would be a very powerful god—a giver of life and death."

Hades ground his teeth.

"There is no child. There will be *no* children."

Poseidon offered a humorless laugh. "Even the most careful of men have children, Hades. How can you possibly ensure that when you cannot even get through a dance without leaving to fuck?"

"I do not have to be careful. It is the Fates who have taken my ability to have children. It is the Fates who wove Persephone into my world."

Hera tilted her head as if she were curious, her eyes on Persephone. "Do you *wish* to remain childless?"

"I want to marry Hades," Persephone answered. "If I must remain childless, then I will."

Hades swallowed hard, noting how she didn't offer an outright no, and suddenly he felt like he was taking something away from her.

There was another beat of silence before Zeus looked at Hades. "You are *certain* you cannot have children, Brother?"

"Very."

The Fates rarely reversed their decrees. In fact, Hades could not think of one instance when they had.

"Let them marry, Zeus," Poseidon said, almost dismissively, as if he were bored of this. "Obviously they wish to fuck as husband and wife."

"And if the marriage produces a child?" Zeus asked. "I do not trust the Fates. Their threads are ever-moving, ever-changing."

"Then we take the child," Hera said suddenly, her voice devoid of any emotion, likely because it wasn't the first time she had tried to solve a problem by stealing away or disposing of a child.

Though they had established that Hades could not have children, Persephone's fingers squeezed his hand, nails biting into his skin. He understood—it felt like a violation all the same.

"There will be no child," Hades said again, the words slipping between his gritted teeth. His hatred for everything this meeting stood for burned his blood, and he hoped Zeus could feel that in his stare.

After what seemed like an eternity, Zeus spoke. "I will bless this union, but if the goddess ever becomes pregnant," he said, his eyes slipping to Persephone, "the infant must be terminated."

It was enough.

Hades called up his magic and teleported to the Underworld just as Persephone swayed and fell to her knees, vomiting at his feet.

CHAPTER XL
HADES

He knelt beside her and took her into his arms, brushing her hair from her face.

"It's okay," he said, though he didn't believe his own words. He understood why this was devastating, even given that they would not...*could* not have children. It was the violation of the whole thing. They had to admit to things that should have remained between them.

"It's not. It isn't," she sobbed. "I will *destroy* him. I will *end* him."

"My darling," he said. "I have no doubt. Come, on your feet." He urged her to her feet and took her face between his hands, holding her teary gaze. "Persephone, I would never—will never—let them have any part of you. Do you understand?"

She nodded, taking a breath but clearly overwhelmed, so he took her to the baths and helped her out of her dress and into the tub. She sat with her knees to her chest and seemed to relax the longer she remained in the warm water.

Hades lowered to his knees beside the pool and ran soap and water over her skin. He worked slowly, in time with her breaths, which became deep and shallow, and then her hand came down on his wrist, halting his touch as it passed over her breasts.

"Hades," she murmured, her eyes falling to his mouth.

The tension between them was thick and burning, and they seemed to move at the same time, each of them dragging the other closer. Their lips collided in a hard kiss that sent a wave of heat straight to his groin.

"I want you," she said, gripping him tight.

"Marry me."

She gave a breathless laugh. "I already said yes."

"You have, so marry me. Tonight." She just stared, so he explained, "I do not trust Zeus or Poseidon or Hera, but I trust us. Marry me tonight, and they cannot take it away."

He knew it was far more sudden than either of them had expected, but what difference did it make if they waited? Besides, if she married him now, she would have power over his realm.

She studied him a moment before a smile spread across her face as she answered, "Yes."

His grin matched hers, and he drew her to him once more, kissing her until he ached for her.

"I will have you tonight as my wife," he promised. "Come. I will summon Hecate."

Hades retrieved a robe for her and as they left the baths, Hecate was waiting.

"Oh, my dear!" she said, embracing Persephone. "Can you believe it? You will be married tonight!

Let's get you ready." Then her eyes slipped to him and narrowed. "And if I see—or sense—you anywhere near the queen's suite, I will banish you to Arachne's Pit."

Hades chuckled.

"I will not peek," he promised, his gaze shifting to Persephone, as there was a part of him that was still trying to grasp the fact that by the end of this night, she would be his wife. "I'll see you soon."

"I'm not going to lie," said Hermes. "I'm a little salty you let Hecate dress you for what is likely the most fashionable event of your life."

"I didn't *let* her do anything," said Hades. "She just did it."

He straightened his jacket for the millionth time.

"Stop pulling on it!" Hermes chided. "Here."

Hermes pushed Hades's hands down and smoothed his collar and the lapels of his jacket. When he was finished, his hands fell to his sides, and he met Hades's gaze.

"I'm really happy for you, Hades," he said, his tone and expression so serious, it was most unnerving. Hermes was rarely sentimental, save for when he was angry.

"Thanks, Hermes," Hades said. "You really are a great friend."

"The best, right?" Hermes asked with a grin.

"Don't push it," Hades replied.

Hermes chuckled. "As for me, I'm not sure I could commit to just one person. I am a god with many needs, if you know what I mean."

He waggled his brows, and Hades rolled his eyes.

"*Everyone* knows what you mean, Hermes. It's not as if you keep it a secret."

There was a knock at the door, and they both looked up as Hecate popped her head in.

"Hades, it's time. You must take your place!"

Hermes led him from the palace. Cerberus, Typhon, and Orthrus followed behind him as they made their way to Hecate's grove. As they neared, he grew increasingly nervous. He wasn't even sure why. Maybe it was the significance of this event. Hades had been desperate for this for so long, and now it was finally here. He almost couldn't believe it.

They came around a line of trees, and Hades halted in his tracks, realizing that he hadn't been prepared for this at all—to find the grove both decorated beautifully and crowded with souls and divinity alike, all gathered to celebrate the great and passionate love that had blossomed between him and Persephone, this incredible goddess who had brought life to his world in ways he had never thought possible.

It was almost overwhelming but in a way that made his chest and throat feel tight.

He made his way down the aisle to the arbor of greenery at the end and took his place on the right. Cerberus, Typhon, and Orthrus remained at his feet. Hermes sat in the front row beside Apollo—both had left the feast upon his summons, because he knew Persephone would want them here.

Hermes leaned forward and half whispered, half yelled, "Don't lock your knees, or you'll pass out."

"I'm not locking my knees," Hades whispered back, though he wasn't sure why. "Why would you tell me that?"

"I'm not saying you are. I'm saying *don't.*"

Well, now he was worried. What if he passed out? He practiced bending his knees just to make sure he knew the difference between bent and locked knees.

"You look like an idiot," said Hermes.

Hades glared, but then the music started—played by a small group of souls who sat off to the side—and his eyes shifted to the end of the aisle.

His heart raced in his chest and throughout his whole body as he waited for Persephone to appear, and then she did, and she was so fucking beautiful it physically *hurt* to look at her. All he could think was that everything he'd ever done or fucked up was worth it for this one moment.

He worked to memorize it—every detail of her approach—from the baby's breath on her head to the silhouette of her gown to the way her eyes lit up when she saw him and the smile that followed.

Gods, he never thought he would be grateful for the Fates.

True to her nature, she stopped to hug those closest to her, including Apollo and Hermes, and then she was finally in front of him, and he felt a profound and euphoric rush of pure joy.

She took a step toward him when Lexa pulled her back to take her bouquet. Hades chuckled, and the crowd laughed.

"Eager, darling?" he asked.

"Always," she said, and when she finally stood opposite him, he took her hands. "Hi."

"Hi," he said, grinning. "You are beautiful."

"So are you."

He thought it would be easier to breathe once she was in front of him, but it wasn't.

Hecate cleared her throat as she stepped between them, looking from him to Persephone.

"I knew this moment would come eventually," Hecate said. "I have seen love—all forms and degrees—but there is something dear about this love—the kind you two share. It is desperate and fierce and passionate." She paused to laugh, and so did everyone behind them. "And perhaps it is because I know you, but it is my favorite kind of love to watch. It blossoms and blazes, challenges and teases, hurts and heals. There are no two souls better matched. Apart, you are light and dark, life and death, a beginning and an end. Together, you are a foundation that will weave an empire, unite a people, and weld worlds together. You are a cycle that never ends—eternal and infinite. Hades."

Hecate gave him Persephone's ring. Her eyes widened when she saw it, and he knew she was just now realizing she didn't have one, but she had no need to worry. He had prepared for this moment.

"Do you take Persephone to be your wife?" Hecate asked.

"I do," he said as he slipped the ring on her finger.

"Persephone," Hecate said, giving her a black ring. "Do you take Hades to be your husband?"

"I do," she said, and as she slid the ring on his finger, Hades felt like she had given him the greatest gift.

He had the honor of being her husband.

"You may kiss the bride, Hades."

He took her radiant face between his hands.

"I love you," he said and pressed his mouth to hers,

gentle at first, thinking it would be enough, but it wasn't. He pulled her against him, parting her mouth with his tongue, deepening the kiss, and it was strange to say, but it felt different. Maybe it was because he had never been so happy. Either way, he was very aware that this was his wife, his goddess, his queen.

"Get a room!" Hermes shouted.

He held her in his embrace a little longer just for that. When he pulled away, he pressed his lips to her forehead before taking her hand and turning to the crowd.

"May I present Hades and Persephone, King and Queen of the Underworld."

The crowd erupted in great applause, and they returned down the aisle as husband and wife. Once they had come around the copse of trees, he paused to kiss her again.

"I have never seen anything more beautiful than you," he said, looking down at her, memorizing her as she stared back just as intently, just as happily.

"I love you. So much," she said.

"Come," Hecate said sharply, teleporting them into the library. "You have a few minutes to yourselves until I return to collect you for the festivities," she said. "If I were you, I'd keep your clothes on…and your feet on the ground."

When they were alone, he looked down at Persephone. "That sounded like a challenge."

"Are you up for it, husband?"

That word tightened his chest, and he closed his eyes against the emotion that welled within his eyes.

"Are you okay?" she whispered.

"Say it again. Call me your husband."

"I said, are you up for the challenge, *husband*?"

When he was sure he could handle it, he looked at her again and drew their hips together.

"As much as I want you now," he said, "I have something else planned for us tonight."

"Does it involve...something new?"

"Are you asking...for something new?"

"Yes," she whispered.

He took one of her hands, which had come to rest on his chest, and kissed the inside of her wrist.

"And what is it you wish to try?"

He wasn't prepared for her answer.

"Restraints."

CHAPTER XLI
HADES

Restraints, she said.

There was an anxious part of him that did not want to try it again, especially on this night—the most memorable one of their lives—but if it went well, then it would be more than anything he'd hoped for, like everything that had happened so far.

He would just have to be more for her tonight—more attentive, more present, more communicative—and he could do that. He *would* do that.

It wasn't long before Hecate retrieved them from the library, which was good because Hades was seconds away from leaving. She led them to the ballroom, and on the other side of the doors, he heard Hermes announce them.

"Introducing your Lord and Lady of the Underworld, King Hades and Queen Persephone."

When the doors opened, it was to great applause and cheering. The ballroom was packed with people, but it did not bother him the way the crowd on Olympus had. They walked along the path the souls had made to the courtyard to dance beneath the moon and stars.

He drew her into his arms, almost too close to do anything beyond sway in place, but he did not care. This was what he wanted—to be near her, to feel her, to know this was real.

"What are you thinking?" she asked after a long moment.

Neither of them had spoken, basking in this moment of quiet happiness.

"I am thinking of many things, wife," he said and could not help smiling when he used the word. It was perhaps his favorite title he had ever bestowed.

"Like?"

"I am thinking of how happy I am," he answered.

"Is that all?"

"I wasn't finished," he said, knowing what she was asking because he had felt it the moment they'd approached the topic of sex. "I am wondering if you are wet for me. If your stomach is wound tight with desire. If you're fantasizing about tonight as much as I am—and are your thoughts just as vulgar?"

Her gaze was unwavering.

"Yes."

His hands flexed on her hips, and he wondered how appropriate it would be to leave this celebration early, though Hades wasn't sure he wanted to risk never hearing the end of it from Hecate, who had put in so much work, along with Yuri and the other souls in Asphodel. In many ways, this was just as much for them, and he did not wish to take away their only chance to celebrate their union, even if he knew what they were most excited about was having Persephone as their queen.

That fact became more evident as the night progressed and the souls drew her into dance after dance.

He watched her for a while when Hecate approached.

"Come, my king," she said. "You should dance on your wedding night."

He took her offered hand, and they joined the others on the floor.

"Thank you, Hecate," he said. "I will forever be grateful for everything."

She smiled. "You're welcome, my dear, but I would do anything for you. I would do anything for Persephone."

There was a weight to her words that was almost threatening. He could feel it, as if she too wanted to promise the end of the world if either of them came to harm.

They danced a while, and then Hades was pulled into a circle of little girls who sang "Ring around the Rosie" over and over again, and while he was trapped there, his attention caught on Apollo, who stood in the shadow of the room with Hyacinth. The two stood close but not touching, and Hades wondered how the God of Music was coping now that he had found a mortal love interest.

Hades was not someone who believed that everyone had one true love in their lifetime. The only reason he believed it for himself was because he wanted it no other way. Sometimes he wondered if Apollo was the same. The thing about Apollo and Hyacinth's love was that it had changed the god on a fundamental level, not only as he fell for the man but also in his death.

Sometimes that was what people were unable to come back from.

When he was finally released from the confines of the ring of Rosie—or whatever it was—he crossed the room toward Apollo, who was now alone.

When he noticed Hades's approach, Apollo stiffened and lifted his chin, his throat bobbing up and down.

"Are you all right?" Hades asked.

"Do not be concerned for me," Apollo said. "This is your wedding."

"If Persephone saw you, she would be concerned," Hades said.

Apollo angled himself away from the crowd, his face splotchy red.

"What did you tell Hyacinth?"

He took a breath. "I told him about Ajax," he said and paused, his voice thick with emotion. "It isn't at all bad. He was so happy for me."

"It has been a long time, Apollo," Hades said as gently as possible.

"I know. The thing is, I just…don't know that I expected him to be happy."

Hades frowned. "What do you mean?"

Apollo was quiet before he answered. "I don't know. I guess I thought…if he still loved me, he would be angry…but that's not what happened."

"Hyacinth loves you, Apollo," Hades said. "And just because you move on in life does not mean you love him any less."

"It felt wrong, you know?" Apollo said, meeting Hades's gaze. "Until now."

"You know you always had his blessing."

Apollo nodded, and Hades's gaze shifted to Hyacinth, who had returned, two drinks in hand.

"Lord Hades, congratulations!" he said, his eyes bright with mirth.

Apollo took a breath to compose himself and then turned to face the mortal prince.

"Thank you, Hyacinth," Hades said, nodding once. "I'll leave you two to the festivities."

Hades wandered outside into the Underworld night, leaving behind the clamor of the crowd. He needed the space and the quiet. He wasn't overwhelmed exactly, but there came a point when he only wanted to sit with his thoughts.

He was eager to be alone with his bride. When he thought of how this evening had begun, he had no idea it would escalate to this. He doubted his brother expected him to marry so quickly. Zeus had likely anticipated that they would wed publicly, both in the Upperworld and on Olympus.

Weddings between gods among the Olympians were rare and celebrated as monumental occasions, and while it was a monumental occasion in his life, Hades was not so certain he wished to share that with anyone beyond his realm, especially in the climate that existed in the Upperworld right now. It was likely, if word was to get out about their marriage, it would be seen as a selfish choice, given Demeter's snowstorm.

But Hades hated the politics. He hated that their union had been about power at all, when all he wanted was to marry the woman he loved. And so he had, come what may.

He heard the familiar sounds of his dogs' loud

sniffing, and when he turned, Persephone was walking down the path toward him, and it was like being back in that moment when she'd rounded the tree line to marry him.

He smiled at her as she approached and then asked quietly, "Are you well?"

"I am," she replied.

"Are you ready?"

"I am."

He offered his hand, and when she took it, they vanished.

Hades had planned no part of the wedding, but that did not mean he hadn't planned for the night. He had only thought of one thing when he considered where to take her, and that was some place beyond this world, to a place that had not been touched by terror or strife.

He wanted to take her to the stars.

He was pleased with the illusion, and as they stood on the platform of their marriage bed, stars glittered all around.

"Are we...in the middle of a lake?" Persephone asked.

"Yes," he answered.

"Is this your magic?"

"It is," he said. "Do you like it?"

"It is beautiful," she said. "But where are we, really?"

"We are in the Underworld. In a space I made."

"How long have you planned this?"

"I have thought about it for a while," he said, just as he'd thought about her ring for a while.

Persephone's lips curled, and she approached the bed, smoothing her hand over the soft silk sheets. He wondered what she was doing—perhaps making sure it was real—but then she straightened and looked at him over her shoulder.

"Help me out of my dress," she said.

He obliged happily and approached, drawing the zipper down, letting his fingers drift along her spine as he returned to guide the thin straps of her gown from her shoulders. As it pooled to the ground, he realized she wore nothing beneath.

She turned to him slowly and met his gaze. There was a strange and nervous energy between them. He wasn't sure why; it was not as if they were new to this, but perhaps it had something to do with her earlier request.

He drew her nearer, the tension a physical thing. He could feel it in the space between them even as he closed it, even as he pressed his mouth to hers and touched her soft skin. He smoothed his hands up her sides to her breasts, then to her back so he could pull her even closer.

He didn't want to stop but he had to. When he drew away, he pulled a small, black box from his pocket.

"These are Chains of Truth," he said. "They are a powerful weapon against any god unless they have the password. I am telling you that password now so that if you begin to feel afraid, you can release yourself from their grasp. Eleftherose ton—say it."

She looked at him and then at the box.

"Eleftherose ton."

He watched her lips as she repeated the words. "Perfect."

"Why are they called Chains of Truth?"

"The only truth they shall draw from your lips is your pleasure," he promised. "Lie down."

She turned and gave him her ass as she crawled onto the bed. He had to restrain himself from dragging her back to him by her hips to swat her and fuck her from behind—there would be enough time for that later. Right now, he had an obligation to make sure she felt safe and comfortable, and he would do nothing else until that happened.

Even if his cock was raging.

She shifted onto her back and spread her arms when Hades instructed. He hovered over her, unable to take his eyes off her glorious body. Preparing her for this process was just as fucking erotic.

When he placed the box over her head, the restraints materialized. At first, they were heavy manacles made of iron, meant for restraining a god. Hades touched them, turning them into soft bindings.

"Forgive me, my darling," he said and then met her gaze. "Are you ready?"

"For you?" she asked. "Always."

"Always," he said, the word shuddering through him.

He sat back, admiring her as he removed his jacket and shirt. He was thinking that he liked this, that he could do this now that she had a safe word.

Her eyes were dark despite their color and tracked his every move.

"What are you thinking?" he asked.

"I want you to move faster," she said, and her eyes widened as those words fell from her mouth. She looked up at the restraints around her wrists and tugged on one before looking at him again. "Is there any chance you get to wear these?"

"If that is what you want," he said as he discarded his shirt. "But you do not need chains to draw the truth from me, especially when it comes to what I plan to do to you."

"I'd rather not hear your plans," she said.

He smirked. He knew she just wanted him to begin. "What do you want, wife?"

"Action," she said, moving beneath him.

Fuck, she was beautiful and so tempting.

He laughed as he pressed a kiss between her breasts, then on each of them. Her legs closed around him, her hips grinding into his erection.

He liked her eagerness. He hoped it meant that by the time he made it between her legs, she was so wet he could drown. He made his way down her body, and her legs fell open, exposing her wicked flesh to his mouth.

He licked and sucked her there, and she moaned.

"This," he said roughly. "I love this."

He loved the way she tasted and how she smelled, the silkiness of her on his tongue. Mostly, he loved her and how she responded—the way her heels dug into the bed, the way her thighs pressed into him as she felt each wave of pleasure, the way her fingers twined around the chains.

"Oh, it's so good," she breathed.

His finger was inside her, his mouth on her clit. He broke long enough to encourage her words.

"That's it, darling. Tell me how it feels."

"It's good. So good." She managed to look at him before her head fell back against the pillow on a guttural moan.

When she came, her body tightened around him so hard it was like she wanted to trap him between her legs forever. If it meant pleasuring her this way for an eternity, he would gladly stay, but his own need for her pulsed between his legs. He kissed up her body, and with the taste of her on his tongue, he shook with the carnal need to bury himself inside her.

"Where are you going?" she asked when he stood, his hands already on the button of his trousers.

"Not far, wife," he said as he finished undressing, and when he was naked, he was fully aware of her stare. It burned his skin, made his cock grow thicker and his balls heavier. He could not wait to be inside her, to make her his wife in this way. It did not matter that they'd had sex so many times before; this was still different.

"Tell me your thoughts," he prompted her again, curious as to what was behind that heated gaze.

"It doesn't matter how often you are inside me," she said. "I can't…it's not enough."

He climbed on top of her, letting his body rest against hers, reveling in the warmth and wild energy between them.

"I love you," he said as he stared down at her.

"I love you."

He would never tire of hearing those words returned, and for the first time tonight, he wanted her hands free so she could touch him, but he would wait.

That was a reward in and of itself.

"Are you well?" he asked, wanting to make sure.

"Yes." She nodded, though her voice trembled slightly. "I am just thinking of how much I truly love you."

He did not doubt her love, but he mourned that she would never know how much it meant to him. He had waited for her. He had ached for her. He had dreamed of her, and here she was—real and warm, lying beneath him.

And now he wanted inside.

He kissed her hard and then guided his length to her opening. She lifted her legs, digging her heels into his ass, trying in vain to push him inside harder and faster, but he resisted her urging and slid inside in one slow stroke. When his balls settled against her, he shifted her legs so that they were propped against his shoulders and pumped into her.

He focused on her, how she quaked beneath him, how her breasts bounced with his thrusts, how her eyes held his and then closed in pleasure, her mouth following the same sort of pattern. Her reactions were everything he wanted. She made it hard to focus, harder to maintain this for long.

"You feel so good. So tight, so wet," he said, increasing his pace from a steady and methodical movement to something far more possessive and carnal. Fuck, he was ready to have her hands on him. "Eleftherose ton!"

He let her legs go and leaned down to take her mouth against his in a messy kiss as her fingers threaded through his hair before she moved down to grip his ass, pulling him against her harder.

"Fuck!"

He broke away and sat back on his heels, bringing her with him. He helped her sit on his cock as she wrapped her legs around him. They held each other tightly as they both moved, grinding together, and he knew he could not hold on for much longer. It was the way she breathed, the way her nipples scraped against his chest, the way she felt around him.

They both tensed and tightened, their fingers pressing hard into their bodies the harder they moved, the more they chased the feeling of ecstasy erupting between them. When she tightened around him in release, he came in a rush that went straight to his head.

He was dizzy as he fell back against the bed with Persephone in his arms, bodies heavy.

Persephone started to laugh.

"I will refrain from thinking you are laughing at my performance, wife," he said.

She laughed harder and finally stopped to look at him.

"No," she said, tracing his features. "You were everything."

He shifted them to their sides so they could face each other.

"You are my everything," he said. "My first love, my wife, the first and last Queen of the Underworld."

CHAPTER XLII
HADES

The next morning, Hades rose with Persephone to get ready for the day. It felt strange to do something so routine after the evening they'd had. Hades felt like they should continue to celebrate, and by celebrate, he meant *remain in bed*. But he knew that was not possible given the circumstances.

He made a drink and waited near the fire while she continued getting ready, preferring to dress the mortal way.

"You're quiet," he said, sipping his whiskey.

Persephone paused to look at him as she rolled a pair of thick stockings over her knees.

"I am just thinking of how surreal this is," she said. "I am your wife."

He set the drink on the mantle and crossed to her, letting his fingers linger on her cheek.

"It is surreal," he said.

"What are you thinking?" she asked.

He considered lying, but he answered truthfully. "That I will do anything to keep you."

"You are thinking Zeus will try to separate us?"

"Yes," he said, tipping her head back farther. "But you are mine and I intend to keep you forever."

"Why do you think he let us leave?" she asked.

"Because of who I am," he said. "Challenging me is not like challenging another god. I am one of the three—our power is equal. He will have to take time deciding how to punish me."

She swallowed hard, and he hated that he had given her anxiety.

He kissed her forehead. "Do not worry, my darling. All will be well."

"Eventually," she said.

"Shall I take you to work?" Hades asked.

"No," she said, standing and straightening her skirt. "I am going to breakfast with Sybil."

He paused and then asked, "Will you tell her that we are married?"

"Can I?"

"Sybil is trustworthy," Hades said. "It is her greatest attribute."

Persephone smiled. "She will be ecstatic."

While he did not take her to work, he did see her off to breakfast with her friend, teleporting outside Nevernight where Antoni waited to drive her.

"I shall see you tonight, my wife," Hades said and drew her in for a kiss. Then he reached for the door and helped her into the cabin.

"I love you," she whispered.

"I love you," he said and shut the door.

He watched the car until it was out of sight and then spoke.

"What is it, Ilias?" he asked, already feeling dread at the satyr's presence.

"I couldn't tell you until Persephone left," he said. "But this morning, we found five nymphs on our doorstep, frozen to death."

"Fuck."

"She's out of control," said Hades, watching video from last night when the five nymphs appeared out of thin air and land on the doorstep of his club.

"Five lives," said Ilias, his voice quiet and mournful. "And for what? To send a message?"

"No," he said. "The message has been sent. Now she is just being cruel."

Demeter had played on Persephone's sense of responsibility to the world with the snowstorm, but now that it had not worked, she had changed tactics and would hurt her directly.

Hades's hands fisted and his jaw tightened.

"Do you think Demeter knows?" Ilias asked.

He did not need to be specific. Hades knew he was asking about their marriage.

"No, but she likely knows that Zeus gave us his blessing."

Fuck.

He had no doubt that despite their quick departure, Zeus had announced the union publicly, heedless of the consequences. It wasn't that he did not know them; it was that he did not care. Any fallout from Demeter meant that Zeus could blame the Goddess of Harvest when they were forced to part.

Now Hades had to think about how to tell Persephone five of the women she had essentially grown up with were dead because of them, and only hours after they had become husband and wife.

Gods, he hated Demeter.

It was one thing to pummel the world with her magic. It only fed his power. It was another to hurt his wife in such a cruel and cold manner.

It was unforgivable.

It was madness, and he wondered—dreaded—what came next.

"What would you like for me to do?" Ilias asked.

Hades did not know. He could attempt to seek Demeter out again but confronting her would have no impact upon the goddess. She'd made the decision to hurt Persephone because of him. His pleas would go unheard. Besides, the damage was done. When his wife returned home later, she would have to burying five of her friends.

Guilt welled in his chest, rising thickly into the back of his throat.

He should have never ordered those women to find Demeter but the last thing he'd expected was murder.

Fuck.

"I shall have to inform their father," he said distantly.

Though it was likely Nereus already knew. Gods could feel this sort of thing—the end of life they had given.

"Perhaps I should," Ilias suggested.

Hades did not accept or deny his offer, his mind

racing. He had been so nonchalant about their fear of death because he had not believed they would die—he had not seen in their soul or in their threads. Demeter's ending of five immortal lives would have great consequences. He wondered if the Fates would take a life or grant one. Would the sacrifice be as dangerous as the resurrection of the Ophiotaurus?

"Prepare them for burial," Hades said. "I...have no doubt Persephone will wish to see them."

She will want to say goodbye and then she will rage—whether at him or Demeter was yet to be determined.

Hades was still thinking about the five nymphs an hour later when Ilias returned. He expected the satyr to inform him that the work was finished and to inquire after a visit to Nereus, but his expression communicated something far more concerning.

"Persephone has been revealed as a goddess," he said.

Hades brows lowered. "What?"

"New Athens News," he said, unable to verbalize much else. "It's their top story."

Fucking Helen.

Hades rose from his seat. Together, they headed downstairs to the main floor of Nevernight and switched on a television. The top headline was about Persephone.

Woman Outed as the Daughter of Demeter

The anchor on television reported, *"The woman, Persephone Rossi, who is engaged to Hades, the God of the Dead, assumed an identity as a mortal journalist. She made headlines earlier this year by writing critiques about the Divine."*

"Do you think she's prepared for this?" Ilias asked.

"To be outed as goddess to the world?" Hades asked. "No."

Persephone had only started to come to terms with her own divinity. Now, the world would be even more interested in her than they were before when they assumed he'd fallen in love with a mortal woman, even those who were angry at her for her so-called deception. She would face obsession and hate—ultimately all of it was worship which meant her power would only grow in strength...the power she could barely control.

As they watched, the broadcast shifted suddenly, and the anchor announced breaking news.

"We are receiving reports of an avalanche near Sparta and Thebes. The cities are buried under several feet of snow. Rescue workers have been dispatched."

Fuck.

Fuck. Fuck.

That meant thousands of souls were about to flood the Underworld—but not just mortals, animals, too, and it was all because of Demeter's fucking snowstorm.

Persephone would be devastated and he wondered what she would do when she discovered the horror her mother had inflicted upon the world.

Though he did not have to wait long to find out because he felt Persephone's power erupted, far stronger than ever before. It felt anguished and angry and it shook him to the soul.

Fucking Fates.

"I have to go to Persephone," he said.

He knew her capabilities when she was pushed too far and this time, it get the attention of Olympus.

He let his magic unfurl, seeking the energy of the stones in her ring, and when he latched on to it, he went to her, finding her at the center of eight Olympians. Apollo and Hermes stood slightly in front of Persephone, blocking her from the others.

Hades placed a possessive hand on her stomach and drew her against him.

"Angry, darling?" he asked, his lips near her ear.

"A little," she replied.

Despite their casual exchange, Hades's heart was racing. He glared at Zeus, who stood directly across from them with Hera on one side and Poseidon on the other. The rest of the Olympians fell in line.

Demeter was noticeably absent.

"That was quite a display of power, little goddess," said Zeus.

"Call me little one more time," Persephone said, her body tensing beneath Hades's hand.

Zeus chuckled.

"I am not sure why you are laughing," she said. "I have asked for your respect before. I will not ask again."

"Are you threatening your king?" Hera asked.

"He is not my king," Persephone said, her tone vicious.

The lines on Zeus's face seemed to darken. "I should never have allowed you to leave that temple. That prophecy was not about your children. It was about you."

"Leave it, Zeus," Hades said. He held Persephone tighter. "This will not end well for you."

"Your goddess is a threat to all Olympians," Zeus said.

"She is a threat to *you*," Hades said.

"Step away, Hades," Zeus ordered. "I will not hesitate to end you too."

Hades had expected this moment. He had prepared for it, but not so soon, and now his mind raced, wondering if they were ready.

If Persephone was ready.

"If you make war against them, you make war against me," said Apollo, summoning his golden bow.

"And me," Hermes said, drawing his blade.

The silence was quiet and heavy. "You would commit treason?" Zeus asked.

"It wouldn't be the first time," Apollo said.

"You would protect a goddess whose power might destroy you?" Hera asked.

"With my life," Hermes said. "Sephy is my friend."

"And mine," said Apollo.

"And mine," said Aphrodite, who broke from the line and crossed to stand beside Apollo, calling Hephaestus's name. The God of Fire also appeared, filling the space beside her.

"I will not battle," Hestia said.

"Nor I," Athena said.

"Cowards," Ares shot back.

"Battle should serve a purpose beyond bloodshed," said Athena.

"The oracle has spoken and pinned this goddess as a threat," Ares argued. "War eliminates threats."

"So does peace," said Hestia.

Hades was not surprised by their decision, and the two left. They faced Zeus, Hera, Poseidon, Artemis, and Ares.

When they began, Hades would focus on subduing

his brothers. He just hoped he could keep them both engaged in battle and away from Persephone.

"You are sure this is what you want, Apollo?" Artemis asked from across the field.

"Seph gave me a chance when she shouldn't have. I owe her."

"Is her chance worth your life?"

"In my case?" Apollo asked. "Yes."

"You will regret this, little goddess," Zeus promised, and Hades could feel his magic charging the air. It raised the hair on his arms and the back of his neck.

"I *said* don't call me little."

Her power broke the earth beneath their feet, and the Olympians scrambled back, rising into the air. Hades remained behind Persephone, waiting to see how she would defend herself, needing to know that she could hold her own in this fight.

Zeus's magic flashed in his hands as he summoned a bolt of lightning and hurled it at her feet, causing the earth to shake. He had done it to scare her, thinking that she would wilt at his powerful display, but Persephone remained firm before him.

"You are as dogged as your mother," Zeus snarled.

"I believe the word you are looking for is strong willed," Persephone replied.

Zeus moved to strike again, and Persephone called up a wall of sharp thorns to stop the blow. That was enough.

Hades stepped between them and dropped his glamour, his shadows falling away, barreling toward Zeus. One managed to pass through his body, stealing his breath, but Zeus recovered in time to deflect the other two with the cuffs that braced his arms.

"The rule of women, Hades, is you never give them your heart." Zeus summoned another lightning bolt.

"I have never taken advice from you, Brother. Why would I start now?" Hades said, calling for his bident.

"Perhaps you should have. Then we would not be here today."

There was a lot of truth to those words.

"I like it here," Hades said, glancing around at the other Olympians locked in battle. "Feels like home."

Neither of them hesitated, their weapons meeting so violently, they were both jarred by the power. They thrust their hands out at the same time, Zeus striking with lightning and Hades with his shadows. Each of them were thrown back by their blasts, feet skidding over the ground, creating deep fissures. They stopped at the same time and then charged one another, slamming together, the impact shaking the very earth.

They both swung, using their fists to fight now.

"You would betray me for her?" Zeus said between his teeth.

"I would betray you for a lot less," Hades hissed.

Zeus snarled and his energy felt nuclear as it erupted around him, throwing Hades back. The earth bloomed up around him as he landed in a cavity created by his own impact. Before the dust had cleared, he saw Zeus's silhouette flash over him as the god came down on him. Hades teleported quickly, but Zeus followed, their bodies slamming into each other again.

Hades thrust his hand out, gripping Zeus's neck. The skin beneath his hold blackened, rotting away beneath his touch. His brother's hands came down on his arms, and as they did, Hades's claws thrust into him, and he tore away, taking Zeus's throat with him.

Zeus clutched at his neck, his eyes gleaming with fury as he glared at Hades, his breathing ragged and wet. He roared and struck, slamming into Hades so hard, he felt his bones break and heal and break and heal in a jarring succession. He squeezed his fists and ground his teeth, shoving his hand toward his brother, sending shadows through him. His body convulsed beneath the magic and then he vanished, reappearing behind Zeus with his bident. Hades brought the two-pronged staff down on his brother, who turned in time to stop the blow with his bolt.

Then Persephone's vines rose up around Zeus's ankles, and though he broke free of them easily, they continued to climb. It distracted him enough, and Hades sent his shadows flying through him again. Zeus stumbled back with each hit and then fell. The ground opened and swallowed him, burying him alive.

Hades started toward Persephone when the ground began to rumble, and Zeus shot from the earth wreathed in an aura of lightning, his eyes glowing fiercely.

"Persephone!" Hades roared, but he couldn't move fast enough, and the lightning struck. Her body shook and the smell of her hair and flesh burning reached his nose. Hades shot toward her when a hand came down on his shoulder.

"Oh, no, Brother," said Poseidon. "This is your punishment. Watch her burn."

Hades started to move, to fight his brother, but then he noticed something strange about Persephone. The magic did not seem to be harming her anymore. Her body no longer shook beneath Zeus's power. It glowed with it.

She was harnessing it.

Oh, fuck.

She sent the bolt back to Zeus, and the God of the Skies fell to the earth.

Hades twisted quickly, sending his shadows barreling toward Poseidon, but they shattered at the end of his trident. Hades summoned his bident again, and their weapons met in a fury of blows. Hades fought fiercely, hate raging in his blood, fueling the frenzy with which he fought. His bident landed a blow across Poseidon's face, cutting his cheek so fiercely, it hung from his face. The blow dazed his brother, and as he stumbled back, Hades buried his bident in Poseidon's chest and kicked him to the ground.

Hovering over him, he pulled his weapon out of his brother's body and shoved it in again and again, and the only thing that stopped him was a bellow of pain.

Hades whirled and found Aphrodite impaled by Ares's golden spear.

Hephaestus was the one screaming. He tore his way toward her, wreathed in flame. He pulled the spear from her body, his hand covering the wound as her blood seeped between his fingers.

Ares neared. "Aphrodite...I didn't mean—"

"If you take another step," Hephaestus threatened, "I will slit your throat."

On the ground nearby was Persephone. Hades teleported to her and urged her to her feet.

"Persephone, come," he said.

They had to get out of there. It was the first of many battles they would fight, and for now, this one was over.

"Aphrodite!" Persephone tried to go to her, but Hades held her back.

"We must go," he said.

"Apollo! Heal her!" she screamed.

Hades gathered her into his arms and vanished even as she screamed.

CHAPTER XLIII
HADES

Persephone was still screaming when they made it to the Underworld.

"It's going to be okay," Hades said. He knew those were the wrong words, but he did not know what else to offer. There was nothing that could quite quell the hysteria of battle—not even time.

"She took that spear for me," she said, leaning heavily against him.

"Aphrodite will be well. It is not yet her time to die," Hades promised, though he could not discount the terror of seeing the goddess injured and in such a violent manner. Persephone had never seen Olympians battle before. "Sit."

She followed his directions but spoke as he knelt before her. "Hades, we cannot stay here. We have to find Sybil."

"I know, I know," he said, though he had no idea what she was talking about. He just needed her to sit still for a few moments. Her shirt was covered in blood, and he would not feel at ease until he knew she was not injured. "Just let me make sure you are well."

"I'm fine," she argued. "I healed myself."

"*Please.*"

He knew she'd been practicing her healing skills, but he had to be sure, because he could already feel his body shaking and his heart racing at the sight of her blood.

She stared at him for a moment and then relented, unbuttoning her shirt to show him her smooth skin. He took a breath and then shot to his feet, that strange terror roiling through him turning to anger.

"Fuck!" he roared. "I never fucking wanted this for you!"

"Hades, this is not your fault."

"I wanted to protect you from this," he said.

He had tried so hard, but at some point, it seemed inevitable that things would come to this.

"You had no control over how the gods would act today, Hades. I made a choice to use my power. Zeus made a choice to end me."

"I will destroy him," Hades swore.

"I have no doubt," she said. "And I will be beside you when you do."

"Beside me," he said and stroked her cheek. Then he let his hand fall. "Tell me about Sybil."

"This morning, Sybil never showed for breakfast," she explained. "I went in to work hoping she might be there and had just forgotten, but she wasn't. Then when I arrived at my office, there was a box on my desk." She paused and swallowed, her voice shaking slightly. "Sybil's severed finger was inside."

Hades's blood ran cold. He thought of the nymphs Demeter had killed; had she gotten Sybil too? Was this her way of luring Persephone into a trap?

"You are certain it was Sybil's?"

"Yes."

"Where is it now?"

"It's still in my office."

"We'll have to retrieve it," Hades said. "Hecate can cast a tracing spell that will at least tell us where her finger was removed."

"What do we do if she isn't there?"

"I cannot say," Hades said. "It depends on what we find when we trace her."

The point was they needed a place to start.

"Come. We must hurry. We cannot spend much time outside the Underworld given how we left the Olympians."

Hades had expected the retrieval of Sybil's finger to be easy. The hard part would come when Hecate conducted the trace and her rescue, but as soon as they arrived at Persephone's office, he realized he had guessed wrong.

Demeter was not responsible.

It was Theseus.

He should have known.

Demeter used her magic to hurt.

Theseus used weapons.

Gods-dammit.

Theseus sat across from Persephone's desk, reclined on her couch as if he belonged there.

"You," Persephone seethed.

Hades kept his hands planted firmly around her.

"Me," Theseus said in an almost singsong voice. His arrogance permeated the air, an oily feeling that slid over Hades's skin.

"Where is Sybil?" Persephone demanded.

"She's right here," Theseus said, holding up her severed finger.

"What do you want with her?"

"Your cooperation," the demigod said, and then his eyes shifted to Hades. "I will need it after I collect my favor."

Hades went cold, and he dug his hands into Persephone's waist, holding her tighter. He had known this day would come eventually.

Theseus had captured Sisyphus, the mortal responsible for using a spindle to extend his own life. The Fates had been furious and Hades knew that if he did not contain the threat, they would retaliate. So when Theseus brought the mortal and the stolen relic to his doorstep, requested a favor in return, Hades had granted it.

"What favor?" Persephone asked.

"The favor Hades owes me," Theseus said, a smile playing on his thin lips. "For my aid in saving your relationship."

"What is he talking about?" Persephone asked.

Hades did not respond. He was thinking about how he was going to kill Theseus and the best way to engage in the fight without Persephone and Sybil coming to harm.

"Hades?"

"He returned a relic that fell into the wrong hands to me. You have learned the devastation such a piece can cause."

There were no coincidences here. The spindle was the first relic Poseidon and Theseus had introduced to the world as a test. When it had wreaked enough havoc and they were done with their game, Theseus had brought him Sisyphus and the spindle in exchange for the favor.

It was a trap.

It had worked.

"What is it you want from him?" Persephone asked.

"You," Theseus answered.

Hades shook. His bones rattled in his body. He did not think he could hold Persephone any tighter.

"Me?" she asked breathlessly.

"No." Hades's voice was dark but resonant, and his magic rose, thickening the air.

"Favors are binding, Hades," Theseus reminded, as if he were chiding him. "You are obligated to fulfill my request."

"I know the nature of favors, Theseus," Hades hissed.

"You would face Divine death?" Theseus asked, rising from his spot on the couch.

"Hades, no!"

Hades ignored her pleas. "For Persephone? Yes."

"I'm only asking to borrow her. You can have her back when I'm through."

Hades knew too well what that meant.

"Why me?" she asked.

"That is a conversation for another time. For now, you must leave here with me, and Hades cannot follow. If you do not do as I say, I will murder your friend in front of you."

She managed to turn in his arms. He didn't want to look at her.

Don't make me do this, he thought. *Don't make me watch you leave.*

"Persephone," he said, his teeth clenched. There was a thickness in his throat that burned his nose and his eyes.

"It's going to be okay," she whispered.

"No, Persephone." His chest felt heavy, his heart racing in his chest.

"I have lost too many people," she said. "This way...I can keep you all."

He had lost too many people and yet she asked this of him. He couldn't do it. He could not let her go—how was he supposed to watch her walk away with a man who had the power to kill gods?

Persephone rose onto the tips of her toes and pressed a kiss to his lips. He did not return the kiss and he did not release his hold as she pulled away.

"Trust me," she whispered.

"I trust you."

It was Theseus he did not trust.

"Then let me go," she said and he wasn't sure what it was about how she spoke, but he found himself relaxing his fingers but it was as though he'd been spelled, his heart at war with his mind.

Theseus chuckled and opened the door. "You have made the right decision."

Hades held her gaze, unable to look away. She took a few steps back, eyes wide and pleading. She was asking him to let her leave, begging him to stay. When she turned away from him, she took his heart with her..

"Persephone," he said, desperate to call her back.

Do not leave with him, he wanted to say. *We will figure this out*, but he knew there was no escaping Divine Justice if he did not let this transaction take place. As much as he hated to admit it, letting her go was likely the best option. It would leave him free to find her, to save her, to tear Theseus to pieces.

She came to stand beside Theseus, and she held his stare.

"I love you," she said. "And I know you."

He knew what she was saying, because he felt her magic a second before it burst through the ground and took hold of him. His arms and legs suddenly anchored him to the floor, which was quickly buckling beneath his feet.

"Persephone!" he roared though she was right. He'd have likely not let them leave the building before he came after them and she wasn't willing to risk Sybil's life.

As he struggled against her restraints, his muscles shaking, he looked up in time to see her stricken face before the door slammed shut.

CHAPTER XLIV
THESEUS

Theseus ushered Persephone out of Alexandria Tower and into a waiting SUV and climbed into the vehicle behind her. As soon as they were seated, he held out his hand.

"Your ring," he said.

"My—why?"

"Your *ring*," he said sharply. He did not like repeating himself. "Or I will cut your finger off too."

It was not an empty threat. He was a man of his word.

She glared but pulled the ring off. He dropped it into the pocket of his jacket.

"Where are you taking me?" she asked.

He had expected his question. They always wanted to know, as if it the knowledge somehow mattered.

It didn't.

It was not as if she could escape him. By the time they reached their destination and she saw what he was capable of, she would be too afraid to move against him.

"We will be going to the Diadem Hotel until I am ready to execute my plans with you."

"And what are those?"

"I am not one to show my hand before I am ready, *Queen* Persephone."

He'd hoped she would react a little more to the use of her title, but she ignored it. He didn't like that and a wave of irritation rushed to his head, making his face burn.

"Is Sybil there? At the hotel?"

"Yes. You will get to see her. You will need to see her so you can remember why you must follow through on your mission."

The mortal was in bad shape, but that was to be expected. She was the lamb—a sacrifice sent to slaughter. Without her, he had no compliance from Persephone. Demeter had been right about the goddess, she would do anything to save her friends, anything for the world.

Her righteousness would be the end of her—it would be the end of Hades.

She was finally quiet, at least for a moment, though there was a part of him that wanted her to continue preaching to him as if her values were not her weaknesses. He would use each of them against her later as *he* became Fate, weaving a tortuous existence for the Goddess of Spring until she begged for mercy at his feet.

That was what he wanted from her, what he wanted from the world—submission, obedience.

The thought made his cock swell and he glanced at Persephone. She had crammed herself into the corner of the vehicle as far away from him as possible, though she was angled toward him, as if she expected him to attack.

She was prepared to fight him. He liked that. It made his mouth water, it made his dick twitch.

But he knew self-control and understood his

priorities. He had to execute a plan before he could break her.

And break her he would. He would shatter her so thoroughly she would never find all the pieces.

"You are working with my mother?"

He would not exactly call it working. He did not work with anyone. He used what they offered, and when he was done, he discarded what was left. It was simple. No waste.

"We have common goals," he said.

"You both want to overthrow the gods," she said.

"Not overthrow," he said. "Destroy."

"Why? What do you have against the gods? You were born from one."

"I do not hate all gods," he said. "Just the inflexible ones."

There were plenty who were willing to concede to his desires to maintain their existence as they had done when the Olympians first overthrew the Titans. Unlike her, they did not care about humanity, only that they could continue to live in comfort upon the Earth.

"You mean the ones who will not let you have your way?"

"You make me sound selfish. Have I not always spoken of helping the greater good?"

And the greater good was of benefit to all, even those who did not realize it.

But it was just a matter of time before they understood—it was either his idea of the future or war—and who wouldn't want what he had planned? He would bring about a golden age, much like when Cronos ruled. There would peace and prosperity. There would be no need for rules or laws outside of the expectations he had for the world, and his worshippers would listen because he would provide their every need.

And Persephone, whether she wanted to or not, would bring about eternal spring. He would use her as he used all gods—the ones he could force, of course.

"We both know you want power, Theseus. You are only playing at offering mortals what other gods will not grant."

He played at nothing but she was soon to realize that.

Theseus grinned. "Ever the skeptic, Lady Persephone."

His smile did not work on her the way it worked on others. She did not relax or stop scowling. She continued to glare, angry and defiant. Usually, he liked defiance because he could punish it, but right now, he needed her to obey so he could execute his plan.

She did not seem scared so much as angry, which annoyed him.

It did not matter, he supposed, because by the end of this, she would fear him *and* she would hate him.

Then she would be perfect.

When they arrived at the Diadem, he reached across and wrenched her face between his fingers, forcing her to look at him. She stiffened beneath his touch, and he knew no matter how he coaxed, she would never ease beneath him. That was fine. He only needed her willing to a point, beyond tonight, he did not care.

"We have a bit of a stroll to make. Just know I will be counting the number of times you misbehave, and for each offense, I will cut another finger from your friend. If I run out of fingers, I will move on to toes." He released her with a jerk. "I trust you will obey."

They left the vehicle, and as he came around the SUV, he offered his hand to Persephone. Her eyes were bright with hatred. Very few mortals knew the difference between that and passion.

Like a good girl, she accepted him, and they entered the hotel.

"Does Hera know you are using her facility for treasonous activities?"

She spoke quietly as they made their way through the bright lobby.

He laughed—genuinely. That was rare, but he found her question amusing. Clearly Hades did not tell her anything. Hera had offered several floors to him for his own private use. And use them he did—for sex, murder, hostages, whatever he wanted.

"Of all the gods, Hera has been on our side the longest," he said.

It helped that she despised her husband and that he continued to forgive her despite her many betrayals—but that was the nature of love, the greatest weakness of all. It would be Zeus's downfall just as much as it would be Hades's.

"I assumed you would be more discreet," Persephone said. "Since you are breaking the law."

He leaned close, enjoying how she cringed as he neared.

"You broke the law," he pointed out, his lips grazing her ear. "*You* engaged in battle with the gods."

"*You* kidnapped my friend."

"Is it a crime if no one knows?" Her jaw tightened, and he could feel her seething hatred. He wanted to taste it, and he would. Soon. "Do not waste your thoughts on how you will torture me when I die. Hades has already claimed that honor."

She offered a bark of laugh. "Oh, I will not torture you when you die. I will torture you while you live."

He hoped she did. He liked pain.

He dragged her upstairs, forcing her to keep pace with him. When they made it to the room, he held the door open for her. It was the least he could do—the absolute least.

She kept her eyes on him as she entered until she caught sight of her friend in the corner.

"Sybil!"

He knew he had her obedience by the tone of her voice. He'd heard that sharp cry too many times in the past not to know what it meant. She was horrified, and she understood the threat.

He let her go to her friend, who was barely awake, bloodied and beaten. She knelt at her feet and spoke her name quietly, desperately. Theseus liked the sound and his head tipped with pride. It was a mournful song and he had been the composer.

He waited.

When she turned on him, she finally caught sight of the other body.

"Harmonia!"

"Oh yes," he said. "That one was with her when we showed up. Made a mess of things, so I was forced to make a mess of her."

"You didn't have to hurt them," Persephone said, her voice trembling.

Good.

"But I did. You will understand what it takes one

day to win a war," he said, then pointed to the large man in the room. "Tannis here is your bodyguard. Tannis."

The man brandished a knife and placed the blade against one of Sybil's fingers as a demonstration.

"No!" Persephone lunged.

"Ah-ah-ah," Theseus said, holding out his hand, palm flat. She froze, breathing hard. Her eyes bright with fury. "Tannis is a butcher's son. He is an expert carver. He has been ordered to dismember your friend if you misbehave. Of course, not all at once. I will return shortly."

Theseus left the hotel, his skin buzzing.

If he'd had time, he would have summoned Helen and fucked her on the way to his next destination. She wouldn't fight him unless he asked, but it wasn't as fun if it wasn't real—no, she was merely a vessel for his pleasure, a way to release when he found himself in situations like this. Right now, he'd much prefer the resistance that only a woman like Ariadne or Persephone could provide.

Except he had no time. Persephone's magic would not hold Hades long and once he was free, Theseus knew exactly what he would search for—the energy signatures of her engagement ring.

He entered the back of the SUV. Once the door was shut, Hera appeared beside him.

Theseus did not look at the goddess, but he felt her suspicious gaze. There was nothing quite like it and it killed the high he'd had from his time with the Goddess of Spring.

"There is no going back from this," she said.

"Having second thoughts?" he asked mildly.

"Questioning if I was wrong to put my faith in a demigod."

Theseus chuckled humorlessly. "Faith requires trust, and let's be honest. Neither of us trust the other."

He was not stupid. If Hera was caught before they could imprison Zeus, she would fold and blame him for the uprising. If they succeeded, she would attempt to kill him to take the Olympian throne. Her predictability was boring.

They arrived at the Palace of Knossos, the exterior of which was nothing more than crumbling ruins.

"This is where you intend to trap Hades?" Hera scoffed. "He will hardly fall for this."

Theseus pulled out Persephone's ring. It was cold against his skin, no longer warm from the heat of her body.

"He will go anywhere if he thinks Persephone is there."

Theseus closed his fingers around the ring and strode into the palace. Beneath its derelict exterior was an ancient labyrinth, and Theseus had spent the last few years creating an extensive network of cells powerful enough to contain gods.

It was his own version of Tartarus, housed within a labyrinth, and they were about to see just how well it worked.

Hera followed behind him at a distance, likely not trusting that he wouldn't attempt to take her prisoner, but he was not yet interested in her.

Hades was the problem, the thorn.

Theseus knew the God of the Dead had been working on executing his own plan, not only to combat him but to eventually overthrow his brother, but Hades was about to realize he had not worked fast enough.

He took a set of crumbling stairs down into the dark

depths of the palace, until he came to a great metal door that he opened with a press of his palm, revealing a long row of cells. He could already hear the heavy and gruff breathing of the Minotaur as he made his way to the middle of the hall where he faced the monster.

He was large and towered over him. He had the head of a bull, his snout was wet and dripping as he bellowed, charging the metal bars, jamming his horns through them, not caring as he ricocheted against them. His human hands gripped the bars instead, shaking as he attempted to pry them apart, but they did not move—and they wouldn't. They were completely composed of adamant. It was the only metal that could harm a god, the only metal that could contain a god.

"Asterion?" Hera asked.

He was the first Minotaur—the one who had originally existed in the bowels of this very palace, in the labyrinth beyond these cells.

"Oh no, he is long dead. This is my creation."

"Your creation?"

Theseus said nothing; he did not need to explain himself. Minotaurs were created as they always had been—from the coupling of a bull and a woman.

"You are no different from your father," she sneered.

"Whatever it takes," said Theseus, and then he looked at the goddess whose sharp features were still narrowed in disgust, as if she had committed no horrors in her long life. "Isn't that what you said? Do whatever it takes? I'm willing. Are you?"

Hera only stared, and then Theseus turned his attention to the Minotaur again.

"Open it," he said.

"What are you thinking?" Hera demanded, her magic rising to fight.

He chuckled as a door within the cell opened which spilled out into the labyrinth.

The Minotaur whirled to face it, stance wide, breathing hard.

"Did I frighten you, Hera?" Theseus asked, and then he left the floor, heading up a set of stairs to the second floor of the prison where a platform overlooked the vast and complicated maze. It was extensive and dark with no uniformity to its shape or the size of the corridors.

They watched as the Minotaur crept into it and saw how he raged when the door to his cell shut, trapping him inside.

"Hades can kill a Minotaur," said Hera.

"I know," said Theseus.

He was counting on that.

CHAPTER XLV
HADES

Motherfucking Theseus.

Forget an eternity of misery in Tartarus. Hades would not rest until his nephew ceased to exist. He would shatter his soul, cut his thread into a million pieces, and consume them. It would be the most savory meal he'd ever eaten.

Fucking favor.

Fucking Fates.

He strained against Persephone's bindings, his limbs shook, and his muscles tightened, but they would not give.

Fuck. Fuck. Fuck.

She was powerful, and he would have felt more pride if she hadn't left with that bastard demigod. He knew why she'd done it. She'd wanted to protect him, and the thought filled him with a conflict that made his chest ache. He loved her so much, and he raged that she would put herself in danger, even if he understood it.

What would Theseus do to her?

The thought sent another wave of fury through him, and he fought against her bindings once more. This time, he heard the distinct snap of one, and his foot was free. He wrenched his arm, veins rising to the surface of his skin, and the vine cut into his wrist until it finally broke. He tore at the remaining bindings after that, and once he was free, he teleported.

Persephone had a knack for hiding her own personal energy signature. He had not yet discovered if it was merely one of her powers or a result of having her powers dormant for so long. Either way, it made it impossible to find her—except when she wore her ring. He focused on the unique energy of the stones—the pureness of the tourmaline and the sweet caress of the dioptase.

He manifested among ruins.

It did not take him long to recognize where he'd arrived: the crumbling Palace of Knossos. In the night, it was impossible to make out the detailed and colorful paintings that covered what was left of the ancient walls or exactly how many miles the grounds stretched, but Hades knew because he'd known this place in its prime and throughout its inevitable destruction.

It was here he sensed Persephone's ring, but faintly. He knew these ruins went deep into the belly of the earth, a twisted maze meant to confuse. He imagined Persephone somewhere within, and his anger drew him into the shell of the palace.

Though it was dark, his eyes adjusted, and as he crossed a broken blue mosaic floor, he came to a dark pit. It seemed to be a part of the floor that had given way. He spoke to the shadows, commanding them to descend. He watched through them as the chasm turned into another level of the palace, then dipped farther into an even deeper level.

Hades jumped, landing quietly on another mosaic floor. Here, the palace was more intact, its columned walls and rooms more pronounced. As Hades crept through each, following the energies from Persephone's ring, unease crept through him. He sensed life here—ancient life—and profound death. That was not unusual, given this site dated back to antiquity. Hundreds had died here, but this death, some of it was fresh—harsh, acute, acidic.

Hades continued to descend until he came to the edge of another dark pit. The smell of death was stronger here, but so was Persephone's ring. Hades's rage and fear twined through his body; a dread thick and foul gathered in the back of his throat. Memories from the night he'd found her in the basement of Club Aphrodisia accosted him, and for a moment, it was like he was there again, Persephone on her knees before him, broken. He could smell her blood, and his mind spiraled into a dark and violent place. It was the kind of anger he needed, the rush he would use to tear the world to pieces if he found her harmed.

He stepped into the darkness, and this time when he landed, it shook the earth. As he straightened, he found several narrow hallways.

A labyrinth.

He was familiar with this craftsmanship too, recognizing Daedalus's work, an ancient inventor and architect known for his innovation—innovation that eventually led to the death of his son.

Fuck, Hades thought, turning in a circle, studying each path. It was colder here, and the air was full of dust. It felt unclean and a little suffocating. Still, he could sense Persephone's ring, and the energy was strongest down the path that stretched out to his right. As he stepped into the deeper dark, he noted that parts of the tunnel were broken, as if it had been hit by a large object.

Something monstrous had lived here.

Perhaps it still did.

Hades gathered his shadows to him and sent them down the corridor, but they seemed to become disoriented and faded into the darkness. Their behavior raised the hair on the back of Hades's neck. There was a wrongness here, and he didn't like it.

Suddenly, the wall to his left exploded, sending him flying through the opposite barrier, and as he landed, he came face-to-face with a bull—or at least the head of one. The rest of its body was human.

It was a Minotaur, a monster.

It bellowed and clawed the ground with one of its hoofed feet, wielding a double ax that was chipped and caked with blood. Hades imagined the creature had been using it to kill since his imprisonment here, which, if he had to guess by the state of the creature—matted hair, filthy skin, and crazed eyes—was a very long time.

The creature roared and swung his ax. Hades pushed off the wall and ducked, sending his shadow-wraiths barreling toward him. If it had been any other creature, his magic would have jarred it to the soul. The usual reaction was a complete loss of the senses, but as they passed through this monster, he only seemed to grow angrier, losing his balance momentarily.

Hades charged, slamming into the Minotaur. They flew backward, hitting wall after wall after wall. When they finally landed, it was in a pile of rubble, and Hades rolled away, creating as much distance between them as possible.

The Minotaur was also quick and rose to his hoofed feet. He might not have magic, but he was fast and seemed to draw from a never-ending well of strength. He roared, snorted, and charged again, this time keeping his head down, his horns on display. Hades crossed his arms over his chest, creating a field of energy that sent the creature soaring once more.

As quick as he crashed, the Minotaur was on his feet, and this time the snarl that came from the monster was deafening and full of fury. He tossed his ax, the weapon cutting through the air audibly. At the same time, he charged at Hades, who braced himself for impact. As the creature barreled into him, Hades called forth his magic, digging the sharp ends of his fingers into the Minotaur's neck. As he pulled free, blood spattered his face. The creature roared but continued to run at full speed into each labyrinth wall. The impact against Hades's back began to send a sharp pain down his spine. He gritted his teeth against it and continued to shove the spikes into the Minotaur's neck over and over again.

Hades could tell when the creature began to lose his energy. He slowed; his breath came roughly, snorting exhales through his nose and mouth where blood also dripped. Just as Hades was about to let go, the Minotaur stumbled, and Hades found himself falling with the monster into another pit. This one narrowed quickly, causing him to hit the sides like a pinball, knocking the air from his lungs. They twisted and turned sharply until they were both thrown from the tunnel into a larger room. The Minotaur landed first, and Hades after, hitting a wall that did not give, which told him whatever they'd landed in wasn't concrete or stone.

Adamant, Hades realized.

Adamant was a material used to create many ancient weapons. It was also the only metal that could bind gods.

Hades rose to his feet quickly, ready to continue the fight with the Minotaur, but the creature did not rise.

He was dead.

Hades's eyes adjusted to this new darkness. It was somehow thicker. Perhaps that had something to do with how far below the earth they were located, or maybe it was the adamant. Either way, the cell was simple—a small square with a sandy floor. At first glance, as far as Hades could tell, there was no way out, but he'd have to look longer. For the moment, his attention was drawn to Persephone's presence. It was strong here, as if her heart beat within the walls of this cell. Then he saw it—a gleam from one of the jewels in her ring.

If her ring was here, where was she? What had Theseus done?

As he started toward it, there was a faint mechanical sound, and a net fell from the ceiling above, sending him to the ground. He landed with a harsh crack against the floor. As he tried to call on his magic, his body convulsed—the net paralyzed him.

He had never felt so helpless, and that made him angry.

He thrashed and cursed but to no avail. Finally, he lay still, not because he did not wish to fight but because he was too exhausted to move. He closed his eyes for a moment. When he opened them again, he had the sense that he'd fallen asleep. It took him a moment to adjust, his vision swimming even in the darkness. As he lay there, breathing shallow, he noticed a faint flicker of light a short distance from him.

Persephone's ring.

He started to reach for it, but the net kept his arm locked in place. Sweat broke out across his forehead, his body losing strength. Once again, he closed his eyes, the sand from the floor coating his lips and tongue as he worked to catch his breath.

"Persephone," he whispered.

His wife, his queen.

He thought of how stunning she'd looked in her white gown as she had walked to him down the aisle, flanked by souls and gods who'd come to love her. He remembered how her smile had made his heart race, how her bottle-green eyes, aglow and so happy, had made his chest swell with pride. He thought of everything they'd been through and fought for—the promises they'd made to burn worlds and love forever—and here he was, parted from her, not knowing if she was safe.

He gritted his teeth, a fresh wave of anger coursing through his veins. He ripped open his eyes and reached for the ring again. This time, though his hand shook, he managed to strain and grasp a handful of sand, and as he let it sift through his fingers, he found the gem-encrusted ring.

Breathing hard and shaking, he brought the ring to his lips, curled it safely in his palm, and held it to his heart before he fell into darkness once more.

Author's Note

I only have a couple of additions to make in this author's note given that most what features in *A Game of Gods* is also in *A Touch of Malice*. If you haven't read the author's note at the back of *Malice*, please take a look as it gives an overview of many of the myths that were used or referenced in both of these stories.

The Ophiotaurus:
If you are wondering how to pronounce it, you can google it. I, personally, say "oh-fi-o-taurus" but just know that pronunciation differs across countries.

There isn't a lot of information on the ophiotaurus except that it was a half bull/half serpent monster likely born of Gaia. Its existence was accompanied by a prophecy, "Whoever fed the bull's guts to consuming flames was destined to defeat the eternal gods." Sometimes it's reported that the Titans slayed the monster, but Ovid says that it was Briareus. As he is about to feed the intestines to the flames, Zeus's eagles swoop in and steal them away.

After this death, the ophiotaurus is set among the stars as the constellation Taurus.

It is thought that this story is part of *Titanomachia* which is a lost Greek Epic about the War of the Titans.

Ariadne x Dionysus:

I chose to include Dionysus's point of view in *A Game of Gods* because it connects to *Chaos*. Plus, I love the juxtaposition of Hades and Persephone's established love story and Ariadne and Dionysus's new love.

For this story, I referenced *The Odyssey*. The parallels might be obvious, but I'll go through them anyway. First, the fact that the two are swept out to sea by Poseidon just like Odysseus who is trying to get home after the Trojan War.

Let's just make a note here that Odysseus, who is considered a "hero" of Greek Mythology also tried to get out of going to battle by pretending to be insane, sowing his fields with salt. Now, you could argue he did this because it was prophesized that if he participated, he would be away from home for twenty years, but I don't know...doesn't seem very heroic to me.

We all know the true hero of that story is his wife, Penelope.

Anyway, Dionysus and Ariadne are swept out to sea and arrive at an island that is later identified as Thrinacia which is technically owned by Helios in mythology (it's where he keeps his cattle). When they arrive, they encounter an old man who Dionysus believes is a god. This is Nereus who is also referred to as "the old man of the sea." He is the father of the Nereids (sea nymphs). He says he will help Dionysus if he kills the cyclops who steals his sheep.

The cyclops is Polyphemos who is one of Odysseus's foes in The Odyssey. Similar to what unfolds in the epic, Dionysus offers the cyclops wine (which was such a perfect situational reference considering Dionysus is the God of Wine). When the monster asks Dionysus his name, he replies, "no one," which is a reference to Odysseus replying that his name is "no body."

When Polyphemos passes out from drunkenness, Odysseus blinds him. When he is asked who hurt him, he replies, "no body!" In *Gods*, I did not have Dionysus fulfill his debt which will likely come back to bite him in the ass...but that's for another story.

I LOVED Ari and Dionysus's storyline in this book, and it was actually the easiest part of the book to write.

A Quick Note on Hypnos:

I like to offer more depth to characters in the Hades Saga because the series just makes it easier given that Hades knows so much about so many things.

Anyway, Hypnos was known in mythology as a very gentle god but during my first encounter with him, he was *so* grumpy. When I started to write the chapters for him in *Gods*, I realized why—he just missed his wife.

Pasithea is the youngest charity, and she was given to Hypnos as a gift by Hera when he helped put Zeus to sleep a second time. Hera did this so the gods could interfere in the Trojan War. Technically, he never found out about this trick.

Read ahead for a sneak peek into *A TOUCH OF CHAOS*, coming from Bloom Books, September 2023

The burn in his wrists woke him.

The headache splitting his skull made opening his eyes nearly impossible, but he tried, groaning, his thoughts scattering like glass. He had no ability to pick at the pieces, to recall how he had gotten here, so he focused instead on the pain in his body—the metal digging into the raw skin on his wrists, the way his nails pierced his palm, the way his fingers throbbed from being curled into themselves when they should be coiled around Persephone's ring.

The ring. It was gone.

Hysteria built inside him, a fissure that had him straining against his manacles, and he finally tore open his eyes to find that he was restrained in a small, dark cell. As he dangled from the ceiling, body draped in the same heavy net that had sent him to the ground in the Minotaur's prison, his gaze locked with familiar aqua eyes. He was not alone.

"Theseus," Hades growled, though even to him, his voice sounded weak. He was so tired and so full of pain, he could not vocalize the way he wished; otherwise, he would rage.

The demigod was not looking at him, but at a small object clutched between his thumb and forefinger. He looked so at ease—and why not? He had the advantage.

"This is a beautiful ring," he said and paused, twisting it so that even beneath the dim light, the gems glittered. Hades watched it, his stomach knotting with each movement. "Who would have guessed it would be your downfall?"

"Persephone will come," he said, certain.

Theseus laughed. "You think your bride can go up against me? When I have managed to ensnare you?"

Hades took a breath, as deep as he could manage, though the weight of the net pushed against his sternum—it pushed against his whole body, made him feel like he was crumbling. Then he spoke, a quiet promise that shook his bones.

"She will be your ruin."

Have you discovered Scarlett St. Clair's fairy-tale world yet? Read on for a sneak peek of

Mountains Made of Glass

CHAPTER ONE
The Toad in the Well

The goose hung suspended by its feet from a low limb, bleeding into a bucket. Each wet plop of blood made me flinch, the sound inescapable even as I chopped wood to feed my hearth for the coming storm. The air had grown colder in the few minutes I had been outside, and yet perspiration beaded across my forehead and dampened all the parts of my body.

I was hot and the blood was dripping, and the strike of my ax sounded like lightning in the hollow where I lived before the Enchanted Forest. I could feel her gaze, a dark and evil thing, but it was familiar. I had been raised beneath her eyes. She had witnessed my birth, the death of my mother and father, and the murder of my sister.

Father used to say the forest was magic, but I

believed otherwise. In fact, I did not think the forest was enchanted at all. She was alive, just as real and sentient as the fae who lived within. It was the fae who were magic, and they were as evil as she was.

My muscles grew more rigid, my jaw more tense, my mind spiraling with flashes of memories bathed in red as the blood continued to drip.

Plink.

A flash of white skin spattered with blood.

Plink.

Hair like spun gold turned red.

Plink.

An arrow lodged in a woman's breast.

But not just a woman—my sister.

Winter.

My chest ached, hollow from each loss.

My mother was the first to go on the heels of my birth. My sister was next, and my father followed shortly after, sick with grief. I had not been enough to save him, to keep him here on this earth, and while the forest had not taken them all by her hand, I blamed her for it.

I blamed her for my pain.

A deep groan shook the ground at my feet, and I paused, lowering my ax, searching the darkened wood for the source of the sound. The forest seemed to creep closer, the grove in which my house was nestled growing smaller and smaller day by day. Soon, her evil would consume us all.

I snatched the bucket from beneath the goose and slung the contents into the forest, a line of crimson now darkening the leaf-covered ground.

"Have you not had enough blood?" I seethed, my

insides shaking with rage, but the forest remained quiet in the aftermath of my sacrifice, and I was left feeling drained.

"Gesela?"

I stiffened at the sound of Elsie's soft voice and waited until the pressure in my eyes subsided to face her, swallowing the hard lump in my throat. I would have called her a friend, but that was before my sister was taken by the forest, because once she was gone, everyone abandoned me. There was a part of me that could not blame Elsie. I knew she had been pressured to distance herself, first by her parents and then by the villagers who met monthly. They believed I was cursed to lose everyone I loved, and I was not so certain they were wrong.

Elsie was pale except for her cheeks which were rosy red. Her coloring made her eyes look darker, almost stormy. Her hair had come loose from her bun and made a wispy halo around her head.

"What is it, Elsie?"

Her eyes were wide, much like my sister's had been at death. Something had frightened her. Perhaps it had been me.

"The well's gone dry," she said, her voice hoarse. She licked her cracked lips.

"What am I supposed to do about it?" I asked, though her words carved out a deep sense of dread in the bottom of my stomach.

She paused for a moment and then said quietly, "It's your turn, Gesela."

I heard the words but ignored them, bending to pick up my ax. I knew what she meant without explanation. It was my turn to bear the consequences of the curse on our village, Elk.

Since I was a child, Elk had been under a curse of curses. No one agreed on how or why the curse began. Some blamed a merchant who broke his promise to a witch. Some said it was a tailor. Others said it was a maiden, and a few blamed the fae and a bargain gone wrong.

Whatever the cause, a villager of Elk was always chosen to end each curse—some as simple as a case of painful boils, others as devastating as a harvest destroyed by locust. It was said to be a random selection, but everyone knew better. The mayor of Elk used the curses to rid his town of those he did not deem worthy, because in the end, no villager could break a curse without a consequence.

Like my sister.

I brought my ax down, splitting the wood so hard, the blade cracked the log beneath.

"I do not use the well," I said. "I have my own."

"It cannot be helped, Gesela," Elsie said.

"But it is not fair," I said, looking at her.

Her eyes darted to the right. I froze and turned to see that the villagers of Elk had gathered behind me like a row of pale ghosts, save Sheriff Roland, who was at their head. He wore a fine uniform, blue like the spring sky, and his hair was golden like the sun, curling like wild vines.

The women of Elk called him handsome. They liked his dimpled smile and that he had teeth.

"Gesela," he said as he approached. "The well's gone dry."

"I do not use the well," I repeated.

His expression was passive as he responded, "It cannot be helped."

My throat was parched. I was well aware of how Elsie and Roland had positioned themselves around me, Elsie to my back, Roland angled in front. There was no escape. Even if I had wanted, the only refuge was the forest behind me, and to race beneath its eaves was to embrace death with open arms.

I should want to die, I thought. It was not as if I had anything left, and yet I did not wish to give the forest the satisfaction of my bones.

I gathered my apron into my hands to dry my sweaty palms as Roland stepped aside, holding my gaze. Elsie's hand pressed into the small of my back. I hated the touch and I moved to escape it. Once I had passed Roland, he and Elsie fell into step behind me, herding me toward the villagers, who were as still as a fence row.

I knew them all, and their secrets, but I had never told them because they also knew mine.

No one spoke, but as I drew near, the people of Elk moved—some ahead, some beside, some behind, caging me.

Roland and Elsie remained close. My heart felt as though it were beating in my entire body. I thought of the other curses that had been broken. They were all so different. One villager had wandered through the Enchanted Forest and picked a flower from the garden of a witch. She cursed him to become a bear. In despair, he returned to Elk and was shot with an arrow through the eye. It was only after he died that we learned who he was. The next morning, a swarm of sparrows attacked the hunter who had killed the bear and pecked out his eyes.

There was also a tree that had once grown golden apples, but over time, it ceased to produce the coveted fruit. One day, a young man wandered through the village and said a mouse gnawed at its roots. He claimed if we killed the mouse, the fruit would thrive, so our previous mayor killed the mouse, and the fruit returned. The mayor picked an apple, bit into it, and was consumed with such hunger, he gorged himself to death.

No one else touched the fruit of the tree or the mayor who died beneath its boughs.

There were no happy endings, that much I knew. Whatever I faced after this would surely lead to my death.

The villagers spilled into the center of town like phantoms. They kept me within their ghostly circle, surrounding the well, which was open to the sky and only a cold, stone circle that went deep into the ground. I approached and looked down, the bottom dry as a bone.

Roland stood beside me, too close, too warm.

"Who will you sacrifice when everyone you hate is dead?" I asked, looking at him.

"I do not hate you," Roland said, and his eyes dipped, glittering shamelessly as he stared at my breasts. "Quite the opposite."

Revulsion twisted my gut.

I had known Roland my whole life just as I knew everyone in Elk. He was the son of a wealthy merchant. That money had bought him status among the villagers and placed him at the mayor's side, which gave him power over every woman he ever laid eyes on and ensured he never had to face a curse.

My own misfortune had never deterred Roland. He had often offered to *help my case* if only I'd fuck him.

"You are disgusting."

"Oh, Gesela, do not pretend you despise my attention."

"I do," I said. "I am telling you."

Roland's face hardened, but he drew nearer, and it took everything in me not to push him away. I hated how he smelled, like wet hay and leather.

"I could make this go away. Say the word."

"What word?" I asked between my teeth.

"Say you will marry me."

I shoved him.

It was not as if he were serious either. He had made many proposals to women under the guise that he would save them, only to shame them later for believing he was serious.

If anyone was a curse on this land, it was Roland Richter.

"That is more than one word, idiot," I seethed. "But I shall give you one—never!"

Roland ground his teeth and then pushed me toward the well.

"Then you will face this curse."

I stumbled, catching myself against the side of the well, my palms braced against the slimy stone as I faced the endless darkness below.

"The crone in the wood says there is a toad in the well. Kill it and we will have water again."

"And did the crone say what will happen to me?"

"I gave you an out and you refused."

"You did not give me an out," I snapped. "You offered another curse."

"You think marriage to me is equal to what the forest would do?"

"Yes," I hissed. "I might consider it if I found you the least bit handsome, but as it is, I would vomit the moment your cock entered my body."

Acknowledgments

First, I must thank my editor, Christa, who lets me write in her she shed when I am on deadline, which goes well above and beyond anything a "normal" editor would do for their author and yet you do that and so much more. Thank you for letting me crash your space, helping me write through these incredible deadlines, and for Spaghetti Sundays. I'm so grateful for everything, but especially your friendship.

Thank you to Leslie whose encouragement kept me going day after day. When you told me I would finish this book on time, I believed you, but you also knew how often I needed to hear it. Without you, much of this journey would not have been realized in the first place. Thanks for repeating yourself. Lol.

Thank you to Lexi for keeping my social media and calendar. I would not appear half as organized without you. Also, for the accountability. Waking up at 4:00 a.m. is easier when you're up with me.

As always, I am thankful to my friends for sticking with me through the ups and downs of writing a book. I always look forward to finishing because y'all are on the other side and ready for brunch.

To my readers: every author dreams of the demand you all have for my books and this part of the series would have never happened without you. Thank you for wanting to see *A Touch of Darkness* from Hades's point of view. This saga has become more than I ever imagined and it's all because of you.

About the Author

Scarlett St. Clair is a *USA Today* bestselling author, a citizen of the Muscogee Nation, and the author of the Hades X Persephone series, the Hades Saga, the Adrian X Isolde series, *Mountains Made of Glass*, and *When Stars Come Out*.

She has a master's degree in library science and information studies and a bachelor's in English writing. She is obsessed with Greek mythology, murder mysteries, and the afterlife. For information on books, tour dates, and content, please visit scarlettstclair.com.

Find her on social media:
Facebook: AuthorScarlettStClair
Instagram: @authorscarlettstclair
TikTok: @authorscarlettstclair

See yourself *in* Bloom

every story is a celebration.

Visit **bloombooks.com**
for more information about

SCARLETT ST. CLAIR

and more of your favorite authors!

 bloombooks   @read_bloom   @read_bloom   read_bloom

Bloom *books*